CLAVEL, B.

Spaniard

F

26/11/69   6

AUTHOR CLAVEL, B	CLASS No. G F
TITLE THE SPANIARD	BOOK No. 86926034

THE SPANIARD

*Pablo Sanchez is an embittered and persecuted man.
The death of his wife in the Spanish Civil War and his
own subsequent imprisonment in a detention camp
have robbed his life of any sense of meaning, purpose,
or peace. Even when he escapes into France and finds
refuge in a small vineyard he consents to stay and
work for the peasant owners only for lack of anything
else to do. Gradually, however, the simple rhythmic
life of the vineyard restores his capacity to be involved
in the people and things around him with a strength
enabling him to survive the new trials he undergoes
in German-occupied France.*

*This original and sensitive account of a man's
instinctive struggle against his own chaotic past is
Clavel's first novel to appear in English in this country.
He is the 1969 winner of the Prix Goncourt, France's
most famous literary prize.*

Bernard Clavel

THE SPANIARD

Translated by

W. G. CORP

GEORGE G. HARRAP & CO. LTD
London · Toronto · Wellington · Sydney

DRJAR

Published in France 1959
© *Robert Laffont* 1959

First published in Great Britain 1969
by GEORGE G. HARRAP & CO. LTD
182 High Holborn, London, W.C.1

English translation © *George G. Harrap & Co. Ltd* 1969
Copyright. All rights reserved

SBN 245 59814 6

Composed in Caledonia type and printed by
Western Printing Services Ltd, Bristol
Made in Great Britain

PART ONE

PART ONE

I

Enrique muttered something which was lost in the noise and turned round to lift the tarpaulin. The van had slowed down and was now tilting in the dip at the side of the road. Pablo, also tilting sideways, was staring out. The glare of the headlights picked out vague shapes which were swallowed again almost immediately by the night. Squalls of wind flapped the tarpaulin, producing a wave-like sound, and the rain pattered on the metal roof of the cab.

There was a noisy spluttering, and the van stopped. The door of the cab opened, and they heard the driver splash about in water, hesitate, and then walk off. Enrique shifted his position.

"This is us," he said.

He again lifted the tarpaulin, and Pablo again turned towards it to look out. The driver was standing at the door of a house a few yards down the road. With one hand on the frame of the door and the other on the door-handle, he seemed to be talking to someone out of sight, but the wind and the rain carried away what he was saying.

"It's a café," said Enrique, letting the tarpaulin drop. "There's an advert for some wine or other stuck on the door."

"If it's a café," said one of the others, "we certainly won't stop there."

His companion laughed derisively, saying, "It'd be too good to be true if they sent us to cafés. I had a pal once who was a waiter in Teruel. He made a packet."

"Couldn't have been that sort of café then," growled Enrique.

The other did not seem to have understood. A moment slipped by, with the noise of the storm and the throbbing of the engine continuing.

Pablo had bent his legs and was resting his chin on his knees. He felt almost comfortable. On his left he could sense the warmth of Enrique, and opposite he could see the movement of the glowing tip of a cigarette the others were passing to each other.

7

After a few minutes the driver returned. Together with the sound of his boots on the road there was also the sound of clogs. The tarpaulin at the far end was lifted. There was a glimpse of three stars and the flame of a lighter shielded by a hand. The driver leaned towards the inside and took a paper from his pocket. The lighter flame fluttered. The driver hesitated and then said slowly:

"Pedrel, Enrique, and Sanchez, Pablo."

The two men stood up. The others wished them goodbye and good luck, and as they jumped down into the road a voice called after them:

"If you do buy the café I'm pretty good at drawing wine."

Immediately afterwards they received an icy slap in the face from the wind. All the comforting warmth they had managed to conserve by remaining immobile vanished immediately at the first touch of the wind.

Pablo tried to see the man with the driver, but the night was too dark and the light from the café did not reach as far as the road. It picked out two stone steps and ended at a large puddle which seemed to be boiling under the gusts of wind.

"Someone'll tell you where you're to go," said the driver.

"Isn't it here?" asked Pablo.

"No, but it's not far. To get there in the van I'd have had to swing off to the left some two miles back. But I can't turn back now. It'd take too long."

"Sure," said the man in clogs. "It's best to go from here on foot, taking the short cut. It's a bit of a climb, but you can't miss your way. I'll tell you."

He spoke quickly and not very clearly.

"What did he say?" asked Enrique.

As soon as Pablo had told him Enrique moved off a few paces, swearing vigorously.

The driver thanked the man, said good-night, and climbed back into the driving-seat.

The lorry drew away. The yellow light of its headlamps picked out for an instant two small houses and then a line of trees with white marks on their trunks. The reflection of the red tail-light fluttered across the puddles, and then all was dark again.

The man in clogs walked as far as the path leading to the café doorway. He then stopped and turned round to ask:

"Like a drink?"

Pablo didn't feel like a drink, but he hesitated. It would be warm and dry inside the café. Enrique had not understood what had been said. The man took a step towards the house.

"Come on," he said.

Pablo could not make up his mind. It would be good to be inside, but then, afterwards, it would mean coming out again. It was still raining and the night seemed darker than ever.

"No," he said. "Best to go straight away."

The man did not insist. He walked on by the side of the road. Pablo had not at any time been able to see his face. He had only been able to make out that he was wearing black oilskins with a hood which came down very low. They walked to the beginning of a barely discernible pathway on the left, which disappeared between two shadowy humps along the ditch.

"Now," said the man, "you take this road. You can't lose your way—there are hedges all along it. You go over a little bridge, and immediately afterwards the path divides. You take the right fork and go up as far as another road. You'll have to be careful because the path twists quite a bit. Once you're on the road, you keep on bearing right, and it's the first house . . . on the right."

He had hesitated a moment before saying the last "right". He was silent for a moment, and then he added with a laugh, "Perhaps you're not too keen on keeping to the right. I'm not either. But what can you do? That's the way it goes."

Pablo thanked him and led the way up the path where they had to walk in single file. Behind them the man's laugh still sounded, almost lost in the drenching night.

"What's he got to laugh about?" asked Enrique.

Pablo tried to explain the joke, but his companion didn't understand. The gusts of wind increased, whistling through the hedges. Long, supple branches, heavy with rain, swayed up and down, hooking on to their clothes.

They walked for a long while without speaking, merely groaning when a foot got caught in a muddy rut.

Pablo could feel the rain running through his hair, on to his neck, and down his spine. Shortly afterwards he could feel nothing: his shirt was sodden, and so was his vest. Nevertheless he was warm. Inside his clothes his sweat was warmer than the rain.

"What's that?" shouted Enrique.

Pablo came to a halt. Somewhere ahead of them there was a

9

rumbling in the night which they heard intermittently, between the squalls of wind. They walked on again.

"That must be the stream," said Pablo a moment later.

The path sloped downwards, and, as they advanced, the rumbling sound grew louder. Soon it was louder than the wind. They pushed on further, and, suddenly, they realized that the stream was at their feet.

Pablo put up one hand and felt about, his fingers soon touching the stone of the parapet. He leaned forward. The water was there, quite close. He could feel it lapping strongly against the bridge, but it remained invisible. He straightened up. The rain-filled wind spattered against his rain-wet face. The wind had not slackened, but they could no longer hear it. The earth here was noisier than the heavens.

"Well," said Enrique, "are we going on?"

He went a little way, then, since Pablo did not budge, added in a louder tone, "What's the matter? Have you taken the wrong road?"

"No, this is where we must fork right."

They pressed on, and the sound of the stream began to fade quickly.

The path was wider and less muddy. The water seemed to be running over small stones, and only now and then did their feet slide on muddy patches. The path also rose and wound quite a bit before reaching the main road.

When they felt tarmac again beneath their feet they stopped, both out of breath. The cords which each was using to carry his belongings were chafing their shoulders.

"With this stuff we've got on our back," said Enrique, "and with the rain soaking everything, it's really starting to feel heavy."

They got their breath back and Enrique went on: "Which way now?"

Pablo hesitated for a moment and said, "To think that we are free at last!"

"What's that?"

"I was saying that now, if we want to, we can go anywhere we like."

"Go where?"

Pablo sighed. "Absolutely anywhere."

"I'd like to know where we *can* go."

"Absolutely anywhere," repeated Pablo. "Absolutely anywhere."

10

Enrique laughed derisively. "Do you think the driver who was supposed to take us to these people is losing any sleep? He knows damn well we're not likely to bugger off on a night like this." He caught hold of Pablo's arm and said, "Don't talk cock. Which way *do* we go?"

"Over there."

Then Pablo began to walk on again, trying to distinguish the shadowy shapes bordering the path. After a few steps he asked, without breaking his stride, "Don't you find it funny that here we are, just us two, here on this path free to go anywhere?"

"Don't make me laugh! What I want is to get to shelter, to dry myself, to eat and sleep. I don't give a damn about anything else."

Pablo did not reply. From time to time he stopped, trying to see, always on the right-hand side of the road.

"D'you really mean to tell me you want to get away?" asked Enrique.

"This could well be the moment for it."

"But where would you go?"

"I don't know."

"There you are then—it's better to go to these people. You could just as easily get away tomorrow. D'you think they're going to tie us up?"

Trying to joke, Enrique went on: "The best thing is to take a look, see what it's like. Apparently it's a place with plenty of vines, so we shouldn't go short of wine, and that's something. When we've put on a bit of flesh we can do just what we like. Let's give ourselves time to look around."

Pablo walked a few paces without speaking, and then he sighed: "One can never tell about the future!"

"Listen, we might just as well have a quiet week. After that, we'll see. But one thing's certain: country people usually manage to eat well. Right now that's what's most important to us."

They walked on further, keeping to the right-hand side of the path. They passed beneath vaulting trees whose trunks were scarcely discernible. The branches cracked above their heads, and the wind in the branches led a saraband. Larger raindrops fell on them. The tarmac was covered with leaves sticking to the surface, twigs and branches among them to trap unwary feet.

Once they were through the trees the wind was gentler. They could still feel it, but less bitterly. The night now seemed even darker, and their footsteps sounded louder, the noise seeming to follow and sometimes even precede them a little. Pablo realized that the road must be passing between two very high walls which forced the wind upwards.

"Perhaps it's over there," said Enrique.

"You can't see anything?"

"No, but there should be a light of some kind."

"This must be just a surrounding wall. The house must be behind it."

"Then we'd better try to find the gate."

Pablo climbed up the bank and, walking slowly along the grass, went forward feeling the wall. He took about a dozen paces, and then, as his hand touched a pillar, found himself facing the fury of a fierce, icy wind. He lowered his head, felt further along the wall, and found the bars of an open iron gate.

"This must be it," he said.

"They might have left a light on."

"It's probably forbidden up here, too."

"Don't talk daft. They didn't seem to give a damn about the light at the café, and that was on the main road."

They moved forward a little.

"It's open, so we might as well go in. If there is a house we'll find it all right."

They were no longer on tarmac, but on mud again, and the ground sloped downwards slightly.

"I've a feeling it's not here," said Pablo.

"If you can see anything at all you're lucky. I can't even remember being out on such a pitch-black night."

"Anyhow, if it's here the house must be further on, or else somewhere on the side."

"How d'you know?"

"By sniffing the wind."

The wind was blowing straight into their faces in sustained gusts, driving the rain and making their eyes smart. Coming across open space with no obstacles, the wind was sweeping along as if roaring across flat, desolate plains.

Pablo suddenly stood still.

"Listen."

Enrique stood still and listened in turn.

"What is it?"

"It sounds as if someone has shut the gate."

12

"Hi, there!" shouted Pablo. "Anyone about?"

The sound was repeated.

"It must be the gate," said Enrique, "but it's only the wind rattling it."

He went a few steps forward. The ground became more miry, and he slipped, but without falling.

"Christ, I've had enough!" he shouted. "That driver was a sod. He should have brought us right here. That's his job. All these Frenchmen are rotten sods."

"Shut up! We can't be far off now; we must find the gate."

Enrique was still furious and let loose another long string of Catalan oaths. Pablo called to him:

"Over here; this is it!"

Enrique went forward and bumped into a metal upright. The clicking sound was heard again, and the barbed wire vibrated for a long time.

"Try to get it open."

Pablo's hand was feeling along a flat, horizontal bar. Soon he touched an upright. Something was creaking above their heads, something swinging in the wind. It was from this that the sound they had heard had been coming.

"It's not a door," said Pablo. "Here's the end."

He went forward, feeling through the night with the toe of his boot. His foot knocked against stone. He raised his foot and explored again.

"Steps."

"Be careful; might go down to a pool."

"No, they're rising steps."

"You're crazy. There's nothing ahead."

With one foot Pablo found the stone above the second step, but the next stone was too high. He reached forward with one hand, holding the rusty iron rail with the other. He felt down and touched the coldness of smooth stone. He released his grip on the metal upright and rested both hands on the stone. He gave a sigh.

"Well?" asked Enrique, who was still holding the railings.

"Of all places!" muttered Pablo. "We're in a cemetery."

Enrique also felt the tombstone. He returned afterwards to the railings, where the metal-mounted wreath of artificial pearls was still hanging on the wire.

They were silent for a moment, standing with their backs

13

turned to the wind. Pablo was sitting on the stone beside which water was gurgling.

Suddenly Enrique's anger burst out. "Christ! We'll never get out of here. That old man way back was laughing himself sick because of this. The filthy dog! Worse even than that blasted driver!"

He choked. Then he swore about everything—the lorry-driver, the man in clogs, and the country people who hadn't shown a light. He even swore at the night and the wind.

Pablo remained still, and Enrique too became silent finally, and remained so for a while. The wind was pressing against him, holding his wet clothes against his body. He was being moulded by the wind and icy water pressing his clothes against his straight spine. The wind was gathering strength again. It swept round once more, catching Pablo this time.

"Are you going to let us stay here and croak? You can't remember a thing about what he told you. You're always making out you're the one who understands everything, and then, when it comes to the point, you don't know any more than I do."

Pablo stood up slowly.

"He said the first house on the right, that's all I know."

Pablo did not shout. He didn't feel any desire to shout, but he could well understand his companion's fury.

"Now we've got to start finding the way again."

Pablo did not reply. He marched on, the wind behind him. He sensed that he was going straight towards the main door.

They were soon back on the tarmac road, and they started walking blindly again, sheltered by the wall.

A short distance further on the wall came to an end, and they felt again the full force of the wind. There were still a few trees about, their branches creaking overhead, and then, suddenly, a light shone through the darkness. It was only a short distance from them, on the right, and its warm reflection flickered towards them in a zig-zag down the road.

They walked more quickly. Bushes loomed out of the shadows, and then railings appeared on the top of the low wall.

The light was coming from a bulb which lit up the front of a house. It was placed very high, just below the eaves, from which a few stalks of maize were hanging.

The courtyard was fairly large and was closed by a wooden gate. Enrique shook the gate violently.

14

"Don't shake it! There's a latch."

Pablo raised the metal latch, and the gate opened. Before they crossed the courtyard, Enrique said:

"You're sure this is it?"

"Let's go in anyway. We'll soon find out."

They took a few steps forward, and then Enrique stopped again.

"D'you think they'll give us something to eat straight away?"

"I don't know."

"If they don't think of it we'd better ask."

Pablo walked towards the door.

"We will," he said, "but come on. We must find out if it's the right place."

"Of course it is. That's why they had the light on. They must be waiting for us."

They were only a few steps from the door when there was a sound of clogs on their right. Someone was coming near, walking beside a building they had not noticed till now, which extended the line of the house, but was set slightly back.

They saw that the newcomer was a very small woman. She waddled as she walked along carrying a pail in either hand. Her black hair was untidy, and the wind was blowing a lock of it across her face. She approached, still waddling and looking as if she was being pulled forward by the weight of the two pails. She went close to the wall, looking at the two men, but without turning her head towards them.

As she passed in front of them Pablo asked:

"Is this Monsieur Bichat's place?"

They could not tell whether she was a child or a very small woman, but she did not answer them.

When she reached the door she put down her pails, opened the door, and went inside. She had large hips and her frock was too short to cover her bandy legs. Her ankles were almost as thick as her knees.

"She's deaf, she is," growled Enrique.

"But she saw us all right."

She went in, leaving the door ajar behind her. Enrique and Pablo moved forward. From inside a man's voice shouted:

"The door, Jeannette, the door!"

Pablo stepped forward quickly. Again the voice shouted:

"What? What's the matter?"

15

Pablo saw a woman in the lighted room. He tapped the door and walked in.

II

"EXCUSE ME," said Pablo on the threshold, "is this Monsieur Bichat's house?"

A woman came forward.

"It is," she said.

Pablo brushed his forearm across his wet face, using the sleeve of his jacket as a towel.

"Good Lord," exclaimed the man, "they must be our two Spaniards! But how do they come to be in such a state?" He began to chuckle and added: "Well, old chap, if you have to be paid for by weight I'm not having any." Then he began to laugh again.

"How *did* you come?" asked his wife.

"In a lorry," said Pablo, "but they left us on the road. We came up by a path which a man in a café told us about."

"They must have come up through the pigsty," said the woman. "On a night like this, they were lucky not to have fallen into the stream."

The man began to laugh once more. "They couldn't have got wetter than they already are!" he exclaimed.

They had put their bundles beside them and stood there unmoving, in the centre of a puddle growing steadily larger on the stone floor.

"Have you got a change of clothes?" the woman asked.

Pablo nodded towards the bundles. "Yes," he said, "but they are wet through too."

"Undo them anyway; we'll see. Just a moment. Come here."

She pushed back a large round loaf of bread and two bottles which were standing on the end of a long table covered with American cloth, patterned in red and white squares, faded and worn. At the other end a place was set and the man was sitting there.

Pablo and his companion put their bundles on the table. Their

16

fingers were numb, and the water had tightened the knots of the cord.

"Cut it," said the man, "cut it."

He threw a pocket-knife on the table, and it skidded down to them. Once the cords had been cut, they unfolded their clothes. The rain had got into everything, and the boiler-suits they had been given when setting out were as wet as the clothes on their backs.

Pablo looked at the woman and made a gesture with both hands, as if excusing himself.

"Those two can't stay like this," said the man. "We'll have to try and find something."

The woman went to the end of the room, where, against the wall, there were several bulky portmanteaux. She brought back two jackets, one of blue linen and the other in brown corduroy.

"That'll do," said the man. "Go on, put them on and get warm. The lower part doesn't matter. It's always at the top you catch your death of cold."

The woman had gone across to the stove and was putting vine-shoot cuttings on the fire. Flames rose from the stove and sparks spluttered.

They stripped off their clothes above the waist. The man stared at them, both elbows on the table, his chin between his hands.

The girl they had seen outside also stared at them, as she stood between her two pails which she had put down in front of a large stone sink.

Their trousers were clinging to their legs, and as soon as they were near the fire the material began to steam. They remained by the fire for some time, turning from time to time to get warmed all round.

"You're both Spanish?" asked the man.

"Catalans," said Pablo.

"What?"

Pablo hesitated for a second or two, and then said, "Yes, we're Spaniards."

"But you've hardly any accent. You must have known French a long time."

"Yes, a long time."

"And your friend doesn't speak French?"

"Yes, a little, but you talk too quickly. He can't understand you."

The man had not moved. He was still holding his head between his hands. He was big and thickly built. His face was ruddy, and he had a large, fair, nicotine-stained moustache. He was wearing a cap thrust towards the back of his head, showing all his forehead and part of his bald head.

"Want a glass of wine?" he asked.

Enrique had understood. In Catalan he said to Pablo, "Tell them that we're hungry most of all."

"What's he saying?" asked the man.

Pablo hesitated. Enrique looked at him and said, pointing to the round loaf of bread, "Hungry, want food."

The man began to laugh again, saying, "He's damned funny, that chap. When it's a question of food he both understands and can speak French. He'll go a long way."

The woman went across to the table. "Come along, Jeannette," she said. "Help me to clear away." Then, turning towards the man, she added: "If they haven't eaten we must give them something."

"Of course we must give them something. But it's a bit thick that they made them come in weather like that with nothing warm in their bellies. Must be pretty rough in those camps."

As he was speaking the man stood up. For a second his chin remained white where his fingers had been resting, then the blood began to circulate again.

The girl they had seen in the yard, whom the woman had called Jeannette, made no move. Standing with her hands dangling and her mouth slightly open over large teeth, she stared at the two men. Her eyes were large and round, with dull, lifeless, black pupils, and she had scarcely any eyebrows. Pablo had turned his head her way several times, but he had been unable to bear her fixed, empty stare.

"Come on," shouted the woman. "Are you going to move, Jeannette?"

The girl jumped, swayed two or three times from left to right, and then walked over to the table. She was no longer carrying her two pails, but, nevertheless, all her body seemed to be dragged towards the ground by her hanging hands. Her chest was completely flat.

Pablo's eyes followed her as she cleared the table. Now and again she looked in their direction, and then got on with her work again. When she carried away two plates Pablo had the

18

feeling that she was bound to fall forwards. She arrived at the stone sink, however, without mishap.

The woman told her to set two places, and then, taking a carving-knife and a plate, she went out through a low door in a corner of the room which the lamp left in shadow.

Jeannette put out the plates, forks, and spoons, and then went towards the sink and stood again between her two pails. Standing quite still, she began to stare again at Enrique and Pablo.

"Come and sit down," said the man.

They took their places at the table. Their trousers were still wet, but no longer cold.

"Well, my girl," called out the man, turning towards Jeannette, "what are they going to drink from—out of my clogs, eh?"

She walked forward at her usual pace. She took two glasses from the cupboard and put them beside the two plates.

"Thank you," said Pablo.

The girl grunted, and her mouth opened slightly.

The man had now crossed his arms, resting his elbows on the table. He had just lit a half-smoked cigarette which he had taken from beneath the leather band inside his cap.

"Don't pay any attention to her," he said. "She never speaks. She's like that, and there's nothing to be done about it."

He hesitated a moment, rolled the cigarette in his mouth between his tongue and upper lip, then, having brought it back to the spot where his moustache was yellowed, he went on: "She'll always be like that, they say. It's not that she's really dumb; she just doesn't speak. But she understands all right, and you can give her jobs to do. She's not very quick, but she works well."

He looked at the girl, who had returned to stand by the sink. "Come along," he said, "get on with the washing-up. No need to wait till your mother gets back."

The girl started to do the washing-up. The man drew twice on his cigarette, which had gone out, and he re-lit it with a large, brass lighter. After that he filled the two Spaniards' glasses and poured the rest of the bottle into his own glass.

"She's gone to bring up more wine," he said, with a jerk of his chin towards the door through which the woman had left.

He raised his glass, saying, "Your health, my boys!"

"Good health!" said Pablo.

The woman soon returned. She put a bottle of red wine on the table, together with a large knife and a plate. On the plate were

19

slices of cold boiled bacon, as thick as a man's hand, and two small mould-covered cheeses. The woman also took from the pocket of her apron four eggs, which she showed to the man, asking, "Shall I make them an omelette?"

"Haven't you any soup?"

"I've enough for tomorrow morning, but no more."

"All right, give them eggs."

She went and broke the eggs in a bowl, and then put her frying-pan on the stove.

"Go on and eat," she said. "That's what'll warm you up best."

"That and a good fill of wine," said the man, refilling the glasses.

He emptied his own in a single gulp, wiped the back of his hand across his mouth, and then pulled from his pocket a packet of tobacco and some cigarette-papers.

As he ate, Pablo looked at the woman. She looked very much younger than the man. She was well built, and her blue bodice was pleasantly filled. She had round, bronzed arms, with dimples at her elbows. There was another dimple in the middle of her chin. She had black hair and dark eyes which bore some resemblance to those of her daughter, except that hers were smaller and her eyebrows fuller.

When they had eaten the bacon she served the omelette. As she smiled Pablo noticed that she had several teeth missing on one side.

The man had begun to smoke again and to talk about the work to be done. After a moment or two Enrique, who was trying to follow what he was saying, pointed to the window behind its closed shutters, saying, "Rain, rain."

The man looked at him with a smile, and then, turning towards Pablo, he said, "That pal of yours is a bit of a card. He's scarcely inside the door before he says, 'Hungry, want food'! When I talk about work he decides it's raining too much. Oh yes, he's a card all right!"

Pablo smiled. Enrique puckered his forehead.

"Don't you worry about the work," said Pablo. "He only meant to say that the bad weather's a nuisance."

"It'll be fine tomorrow," declared the countryman. "But I ought to tell you right away that it'll have to rain pretty hard to stop us gathering the grapes. That's because they're ripe, and with a wind like this they'll all be on the ground soon."

The man became irritable as he spoke of the bad weather and

the danger to the wine-harvest. He poured two glasses of wine quickly, one after another, and drank each in a single gulp.

"Perhaps you'd better go to bed," said the woman. "It's pretty late."

"You're right; I'll go up," he said. "You can show them where they're to sleep. And remind them there's to be no smoking."

"I will; don't worry," said his wife.

The man put both his fists on the table, leaned forward, and got to his feet, pushing the chair away with one foot. He took the stick hanging on the back of his chair and made his way to the end of the room. His right leg was absolutely rigid, and he appeared to be able to use it only with great difficulty. He was shorter than his wife, and his belly jigged with every step. He also went out through the low door, and Pablo heard him climbing a wooden stairway.

"My husband had an accident two years ago," explained the woman. "He fell under his cart one night as he was coming back from the fair, and his leg has been stiff ever since."

Pablo wondered for a moment what he could say. "It might still get better," he said. "Things like that often take a long time."

"No, it won't get any better. Nor will he get any better, either. He can't get used to it. He'd like to, but he can't, and that makes him irritable."

She became silent long enough to take a cast-iron pot from the stove and carry it across to the sink. "Leave the stew-pan to soak," she told her daughter. "That'll be all for now, so you can go up to bed."

She came back towards the two men and leaned with one hand on the bar of the stove. She remained still for a moment, and then went on, speaking in a lower voice: "The worst thing is that since his accident he can't carry his drink like he used to."

She looked in particular at Pablo, who thought for a moment and said simply, "That certainly makes it rather difficult."

"In any case, I thought it better to tell you that if he gets annoyed don't say anything. Not even if he's in the wrong. He gets quarrelsome when he's been drinking, but when it's over it's over. He's soon his proper self again."

The two men looked at each other. The woman turned round. Behind her the daughter remained standing, her eyes still on Pablo, who had noticed this, but had refrained from turning his head towards her.

21

"What are you doing here?" shouted the mother. "Not taking root, eh? I told you to go upstairs, so go up, and go quickly!"

Jeannette grunted, swayed three times on her feet, and turned on the spot in a curious manner, taking five or six short steps. Then, still leaning forwards with her hands hanging, she reached the low door. As soon as she had gone out she could be heard going up the wooden stairway. She trod heavily on each stair.

The mother sighed, pulled up a seat, and, sitting sideways, one elbow on the table, said, "It's a martyrdom, you know. A martyrdom. At thirteen she's like she was at four. And obstinate as well. Even when she understands what you ask she makes you repeat it. It's a real calvary to have a child like that. You can't trust her a moment; she does everything wrong."

Pablo and Enrique, who had finished eating, remained motionless. Enrique, after some hesitation, stood up and went over to the stove. He felt in the pockets of his jacket and managed to pick out a few scraps of damp tobacco, which he put in the palm of his hand.

"What are you looking for?" asked the woman. "Tobacco?"

"Yes," he said, "tobacco."

She stood up and took from the ledge above the fireplace a glazed earthenware pot with a plate on top to close it.

"Here you are," she said, "but I haven't any cigarette-papers."

Enrique looked round the room and walked across to the window. He took a newspaper from the window-ledge and held it out to show the woman, asking, "Can I have this?"

She began to laugh. "But that'll be nasty. You should have asked the *patron* for some cigarette-papers before he went up."

"It'll be all right," said Pablo. "If the newspaper's no longer wanted it'll do us. We're used to it, you know."

The woman looked from one to the other of them. "You can have it," she said.

Enrique sat down again, put the newspaper on the table, and tore off a small square. The woman watched them roll their cigarettes and then asked, "Were you well treated in the camp?"

Pablo shrugged his shoulders. "Not bad."

"And the war?" she asked. "What really happened?"

They looked at each other.

"Tell me a little," she insisted. "I'm interested because of my son."

"Your son?" asked Pablo.

"Yes, he was just nineteen when the Germans invaded Poland. As he was very bright he was attending an agricultural course. Someone must have put ideas into his head one day, and he wanted to volunteer. We did all we could to stop him, but he's as obstinate as his father. Then he went. In no time at all he was in the Maginot Line."

Pablo stared down. Enrique made a vague gesture with his hands and shrugged his shoulders. Since the woman insisted he pointed to Pablo. The woman thought that he was suggesting she should ask his comrade. She stretched out her arm and touched the fingers of Pablo's hand resting on the table. Pablo withdrew his hand and, lifting his head, looked at the woman, frowning. There was almost anger in his thin, angular face. Then he lowered his head again.

There was a heavy silence which seemed to come from the corners of the room where the light reached only half-way up the walls. The ceiling of heavy beams was dark, and the shaded lamp threw only a tiny circle of light in the centre of the room. All else was like a vault of night, and it was from this that the silence came—this vault which shut out the sound of the wind and the rain.

When Pablo lifted his head he was smiling. Slowly, almost whispering, he explained: "You must understand that we can't tell you anything. The war you're fighting has nothing to do with the one we fought.... I'll be surprised if it lasts very long."

"Our boy, if he has to fight, will be in the Maginot Line. It seems it's pretty good there, and they're in hardly any danger."

"It's certainly better than being outside. I've heard talk about it—that the Germans won't be able to break through."

"A good job too. It wouldn't be very funny if they were able to do again what they did in 1914."

They were silent for a moment, and then the woman asked again, "You really think it's not at all like it was in Spain?"

"No, for the moment there's hardly any fighting at all, and even when they do fight, they don't kill women and children."

The woman's eyes had lit up. She leaned a little forward over the table, resting her breasts on her forearms. "Did you see women killed in your country?"

Pablo lowered his head once more. He remained motionless for a few seconds. The woman was waiting, her eyes fixed on him.

23

Abruptly he pushed back his chair and stood up. His face had hardened again. "We want to go to bed," he said.

She seemed put out, and stared at Enrique, who had stood up in turn.

"Very tired," said Enrique, indicating Pablo with a movement of his chin.

"I'll show you the way," she said. "Just give me time to light the lantern."

She went across to the cupboard, opened the door, and squatted down. She pulled out several pairs of shoes, shifted some tin boxes, and then came back to them carrying a large, square lantern with one panel of red glass.

She took a candle from a drawer and fixed it in the lantern.

"You heard what the *patron* said. I'm trusting you, but there's fodder stored, and the whole place would go up in smoke if you set fire to it."

"You can sleep peacefully, *madame*," said Pablo.

She looked at him for a second, seemed to hesitate, and then said, "Don't call me *madame*; say *patronne*."

As they approached the stove to take their boiler-suits, stretched over chairs, the woman put a hand on the material. "No," she said, "they're still damp. Leave them here, and I'll iron them to-morrow, before I call you."

Pablo thanked her, and they followed her. Before opening the door she threw a large black woollen shawl over her head and shoulders and pulled on her clogs.

The wind had not dropped, but the rain was lighter. They crossed the courtyard, which was lit by the lamp under the eaves.

"It was a good thing you left the light on outside to help us find you," said Pablo. "Without it we wouldn't have found you very easily."

"A light on?"

"Yes, when we arrived."

She thought for a moment. "Oh no!" she said, "the child had lit it to go to the stable." She seemed to regret what she had said and added quickly, "You see, we didn't know exactly when you would come, and as we're forbidden to show a light after dark we didn't dare leave it on too long. And, to tell you the truth, we no longer expected you so late. We said: they'll arrive to-morrow morning first thing."

24

They had crossed the road and were now marching in single file down a muddy, slippery path. The woman was going ahead, lighting the path with the flickering lamp.

They soon arrived in front of an old barn. The woman turned round and held out the lantern to Pablo.

"Hold it a minute," she said. "The door always has to be forced a bit before it'll open."

Pablo took the lantern. Enrique, who was behind him, rushed forward. "Leave it," he said. "I'll do it."

Pablo held the light for them. The woman had her back to the door to raise it as she pushed against it. Enrique pressed himself close to her and pushed with her. The door opened.

They entered a space where there was an earthen floor. Enrique and the *patronne* could stand upright, but Pablo had to hold his head low to avoid the beams. He felt cobwebs on his face, and wiped them away with his handkerchief. The woman was already going up a wooden stairway with high, narrow steps which creaked. When she arrived at the top she turned round to light their way. They walked up.

"You must be careful," she said, pointing to one corner. "The flooring over there is weak." She directed the beam of light towards a low door and added, "You mustn't open that; there's nothing behind it. That's where the straw's passed in."

Then she put the lantern on the floor, took two coverlets hanging on a length of wire, and put them on the straw, which was in heaps, some reaching the roof.

"D'you think you'll be all right?" she asked. "I'm going to leave you the lantern, but I count on you to be very careful." She took a few steps towards the stairway, and then, suddenly, turning back, she went on: "Ah! I've remembered. The *patron* forgot to speak to you about it, but if one of you wants to carry he'd better say so."

The two men stared at each other.

"We don't understand," said Pablo.

"Well, you, for example, you look strong enough to carry."

"Carry what?" asked Pablo.

The woman began to laugh. "To carry the *bouille*, of course. It's a sort of big pannier made of iron."

"I'll do anything I'm asked," said Pablo.

"That's not the point. It's just that whoever carries gets an extra ten francs a day. So if it interests you I'd like you to do the job.

25

I expect you need money. In any case, with this war on, we'll have only old people and children helping."

"Very well," said Pablo, "I'll carry. I hope I'll manage all right."

"Of course you will," said the woman, "of course you will."

She moved away and began to go down the stairway. Enrique took the lantern and went towards her to light the way.

"Don't bother," she said. "I know the way. Good night, and mind you don't set the place on fire. Be careful."

"Good night, *madame*," called out Pablo. "Don't worry."

She closed the door by pulling it sharply. The whole building vibrated. Then the two men heard her clogs slapping in the patches of mud as she walked hurriedly away.

III

ABOVE THEM the rain, still driven by the wind, spattered on the tiles.

Pablo raised the lantern and inspected the barn.

"What are you looking for?" asked Enrique.

"Nothing. I'm just looking."

He put down the lantern and sat beside Enrique on the straw. They remained silent for a moment or two, unlacing their sodden boots.

"We must stuff 'em with dry straw," said Enrique, "otherwise we'll never get them on again tomorrow."

They filled their boots with straw and stood them on the floorboards. Then, struggling out of their still-damp trousers, they hung them over the wire from which the woman had taken the coverlets.

"The old man's jacket will make a splendid pillow," said Enrique. Pablo watched him. He had taken a big armful of straw and was wrapping it in the jacket.

"That's going to be in a fine state tomorrow."

"As if I give a damn," replied Enrique. "Anyhow, it's not his Sunday jacket. Come on, don't show off. Do like me—you'll find it's a good idea."

Pablo made up his mind and made himself a pillow in the same way. Then they rolled themselves in the coverlets and pulled a few armfuls of straw over themselves.

"I'm warm already," said Enrique, after a few minutes of lying motionless.

"So am I."

Pablo stretched out an arm, lifted the lantern, opened it, and blew out the candle. He put the lantern back on the floor and stared at the red tip of wick which gradually faded before disappearing.

"Pity we couldn't have pinched a bit of the tobacco in that pot. I thought about it, but that bitch kept her eye on us the whole time."

"She did give us some," Pablo reminded him. "That was something. She didn't have to, and in any case it wouldn't be wise to smoke here."

"Oh, yeah! I'm not going without when I've got some!"

Pablo did not reply. He was not really sleepy, but his fatigue increased with the warmth and he gradually became relaxed.

"What d'you think of the woman?" asked Enrique.

"They don't seem a bad couple. I think we could have come off worse."

"I'm not talking about that, but about the woman. Wouldn't you like a bit with her, eh?"

Although Pablo remained silent, Enrique persisted: "Just now, down below, when she was opening the door, I got close to her and touched her tits. They're firmer than you'd think."

"You'd better stop acting so dumb, otherwise it won't be long before we're slung out."

"That's what you think. But I knew the very first moment what she was after. I'm certain her old man's no good for it now. Stands out a mile that she wants it. You can see it first glance."

"Shut up," said Pablo. "You'll get worked up, and you'll only bring us trouble."

Enrique, however, was off, refusing to listen. Raising himself on one elbow, he began to speak again.

"I tell you she wants it. And I'll bet you that within three days I'll have her. But there's no need for you to worry. I'm not going to make her any propositions in front of her old man. All I need is the chance to get her in a corner on her own."

He stopped for a moment, wriggled around, and then went on: "Look, just a little while ago, when she brought us here, if I'd

27

been alone with her she'd've had it. What's more, I'm not sure that she wouldn't have been ready for both of us."

Pablo turned round and, raising his voice a little, said, "Listen, d'you mind shutting up about it?"

"You know what I say to that. Anyway, I'd rather have her than a tart in a brothel. I don't know how you find her, but she's not as bad as all that."

Pablo's anger exploded suddenly. Sitting up in turn, he shouted, "I don't give a damn, d'you hear? I just want you to shut up about it."

"No need to get shirty. I don't know what you're made of."

Pablo gave a long sigh. His anger was already abating. Slowly, almost in a whisper, he said, "I had a wife, see? They killed her. No, it's finished for me. Other women..."

He did not finish the sentence.

"I know," said Enrique, after a short silence, "I know. But for God's sake that's over a year ago; you ought to try and think about it a bit less. It's no good going on and on thinking about misfortunes; it can't do any good."

Pablo laughed derisively. "In any case, all that can happen to me now..."

"Of course, if you talk like that nothing good will ever come to you. But to me, talking like you do at thirty-five doesn't seem to make any sense at all."

Without being really annoyed Pablo raised his voice again. "What really makes no sense is making war. Killing women and the children they have in their bellies. And leaving behind men like me with nothing to live for."

He stopped abruptly and lay down again, turning his back on Enrique. For a few moments there was only the sound of the wind, which was still blowing and sending long waves of rain across the tiles.

In this sound of water there was another sound of water. From one corner of the roof there must have been a gutter-pipe going down to a tank. The gurgling could be heard, stopping at each gust of wind and beginning again afterwards.

"Are you asleep?" asked Enrique after some minutes.

"No."

"Can't you understand that I want a woman?"

Pablo listened again to the stop-and-go sound of the gutter, and then said, "Yes, I understand, but don't rush it; it's not worth bringing a lot of trouble on yourself."

28

"How old d'you think she is?"

"I don't know—forty, perhaps."

"Go on! She's certainly less than that, but with countrywomen they always look older than they are. They don't know how to look after themselves. But I'm sure if she had a good hair-do and some decent clothes she wouldn't be at all bad."

Pablo did not reply. Above all else he wanted silence. But Enrique was calculating. He remained silent for a few moments, and then, suddenly, he took up again the threads of the conversation that so obsessed him.

"Nevertheless, if she has a son of nineteen...well, if she had him when she was eighteen..."

He started calculating, kept silent, then went on: "She's certainly over thirty-five.... But at thirty-five a woman's not too old."

He continued his monologue for a long time. At last he lay down again, pulled the straw over himself, and said again, "Ah, well! Good night, old chap. I can see you hate me talking about women. But in any case I'd rather the mother than the daughter."

He ended his words with a derisive laugh.

Pablo was not asleep. Motionless, his eyes wide open, he listened to the rain in the night.

He remained thus for a long time. He was very warm now. Soon Enrique began to breathe more heavily, more regularly. He was asleep.

Pablo listened with one ear to the light tapping of rain which continued on the roof; with the other he listened to the straw beneath his head crackling like a large fire.

The man's jacket smelt strongly of stale sweat and tobacco. Pablo turned on his back.

Enrique's last words had mocked the daughter. Pablo could see her again, motionless, mute, leaning slightly forward with her arms dangling. He saw particularly her fixed, empty stare, her lips slightly parted for a smile which never came.

Pablo closed and opened his eyes many times in an attempt to cease picturing her.

Jeannette. She was called Jeannette. In French it was *the name of a flower*. A flower which smelled sweet. Which smiled like all flowers. Pablo found himself thinking that no person should ever be given a flower name. It was too risky.

The girl must be dirty. She must certainly smell unpleasant. At this instant she must be sleeping with her mouth open.

29

Possibly because he had evoked the memory of this sleeping girl Pablo thought anew of dead Mariana. Mariana whom he had not seen dead, but whom he tried constantly to imagine. He could see her again, brown-haired also, with dark eyes. But in no way resembling this repulsive girl.

He tried again to free himself from these two faces. He decided to think of nothing but the rain on the tiles—the rain which ran on the tiles. He had seen from inside that the tiles were flat. They must be old and moss-covered. He had also noticed several new tiles. And these, he thought, must be smooth. With the pitch of the roof the rain must run down very quickly. He, Pablo, was now very warm. He thought about the slippery path. Hoping by the same means to get to sleep, he thought back over the whole journey, trying not to forget any detail. The man's laugh in the café; the heavy slaps from branches along the path bordered by hedges; the sounds of the almost overflowing stream; the climb; the silence between the walls. There his thoughts moved more quickly. He was suddenly in the cemetery. He thought suddenly how he had sat on a stone.

That stone had been a tomb.

No-one should ever sit on a tomb. Earlier he had not thought about it.

If some unknown person was to sit on the tomb of Mariana!

But first of all, had Mariana a grave? Was she buried in a cemetery? Had her body remained buried under the stones of the house?

Down there the whole village was perhaps a cemetery. All Catalonia.

Pablo tried to start again. He wanted to follow the interrupted path. But he arrived immediately at the farm. There was light and strangers. The face of the dirty idiot girl. Her mouth with lips just parted.

And now again it was Mariana. Mariana who had beautifully shaped lips. Lips, perhaps open in death, with blood running from the mouth.

In war the dead often have blood running from their parted lips.

For Mariana there should have been a great grave, a grave with two crosses. One for her and one for the little one she was carrying in her womb at the moment of her death.

For Mariana and her little one there should have been a grave
30

with a stone. A solid stone, a stone like a roof, to stop the water entering into the earth.

IV

PABLO had gone to sleep very late, and he had awakened several times during the night. Each time he had envied Enrique snoring beside him.

Enrique was still sleeping, although it was now daylight. Pablo had been watching it for some little while as it advanced across the floor beneath the low door which the woman had told them not to open.

It was no longer raining. The wind had also dropped.

Before dawn several cocks had crowed, but now all was silence. Deep silence, with the daylight continuing its advance across the floor, picking out one by one the bits of straw.

Pablo waited a little longer, then he got up noiselessly. He had slept naked, so that all his clothes could dry out. He touched his stretched-out trousers. The material was still slightly damp. He went back towards the straw and unstuffed his pillow to get the man's jacket. It was slightly warm.

Pablo went across to the shutter, put his eye to a crack, and then, as he could see nothing, looked between the tiles and the top of the wall. There a little daylight was also coming in, but he had been unable to see it from where he was lying because of the heap of straw. The roof, projecting a long way, made it impossible to see anything other than the ground. There was some grass and a few scattered black twigs. Pablo was about to draw back when a white hen crossed the space he was able to see. She moved slowly, lifting her feet and curving her claws. She looked in all directions nervously, scratched the soil, pecked at something, and then made off.

Pablo went back to the small shutter and tried to find the bolt. His hand first encountered a festoon of spiders' webs. He got rid of them by wiping himself with the jacket. Finally, he found the shutter-bolt. He tugged it gently, but the rusty iron resisted. He pulled harder, and it slid back, squeaking. He remained quite still for a moment, but Enrique slept on.

Pablo pulled the shutter, lifting it a little. It opened noiselessly. Kneeling on the floor, a little way back, Pablo stared out.

In the foreground was a piece of land, covered with thin, weak grass, and a path leading to the road. There was a low stone wall, and then, immediately after it, a larger meadow running downhill. The meadow was almost covered with mist which grew denser, hiding it behind what looked like a cloud.

Pablo listened. Nothing was moving. There was only, here and there, the brief cackling of a hen. He opened the shutter wider, moved nearer the edge, and hung out a little way. On the right was the house, which seemed in the white mist to be painted in grey. On the left there were houses also, but farther off, as vague and pale as the bushes bordering the road.

Once again Pablo stared at the farmhouse. It looked old, and the ridge of the roof sagged. Grass sprouted from the guttering at many points. On the façade there were three windows on the first floor, and two on the ground floor, with between them the door through which he and Enrique had entered. The shutters of the first floor were open, but those of the ground floor were closed. Leaning out a little farther, Pablo was able to see a building which formed an extension to the house. It seemed to be of a later date. All the tiles were new. The main door opened on the barn. Farther off he saw another door and a dormer window. Beneath the window a tap stood out from the wall, above a stone basin. Pablo noticed also the tools left about in the courtyard. There was also a wheelbarrow and two large tubs, turned upside down, with their bottoms full of water. The door was open, and some chickens were coming and going, while others stood with their feathers ruffled outside the kitchen door.

Pablo shivered. He straightened up and went back to the centre of the barn, rubbing his naked thighs vigorously. He felt his trousers again, hesitated, then, clenching his teeth, he drew them on. As he buckled his belt he gasped, so cold was the cloth against his skin. He tugged the straw out of his boots and pulled them on too.

"What are you doing?" asked Enrique, stretching himself.

Pablo turned round. "Nothing, I must go down. I'm dressing."

"What's the time?"

"I don't know, but it's daylight."

"It's not raining any more, but I've got the feeling that it must be very cold."

32

"It is a bit, and there's a lot of mist."

"They've already called us?"

"No, there's no-one up."

"Then don't make a noise and wake them; we'll begin work soon enough anyway."

Pablo went down. As he opened the door the shutters of the house creaked. The woman saw him and waved a hand, shouting, "Good morning! Up already! The youngster was going to bring your overalls over to you. They're quite dry."

Pablo went towards the house. The *patronne* was opening the other shutters as he entered the courtyard.

"Come in," she said. "The *patron* has just gone down to the cellar. I'll give you your overalls, and then you can go down and see. He'll certainly need you."

Pablo went in. The fire was already roaring, and it was pleasant in the kitchen. There was a curious but pleasing odour—a mixture of coffee and wood-smoke.

Jeannette was standing behind a bench on which there was a large cast-iron pot and a wicker basket. She was motionless, a pointed knife in her right hand, the half of an apple in her left. Her mouth still slightly open, her eyes still empty, she stared at Pablo. He nodded to her. She grunted, but did not move.

"Here you are. They're quite dry," said the woman.

She held out the overalls to Pablo, together with the remainder of their clothes, which she had already collected.

"Thank you, *madame*," he said.

"Call me *patronne*."

Pablo went as far as the door, and then, turning round, he asked, "Where can I wash?"

The *patronne* stared at him in astonishment for a moment. She appeared to reflect, walked round the sink, and then, looking at Pablo again, asked, "You want to wash now?"

"Yes, if it isn't too much trouble."

"There are two taps, one in the courtyard, the other in the stable. Use whichever one you like."

Pablo thanked her and went out as the woman added, "But hurry, the *patron* is certainly waiting for you."

As soon as he was outside he heard the woman shout, "Well, are you coming too, eh? Have you never seen a man before?"

Pablo went back to the barn. Enrique had not budged.

"Get up, the *patron* is waiting for us."

33

"What for? For eats?"

"No, for the cellar, but I don't know what he wants done."

Pablo threw his comrade's overalls on the straw. He took off his own damp trousers and pulled on the dry ones. Enrique was still yawning. As soon as Pablo was dressed he began to go down the stairs.

"Hurry up," he said. "Don't start off by upsetting these people the very first day."

"O.K.!" shouted Enrique. "You're just showing off to get the old girl to fall for you!"

As Pablo reached the courtyard the *patronne* came out of the kitchen, a pail in one hand and a large milk-can in the other.

"D'you see," she said, "the tap is down there."

She pointed out the tap, which Pablo had noticed under the window of the adjoining building. They walked a few steps together, and then, hearing Enrique's voice, they looked back. Hanging out of the opening in the wall of the barn, his torso bare, he was shouting in Catalan, "When you've finished trying to charm her tell her to bring up my coffee, I've got a surprise for her." He then began to laugh very loudly.

"What did he say?" she asked.

"He said he's just coming down and is sorry to be a bit late, he couldn't find his boots."

"There's no hurry," she said, "providing there's someone to help the *patron* if needed."

"I'll go down to him now," said Pablo. "I can wash later."

The *patronne* put her pail in the stone basin and turned on the water. Afterwards she opened the small door and went in. Pablo followed her. It was the stable, very warm, and the odour of the animals surprised him. He had time to catch sight of a cow and a horse separated by a swinging bail. At the end where there was scarcely any light several goats tugged at their chains, bleating.

The woman pushed another door, which opened on another barn, where there was a lamp alight.

"Look," she said, "if you open the big door the cart can be brought out; that'll make some room. After that you won't need the lamp on."

Pablo opened the two large wooden doors and looked round the side of the building. There was still no sign of Enrique.

Having done that, he made towards the door from which a sound of bottles being moved was coming. A stone stairway with

34

some twenty steps, quite wide and level, led to the wine-cellar. On the right was the wine-press, and all around were barrels of every size.

"Come round here," shouted the *patron.*

His voice came from behind a line of four large casks, each above a man's height, which filled the centre of the cellar and almost reached the vault of black stone. Pablo walked round the casks.

"Hullo!" said the man.

"Good morning, *monsieur.*"

"Call me *patron.* And what's your name?"

"Pablo Sanchez."

"Pablo what did you say?"

"Pablo Sanchez."

"Good old Sanchez," he said, clapping a hand on Pablo's shoulder. "You Spaniards are a funny lot. We like to have a joke here. You'll see, there's a good crowd coming."

He became silent for a moment, leaning forward to look round the door which Pablo had left open, then, half whispering, he went on with a wink, "During the wine-harvest there's always plenty of fat bottom."

He laughed again, repeating several times: "Good old Sanchez!" When his chuckling ended he asked, "What about your pal? Isn't he coming?"

"Yes, he'll be down in a minute."

"He doesn't seem to rush to work."

As he was talking he had approached a small cask standing on two larger ones.

"Lift the bottom a bit so we can finish emptying it completely."

Pablo tipped the cask gently. The man held a bottle under the tap.

"What's his name, your pal?"

"Enrique Pedrel."

"Enrique, that's not a name. We'll call him Henri."

The bottle was full. The man turned the tap off.

"Don't move!"

He took another bottle; Pablo titled the cask a little more. The wine now ran cloudy and thick.

"That'll do for the *patronne* to use with her vinegar."

He put down the bottle. "What's your trade?"

35

Pablo hesitated, then he said, "I used to work for a transport firm."

"What did you do?"

Pablo looked at the man and hesitated for some seconds again before saying, "It's difficult to explain....I dealt with correspondence....I received customers...."

"If I understand you aright, you were a pen-pusher."

"If you like."

The man laughed derisively. "If I like, if I like! I've got to take you as you are. But my wife said you were prepared to carry, so I'd better warn you that it's no girl's job."

"I'll do what you tell me to do."

The man swung his hand as if to brush away any explanations. "No, no," he said, "you wanted to carry, and you will carry. You'll be paid accordingly, but I warn you that it'll be no good coming to me at midday and saying you want to change."

Enrique came down the stairs. Turning to him, the *patron* called out: "Ah, here's the bright spark. He turns up when the work's done. Come on, take the bottles; we're going up. We're going to get the cart ready, and after that you'll come down and scrub out the barrel we've just emptied."

The man went first. He climbed the steps slowly, helping himself with a stick and holding on to the iron rail. Without stopping or looking back he asked, "And Henri, what was he, eh? Gendarme, I'll bet!" He ended with a laugh.

Enrique had not fully understood. When Pablo translated the man's words for him and explained why he had spoken like that, Enrique shrugged his shoulders. "Tell him he gives me the gripes," he said. "Tell him also that within three days he'll be a cuckold."

"What's he saying?" asked the man.

Pablo replied immediately, "He says that he was a taxi-driver. And it's true. That's what he did."

"Since he can talk French he ought to talk French."

As they reached the barn three women began to cross the courtyard. One was old, bent-backed, and dressed entirely in black. The second woman appeared to be about forty, and the third a little more than twenty. All three were wearing clogs.

"Hallo there! Marguerite," shouted the *patron*.

The women changed direction and entered the barn.

"I see you've got your Spaniards," said the old woman.

36

"Yes," said the man. "An office clerk and a taxi-driver; I've got a right pair, I can tell you."

The old woman stared at them. She had very small, quick eyes. Her sharp stare passed rapidly from one to the other. Her seemingly lipless mouth chewed constantly. On her wrinkled cheek a large wart rose and fell, shaking a long, curly hair.

"The tall one is rather skinny, but he must be pretty strong," she said. Then, giving a nod in the direction of Enrique, she added, "That chap looks like my grand-daughter's husband. You know, Denise, the one who lives at Saint-Claude. He's got a chest that caves in like that fellow's. It's a sign their health's no good."

She took a few steps towards the kitchen, then she turned round to add, "I say the sickness they've got comes from always living indoors. Denise's husband is a chemist, so what can you expect?"

When the three women had left the *patron* began to laugh. Turning towards Pablo, he explained: "We're going to have a bit of fun later. The old woman must have thought you didn't understand a word of French." He winked again and, lowering his voice went on: "The two others are her daughter and grand-daughter. They're both good for a tumble."

Pablo could not restrain a shrug of his shoulders. He turned towards the cart and asked, "What can I do now?"

The man made them pull the cart to the centre of the courtyard. After that they loaded the two large wine-tubs called *sapines*, putting a small ladder and the *bouille* in the first. In the other they piled the wooden pails.

The man followed them round, giving orders and advice, pointing out with his stick what had to be done. He became irritated for very trivial reasons, and swore unceasingly. Pablo tried to understand everything he said, but from time to time the man used strange words to indicate a tool or an object. Pablo would then ask the man to repeat what he had said, and the man shouted back his reply.

Enrique did very little. Now and again he made rude comments about the man in Catalan.

"You see," he said at one moment, "he's on edge because he senses I'm going to get going on his wife. Reassure him, tell him I prefer the couple of birds who've just arrived. Explain to him that he can have his wife and the old woman."

"Shut up!" said Pablo. "It's you standing there doing nothing that's getting on his nerves. And the way you keep speaking Catalan."

The cart was ready. Everything was ready, even the bag of hay for the horse.

"When the *patronne* has prepared the food you'll hang the basket at the rear. We'll see to the harness at the last moment. Come on now, let's have breakfast."

The man went towards the kitchen.

V

WHILE they were having their breakfast an old man with a limp arrived. The *patron* called him Clopineau.

"You see," the *patron* explained, "so long as he's alive they'll keep calling me by my proper name in the village. You can't have two 'hobblers' in one village. But as soon as he's dead it's me who'll get the name. He limps because he was kicked by a horse, but with time he's got accustomed to it: he doesn't need a stick."

"You'll get used to it too," said the old man, "but it'll take you longer. Your leg's worse than mine."

Old Marguerite, who had remained by the stove with her daughter and grand-daughter and the *patronne*, approached the table. "Tell me, Lucien," she asked the *patron*, "who are you explaining all this for?"

Her old face was even more wrinkled than a little earlier. Her eyes were almost closed. The *patron* looked at her, looked at Clopineau, and then, turning to Pablo, he burst out laughing.

The old woman began to gesticulate. "What are you laughing about? What's so funny? You're explaining for them."

"Of course, it's for them."

She was becoming more and more angry. "And what was that cock-and-bull story about them being Spaniards?"

"They are Spaniards, but they speak French."

Old Marguerite's daughter, who was standing by the stove, said a few words in a low voice to the *patronne*, and then all three burst out laughing in turn. The old woman turned round and shouted something to them in the local dialect which Pablo did not understand. Everyone laughed louder than ever. Then, shrugging her shoulders, the old woman sat down facing Pablo. She waited for the roar of laughter to finish, and then, scornfully, she stared at the *patron*. "Well," she said, "what did I say? Nothing bad. I said that the big one was certainly strong and that the other was like the husband of my grand-daughter. That's nothing to be ashamed of."

Pablo looked at the old woman; he looked also at old Clopineau. These two must be just about the same age. Clopineau was less wrinkled than Marguerite, but he had a large walrus moustache which his lower lip sucked constantly.

Pablo looked at them for a long while. He would have liked to say something friendly to them, but he couldn't find the words.

The *patron* had stopped laughing, and the women were preparing, on the end of the table which was free, what would be needed for the midday meal. The *patronne* had unfolded several clean napkins in which to wrap the food. First there was a large piece of ham, two huge home-made sausages, several small cheeses, and a large pot of jam.

They put everything in a large basket. The two large, round loaves of bread were wrapped separately.

"We'll put those in the *sapine*," said the *patronne*.

They were about to rise from the table when another woman came in. She was very fat, with a goitre as big as her chignon. She was out of breath. "I thought we were late," she said.

"You're just in time," said the man. "We're just off."

"*Bonjour*," continued the fat woman. "The boy made me run. I can't get my breath."

"Give her a glass of wine, Jeannette," shouted the *patron*.

Jeannette left the corner by the sink, where she had stood for a long time, as if frightened by so many people and so much noise.

The fat woman drank her glass of red wine at a single gulp, and everyone filed out.

A lad of about fifteen was waiting outside, sitting on the shaft of the cart.

"Jump to it, my fine fellow," shouted the *patron*. "Go and fetch La Noire."

The lad ran to the stable, and soon came out leading the mare. She was a slightly heavy animal, with a beautiful coat and jet

39

black. Only in her mane were there a few reddish hairs. She backed docilely and let Pablo pat her, while the lad helped the *patron* to harness her.

"D'you like horses?" asked the *patron*.

"I like all animals," said Pablo.

"That doesn't mean a thing. It's not the same at all. I mean, d'you know horses well?"

"No," admitted Pablo, "but I'd like to know them better."

"Well, La Noire is the finest animal I've ever had."

"That's true," said Clopineau, who had come across.

"She's an exceptionally fine animal. And I'm talking of gentleness as well as strength."

As he was speaking he gave the animal some crusts of bread he had picked up from the table before leaving.

"Actually, gentlemen," said the *patron*, "I'm quite certain if I'd had that animal the night of my accident I'd still have my leg intact to this day."

The harnessing completed, he hooked his stick on the edge of the *sapine*, put his hand on the mare's croup, and managed thus to climb on the front of the cart.

"Come up!" he shouted. "Jump on!"

The boy climbed up on the wheel and settled himself in the *sapine*. The *patron* picked up the reins, and everyone started to walk behind the cart.

All around them the mist seemed to have thickened. They walked in a white circle which seemed to move forward at the same pace as they did themselves, revealing the road yard by yard. They passed underneath trees the tops of which were invisible and which dripped down water on a carpet of sticky and muddy leaves. Later on they passed between two houses. There the mist was scented with woodsmoke. A woman opened a door.

"You're going?" she asked.

"We're going to try," replied the *patronne*. "Have your people gone?"

"They started five minutes ago. The mud must be up to their knees."

The *patronne* stopped for a moment, and Pablo, who was passing, heard her saying, "Let's hope the wind hasn't beaten everything down. We've not as many people as we'd like to have."

She caught up with the party and asked them, as she passed, if they were cold.

"Not too bad," said Pablo as he marched along.

She smiled at them and lengthened her stride to rejoin the group of women who were walking a few clogs' lengths behind the cart. Pablo could hear them chattering endlessly, but he was too far away to be able to follow their conversation. From time to time they passed through thicker patches of mist. The cart then faded from view, and, sometimes, even the silhouettes of the women became blurred.

Soon the road began to climb. Old Clopineau, who till then had walked beside Pablo and Enrique without speaking, stopped. Taking a deep breath, he said, "It's making me puff. You push on ahead; you're young, you two."

He lifted his cap. His white head was moist with sweat. He wiped it with the back of his sleeve and added, "It's not far now, but all the same, Marguerite's still trotting along well. As for me, I'll wait for Jeannette, and we'll walk the rest of the way together."

Before starting off again Pablo looked back. The girl was coming along, still with her duck-like gait and her drooping lip. When she caught Pablo's eye she opened her mouth a little more, and Pablo thought she must have grunted.

As they advanced the mist became whiter. Eddies of wind revealed a tree, a bush, or a heap of vine-cuttings.

"There are some vines," said Pablo.

"They aren't like those back home," said Enrique.

They were the first they had seen since arriving in France. They could distinguish only the beginnings of rows which disappeared into the grey mist. The leaves were red and yellow, all shining with moisture.

As they passed a spot where the road overlooked a vineyard they heard muffled voices which seemed to be coming out of the ground itself.

"Hallo! Hallo! Noémie!" shouted the *patronne*. "They're not too blown about?"

A voice rose. "Is that you, Germaine?"

"Yes."

"It's not too bad, but it's a good job the rain has stopped; the grapes are very ripe."

"You've got everyone with you?"

"Yes, and you?"

"Us, too."

They had not halted; nothing had come from the mist except

this voice, other voices, a girl's laugh, and the sounds of the *seilles*, the wooden wine-harvesting buckets, striking against each other. They were already some way farther on when the voice sounded again, more muffled: "And your boy, Germaine? Any news?"

"No, nothing for three days," shouted the *patronne*.

Pablo had turned round. The old man and the girl were not yet in sight.

When they caught up with the cart, standing at the side of the road, the *patron* and the boy were already unhitching the horse.

"Come on, get everything off."

Once the *seilles* had been distributed, the *patron* told everyone his place, two persons to each row. In the middle row he placed Enrique and the *patronne*.

"You'll show Henri how to empty the *seilles*. Jump to it!"

Each pair went along the vines. Clopineau and Jeannette arrived when the others were together—at the far end of the rows.

"You," said the *patron* to Pablo, "stay there; I'm going to show you how to empty the *bouille*."

He looked round again to be sure that everyone was in their right place, then returned to the cart.

"I put the old man with Jeannette," he explained in a low voice. "He's the only one who can bear to be with her; the others shout out all the time that she doesn't work fast enough. As I can't bend there's no question of me taking a row. So I go along with them, and I cut anything that's high; that helps the old man a bit, and no-one falls behind the rest."

He had hooked his stick onto the wheels and put on the straps of the *bouille*, which was standing at the edge of the cart. "It's like this," he explained. "When you get here you climb the ladder, you hold on to the edge of the *sapine* with one hand, and with the other you push the bottom of the *bouille* round. At the same time you lean to the side."

He demonstrated the movement several times, holding with one hand to a vine-stake.

"Understand?"

"I think so," said Pablo.

"That's fine. Now try."

Pablo put the *bouille* on his back, climbed on the ladder, and made the motions of emptying it.

42

"A bit further forward," said the *patron*. "Otherwise every-thing'll go on the ground."

Pablo tried again several times.

"That's fine; I think you'll manage. Remains to be seen whether you can stand up to the job."

"I hope I can."

"Me too, because with the team I've got, apart from your pal, no-one can carry except the *patronne*, but if she had to do it there'd be a lot of gossip in the village."

"The *bouille*," shouted the *patronne*.

They turned in the direction of the vines. A few yards away from them the harvesters were standing up.

"Go on, quick!" said the *patron*.

Pablo climbed between the vines. He almost ran, glad of the chance to get warm. The earth was soft and clung to his feet. When he reached the *patronne* he turned his back and bent his knees.

"Don't go down," shouted the *patron*, who had stayed near the cart, "otherwise in an hour or two your knees'll be absolutely stiff. Get your feet apart and hold on to a post."

The *patronne* emptied the first few *seilles*.

"Try it," she said to Enrique.

He took a *seille*, raised it, and let it fall upside down in the *bouille*.

Pablo staggered. He felt grape-seeds on his neck and icy juice running down his back.

"Be careful!" he shouted.

The others laughed.

"Show him again, Germaine," shouted the *patron*. "And don't fool about or everything'll go wrong."

As soon as the *bouille* was full Pablo had to shake it down to make room for the last two pailfuls. The *patronne* emptied them in.

"Off you go," she said.

Pablo set off with long strides. His feet dug in more than when he came up because of the load he was carrying.

"Scrape your soles at the first rung before you start to climb, otherwise you'll have the whole lot on the ground."

Pablo obeyed. He climbed and emptied, carrying out the move-ment the *patron* had shown him.

"That's fine. You're doing it right. I think you'll be able to

43

manage. Only what you must do is to get a proper rhythm. Don't try to run when you're going up. Coming down, lengthen your stride, let yourself be pushed along by the load. You'll find out that when they are at the far end of the rows you'll have just time to do the journey."

Pablo went up again. The *patron* took his stick and went up at the same time, but along the row where his daughter was helping. When Pablo came near the pickers Enrique asked him, "Aren't you cold?"

"No, I'm all right."

"Well, I can't feel my fingers any more. Let me do a trip; it'll warm me up."

"You'll have to ask the boss."

"What's he saying?" asked the *patronne*.

"He wants to carry for a while, to warm himself up."

The *patron* had stiffened. Shaking his secateurs, he began to shout, "Oh, no, not that! Tell him not to make a nuisance of himself. I'm going down to telephone for them to take him away."

Enrique did not persist. He rubbed his numbed hands together and started again to cut the bunches of sodden grapes.

"Don't worry," said the *patronne*. "The sun'll be through very soon."

With each journey the distance became greater, but Pablo had to wait a little while between each loaded *bouille*. At the beginning he had asked for secateurs, so that he could lend Enrique and the *patronne* a hand, but the *patron* was firmly against it.

"The one who carries never cuts. That's the rule. If you've nothing to do, roll yourself a cigarette."

He passed over his tobacco-pouch and cigarette-papers.

"You could roll one for your pal as well. That'll at least warm the tip of his nose."

The others laughed. They were laughing constantly at the slightest excuse. From time to time the *patron* shouted, "A little less chatter! When tongues are busy hands are idle."

There would be silence for a few minutes, and then the chattering would recommence. The *patron* also chatted to old Clopineau.

Only Pablo and Enrique were silent. Pablo had the feeling of not quite belonging to the group. Now, when he reached the cart and turned to empty the *bouille*, he could no longer see the others, lost in the mist above him. He heard only an occasional laugh from one of the women or the *patron* shouting. He

44

was alone. No-one could see him. The mare, hitched to a post on the other side of the road, was the only other living thing in this little world confined in a circle of mist. La Noire turned her head towards him. Each time before going back up the slope he went across to her and stroked her neck or her head.

"D'you like grapes?" he asked her.

La Noire nodded her head. Pablo smiled. He had spoken in Catalan. "D'you understand Catalan?" he asked.

La Noire nodded her head again. This time Pablo laughed loudly. He gave her a bunch of grapes, which she munched, dribbling red juice.

On that trip, when Pablo arrived, all the *seilles* were already filled.

"Taking longer," said the *patron*.

"It's all right," said Pablo. "I just stopped a minute or two with the mare."

As if he had guessed, the *patron* advised him: "Don't give her too many cold grapes; they won't do her much good."

Pablo made several more trips, then as he climbed, his back bent, looking at the sun ahead of him, he suddenly had a feeling that the sky had split open. It was like a rain of light.

He stopped and raised his head.

The mist, however, was still moving across the face of the sun in huge, soft waves which clung to the vines.

The pickers had also straightened up. It was now possible to see beyond them. The first trees emerged, still pale but sparkling.

Pablo turned round and remained almost breathless for some seconds.

All the golden vines were gleaming. Everything was moving. The leaves were rising in a shower of sun-drops, and they were like that as far as that part of the road where La Noire made a black patch, and even farther on, lower down, where there were other vines, green hedges, and trees. Beyond this, at the very foot of the hillside, there was a sea of white mist with blue swirls and long grey alleys in it. And from the other side, lighting up this compact white frost, the sun was rising. It was at the line between the mist and the sky—a sky, still pale, but already blue and clearing of a few fragments of transparent cloud.

Everything was alive. In the stretch of vines which Pablo had before him, in the sea of mist in which the foot of the slope was

45

bathed, nothing was truly still. Nothing. Except the cart and the mare.

The vapour which rose from the ground disturbed the vines as it passed. Everything moved; even the branches of the trees straightened one by one. Everything took on colour, each plant showing in its place, which it marked on the ground by throwing a blue shadow.

"Hey, down there! Sleeping on your feet?"

There was a burst of laughter. It sounded clearer.

Pablo turned about and began to climb again. The laughter continued and greeted him.

"Well," said the *patron*, "haven't you ever seen a sunrise before?"

Pablo smiled, but did not speak.

No, he had never seen such a sunrise. He had seen the sun rise over a town, sometimes at sea, sometimes on a mountain, but never like this.

His *bouille* loaded, he went down again. He walked facing a huge emptiness which ended only just below the sun.

He emptied his *bouille*, went up again, made several more trips, and, each time he turned round to go down he discovered something new. First it was the tower of the village church, then another tower farther off. After that the poplars isolated or in groups. And each time there was a blue patch lengthening on the mist.

At midday the gang of workers had picked three complete rows. The first *sapine* was full.

The *patron* was well pleased. The storm had not done as much damage as might have been expected.

The sun was very warm. The earth was no longer steaming, but was already drying in places, sticking less to the feet and to the bottoms of the pails.

Pablo had set down his *bouille* only once, just long enough to take off his jacket and to drink a glass of wine at the moment when the pickers began the second row. He had a burning sensation on his shoulders and the base of his neck was painful. Nevertheless the time had not seemed long to him.

On each trip he was able to see a little more of the immense Bressan plain which stretched now as far as the blue line of the first foothills of the Massif Central. Miles and miles of plain to be discovered everywhere—sections of black or yellow roads,

46

villages, isolated farms, and the lighter patch coming from a pond with a veil of mist lingering over it longer than elsewhere. Kilometres of earth and vegetation smiling in the brilliant sunshine.

When he was going up, the summit was immediately ahead of him. Above the vines there was a stretch of russet-coloured fallow land which extended as far as the wood, where the first trees stood out clear and sharp against the blue of the sky. The sky seemed very close. Beyond the wood it seemed one might touch it by stretching out a hand. To the left the line of slopes fell back on the plain surrounding the village. Down there the greyness still persisted. It was to the north, and the base of the sky remained cold. To the right the slope stretched very far, with hollows which made the shadow and light more sharp.

Now and then patches of colour, in groups, rose in the rustiness of the vines. On the road wagons waited, and horses too.

When Pablo had taken off his jacket the *patron* said to him, "You can take the blanket off La Noire too."

He had lifted off the blanket which had been thrown across La Noire's back when they arrived. She had scarcely touched the hay which the boy had put down for her. She preferred to tear pieces off the hedge or to beg a grape from Pablo, who continued to caress and speak to her on every trip.

They remained near the cart to eat. The *patron* upturned three pails and placed a plank across the top of them. He told Clopineau to sit down and sat beside him.

"Come on, Marguerite," he shouted. "There's room for you here."

She began to laugh. "I'm not so old that I need to be given a seat," she declared.

Enrique and Pablo had sat down on the grass, their backs against a slope. The earth was warm on the surface, but they had to change their place often because of the rising damp.

The women were sitting on pails, except the *patronne*, who was eating leaning against the cart where she had spread out the provisions. She was cutting large chunks of bread, putting bacon, sausage, or cheese on them, and handing them round. She was also pouring out drinks.

Jeannette was not sitting down either. Slightly away from them, she remained standing at the edge of the road, legs apart, leaning forward and eating open-mouthed, her eyes on Pablo and her father and old Clopineau.

47

Pablo looked at her for a moment. When whoever she was looking at looked back at her she made an odd movement of her lips and stared at one of the others. Pablo stopped looking at her; she was repugnant when she ate.

The meal lasted a long time. They ate a great deal very slowly, at first without speaking, then commenting on the harvest or listening to the gross jokes of the *patron*.

As soon as the meal was over the *patronne* offered glasses of brandy, and the *patron* passed round his tobacco-pouch. Then, while the women put the left-overs, the glasses, and the empty bottles into baskets, the men smoked a cigarette.

When Pablo stood up a sharp pain gripped the small of his back. He gritted his teeth and walked as far as the cart. The wine-harvesters were already at work. Pablo made sure that no-one was watching him, and then, opening his shirt, he looked at his shoulders. They were very red, and the mark left by the straps showed distinctly. Just above the bone some of the skin had come away, and his flesh was raw. He buttoned up his shirt, walked across to La Noire, and gave her a piece of bread he had kept for her. While she munched it, tossing her large head, Pablo looked at the plain.

The earth was still steaming, but the rising mist was transparent. In the distance the blue line of the mountains rose, undulated, and became merged with the lower sky at times. The shadows were closer, denser.

Pablo's eyes again sought the house he had noticed that morning. It was easy to find because of the cemetery. In the yard and in the fields light and dark shapes moved about—chickens, geese, ducks. On the road a few glittering cars passed along. There was not a breath of wind. There was no noise except the clicking of secateurs, a vibrating wire, a pail dragged across stones, a few words or a laugh.

Pablo sighed. He stroked La Noire's head, and she begged by thrusting her muzzle against his chest, then he walked towards the cart. He slipped the straps on again and set off, his teeth clenched, his hands on his back to support the *bouille* a little.

As the first pail was poured in he almost screamed. He had to move his hands, and the burning on his shoulders redoubled. Enrique was loading him. The *patronne* had probably noticed Pablo's grimaces.

"Be careful," she said. "Don't bang the *seilles* on the *bouille*

48

Enrique did not reply and emptied another *seille* the same way.

"Don't you understand?" asked the *patronne,* raising her voice a little.

"If he hasn't understood I'll explain it to him!" shouted the *patron.*

Enrique took a little more care. "My word," he said to Pablo in Catalan, "she's certainly got a soft spot for you, the old girl."

"What's he saying?" demanded the *patron.*

"He said that he didn't understand the first time."

"Shake the *bouille,*" said the *patronne.*

He shook it.

"Are you tired?" she asked.

Pablo shook it more vigorously. Without parting his teeth he said, "No, I'm fine."

Then he set off again, pushed along by the weight of grapes, with straps which seemed at every step to cut more deeply into his flesh.

After a moment or two the burning sensation was less sharp. He tried to look at the plain, fixing his eyes on a single point and keeping them fixed to avoid thinking.

Like an automaton he walked like this until evening. On the last ascent to the vines the road was longer than ever. He had to go up through the whole length of vines. That was a short distance, really, a few dozen yards at most, but he was so tired. The earth no longer stuck to his soles, but nevertheless Pablo felt it getting heavier with every trip. His knees were stiff. He climbed again, his back bent, his thumbs under the straps of the *bouille.* The sweat was running down his whole body, and the evening breeze made his shirt stick to his chest each time that he straightened up. The cold contact refreshed him a little.

When descending he almost ran, staggering, grabbing at a stake here and a post there, to balance himself. He emptied the *bouille,* went back again, came down immediately, then someone would shout "Off you go!"

He was no longer even taking the four paces which separated the cart from the mare. However she shook her head and made her snaffle click, Pablo no longer even looked towards her.

In the end the others were shouting for him when he still had a quarter of the distance to cover. Pablo pushed on, sometimes closing his eyes, blinded by sweat.

"The *bouille!* The *bouille!*"

49

Pablo mouthed a few curses in Catalan, but he arrived at the top with a smile.

"You can't manage any more," said the *patronne*. "Hand it over; I'll take your place. There's very little left."

"No, I'm all right. I assure you I can manage."

"Would you like me to take over?" enquired Enrique.

"Come on, come on!" shouted the *patron*. "Don't waste time. He's got the rhythm; he'll manage. The main thing is not to stop. What d'you think he is, a girl?"

Nobody laughed. Weariness was also making the *seilles* heavier, making backs and arms ache.

"Very well," said the *patronne* at last. "There's little more to do. Don't come up again; we'll bring down our *seilles*."

Pablo straightened up. They were only a few yards from the fallow land. Then, as soon as his *bouille* was full, he let himself be pushed down the slope. He emptied his load into the almost full *sapine* and left his *bouille* lying on top of the grapes. As soon as he was back on the ground he leaned against the ladder and looked towards the distant plain, breathing deeply.

The sun had long since set. Some lights had already appeared. Smoke rose from village chimneys. Over all the land there was a great weariness which rose from the earth, which flowed from the hillsides in billows of sound-like waves. Waves which swept through Pablo's legs, gripped his body, echoed in his head, and let their whole weight sink into his hanging hands on either side of the ladder.

Over everything the evening breeze sent other waves, soft and fresh.

On all the plain was an immense weariness like the promise of a deep sleep.

VI

THEY got back when night had already fallen. In silence they had followed the cart, its woodwork groaning under the weight it was carrying. During the descent the brake fully applied held the wheels, which ploughed furrows in the earth and crushed the pebbles into white powder.

Pablo no longer felt tired. He was simply drunk, just that, and he found it almost agreeable. He staggered a little. He had nothing on his shoulders except the weight of his jacket, and he was surprised by this at every step. He walked with his eyes fixed firmly on the cart. He didn't even notice as women broke away from the group.

When they entered the courtyard there was only the *patronne*, Enrique, and himself behind the cart. The *patronne* hurried forward, went in through the stable, and opened the double doors of the barn. The man climbed down, took La Noire by the bridle, and made her back to get the loaded cart into the barn.

"And Clopineau?" he asked his wife. "I hope you didn't let him go off."

"No, he must be a bit behind with the child."

"Well, don't let him go. First he can have some soup with us, and then he can provide another pair of hands to unload the grapes."

As Pablo heard the *patron* speaking he became fully alert. He had not thought of that. He had not thought of anything, but had just marched along like a worn-out horse who still finds the strength to trot because he can scent the stable.

He said nothing, as if he had been knocked out.

The *patron* unhitched La Noire and led her to the stable. Pablo, sitting on the edge of the stone basin, heard him giving the horse a drink.

Soon afterwards old Clopineau arrived. He was limping more now than early in the day, and walking more slowly. He had cut himself a stick and was leaning on it. As he entered the courtyard he flung the stick down by the wall.

Jeannette was still with him and had not changed, either in her expression or in her gait. She went immediately to the kitchen, where her mother was busy with casseroles. Pablo heard a shout:

"Hurry and make up the fire and put the soup on."

Then the *patronne* went out to the stable with her two milking pails.

"You'll stay, Clopineau," she said.

The old man went to sit on the edge of the stone basin beside Pablo and Enrique. He remained silent for a moment, pulled out his tobacco-pouch, and rolled a cigarette. Then, offering his pouch and cigarette-papers to Pablo, he said, "Here you are. Roll yourself one. A smoke's refreshing."

"Thanks," said Pablo.

They rolled their cigarettes, and the old man pulled out his lighter. When they had lit up, Pablo asked, "What are we going to do now?"

"Unload the grapes."

"Will it take long?"

"Not very long. Today it's the red grapes, so we don't do any pressing. They're left to ferment."

"And then?" inquired Pablo.

"Then? Well, they're finished more quickly than the white. By the time the *patronne* and the child have got the soup ready it'll be finished. Whereas for the white you have to come back after your meal to do the pressing."

The *patron* came out of the stable. "That's fine," he said. "Come along."

Clopineau and Pablo stood up and followed the *patron* into the barn.

"We must fix up the strainer. You two take—"

He stopped suddenly, looking for Enrique.

"Where is he?"

Pablo called: "Enrique!"

No answer. Pablo went as far as the door. Enrique hadn't moved.

"Come on," he said.

"No, I'm browned off. I'm hungry. I want to eat and then sleep."

The *patron* came over. "What's the matter with him?"

Pablo hesitated. "He's very tired," he said.

The *patron* clenched his fists. The muscles of his jaws moved under his roughly shaven skin. Old Clopineau had also come forward.

"It's natural," he said; "he's not used to it. And in those camps they must have been underfed."

The *patron* looked at the old man, then at Pablo, and he sighed. In the half-light of the courtyard Enrique remained motionless, his back bowed and his hands resting on his knees. Only his eyes were bright. He looked like a sick animal.

There was silence for a few seconds, then the old man spoke again: "If he could just help us to fix the strainer we three could manage afterwards."

"Tell him he's to help for five minutes," explained the *patron*.

"After that he can go and get some food in the kitchen, and then go up to bed."

The *patron* went back into the barn, adding as if to himself, "I'd rather have no-one than someone who works without using his head."

Pablo explained what the *patron* had said, and Enrique got to his feet slowly. He dragged his boots across the concrete of the barn, moving like a sleep-walker. He helped, however, to unhook a long wooden strainer from the ceiling where it was hanging. They then slid it through one of the air-holes of the cellar. Passing under the press, where there was a support for its middle, the strainer went down in a gentle slope to the top of one of the big barrels lined up in the centre of the cellar. Another shorter strainer was joined to the first and went as far as the *sapine* standing on the cart.

As soon as the installation was finished, Enrique went towards the kitchen without a word. The *patron* watched him going, and then, turning to Pablo, he asked, "And you, are you tired?"

Pablo tried to smile. "No, I can manage," he said.

Then the *patron* nodded towards Clopineau. "It's the old 'uns who stick it the best."

Clopineau laughed heartily, and, at the same time, made a gesture with both arms as if to excuse himself for still being so sturdy.

They went down to the cellar, and the two men helped the *patron* to sit astride the barrel.

"The trick is to get everything into place; afterwards it's just a question of having hands to do the job, and where hands are concerned, there are few I couldn't beat."

He had to push the *vendange* into the huge funnel as it came down through the wooden strainer.

The old man and Pablo went up afterwards and climbed on the cart, one on either side of the *sapine*. There, armed with short-handled mattocks, they began to pound the grapes.

"Must make sure we work in the same rhythm," explained Clopineau. "Otherwise we're likely to get in each other's way or to hit each other."

They began slowly, and then, little by little, their movements speeded up. While Pablo dug into the grapes and drew the bunches dripping with juice to his left, the old man drew his own into the strainer. There the grapes were carried along by the juice running in long violet streams.

The grapes were warm. Their hands were sticky with grape juice, but it was clean and not unpleasant, and the smell rising from the *sapine* was like a mixture of sunshine and mist.

When the *sapine* was half emptied the old man was breathless. Pablo could hear his struggle for breath with every movement. He slowed down a little, but the old man still puffed very hard.

Once again Pablo had succeeded in forgetting his own weariness. He felt it, but it remained still and silent.

Soon the *patronne* came out of the stable and went to the cart.

"All right?" she asked.

"Fine," replied Pablo, without stopping.

She hung over the stairway, looked into the cellar, and then turned back.

"And that pal of yours?"

"In bed."

She went off towards the kitchen, and returned after she had put down her cans. She caught hold of the edge of the *sapine* and, one foot on the hub of the wheel, hoisted herself up to look around.

"Send us the ladles," said the old man, straightening up.

Pablo also stopped and brushed his forearm over his sweaty forehead.

"Gets warm," puffed the old man.

They got to the bottom of the vat; there was more juice than grapes and the mattocks drew nothing up. The *patronne* handed them two wooden ladles.

"Well," shouted the *patron*, "how's it going?"

"Going fine," she said; "they're at the bottom."

When they came down to move the cart and put the second *sapine* in place the *patronne* was still there. She supported the strainer while the two men manœuvred it. When all was ready and before the old man had got back she climbed up and took her place opposite Pablo.

"Come down from there," shouted Clopineau.

"No," she said, "let me go on. I want to see if I still know how how to do it."

The old man was annoyed, and his chin was trembling.

"You're making fun of me, or else you think my work's no good."

54

"What's he belly-aching about?" shouted the *patron*, who knew perfectly well. "That'll be the day when someone tries to stop my wife having her share in the vintaging! If that happens she'll drink none of the wine!"

They all began to laugh. The old man shrugged his shoulders and walked off, muttering to himself.

"Go and see that Jeannette isn't letting the soup burn," shouted the *patronne*. "I don't like her left alone near the fire."

As she said the last word she plunged her mattock into the grapes. Pablo and she immediately established a quicker rhythm, and their tools did not clash even once. All that could be heard was the regular 'swoosh' of the mattocks biting into the grapes, and the sound of juice and seeds sliding down the strainer. Soon the sounds of their gasping breath could also be heard.

To the scent of the grapes was now added the strong odour of the woman's sweat.

Pablo noticed his weariness again, but he clenched his teeth to keep from groaning too loudly. The pain screamed, particularly in the small of his back, but it could not be heard, the sound could not escape from his body.

When they were half-way through they had to bend over further. On several occasions Pablo felt a lock of hair brush against his cheek. He stepped back a little.

As soon as they had emptied their last ladleful they stood erect with a sigh.

The woman was smiling. Sweat was making her hair stick to her forehead and cheeks.

"I think we did pretty well," she said, getting her breath back.

"I think so too."

"That's the lot?" shouted the *patron*.

"That the lot, yes!"

"Then come and give me a hand."

They both went to support him as he came down from the top of his barrel. Once on the ground again, he took off his cap and with the back of one sleeve brushed off the cobwebs which covered it.

"You need a feather duster to get rid of them," joked Pablo.

The two others looked at each other and began to laugh.

"What's so funny?" asked Pablo.

"No-one ever removes spiders' webs in a cellar," explained the *patron*. "They help catch insects which might spoil the wine."

Pablo smiled in turn and said, "I'm from the town."

"Anyone can tell that," said the *patron*, "but the main thing is that it doesn't show when you're working."

They came up again, closed the barn, and then, after having washed their hands and arms under the tap in the courtyard, they went towards the kitchen.

"Your pal must be sleeping like a log already," said the *patron*.

"He was certainly very tired."

"He didn't want to wait for his soup," said the *patronne*. "He just asked Jeannette for a slice of bread with some bacon."

When they went into the kitchen old Clopineau was asleep, his head on his arms on the table.

Standing by the stove where the pot of soup was steaming, Jeannette waited, her arms hanging loosely, her mouth a little open, and her eyes on the door.

VII

WHEN Pablo awoke the next morning it was already day, and light was filtering through every crack. He was no longer content, as the day before, to peer under the shutter. He could sense that it was a stronger light advancing over the earth to meet the wind which was already there. But the wind did not rage round the gable of the barn; it went round singing.

Pablo thought it must be very late. He tried to get up.

"Oh!" he cried.

He let his head fall back on the straw.

With that movement he had awakened all the deep pain which had been dormant in him. It flashed madly through his entire body; it became a thousand and one pains all linked together to act in unison. It went from the tips of his toes to his wrists, to his chest, and to the nape of his neck. Now, after the first attack, everything became a little easier, except the small of his back and his shoulders. In them it was more than a pain, it was a deep wound, a hot iron turning and turning deep inside him. It was an animal biting his flesh, tearing his skin and his muscles.

Slowly Pablo turned his head. Stretched out also on his back,

56

Enrique was staring at him, pulling an ugly face. When their eyes met Enrique's face became uglier, and he began to sneer.

"You too? Can't move?" he asked.

"I'm aching all over," Pablo admitted.

"I've had enough, I have. You wanted to show how tough you were. The great carrier! You wanted to show off where the old birds could see you. Fine! They're going to have a good laugh this morning, those old birds. I wonder who'll be carrying their barrel with braces today!"

Pablo did not reply. He was now staring at the beams and tiles above his head. He heard clogs clicking on the road.

He sighed. His great pain was lying, as he was, still and attentive. It had not gone to sleep again. He knew now that it was ready to start again the moment he moved.

"Did you have a good sleep?" asked Enrique.

"Yes, I slept like a log."

Enrique sneered again. Pablo kept silent. It was true: he had slept like a log.

He remembered the quick and silent dinner. He remembered the lantern the *patronne* had got ready. The stairway, Enrique asleep. Then, after that, darkness. A sudden, immediate pit. Heavy sleep, without an instant for reflection. For months and months he had not slept like this. Each night he had always seen, hour after hour, the face of Mariana. Mariana dead. Mariana mutilated. Mariana lost in the ruins. Mariana whom the night brought out of the shadows, thrusting her towards Pablo. A Mariana frightening because of the weight of her sadness and mystery.

Last night she had not come with him as far as the barn. She had not really left him, but she had been crushed by Pablo's weariness. She had slept the same sleep as he had.

This morning she was there, her face between that of Pablo and the tiles. But her face showed no tears. It was not covered with blood and mud.

The face of Mariana was a morning face.

Pablo looked at it for an instant, scarcely surprised, and his astonishment disappeared entirely when he looked at the light.

Mariana's face was not smiling. It was serious, weary, but it was alive with the light of the morning. This light with which it had entered.

There was still the sound of footsteps on the road and voices which Pablo recognized. The woman and her little boy were arriving. The boy kicked at the stones on the road, and his mother shouted that he would break one of his clogs.

Pablo closed his eyes. He bent his knees slowly, putting his feet flat on the straw. Without opening his lips he counted: "One ... two ... three ... !"

The straw flew through the air. The blanket slipped to the floor, and Pablo bit his lips to avoid crying out.

Now he was up. He knew that he'd made a good start.

"Come on, Enrique!"

The other did not budge. He continued to sneer. "You can go to hell," he said, and he closed his eyes.

Pablo opened the shutter.

"Leave that alone!" shouted Enrique. "I haven't slept a wink. I've had such pains in my legs and back. Leave me alone."

Pablo did not reply, but he left the shutter open. He pulled up his trousers and socks, then, with his jacket and shirt on his arm, he went down and washed himself in the icy water of the tap in the yard.

The *patron* came out of the barn accompanied by the boy and the large, fat woman.

"I was going to give you a shout," he told Pablo.

Then, turning towards the boy, he went on, pointing to the cold water, "You see, little 'un, that's the stuff men are made of."

He went towards the kitchen, and then, turning back after a few steps, asked, "And your brave pal, where's he?"

Pablo nodded his chin towards the barn while he continued to soap his arms.

"Try to make him understand that he'd better hurry; the soup's hot, and if he wants to eat before leaving now's the time."

The *patron* went off, and Pablo hurried to the barn. As he hung his towel on the length of wire he explained: "You've got to get up. Once you've had a good wash in cold water you won't feel so tired."

"You make me sick! You want shares in the farm; I don't."

Pablo was ready. He took two steps towards the stairway, turned round, and asked, "So I'm to say you're not coming?"

"They'll notice, won't they?"

Enrique was snappy. Pablo hesitated. "I thought you'd a bit more guts," he said.

The other raised himself on one elbow, grimaced, and began to

58

shout: "Guts! You call that guts, skulking on a farm while others are getting their heads bashed in?"

Pablo had jumped. He seemed to think for some seconds, then he said, "You know very well that for us the war is over, Enrique. There's nothing more to hope for."

"That's easily said. And to hear you no-one would ever believe you'd been a *dinamitero* on the Madrid front. We're in France now, Pablo. And here nobody's forbidden to continue fighting against the Fascists. On the contrary, it's even encouraged. But you have to be keen about it."

Images of the war came back. Pablo turned towards the attic window. On the other side of the road there was the plain which stretched away and rose to the height of the roof. It was alive, filled with blue and mauve vapours, with the sun moving long, dusty rays all over it.

Pablo turned to Enrique, who was lying down again.

"Very well," he said, "just as you like."

The other was a little calmer. "What I say, you know, doesn't stop you from staying free. We each do as we wish."

Pablo wanted to explain. He went across to Enrique. "You know," he began in a low voice, very slowly, "for me the war..."

"Hey, there," shouted the *patronne* from the door of the kitchen.

Pablo went to the open window and leaned out to shout, "Here we are!"

He returned towards Enrique, who asked, anger still simmering in his eyes, "What about the war?"

"The war, for me, you see..."

Pablo became silent, searching for words. Then he went on: "I can't seem to explain to you," he said. "I can't! I can't!"

His voice broke suddenly. He leaned towards his comrade and held out a hand which was trembling slightly.

"So long, Enrique," he said. "Good luck!"

Enrique shook his hand. "Best of luck, Pablo!"

There was less anger in his eyes. His voice had softened. "Got any money?" he asked.

"No," said Pablo, "but I could ask for you to be paid for your work yesterday. And also, if they'll let me have an advance, I'll give you some from my pay."

He waved his hand and went down the stairway.

"Ask them also to leave me a bit of bread," shouted Enrique.

59

In the kitchen two plates of steaming soup were set on the table.

"What the devil have you been doing?" shouted the *patron*. "We should have left by now."

He had just finished chewing a chunk of bacon. All the others were there, ready to start out and watching the *patronne*, who was just finishing the preparation of the baskets of food.

Pablo sat down and began to eat.

"And the other blackguard," asked the *patron*, "is he waiting for me to go and fetch him?"

Pablo stopped eating. He hesitated a moment, and then said very quickly, "He won't be coming down. He doesn't want to stay here. He wants to join the Army and fight."

As he said this he had anticipated an angry response from the *patron*. Everyone looked at Pablo, and then, one by one, looked away at the others. Each seemed to be asking, "Is it true? Did I really understand? Did you hear what I heard?"

With his spoon hanging in the air Pablo looked at them.

Old Marguerite was the first to speak. "But," she said, her face more wrinkled than ever, "does he want to go to the war in your country or to our war?"

"Their war's over," said the *patron*. "And they haven't the right to go back to Spain. Down there Franco's the boss."

"So it's with us. He's going where your boy and the others are?"

"Of course."

There was again a long silence. Marguerite shook her head. Her tiny eyes seemed to retreat into their sockets, in a wrinkle deeper than the others. The *patronne* had started to fill a basket again. The *patron*, pushing his empty plate towards the centre of the table, began to roll a cigarette. Jeannette, standing behind her father, was staring at Pablo, who glanced at her for an instant and then went on eating.

The *patron* lit his cigarette, handed his pouch to old Clopineau, and then said, "Yes. Must have taken him just bang! Like a sudden urge to pee!"

"It's a disease," muttered the old man. "A nasty disease!"

The old woman approached the table. "You shut up, Clopineau," she said. "If there weren't some who had the disease we'd have had the Prussians right here a long time ago. You've never had to go to war, you with your wonky foot!"

Clopineau did not reply. He did not even look up towards

Marguerite, who was spluttering on his cap. The *patronne* intervened: "You're not going to start quarrelling, surely! You're like a couple of children!"

Now everyone was talking at once about the war and those who had gone, volunteers or not.

Pablo finished his soup, put a piece of bacon between two hunks of bread, and said he would eat it as he went along so as not to delay anyone. Before going out he asked the *patron* if he could have an advance on his wages.

"It's for your pal?"

"Yes, he can't go off without anything."

The *patron* went to the dresser, opened a drawer, and took from a black wallet a five-hundred-franc note which he held out to Pablo.

"But..." stammered Pablo, "but..."

"Hop off and give it to him. And say *merde* to him for me. In French it means good luck."

Pablo ran to take the money to Enrique, who had not budged.

"That's fine. The old man's less stupid than I thought," said Enrique.

Pablo wished him good luck again and went down to join the others.

The cart was ready. The *patron* climbed up, and La Noire began to step out. Pablo helped the *patronne* to shut the door of the barn, then they left side by side to catch up with the others who were following the cart.

As they passed the barn Pablo looked at the open attic window. Enrique had obviously not budged. They walked on for a minute or two, and then Pablo pulled the bread from his pocket and began to eat.

"It's surprising, all the same," said the *patronne*, "that he should go off like that."

"Yes," said Pablo. He finished chewing his mouthful of bread and added, "The *patron*'s very kind."

"It was the least he could do."

"When Enrique asked me," said Pablo, "I was afraid the *patron* might be angry."

The woman began to laugh. She looked at Pablo and then said, "Him? Never! What's more, he said to me last night, 'That one's not a trier. He doesn't earn his pay, and I don't want to keep him.'"

"Then you think he would have got rid of him anyway?"

She looked at him, shrugged her shoulders, and said, "That's not certain. With him, you see, you never know. He says black at night and white in the morning. He's been like that since he had his accident. I've gradually got used to it. I never argue with him; that's the best way to get peace."

The woman became silent. They had almost caught up with old Clopineau and Jeannette, who were the last of the walkers. Pablo sensed that the *patronne* was easing her pace a little. He shortened his own step to keep beside her. As he marched along he continued to munch his bread and bacon.

The sun was still behind the slope. It could be sensed near the summit where the trees were fringed with light.

"Today we're going to make white wine," said the *patronne*.

Pablo did not reply. They walked a little way in silence, and then the *patronne* spoke again, "That'll mean going to bed very late; when we get back we'll have to do the pressing. And that's where your pal would have come in useful."

She sighed, and then, since Pablo did not speak, she added, "But there, since he wanted to join up . . ."

They came near to the houses. The woman who had come out the previous day was there again to greet them. When they came level with her the *patronne* stopped. Pablo went on a couple of paces, turned round, and heard the woman asking, "You've only got one Spaniard now?"

As the *patronne* began to explain what had happened Pablo started to walk on. He walked rather faster to catch up with Clopineau and Jeannette. The other group was farther ahead, so Pablo decided to walk with the old man and the girl. He was anxious to avoid any questions from the *patronne*. He knew she would want to talk again about the war. With Clopineau and Jeannette there would be silence, for the old man was too puffed with walking to want to speak.

The *patronne* soon caught them up and walked for a moment alongside them. Then, little by little, she speeded her pace and drew ahead. Twice she looked round at Pablo. Finally, seeing that he intended to go on walking at the same pace as the old man and the girl, she walked ahead more quickly, and soon caught up with the group of women.

Pablo sighed. He looked to his right. They had now reached the flank of the slope, and the plain stretched farther with every step they advanced. They could not yet see the sun, but all the plain was already bathed in sunshine. The shadow-line of the slopes drew back little by little, and soon the sun touched the stream, making it seem aflame.

The face of Mariana was always there, transparent and golden. It remained solemn, but Pablo was no longer fearful of looking at it.

No, this morning, with all that was around him, he would not have been able to speak of war. The woman was some distance away, chatting with the other women. He walked beside the old man and the girl. These two did not embarrass him. They never spoke of the war.

Pablo looked again at the plain, then, as the cart stopped at the end of the long rows of vines on a sharp slope, he looked at the hillside.

Despite himself, his hands went to his shoulders. The pain was there, deep and sharp. Pablo grimaced. He thought of Enrique, who was perhaps still asleep in the straw. Then, seeing the cart and the *sapines*, with the *bouille* projecting, he realized just how much he would be adding to his fatigue. How he would be climbing up between the rows of vines until evening, his eyes fixed on the yellow earth, how he would descend and redescend, pushed by the weight he carried and with his eyes staring towards the blue line where the plain and the sky met! And so on until nightfall, without a thought, with one idea only, to keep on walking.

Later he would again fall exhausted on the straw, crushed by fatigue and sleepiness. There he would sleep, and the pain would be deadened. The weariness of his body would give him once more that heavy sleep which carries one through, without seeing it, the mystery of the night, and takes one in a twinkling to the fresh water of the morning.

VIII

THE DAY was very warm. The soil, as soon as it was touched by the first rays of sunshine, became dusty. Clogs no longer sank in it, mud no longer stuck to the soles, but the pebbles rolled underfoot.

The slope was steeper than the one on which they had worked the previous day, and the water had made ridges in the ground, uncovering stones and cutting deep ruts.

Each step had to be watched. The clods of earth steamed. The south wind carried the dust along the side of the hill.

"It's the white wind," said old Marguerite. "If it lasts three days we'll be able to finish without a drop of rain falling."

"With a sun like that," said Clopineau, "the vintage will gain a degree a day."

The *patron* laughed. He was joking continuously. "If I was sure I'd wait three weeks, then it wouldn't be wine running from the press, it would be spirits. There'd be no need to distil, no need to look after the wine, nor to wonder whether it would sell or not. We'd be on velvet."

Pablo continued to go forwards and backwards, stopping occasionally to pick a grape or two from bunches missed by the pickers. They were warm and sweet. La Noire, in the shade of an elm, continued to try to attract his attention, shaking her head and stamping her hooves, and Pablo went on bringing her grapes.

The *patron* joked, and also drank a great deal. Each time that the workers came down to start a fresh row of vines he offered them a drink. All refused, except the fat woman, who drank almost as much as he did.

"You drink too much," said the *patronne*. "With a sun like this it doesn't do you any good."

"If you could see yourself," put in old Marguerite, "you'd frighten yourself. You're just like a tomato. Upon my word, I wouldn't be surprised if you burst."

Everybody laughed, including the *patron*, who said, "At least it keeps up morale. And it needs something like that when there are so many skirts in the outfit."

Pablo scarcely drank at all. He had never cared very much for wine, and he knew he would last out better on an empty stomach. The *patron* intimidated him rather, but after hearing him laugh and joke so much he decided that he must be getting used to him.

When the time came to return the *patronne* had to harness La Noire and the *patron* had to be helped into the cart.

"It's like that accidents happen," grumbled Clopineau.

But the *patronne* walked along level with the cart.

"It's a good job that Germaine's there to look after everything," said the old man. "She's a really capable woman. She always looks as if she's not doing a thing, but when you watch a bit it's her doing almost everything."

When they arrived at the house they had to unload, and to gain time it was the *patronne* who climbed on to the cart, opposite to Pablo. For the white wine two people were enough, since the strainer led the grapes directly to the wine-press.

While they worked the *patron* sat on a pile of hay, beside Clopineau. At the beginning he shouted continuously.

"Not that like that, for God's sake! You don't know what you're at. You're wasting time. If only I could clamber about . . . Clopineau and me could really show you how to get on if our legs were still strong enough."

Pablo became irritated and lost his rhythm.

"Don't bother about him," whispered the woman. "He's drunk, just drunk and that's that. Let him have a moan. He'll soon get tired of it."

She was right. After a moment or two the *patron* stretched out on the straw and began to snore.

"Would you just have a look at Jeannette," asked the *patronne*. "Tell her to get the milking-cans ready."

Clopineau got up quietly and went out of the barn.

Left alone, they continued to work without a word. The sounds of the work they were doing, and their breathing, mingled with the snoring of the *patron*.

From time to time in his sleep he swore through his teeth.

"Let's hope he isn't too much of a nuisance when we're pressing," said the *patronne*. "Some food might possibly sober him up a bit."

"At a pinch," said Pablo, "we could perhaps manage the pressing without him. He could go to bed as soon as he's eaten."

"He'd never have that. And what's more, as you know, it's not an easy job. The press is in a pretty poor condition. If Clopineau was as strong as you are we three could manage it, but he's old. He soon gets tired."

She was silent for a moment, and then added: "I know very well that the *patron* isn't much good either, with his leg trouble, but the two together are almost as good as one man."

At the beginning of the meal the *patron* was dozy, but after he had swallowed two glasses of wine he began to talk endlessly.

A letter from his son had arrived that morning, and the

patronne had read it aloud as the men began to eat their soup. The son was still behind the Maginot Line. He wrote of how they passed their time playing football and listening to the radio.

This roused the *patron*. "It's a disgrace!" he shouted. "When I think how useful he could be here and they keep him there wasting his time kicking a football about!"

The *patronne* was silent for some time. Pablo looked at her face, tense with anger she could not conceal. She swallowed three or four spoonfuls of soup quickly, and then stopped suddenly. Her eyes became fixed on her husband; she half closed her eyelids, making Pablo think of a cat deprived of its young and ready to leap and scratch anyone. But no-one made any reply to the *patron*. Then, when he stopped talking, there were long moments of silence broken only by the sound of spoons against plates, and of mouths sucking in soup.

The *patron* was at the end of the table; on his right was Pablo, and opposite him old Clopineau, who looked at him from time to time with a nodding of his head and a pursing of his lips, as if saying, "Let him talk. It's of no importance."

Jeannette was beside Clopineau, and Pablo tried not to look at her. But the need to do so was stronger than he was. Each time he lifted his head his eyes turned to her, and quite often he noticed that she was watching him without lifting her nose from her plate. She made a good deal of noise with her mouth as she ate, her elbows well apart and firmly on the table, against which her flat chest was also resting. Her mother was beside her.

When the *patron* had finished his soup he poured out drinks and emptied his own glass in a single gulp. Then, wiping his moustache with the back of his hand, he began to talk again about the war.

"Deep down," he said, "I wasn't surprised your pal wanted to go. It's less hard work than wine-harvesting, and there's scarcely more risk."

He always began talking calmly, but he soon became excited. His gestures became exaggerated and violent.

"War's like the barracks," he shouted; "it's nothing more than a school for vice. The chaps trot around with nothing to do, and they get the habit, so when they return they become layabouts because they don't want to start working again."

He talked for a long while in this strain about how war had, to his mind, many risks for the young. Then, after stopping long enough to have a drink, he began to shout: "It sickens me. You almost kill yourself for your kids, and the Government does its best to ruin them."

The *patronne* had become pale. Her cheeks flushed suddenly and she also began to shout. "You're an idiot. Anyone would think that you're angry because your son isn't running any risks. You'd prefer him to get himself killed or maimed!"

The *patron* remained silent. He stared at his wife with his red-rimmed eyes showing as much astonishment as rage. When she stopped speaking he banged his fist on the table, shouting, "For God's sake! There's no need to blame me for things I didn't say!"

The plates had jumped about on the table, and immediately after her father's first words Jeannette burst into tears.

When the *patron* turned silent all that could be heard was her regular grunting which did not sound at all like sobbing. It was the same strange cry she gave when she seemed happy. The difference was, simply, instead of stopping, it went on unceasingly in rhythm with her breathing. Her face remained unchanged. She wept with her mouth open and almost without lowering her eyelids.

At first no-one said a word, and then her mother, turning towards her, asked without raising her voice, "Are you going to be quiet, eh?"

But Jeannette did not move, and her tears continued. Then her mother began again in a louder voice: "Are you going to be quiet? Yes or no?"

Without shouting this time her father said, "You're not going to bawl her out, are you? If she is blubbering it's my fault, not hers. If you have something to say you'd better say it to me."

The *patronne* contented herself with shrugging her shoulders and standing up to bring to the table a cast-iron saucepan. When she lifted the lid the odour of stew filled the room and the steam rose up to the lamp, chasing away temporarily the moths fluttering about with wings brushing the bulb. The *patronne* served everybody and then sat down again. As she ate she gave her husband and daughter furious looks. The *patron* ate without raising his eyes, limiting himself to muttering between his teeth. Jeannette still continued to weep as she ate her potatoes. Pablo, looking at her, had the feeling that she would never stop, that her sadness was part of her, that it would continue to flow from her like this without changing anything in her existence.

67

The meal was concluded in silence. Clopineau and the *patron* had a last drink, then everyone rose from the table.

"You'll clear the table, wash the dishes, and go to bed," said the *patronne* to Jeannette, who was still weeping.

They went out, and when they reached the door the *patron* turned round. Pablo heard him saying to his daughter, "Don't cry any more, little one, don't cry any more. I didn't mean to frighten you."

Before going up they had tightened the wine-press and emptied the tub. During their absence the tub had become three-quarters filled again. They got into place at the bars, the *patronne* and her husband on one side, Pablo and Clopineau on the other. The *patron* ordered: "Come on! Hu...up!...Hu...up!"

They moved forward about six inches, stopped for breath and to renew their grip, and the *patron* began again:

"Come on! Hu...up!...Hu...up!"

When they could move no more than half an inch or so with each push the *patron* picked up his stick again and let go the bar.

"Now we must empty. Give me a hand. I want to get on top."

"No," said the *patronne*, "that's not your place."

"You make me sick. That's the only place I can help, because the job can be done with arms only."

"You're not going up," said the *patronne* very firmly. "Clopineau is going up, Pablo will go on the ladder, and I'll pass him the *seilles*."

The *patron* went and sat on the stairs grumbling. "Since I'm good for nothing I might as well croak."

Pablo helped the old man to get on a plank fixed between two casks. Then, following the instructions of the *patronne*, he stood upright on the ladder, his back pressed against the rungs.

"You lift above your head and don't bother about anything else," said the old man.

The *patronne* filled the *seille* from the tub and passed it to Pablo, who lifted it up. The old man took it, emptied it, and then passed it back to Pablo. Pablo leaned forward to give it to the *patronne*, and each time he made a movement his eyes, despite himself, turned to the neck-opening of the woman's dress. Below the line of the collar the skin was white and a shadow marked the beginning of her breasts.

From time to time, without budging from the stairs, the *patron* shouted that they were giving themselves too much trouble for the money they would get. He railed at everyone—the Government, the tax-collectors, the politicians, the village priest, and a whole lot of others unknown to Pablo. At one stage he shouted, "How simple it would be to have a pump to do that! All the others have pumps, but we've nothing. We can break our backs."

The *patronne* sighed and shrugged her shoulders.

"But after all," said the old man, "you did have a pump. Has it gone wrong?"

"Everything's going wrong here. You need two pairs of hands to get everything done."

"If you hadn't taken it for the liquid fertilizer," said the *patronne*, "it would still have been useful; it was still working quite well."

"Working? With leaks everywhere, yes! And tubing which pissed at every joint! I only took it for the manure because it was no good for anything else, and because we needed a new one. But you find the money, old know-all."

The *patronne* remained silent. The tub was empty, and they helped old Clopineau to climb down.

From the stone base of the press only a thin thread of juice was now running. When no-one was speaking it could be heard trickling on the wood.

"We'll give another turn," said the *patron*.

He stood up, leaning on his cane with one hand and holding the hand-rail with the other. They took their places again at the bars, and the *patron* began to shout again:

"Come on!...Hu...up! Hu...up!"

After four or five attempts the juice began to flow freely.

"That's fine," said the *patron*, picking up his stick. "Now we can have a drink."

"Not me," said Clopineau. "It's too late."

"It's never too late for drinking."

"But nobody wants to drink," his wife persisted.

"I say there are no drinking hours. Or, rather, there's no time for not drinking."

Then he disappeared behind the row of casks, laughing very loudly. He came back very soon carrying a dust-covered bottle with a cork sealed with yellow sealing-wax.

"You're not going to open that now," said Clopineau. "That'd be stupid. We've said we don't want to drink."

"It'll be nice to see it."

69

He pulled out his pocket-knife and began to break away the seal.

"I just want to see if anyone'll refuse to drink this. It's a 1923. A wonderful year. And it's from the Brûlis vines."

"From Brûlis," said Clopineau, wagging his head. "You've still got some left?"

"About twenty bottles."

Old Clopineau's eyes sparkled. He looked in turn at the bottle and at the *patron*. He passed his tongue over his lips two or three times, nibbled at his moustache with his toothless gums, and then he looked at the *patronne*. She was leaning back against one of the bars of the press on which she had spread her arms apart. She did not move. Her lips were tightly closed. The old man turned towards the *patron*.

"You're wrong to uncork that, Lucien, quite wrong. That's something to save for great occasions."

"The vine-harvest's a great occasion."

"No," said the old man. "A great occasion is a baptism, a first communion, or a marriage."

The *patron* stopped, the bottle in his hand, the corkscrew in the cork. He stared at the old man for a moment, then at his wife, before saying, "A baptism, Clopineau, is not likely to come to us. At least, I hope not. As for the question of marriages, ten bottles for each, that's fine, except that as the young 'un won't be getting married..."

He stopped speaking, lowered his head, and, leaning against a barrel, drew the cork. The veins of his neck swelled and his face became crimson. The cork finally came out.

"Give me glasses," he said to his wife.

The *patronne* took three glasses from the edge of the stone beneath the press and went to rinse them under the tap. She gave one to each of the men.

"What about you?"

"I'm not thirsty."

The *patron*, who was already lifting the bottle, stayed his hand. "Are you trying to make a fool of me? D'you drink a wine like that just to quench your thirst?"

She went and rinsed another glass and came back to them.

Pablo was not thirsty either and had no desire to drink, but it seemed to him that something serious was happening. The silence of the cellar where each word or step echoed; the care the *patron* was taking in pouring the wine; the faces of the two men, and even that of the woman, which were relaxing slowly. There was all that. There was also the colour of the wine. There was also its bouquet.

The bouquet of the wine, indeed, was the first thing to intrigue Pablo, but he wondered where it could have come from. It did not smell like wine. It had a strange bouquet, which he had never smelt before, and which was completely unlike anything he knew.

The *patron* and Clopineau had lifted their glasses towards the lamp. Pablo followed their example.

Seen through the wine, the light-bulb was like a golden sun which had just set on the far edge of the plain. On each side and below, the thickness of the glass gave the blue tint of hills.

"Well?" asked the *patron*.

"Yes," said the old man. "Yes."

They did not drink. They stood there looking at each other, each, from time to time, putting his glass to his nose. They took little sniffs and then held the glass away. The *patron* turned towards Pablo.

"What d'you think of it?"

"I've never seen wine this colour," said Pablo.

"It's the yellow wine," said the old man. "It's unique. It's the Revermont wine."

"Apparently the only wine which resembles it a little," said the *patron*, "is Greek wine."

"Tut, tut, tut," muttered Clopineau. "People say so, but it's not possible."

They still did not drink, and the bouquet of the wine continued to rise, filling the cellar. With it rose a warmth, a sort of peace which calmed everything. The *patron* himself seemed gentler. He spoke in an almost hushed voice and seemed less drunk than a little earlier.

Finally he raised his glass, saying, "To us."

"To us," said the old man, "and may the boy come back soon."

"Your very good health!" said Pablo.

Then they drank.

Pablo tasted the wine and looked at the others. They had done as he had done. They took scarcely a mouthful of wine and kept it in their mouths, letting it flow backwards and forwards, breathing in a little air, pursing their lips.

71

They swallowed, drank another mouthful, and then the old man said, "That's wine!"

Pablo, at the first mouthful, had thought: "That's not wine!"

He found the drink intriguing. It had a taste as indefinable as its bouquet. It was good, better than wine undoubtedly, but Pablo needed several mouthfuls really to appreciate it.

The *patron* refilled the glasses. He did not serve it like the red wine—he barely half filled the glasses.

"It warms," said the old man. "Mustn't trust it."

"Yes, it's the sun," commented the *patron*, nodding his head. "All Brûlis was sunshine."

The old man sighed, swallowed another mouthful, and then he said, "When I think that there's no longer a single acre under cultivation there."

He waited a moment, and then, approaching the *patron*, asked "Have you any idea what it's worth now, a wine like this?"

The other appeared to reflect. He made an odd grimace, saying, "Impossible to say. It's priceless. In any case, I wouldn't sell what I've got left for all the gold in the world."

The *patron* put his glass down beside the bottle, picked up his stick, and went towards the wine-press.

"Come on," he said. "Let's have another go."

They took their places again and pushed as the *patron* ordered. It became more and more difficult, and it took three or four efforts to gain a few inches. However, the juice was still running.

"Shall we empty the tub?" asked Pablo.

"No, wait a little longer; we'll empty it before going up to bed."

The *patron* filled the glasses again.

"You shouldn't," said the old man. "Keep the rest for to-morrow."

"You're joking, Clopineau. You don't leave wine like that once it's opened. If you refuse a glass I shall say to myself, 'Aha! He doesn't think much of it.'"

He went and sat on a small, empty cask. "Sit down," he said.

Then he asked his wife to go and get some nuts and some bread. The *patronne* went out.

Pablo now had in his mouth the strange taste of wine which comes long after tasting it. To bring it out one had to swallow and then, once the mouth was empty, suck one's tongue for a good while. Then one would get the real taste. A very warm taste, a little like that of the mist which comes up from the red earth

72

if it is watered at high noon. Also a little, but very little, of the taste of burnt powder. It was that which had intrigued Pablo most. It was perhaps that which had caused the mistrust he had felt at first. But now he could taste better. His tongue was impregnated with this taste which clung to his palate. It was not the nasty taste of gunpowder, scarcely that of fireworks during an evening fête.

Within himself Pablo felt a pleasant warmth, like the softening of muscles hardened by fatigue.

"Well," the *patron* asked him again, "d'you like it?"

"Yes, it's certainly quite out of the ordinary."

"Have you got anything as good in your own country?"

"No, nothing like it."

"Is it better or not so good as your wines at home?"

Pablo reflected for a few seconds. It was difficult to say. He tasted again slowly. He waited, sucking his tongue for the true taste to come.

"It is so very different," he said, "that it's difficult to decide."

The two others began to laugh.

"But truly," went on Pablo, "truly it's very good."

He looked at the tub where the juice from the wine-press was dripping.

"Is that made from the same grapes?" he asked.

"Near enough, yes."

"And what's the name of the grape?"

"It's a mixture of several. The dominant one is Savagnin, the true, almost wild one, some white Gamey and some Poulsard. But what really counts is the soil. And that wine came from the Brûlis."

The *patronne* returned, handed round chunks of bread, and put in front of them a basket full of nuts and apples.

Pablo found it strange to start eating again like this, two hours after having left the table.

"I'm not very hungry," he declared when the *patronne* offered him some bread.

"You should eat all the same," she said. "It's not for your hunger, but to help you taste the wine better."

Pablo cracked a few nuts and started to eat. Afterwards he drank again, and the wine seemed to him to be even more full-flavoured.

For quite a time they ate without speaking.

73

There was only the sound of the nuts which they were cracking one against another by squeezing them in their clenched hands. They chewed slowly, drinking little sips and waiting a while before beginning to eat again, so as to enjoy to the full the savour of the three things which went together so perfectly—the nuts, the bread, and the wine which enriched everything.

They were seated there a long time, and Pablo was living only in the present moment. He lived it a little as if in a dream which put a pale mist round people and things. The old, time-coloured wine-press seemed far, far away, and when the *patron* spoke his words found a curious echo under the vault of the cellar.

"That's one the Boches won't drink," he said, "and if I knew that they might drink the others I'd finish the rest tonight, even if it killed me."

He was beginning to talk loudly again, and the *patronne* stood up. "Come along," she said; "perhaps we could give another turn and then empty the tub. After that we can go to bed."

"Let's at least finish this," said the *patron*, picking up the bottle beside the lamp. "There's barely a glassful left, so we'll share it."

He held out the bottle, but as the others held back their glasses he filled his own, saying, "If you don't want it, then drink some rough old red. I'm not going to beg you to join me."

Thereupon he emptied his glass in three or four gulps.

IX

THAT NIGHT also Pablo fell asleep quickly. Mainly from fatigue, but also possibly a little because of the wine. The mixture of the two had a curious effect on him. Since he had drunk the wine his fatigue was as if deadened. In the muscles of his legs and shoulders the ache was transformed into weight. He was no longer staggering, but he had taken much longer to climb the stairs in the small barn. The steps had seemed higher to him.

He had let himself flop on the straw, throwing his clothes down haphazardly, and as soon as the candle was blown out the darkness of sleep entered him as swiftly as the night swallowed the barn.

At one moment in his sleep it seemed to him that someone was shouting:

"Pablo! Pablo!"

He did not move. He did not really wake till he heard the door below creaking. Even then, half-opening his eyes, he thought for an instant that he had been dreaming. He listened, however. Clogs were clattering on the stairs.

He raised himself on one elbow.

"What is it?" he asked.

"Come, you must come."

The steps stopped. Pablo had recognized the voice of the *patronne*. Struggling for breath, she went on: "Come...Come quickly...There's something wrong with the *patron*. We must call a doctor. Come quickly."

"I'm coming," he said.

The *patronne* was already going back downstairs in the darkness. She must have run across, and had spoken quickly and jerkily.

Pablo lit the lantern, looked for his clothes, and dressed hastily. His head ached and his tongue felt thick.

The night outside was calm and clear: there was no moon but many stars.

He crossed the path and the courtyard. There was a light in the kitchen, and the door was wide open. Jeannette was there, standing by the table, with a big black shawl over her shoulders and her white nightdress hanging down to her clogs.

"Where is he?"

Jeannette grunted, her mouth twitched, and she started to walk towards the door at the far end, which was also open. Pablo had never yet been through this door. He went up the stairway behind the girl, who kicked each step with her clogs.

Up the stairs was a landing with three doors.

"Come quickly," called the woman.

Pablo went ahead of Jeannette and entered the room. The *patron* was stretched out on the floor in the centre of the room. On her knees close to him, with a bowl at her side, the *patronne* was wiping his face with the corner of a hand-towel.

There was a smell floating in the air of the room which sickened Pablo. The *patron* had vomited.

"Help me to get him back on the bed."

Pablo gritted his teeth and took the *patron* under the arms, while the woman took his legs.

75

Jeannette had remained standing near the door; her hands swinging, her mouth open, she watched what they were doing. Pablo saw her as if through a mist.

When he lifted the *patron* the sharp pain in his back returned. The bed was high and the heavily-built *patron* was completely limp. They managed, however, to get him on to the bed.

"What happened?" asked Pablo. "Did he have a fall?"

"He must have got up because he felt sick."

The man's throat rattled, his eyelids half closed over his globular, blood-flecked eyes.

"Where does the doctor live?" asked Pablo.

"There isn't one anywhere near. We'll have to call the doctor at Saint-Agnès. We'll have to wake the mayor and telephone from there."

"Where does the mayor live?"

The woman turned to the girl, who had not budged. "You must go with Pablo to the Mougeins' house, where Denise Mougein's father lives," she said. "Do you understand?"

Jeannette grunted.

"Go along then," said the *patronne*, "and hurry! I can't leave him alone."

Pablo followed the girl, who walked at her normal pace. She had stopped swinging her hands and now had them crossed on her flat chest, holding the two ends of her shawl.

They followed the road which they had taken to the vines as far as the first crossroads. There they turned left in the direction of the houses. The stars gave enough light, but Pablo had brought a lantern, nevertheless. The light from it looked grubby.

Pablo tried several times to increase the pace, but Jeannette then dragged behind and he had to wait for her.

They passed in front of the church, of which Pablo knew only the bell-tower which he had seen from a distance. In the square there was a large, round stone basin where the water ran in from an iron pipe which jutted from a moss-covered pedestal. The overflow simply ran on to the paving. The noise of the water followed them as far as a crossroads. There they turned to the right along an alley which climbed between houses with balconies and stone stairways, their walls covered with vines. As they arrived in front of an iron gate Jeannette grunted and stopped. Taking hold of the bars in both hands, she began to shake the gate. A dog immediately sprang up, barking and jumping against the gate.

76

Jeannette released the gate and began to bang on a sheet-iron panel with one of her clogs.

A window lit up and was opened, and almost immediately a man appeared in the opening.

"What is it?"

The dog had stopped barking and was now sniffing through the gate.

Pablo explained why he had come.

"Couldn't have had enough to drink!" shouted the man.

"You must telephone," repeated Pablo.

"All right, don't move. I'll phone."

There was a long wait. Pablo could hear the man walking and talking. Some light showed through the shutters on the ground floor, and Pablo heard the man's voice again. Finally the light was extinguished on the ground floor and the man reappeared at the window on the first floor.

"It's all right. The doctor's going to come."

Pablo thanked him.

"He doesn't need me, I think?" said the man.

"I don't think so, thank you."

Pablo returned to the farm with Jeannette, who maintained her slow pace. He wondered if he should hurry on ahead, but he did not like to leave the girl to follow alone.

From the vineyard old Clopineau had pointed out to him all the villages below. He remembered Saint-Agnès. It was not very far. Perhaps the doctor hadn't yet gone to bed. In that case he would soon be at the farm. Pablo had no idea of what the time might be.

Despite himself, he slowed down. The fresh air which rose from the plain with the night helped to wake him fully. His head became less heavy. He thought again of the doctor. In a car you can move quickly, and he would certainly come in a car.

This time the girl had got ahead of him. On she went, swinging always from right to left, her clogs dragging on the stones. Her white nightdress made a curious light patch in the night, the upper part of her body and her head being almost lost in the semi-darkness.

Pablo caught up with her. When he arrived he had to go up again to the bedroom. However, on the threshold of the kitchen he turned round and took some deep breaths of the night air before entering.

77

The *patronne* was there. Leaning over the sink, she was rinsing the floor-cloth.

"Well?" she asked.

"He's coming at once."

"Good."

"How is he?"

"Just the same. I've only left him for five minutes to clear up his vomit before the doctor arrives."

Pablo sniffed. It seemed to him that the sour smell was now in the kitchen.

"Is there anything I can do?" he asked.

The woman threw on the ground the twisted floor-cloth, wiped her hands on her apron, and then said, "I don't think the doctor will need anything. I'll go up again so you can go to bed now if you like."

Pablo looked at the door open to the night which was sending cool air into the kitchen.

"I'll wait. Then we'll see, depending on what he says."

"Then stay here, and as soon as he arrives bring him up . . . but he does know the way."

The *patronne* went to the far end of the room.

"Come along, Jeannette," she said. "You must go back to bed."

They had not reached the door before the sound of the car could be heard.

"Here he is," said Pablo, who was standing in the doorway.

The *patronne* went out into the courtyard. The light of the headlamps showed between the walls of the two cemeteries, shone on the trees along the road, and then the car stopped in front of the house.

As soon as the doctor was in the kitchen Jeannette, who had remained standing beside the table, groaned very loudly and began to cry.

"Be quiet," said the *patronne*.

The doctor nodded his head. He was a small, round-backed, thin old man, dressed entirely in black. He had long-fingered, white hands. In his left hand he was carrying a canvas medical bag, and with his right he was making quick, supple gestures.

"Poor little 'un," he said. "Since her grandmother's death it's always the same. Every time she sees me she begins to cry. She must think that I come to harm someone in the house."

He went towards her slowly, one hand waving gently to and

78

fro like a white dove. Jeannette did not move, but she began to cry more quickly and more loudly, staring at him with wide-open eyes from which tears were running down her pale cheeks.

The doctor's hand dropped again, his shoulders bent a little farther, and he went towards the door at the end, sighing.

"Poor Jeannette, it's impossible to know what to say. One never knows with you."

As he reached the foot of the stairs he stopped and turned to the *patronne*, who was following him.

"What happened?"

"The same as last time. But he's also vomited."

"Any bleeding from the nose?"

"No, not a drop."

They went up. Pablo hesitated for a moment, and then went out again to the doorstep.

The sky vibrated. The entire night breathed gently. There was no view of the slope, but it was there, quite close, beginning where the stars stopped.

Pablo walked a few steps up and down the courtyard, his ear alert each time he passed the door. Jeannette was still crying. Pablo went in and walked across to her.

"You mustn't cry like that," he said.

She had wet cheeks. Her nose was running too. Pablo stared down. Again he felt as if he must be sick. He went once more to the doorstep. The *patronne* came downstairs, opened the cupboard, took a floor-cloth, and went upstairs again.

On her way she had called to Jeannette: "Will you stop whining like that, eh?"

Pablo turned round. The *patronne* had spoken in a very harsh voice, and her eyes showed that she was angry.

When she had gone Pablo went back to Jeannette.

"Don't cry," he told her. "Don't cry, come on!"

He spoke gently. He had never been so close to her.

"You'd better wipe your nose," he told her.

She brushed her hand beneath her nose. A long thread of snot dragged out, sticking shinily to her black shawl. She wiped herself with her apron.

Pablo turned his head away for a moment, then he forced himself to look again at the girl.

The tears had formed white lines on her dirty face. She was still weeping.

Pablo took another step forward. This time he was quite close to her.

"Don't cry," he said. "It's nothing. You mustn't cry."

He looked at her with a smile. She shook her head two or three times as if to say "no," and her sobbing began again louder than before. Pablo sighed deeply, looked towards the courtyard, and then, turning back to the girl, he raised his hand.

"You mustn't cry like that; you'll make yourself ill."

Then he ventured to touch her hair. Once his hand had touched her, he brushed it over her hair two or three times.

She still wept, but a little more quietly.

They remained together like that for a few seconds, then the doctor and the *patronne* came downstairs again. Jeannette's grief increased. Her mother, gritting her teeth, stared at her.

"Go along," she growled. "Up to bed."

"It's nothing," the doctor told her. "You mustn't cry; it's nothing."

Pablo had returned to the doorstep. The doctor and the *patronne* went towards him, and he stepped aside to let them pass. As soon as they were outside they stopped.

"Well?" asked Pablo.

"It's an attack," said the doctor. "I've done what's needed, but I can't say anything yet. I'll come back tomorrow."

"And what can we do about the boy?" asked the woman.

"If I were you I'd have him back. It would at least give him a leave. And one never knows. It is serious, after all. Think about it. I'll give you a certificate tomorrow morning if you decide to."

He went towards his car.

"How many days do you think we can ask for?" inquired the *patronne*.

"I can't tell you. I don't think they're very generous."

They walked a few steps with the doctor, and the woman murmured, "It only needed this! It's the sort of thing that would happen when we were busiest with the wine-harvest."

The doctor came to a halt. "Listen," he said, "I know just what it is. I'm going to tell you frankly: as he is now, there's no chance of him moving, or even falling out of bed. Just find someone who can look in two or three times during the day, and you can go on with your harvesting."

"Still, to leave an invalid like that, all alone..."

"It's as you like, but I can't think of anyone around here who

80

wouldn't do just that. Work is work, and everyone knows it. No-one would question that."

He climbed into his car, switched on the engine, and said again before driving off, "I'll come early tomorrow morning, then you won't be held up.

The car drew away and went out of sight.

"Do you need me?" asked Pablo.

"No," she said.

"If you should need me give me a call."

"I will. Thank you."

Pablo went off. The *patronne* returned to the house, and as soon as she reached the door she began shouting. Pablo stopped to listen to her. She was shouting at Jeannette, who presumably was still crying, standing in the middle of the kitchen. The *patronne* slammed the door, and Pablo heard nothing more.

Then slowly, his legs aching with weariness, he went up again to bed.

This time, however, it took him a long time to get to sleep. The image of Mariana was with him again. A sad Mariana, still living, but already near to death, which Pablo saw her fighting against.

He saw again the face of Mariana as it had appeared to him every night for months and months, beginning from the moment he had heard the news of her death.

Often, then, he had longed to die. Now he knew that he could never kill himself. Nevertheless the sad face of Mariana still kept coming back to him.

X

IT WAS still night when Pablo opened his eyes. He had slept badly. He was very weary, and he tried to force himself to lie there till dawn, to relax. He closed his eyes, trying not to think. But immediately he felt a sense of depression which made it difficult for him to breathe. No effort was needed to know the cause of this feeling. Since the evening death had been near.

Pablo had lived for a long time with death. He knew death

well. He did not need to wait for three cries from an owl or the flight of a crow round the house to identify it. He thought of the days just past, when weariness had made him almost forget it by making him sleep.

Enrique had gone.

Enrique was born to live. To live with life, not with death. Enrique could pass close to death without being affected by it. Or, possibly by instinct, he smelled it coming and went away.

Pablo sometimes repeated the words of old Pérez, whom he had known in Madrid.

"If you ignore Death he gets angry. He goes away. He leaves you alone. He likes easy work."

At that time Pablo had often joked about death with old Pérez. One can always joke about death so long as it has never touched you.

Now that was finished. There had been Mariana.

Death, for Pablo, meant Mariana. War also meant Mariana.

Pablo was like those dogs that death keeps from sleeping and which howl while it is finishing its work, and howl until all is over.

The *patron* was going to die. That was certain. It only remained to be seen how long he would last.

Pablo wondered whether it was he who dragged death with him wherever he went. As a child he had known old women in his own country who claimed that certain people brought misfortune with them.

Pablo shook himself. He threw back his covering and got up in a single bound. In the darkness he sought the shutter, opened it, and hung out to look at the farm. There was a light in the kitchen. The day had not yet begun, but the sky was already getting pale, and Pablo was able to dress and go down without lighting his lantern.

Outside it was cold. The grass was white on the edges of the ditches, and mist was rising from the stream behind the wall of the cemetery.

The *patronne* was alone in the kitchen. The fire was already roaring, and the water for the coffee was singing.

"Good morning," said Pablo.

"Good morning. Up already?"

"How is he?"

82

"He's been gasping most of the night. Now he's asleep, but I'm afraid it'll be a long time before he's well again."

The *patronne* filled the coffee-grinder.

"Give it to me," said Pablo.

He went and sat by the stove, gripped the coffee-mill between his knees, and began to turn the handle.

The *patronne* put the coffee-pot on the stove.

"You know how to make it?" she asked.

"Yes, I think so."

"Well, then, I'll leave you to it. I'll go and milk the cows. I haven't got the girl up. If only she'd sleep till after the doctor's visit. If she sees him this morning that'll be the end—she'll be snivelling all day and we won't be able to do anything with her."

She rinsed out her milking-pail and milk-can in the sink; before going out she said again, "While the coffee is percolating you'd better eat, the soup'll be warm. Everything else is in the cupboard; you know where it is. If there's not enough you've only to cook yourself a couple of eggs. That'll be a help to me."

As soon as she had gone out Pablo put the ground coffee in the percolator and left the water to run through. It was the first time he had ever been alone in the kitchen. Alone with the sound of the coffee dripping into the coffee-pot and the singing of the fire and the water.

All this was life.

Pablo looked towards the end of the room; the door leading to the stairway was ajar. He went across to it silently, put his head round the door, and listened.

The *patron* was moaning feebly.

He pushed the door to and went back to the stove. He lifted the lid of the saucepan. It smelled deliciously of bacon. Pablo took a bowl from the cupboard and at the same time brought the plate of bacon, which he placed on the table. He poured some more water on the coffee, filled his bowl with soup, and began to eat.

He was hungry, yet he had to force himself to finish the soup. The image of the *patron* stretched out on his bed kept coming back to him. And with the image there came back the odour of vomit. Pablo looked at the far end of the table, which was the *patron's* usual place. He stood up slowly, carried his bowl to the sink, and put the bacon back in the cupboard.

83

The *patronne* had hardly entered with her pail of tepid, frothy milk when the doctor's car arrived in front of the door. Pablo went to open it, and the old doctor came in rubbing his hands.

"Good morning. That coffee smells good," he said. "You might pour me a cup. I didn't have time before I left."

He went across to the fire and held his white hands above the oven.

"Well?" he asked.

The *patronne* began to explain how her husband was, but the doctor interrupted her. "I came, and I'm not going without seeing him. Everything you're telling me I know already. And what I don't know I'll soon find out. What I want to hear is what you've decided about your son."

The *patronne* did not hesitate. "To bring him home," she said. "That will be best."

"I think so, yes."

He drank his boiling coffee in little, swift sips, and then, drawing from his pocket a writing-pad and a pen, he wrote out a certificate.

"Take this. You need only to get the mayor to sign before sending it."

The *patronne* put the paper on the sideboard, then went to the door at the end.

"Please don't talk on the stairs; I don't want my daughter to see you, you know how she is."

They went up in silence, but as soon as they were upstairs Pablo heard the *patronne* talking. She was not shouting, but her ill-contained anger could be sensed. He went towards the door; Jeannette was coming down. Pablo drew back. She came into the kitchen and went over to stand by the sink, her hands hanging and her feet apart.

She was weeping.

She was weeping as she had done the previous evening, and Pablo thought that possibly she had not slept; that she had perhaps not stopped crying for a single moment.

It was no longer him she was staring at, but at the door at the end of the room.

He went over to her quietly. She still had a dirty face, and the marks of her tears were more numerous. In places where she had wiped them away with her fingers the dirt looked a little like wood-graining.

84

"Why are you crying?" asked Pablo. "You mustn't cry like that."

He spoke gently, very gently, but Jeannette appeared not to hear him. She looked at him for a second, and then began again to watch the door opening on the stairway.

When the footsteps of her mother and the doctor could be heard the girl's sobbing increased. Her flat chest rose, her neck swelled spasmodically, and her head trembled.

The doctor looked at her and shook his head. The *patronne* also looked at her. She clenched her fists, and the muscles of her jaw moved under her skin.

"That child is harming herself," said the doctor.

"Is there anything I can do?" asked the mother. "You know exactly what it is."

"You must try to get her to take a sedative. Her grief is making her hysterical, but that should calm her a little."

He turned towards the *patronne*. "I'll be back this evening," he said, "or tomorrow morning. In any case there's not much we can do for him now. His heart has held out; it could continue to do so. It's a question of time."

"And you really believe he will be paralysed?"

The old doctor hesitated. His hands fluttered in indecisive gestures, and then he added, "I cannot say anything certain, but I am very much afraid that that may be so."

The *patronne* sighed deeply, looked again at her daughter, and then went towards the door.

"Stay there," said the doctor. "Don't waste your time; you've so much to do as it is."

The *patronne* went back to her oven. The doctor took a few steps, and then, turning towards Pablo, he said to him, "Here, young man, come with me. I must have some medical samples with me. We'll have a look at them and see if I can't find something for that little girl."

They went across the courtyard. The sun would soon be appearing. All the summit of the hill was fringed with red. Higher up the dappled sky was beginning to take on colour.

Once at the car, the doctor opened the boot at the back and brought out an old suitcase tied up with string. His white hands fluttered over it, bringing out and setting down little bottles of every colour. Finally he held one out to Pablo, saying, "A dozen drops with her breakfast. And in the evening, to make her sleep, the same number with her meal."

85

He closed his suitcase, straightened up, and, holding out his hand to Pablo, said, "I don't know if you understand what it means to have a daughter like that."

Pablo nodded his head, and the doctor spoke about her again very slowly, as if he was seeking the right words.

"That little girl is certainly less intelligent than a dog, but she has much instinct. I once had a dog I had to get rid of because he could scent death so well. As soon as I came in from seeing a patient who was near his end, or had just died, he'd howl for hours. Well, you see, that little girl's the same—she senses death."

Pablo looked at the side of the house, and then asked, almost in a whisper, "You really think that it's the end?"

The doctor made an evasive gesture with his hands. "I can't say anything positive, but it's his second attack."

"He's had one already?"

The doctor looked surprised. "Hadn't you noticed his stiff leg?"

"I thought that was the result of an accident."

"Accident, accident, that's easily said. It's true he fell from his cart, but I think it was because he had had an attack. A leg doesn't stay in that condition because of a simple fracture of the tibia. But if he did have an attack he never wanted to listen to me. He never stopped drinking."

The doctor got in his car, and as he pulled the starter he added, "They're all like that. They think they're strong. They all had a grandfather who died at a hundred and drank like a fish, but what they've all forgotten is those who pop off at fifty with a liver like a sponge."

The car backed in the courtyard and moved off slowly as the doctor called out: "A dozen drops, night and morning."

Pablo smiled and nodded his head. The car moved out of sight, and Pablo went in with the little box.

He thought about the doctor's dog. The dog could smell death, the child smelled death, and he, Pablo, had smelled it all night. And already this morning he himself had thought of dogs who could smell death a long way off.

The medicine had no taste, and Jeannette drank her coffee probably without noticing anything. Nevertheless she continued to weep, and her mother was obliged to do all the work alone until the arrival of the first wine-harvesters.

Old Marguerite and Clopineau were the first to arrive. As soon

86

as they had entered the old woman began: "Red sky at morning makes the windmills turn. It'll be blowing hard by midday."

She broke off. She had just caught sight of Jeannette, who was still weeping.

"What's the matter with her?" she asked.

The *patronne* told her what happened the previous evening, and the old lady began to rail against fate which always dogged the same people.

The *patronne* let her have her say and got on with her work, preparing the baskets for midday.

"Shall we harness the horse?" asked Clopineau.

"Yes. I don't think the others will be long."

Pablo went out with the old man, who explained to him how to set about harnessing the mare.

"One never knows," he said. "Supposing something happened to me, it'd be better if you knew how to do it."

When the others arrived all was ready, and it was Clopineau who got in the cart. The *patronne* remained behind. She had to go into the village to give the key to a woman who would come to see the *patron* two or three times in the course of the day.

Pablo walked behind the cart, with old Marguerite and the fat woman. Jeannette followed a few paces behind, still weeping.

"All the same, it's very sad," said the fat woman. "The father at death's door and the child in that state! Let's hope that nothing happens to the boy."

Marguerite turned round and looked at Jeannette. "It's not worth waiting for her," she said. "Nothing will calm her."

Pablo was still thinking about death. Almost despite himself, he told them what the doctor had said.

"She smells death?" exclaimed the old woman. "I'm sure she does. And I'd be surprised if she was wrong. Instinct never betrays. I tell you there's been bad luck about that house since the day when the labourer engaged by Germaine's father hanged himself."

The fat woman nodded assent. "It's certainly true that since then they've always had bad luck."

"Violent death in a house, misfortune for three generations," said the old lady.

"But he didn't hang himself in the house, according to what people say."

87

"No, but it was the same thing. It was the same farm; that comes to the same thing."

They walked on for a while without speaking. Pablo hesitated for a moment, and then, unable to resist, asked, "Where did he hang himself?"

The old woman looked at him with half-closed eyes, then she shrugged her shoulders, but already the fat woman was saying, "He hanged himself in the old stable in the small barn, where you sleep."

Pablo instantly regretted that he had asked the question. The fat woman seemed embarrassed. She hurried to add: "That's what they say. But, well, I wasn't there to see. It's more than fifty years ago it happened."

They were silent for the rest of the journey, and the *patronne* caught up with them as they reached the vines.

Her first concern was to shout at Jeannette, who had not ceased sobbing. But old Clopineau intervened. "Leave her alone," he said. "As soon as I've unhitched the horse I'll look after her."

Pablo helped him and led La Noire close to a hedge, to which he tied her. When he returned to the cart, the vine-harvesters were among the vines. In the farthest row Clopineau was working with Jeannette. For a long time Pablo could hear the murmuring of the old man's voice, regular and gentle as a tireless bell. Then, when the girl stood up to hand over her bucket of grapes, Pablo noticed that she was no longer weeping. She had a face dirtied only by the dust, and the sun was catching a long thread of snot between her nose and her upper lip.

XI

IN THE morning they harvested in silence. At midday the *patronne* opened the hamper, gave some instructions to old Marguerite, and then, taking a slice of bacon on a piece of bread, she went back to the farm while the pickers ate. The old lady distributed the food, and when it was necessary to serve drinks she handed the bottle to Pablo.

In the afternoon they were a little more talkative. At first about the *patron* and their work, and later about everything under the sun, as on the previous days. Then, since it had been impossible to find a man in the village who was free, the fat woman offered to stay to help with the press. The *patronne* accepted her offer, and the picking continued. Each day two substantially full *sapines* were brought back and unloaded by Pablo and the *patronne*, while old Clopineau looked after the animals and the fat woman prepared the evening meal with Jeannette.

The *patron* had recovered consciousness, but he could not move and did nothing but groan. Pablo had not been able to go up and see him, the working days were too long.

Jeannette was no longer weeping. The doctor had been only once while they were up in the vines.

At night Pablo fell asleep quickly. The vines they were picking now were on a very steep slope, and he was exhausted each day by weariness and the sun. The wind blew all the time, the mornings were fresh, and Pablo's lips and hands were chapped. But he had now got into the rhythm of this life, and gradually his body had accustomed itself to all the various strains which had proved so painful at first. His weariness was a part of his life, and he became used to it. When he got back, before he went to bed, he would sometimes shine his lantern on the ceiling of the old stable before going up the stairs. Now he no longer had to search. The reddish light picked out immediately the large iron hook which he had seen the first evening. It was there, it was surely there where the grandfather's labourer had hanged himself.

The first evening Pablo spent a long time staring at the hook. He had thought for a moment of getting his blanket and going off to sleep under a hedge or in the stable with La Noire, but he had forced himself to go up, calling to mind some words of old Pérez:

"You mustn't give a damn for death."

Now his actions were mechanical, almost a rite. As he entered he looked at the hook, but only briefly, went up the stairs, lay down, and, almost immediately, fell asleep.

In the morning, when he woke particularly early, he would sometimes wait to watch the advance of daylight beneath the shutter. Then he would think of Mariana. But he thought at will. He was master of the images which he called up between his eyes and the beam of the barn.

He got up, washed himself in the courtyard, and then took hay to the animals. After that he had breakfast while the *patronne* finished her milking and prepared her cooking. Pablo had got into the habit of serving himself, and the *patronne* never had anything to say to him. They spoke rarely; normally when Pablo arrived he would ask after the *patron*, and the woman would reply invariably, "Still about the same."

Four days passed like this, and then, one evening, just as they had taken their places at the table, the door opened wide and a soldier came in.

"Good evening," he said, closing the door.

The *patronne* stood up, ran to him, and gave him a long kiss.

When she returned to the table with her son Pablo noticed that her eyes were moist. She turned towards the stove and wiped her face with the corner of her apron.

The lad shook the hand of the fat woman and of old Clopineau, then he quickly kissed his sister, who had not moved but whose eyes never left him.

"Well, well," he said to her. "Never seen a soldier before?"

The girl grunted. The lad went across to Pablo.

"He's our Spaniard," said the *patronne*. "I told you about him in a letter."

Pablo shook the young man's hand, saying, "My name is Pablo."

The other gave an almost derisive laugh. "I knew," he said.

His mother came across. "Our boy is called Pierre," she said.

Pierre took off his jacket and threw it on the window-ledge, together with his forage cap.

"I must remember to take advantage of being home to get that washed, it's getting disgusting."

He went and sat in his father's chair and asked, "Well, what is it exactly?"

His mother told him what had happened. When she had finished the lad asked if his father was asleep.

"Perhaps not yet. If you like, we'll go up in a minute."

She put out a plate for her son, served some soup, and then they went upstairs.

The others waited for them before beginning to eat. They did not talk. They all had their elbows on the table, their heads a little hunched into their shoulders, and their eyes looking down at their steaming soup.

As he came down the stairs the son said simply, "Looks as if that turn has hit him badly."

90

They began to eat, and after a while the son asked, "Where are you with the work?"

"It's going along well," his mother told him. "We've finished about three-quarters roughly. It needs two more good days, and the grafts will be finished."

"Yes," said Clopineau, "the weather was just right for us. What's more, it looks as if the wine is going to be pretty good."

"And the quantity?" asked Pierre.

"Good. Not a record, but well above the average, all the same."

"How many barrels?"

"Three at the moment. When we've finished the slope it won't be far off four."

The son looked satisfied. They talked more about the wine-harvest, and then the lad said that he had been given only two days' leave, but if the doctor agreed he could stay till the end of the harvesting.

"Then you'll see him tomorrow morning," said his mother.

"Tomorrow I'm going to Courlans. We'll see after that."

His mother hesitated. "You're not going to stay there all the morning?"

Her son began to laugh. "They're certain to keep me for lunch."

"We could do with you here. That would let me leave a little later and get some work done in the house. I've so many jobs that are all behind."

"What can you expect?" asked Clopineau. "He's come back, so it's normal for him to go and see his fiancée."

Immediately after the meal they rose from the table, and the fat woman, throwing her shawl across her shoulders, declared, "I'm going home. With the boy here you won't need me for the pressing."

She went out very quickly. Pierre grimaced. "Hell!" he said. "I've been travelling most of the day, and I could have done with a quiet evening."

He went down with them, however, and between each turn of the press he went round the cellar, tapped on the barrels, and foraged about in the racks of bottles. He also drank frequently, drawing the wine directly from the small barrel to which Pablo had the habit of going each morning, since the *patron* had been ill, to fill the bottles for the day.

"You aren't drinking?" Pierre asked Pablo several times.

"No, thanks."

91

"Good heavens, it's much better than that muck with sedative in it."

The *patronne* said nothing. She looked at him. All she did from time to time was to ask him, "Are you being fed properly? Do you get my parcels all right?"

At one moment she also asked, "Is it true that you never fight?"

Her son gave a roar of laughter. "Fight? We have to fight among ourselves if we want that. None of us has ever seen a hair of a Boche."

Then he turned to Pablo and asked, "And you, did you fight in Spain?"

Pablo nodded.

"Was it really nasty?"

Pablo hesitated for a moment, and then, because everyone was looking at him, he replied, "Sometimes it was pretty tough."

The lad put a few more questions, but as Pablo replied only in monosyllables or by nods of the head, he grew tired of it and began to walk up, down, and across the cellar.

He was about the same height as his father, but thinner. He also had a thinner face, and his looks were very much like those of his mother.

When the pressing was over, before going up the son went to get a bottle, which he tucked beneath his arm.

"What are you going to do with that?" asked his mother.

"It's marc."

"I can see that, but there's a bottle already opened in the kitchen."

"It's not for me, it's for her father—he's very fond of it. I'll take a chicken too. I don't want to go empty-handed."

The *patronne* seemed embarrassed. However, as they crossed the barn she said, "If you want to take a chicken you'd better catch one now, before they settle down."

"You do it," said the lad, "and don't pick me out your best layer, but don't give me one of your tough old-timers either."

They all went back to the kitchen, except old Clopineau, who left them at the door and disappeared into the night. Pablo lit his lantern. The son opened his kitbag and began to get his things out.

"Before going up," said the woman, "you can let me have the benefit of your lantern to give me some light while I catch that hen."

"By the way," asked Pierre, "where does this chap sleep?"

"Opposite," said the mother with a movement of her chin.

The son began to laugh. "Hasn't the hanged man's ghost ever troubled you?" he asked.

Pablo did not reply.

"Of course, you've probably seen plenty of dead men. But when I was a kid you couldn't have made me go into that barn for all the tea in china."

Pablo went out, followed by the *patronne*. They went round the house to the chicken-shed. The *patronne* opened the door and went in.

"Get the light on the side where the perches are."

Pablo moved the light along the lines of birds. There was some clucking. The *patronne* took several which she felt in turn and put back on their perches. They staggered for a moment, cackling, flapping a wing, and then, having re-established their equilibrium, slept again. Finally she chose a large white bird with a grey neck, and seized it by the legs.

"This'll do," she said.

They went out. She closed the door, walked a few steps with Pablo, and then, coming to a halt, she faced him.

"I wanted to tell you about that man who hanged himself ..."

She struggled to find words.

"I know all about it," said Pablo.

He could not see the woman very well by the light of the lantern which he was holding at about the height of the chicken's legs as its head hung down, almost touching the ground.

"Oh, you know about it?"

"Yes, I heard the women talking about it the other day."

"And you still don't mind sleeping there?"

"No, I don't think about it."

The woman began to walk on. Then, reaching the angle of the house, she asked again, "What were they talking about then, the other day?"

Pablo hesitated, feeling perturbed, and then, trying to recover himself, he mumbled, "I don't know. I didn't hear everything. I think it was simply because they knew I slept there."

They took a few steps in silence, and then the *patronne* stopped again. They were in the middle of the courtyard. The night was dark, and the north wind coming round the corner of the stable made the lantern light flutter. The *patronne* looked towards the kitchen, where the light showed each plank of the shutters, then, moving close to Pablo, she asked in a low voice, "When they said that to you, those women, was it before or after the *patron* became ill?"

"I don't remember," said Pablo. "I can't tell you."

"Try to remember."

"No, honestly, I don't know."

Pablo reflected, and then added, "I don't think it's of any importance in any case."

"That's true, it's not important. What people say usually isn't important at all."

Pablo was anxious to leave, but he did not dare to do so.

"Quite right," he said. "What they said was just small talk, like that."

"They didn't say anything else about the house?"

"No," declared Pablo. "They said nothing."

"That's fine," said the *patronne*. "Good night."

"Good night," said Pablo.

They separated, Pablo carrying the lantern, while she carried the drowsy chicken in the crook of her arm.

XII

THE SON took his push-bike and left in the direction of the main road at the same time as the harvesters left the house.

"Come back through Saint-Agnès and call at the doctor's," his mother shouted to him.

Without turning round he waved a hand to show he had understood.

"And don't get back too late," she shouted again.

He had promised to come up to the vines immediately he returned. Because of this promise, early that afternoon the *patronne* began to glance occasionally in the direction where the road ran between two rows of acacias. When Pablo reclimbed with the empty *bouille* he saw her straighten up, put her hand up to shade her eyes, and stare at the wood. Pablo could not really understand her uneasiness. When the lad was at the front she did not

94

speak of him. She gave the impression that she thought of him only now and then.

Night fell, and the sun disappeared earlier than on other days behind huge clouds which had been lying for some time on the very edge of the plain. The horizon seemed to have caught fire, and all the soil had a red tint for several minutes.

"Red sky at night ponds filled all right," said old Marguerite.

The *patronne* fumed, "It was too good to last. We won't finish without a soaking. There still remains the second crop for us to gather. They are all on the flat land, and if it should rain, we'll be up to our knees in mud."

When they came down the north wind had died out completely, and the old woman declared that this also was a bad sign. Other vintagers who were on the road also complained about the threat in the sky.

"Bloody sun at setting, soon we'll have a wetting," said an old man with a drooping moustache in the other party who was walking along, bent almost double, dragging his huge clogs over the stones.

Pablo, who was walking beside the cart, his hand on the brake, felt a kind of anguish mounting in him. This October evening was not like those which had gone before. In addition to the red sky and the earlier darkness, it seemed to Pablo that something unpleasant was going to happen.

After reaching the plain again, Pablo thought of the *patron* immediately he saw the house. Perhaps the *patron* was dead.

Now that he no longer needed to look after the brake, Pablo let the cart move ahead. The fat woman and Marguerite had gone off towards the village. Jeannette, as ever, must be a long way in the rear, and the *patronne* was walking alone a few paces from the cart.

For an instant, seeing her there in the middle of the road, on this plain where the only noise was that of the horse and the cart, Pablo had the feeling that she was following a hearse which would never stop moving towards the end of its road.

He waited and began to walk beside her, but even in the twilight the cart with its two *sapines* did not resemble a hearse.

When they entered the courtyard old Clopineau, who was beginning to open the barn door, shouted to them, "The boy is back; his bicycle's here. He must have gone up to see his father."

The *patronne* disappeared suddenly, and Pablo caught hold of

La Noire to make her back. The old man had taught him how to handle her, and the mare was docile with him.

They had barely finished putting the cart in position when the *patronne* returned. She was out of breath from having run up, then down, the stairs quickly.

"He's not there," she said. "I'm going to see at the village. Begin to unload both of them."

They unharnessed La Noire, and Pablo led her to the stable. They gave hay to all the animals, and then returned to the wagon.

"I don't understand," said Pablo, "why she's so worried about her son."

"She's afraid he's drinking. He's like his father, he's nasty when he's been drinking. Every time he drinks he has to bash someone."

They began to unload. Then the old man spoke again: "I don't like old wives' tales, but if you think about it, there does seem to be a curse on the house."

They had almost emptied the first *sapine* when the *patronne* came back with her son, who was talking loudly and laughing.

"Hop it, Clopineau!" he shouted as he came in. "That's not a job for you. Let me do it!"

The old man climbed down, mopping his forehead. Pierre climbed on the cart and caught hold of the mattock. The rhythm speeded up immediately. Pablo gritted his teeth. The lad was quite at ease. What was more, he smelt of wine, and what he had drunk must have excited him. They emptied the first *sapine* very quickly and jumped down to move the cart back.

"I think we'll make a famous team," said Pierre, laughing.

"Yes, it's going along well," said Pablo.

They climbed back on the cart and, before they started their task again, Pablo asked, "Did you get your extension?"

"No, the doctor's an old idiot. He said that if he gave me a certificate I would have to stay in the house all day in case the police came to check on me. I don't give a damn. If it's going to be all that trouble, I'll go back."

They began to dig into the grapes with a pick, and the son added, "After all, I do want to get back. I'm in line for corporal, and then I'll go on an N.C.O.'s course."

"Would you like to be in the regular army?"

"Why not? It's not a bad life in peacetime. What's more, I had a talk with Denise this afternoon: since she's been working at the

96

factory she doesn't want to go back to the country. Whether we come here or look for a place in the town's all the same to me."

He stopped speaking and began to speed up their work. When they had finished Pablo was wet with sweat and the blood was pounding in his temples.

"Holy mackerel!" said the lad as he jumped down in the straw. "It's enough to kill you, that job."

They went down to give the first turns to the press.

"This sort of job's O.K.," said Pierre, "when you've got a big estate and a good team of workers. Then it's worth doing. But to do it all yourself, it's too damned hard for the little you get. The old 'uns never stopped to think about it, but it doesn't interest me slogging away like this."

As soon as they had shaken the bucket well and emptied it, they went up to the kitchen. The soup was ready.

"If you want to see your father before eating," said the *patronne*, "he's usually a bit better in the evenings; he still can't talk, but when I went to give him his food he made grimaces with his eyes and moved his one good hand. I couldn't understand what he wanted, but perhaps he wanted you."

The lad was already at the table. He got up slowly and went upstairs, dragging his feet. He did not stay for long.

"It's funny," he said when he returned. "He kept making faces, and when I came out of the room he was trying to talk. I wonder what he wants."

"Perhaps it's something about the work," suggested old Clopineau.

"My goodness," said the *patronne*, "it could well be that. If you'd like to try and understand him, go up."

The old man stood up.

"May I go up, too?" asked Pablo.

"Of course you can."

Pablo followed Clopineau.

The *patron* was lying in the centre of a large, high wooden bed. When they went in he seemed pleased to see them. He tried to speak, but all that came from his open mouth were raucous, inarticulate sounds. He was mouthing "Ayayayay! Ayayayay!" as if he was trying to call someone.

"Don't you worry," said Clopineau, gripping his hand. "Everything will be all right. In a few days you'll be back on your feet again."

"Ayayayay!"

"I can't understand a thing," said the old man.

"Nor can I."

Pablo shook the sick man's left hand. The other was under the sheet. It was obvious that his body was paralysed down one side. His left eye was partly closed, and he had a twitching of the cheek which disfigured him.

"We're having a good harvest," shouted Clopineau. "It's going to be splendid."

"Ayayayay!"

"Yes, it's all good for bottling, and your lad's come. Everything is going to be all right. Don't you worry, we'll look after the cellar for you."

From below the *patronne* called out, "Come on down, the soup is on the table!"

"Well, have a good rest," said the old man. "We'll be back to see you. He's a good workman, you know. He's been hard at it." He nodded towards Pablo.

They went down again, and all down the stairs they could hear the *patron* continuing to shout: "Ayayayay! Ayayayay!"

"Shut the door," said Pierre. "Don't want too much of that sort of music!"

"Well, did you understand anything?" asked the *patronne.*

"No, nothing," said Pablo.

"I think he's worried about the harvest," said Clopineau. "He wants to know if the wine is good and if we'll be able to finish in time."

"Perhaps he doesn't hear what one says," Pablo remarked. "But he appears to see all right, so perhaps we could write on a piece of paper that the work is going well and let him read it."

"Yes, but we'll have to do it later. First we must eat and then do the pressing. I don't want to go to bed at the crack of dawn."

Pierre had spoken coldly. No-one replied, and the meal was concluded hurriedly. As they left the table the *patronne* let Pablo and old Clopineau go out, and then said, "You go ahead and begin to empty out what's in the bucket. We'll join you in a few minutes."

"What are you going to do?" asked Pierre.

"You stay here with me for a couple of minutes."

Pablo went down, followed by the old man. Only a few minutes passed, and then the *patronne* and her son joined them. They applied themselves immediately to the bars, and the *patronne* set the pace.

"Come on! Hup! Hup!"

The juice began to run, gurgling. They gave a few more turns till the screw was tight, and then they waited for a moment or two. The *patronne* looked at her son several times and coughed twice. Then, as the son went to draw a glass of wine from the barrel of red wine, she began, hesitantly, to speak to Pablo. "It's like this. The *patron* won't get well very quickly, according to the doctor. And the war may also go on quite a time."

There she stopped for a moment and looked towards Pierre, as if seeking approval.

"I'm first class," said the youth; "that's to say I can't expect any more promotion. In any case, it's no good counting on me before next summer. According to the officers, there won't be a big offensive till the spring, and it'll take at least two or three months to liquidate the Boches."

He drank his wine, shook the glass to empty the drops, and then, wiping his mouth with the back of his hand, he went on: "And even after that I don't know what I'll be doing. So . . ."

His mother interrupted. "That's just talk."

"It's not just talk; I'm going to do as I want!"

He had shouted. The *patronne* waited a few seconds, and then, very calmly, she said, "Of course you'll do as you want, but we're not at that point yet."

"Well, tell us then! What are you waiting for?"

She turned again to Pablo and went on: "Well, seeing there'll be no man, properly speaking, about the house, we'll have to get someone, so we wondered whether you might like to stay on."

Pablo looked at them without replying. They waited a few seconds, and then the son spoke. "It's up to you. The pay would be rather less than it is during the wine-harvest because in winter the days are short and there's not very much to do. But in any case we'll give you farmhand's pay."

As Pablo still did not speak, the *patronne* added: "Of course, during the winter there'll be no question of you sleeping in the small barn. We'll see what we can arrange."

"There's no difficulty there," said the son. "He can sleep in my room."

Pablo thought for a few seconds more, and then, standing up, said simply, "Done. That'll be all right."

Then they went down to the pressing.

XIII

THE SKY turned cloudy during the night, and the west wind began to blow in the early morning. It brought with it, from the edge of the plain, clouds which were slow to move from the horizon. From time to time the sun sent a beam through an opening. One clear patch in a corner of the plain, bright and shining, advanced rapidly, increasing in size. Then it shrank suddenly and vanished.

From hour to hour the greyness of the sky became more solid, more uniform, and the light diminished.

The first drops of rain began to fall towards midday. There was a sharp shower, and they all took refuge under the cart to finish lunch.

Sitting on upturned *seilles*, backs bowed, they ate silently, staring at their feet where water was beginning to run between the clods of earth and the tufts of grass. On the other side of the road La Noire stood patiently in the rain, turning only occasionally towards the cart. She looked at them all, and it seemed to Pablo that she was asking why she was being left thus, tied to a stake in such miserable weather.

The downpour did not last long, and they were able to start work again. But they had lost the high spirits of the earlier days. They were drenched by the wet vines which were being shaken by the wind. Branches dripped water down their necks.

"The carrier has the best job today," said old Marguerite.

Pablo realized this. The ground was not sodden enough to make walking tricky, and in the last few days his shoulders had become less sore. The vines they were harvesting were well established, and the larger bunches of grapes quickly filled the pails. Pablo had hardly ever to wait for a load. He must have been the only one not to suffer from the cold.

Despite three downpours, which forced them to stop work, they were able to fill the two *sapines* and return before night fell.

100

At the house, already back in uniform, the son, who had spent the day at Coulans, was waiting for them.

"Can't you really put off going till the morning?" asked his mother.

"No, I don't want to risk detention for being late back."

He began to shake hands all round.

"But you've plenty of time; your train doesn't leave till nine o'clock."

"I've to go and say goodbye to my pals."

He kissed his mother and sister, put on his two haversacks, slung his water-bottle across his back, and went off towards the village.

The *patronne*, Jeannette, Clopineau, and Pablo went outside the house to watch him go. When he reached the crossroads he turned round and waved an arm before disappearing behind the hedge. All of them waved their hands, even Jeannette, and the *patronne* shouted, "Au revoir!"

That was all she said, but Pablo looked at her almost in fear. It seemed to him that her whole world was in this hoarse shout which turned almost to a sob at the end. This shout which had flown across the land from which the soldier had already disappeared. The cry which had flown to be lost at the foot of the hillside without finding any echo.

They all turned round and walked slowly towards the house without daring to look at each other.

As they went into the barn rain began to fall again.

Immediately the day's harvest had been unloaded the *patronne* and Pablo returned to the kitchen, where Clopineau and Jeannette had finished preparing the meal and laying the table. The fat woman had gone back to her own house, saying that she would return for the pressing.

"Come along," said the *patronne*, "take your places at table. I'll take food up for the *patron*."

These were the first words she had said since her son had left. She had worked very hard opposite Pablo for more than an hour, her teeth clenched, her lips tight, and her forehead fretted with unusual hard lines. Her voice had not changed, but her words sounded curiously in the silence of the kitchen.

"Is he calling all the time?" asked Pablo.

"I don't know. I haven't been up to him since this morning."

She took a bowl, filled it with clear soup, and disappeared

101

through the door at the end. Pablo now thought of the *patron*. He had thought of him several times in the course of the day.

"If he keeps on like that," he said to Clopineau, "I've a good mind to write on some paper for him that all is going well."

"Yes," said the old man. "That'd do him a lot of good."

When the *patronne* came down Pablo asked, "Well?"

"Still the same. He rolls his eyes all the time and repeats the same thing over and over."

"Would you like me to try to write to him on a piece of paper?" asked Pablo.

The *patronne* shrugged her shoulders. "Write if you like, but that isn't going to cure him."

She gave Pablo a sheet of paper and a pencil, then began to eat her soup.

Pablo set himself to write in large, readable letters: "Everything's all right. The harvest is very good. You'll soon be better."

"That's fine," said Clopineau. "I'll come up with you. Like that he'll see that we aren't forgetting all about him."

As soon as they entered the bedroom the *patron* began to shout again and move his left hand on the coverlet.

"Ayay! Ayay!"

Clopineau shook his hand, and Pablo put the sheet of paper in front of his eyes. He examined it in silence, and then, moving his hand, he began to cry again, louder than ever:

"Ayay! Ayay!"

The two men stared at each other.

"All the same," said the old man, "it's very curious! Surely he must be trying to tell us something?"

"Yes, because it certainly looks as if he can read. I'm pretty sure he's read what we wrote."

As he said this Pablo, with a movement of weariness, had let the hand with which he was holding the paper drop. The *patron* stared steadily at the paper and continued to shout. At the same time he tried to lift his left hand. Moving his fingers as if they were the paws of an animal, he moved his hand in the direction of the paper.

"He wants some paper," said Pablo.

He held out the sheet to him. The *patron* left it on the coverlet and, moving his hand further, made a rough approximation to the movement of someone writing.

Pablo turned back to the old man. They looked at each other

for an instant without a word. They had understood. They both smiled. Pablo went down to the kitchen.

"What does he want?" asked the *patronne.*

"The pencil," said Pablo.

He took the pencil from the table, and then asked, "Give me something hard to put the paper on."

"But what are you trying to do?"

"He wants to write. There's something he wants to tell us."

The *patronne* stood up and took from her drawer the big black book in which she kept her accounts.

"Fine. I'm coming with you."

They put the book on the bed, placed on it the sheet of paper which Pablo had been holding in his hand, and then the *patronne* put the pencil into her husband's hand and put his hand on the sheet of paper.

All three were silent, their eyes fixed on this numb hand which was moving slowly. Outside the rain spattered, driven by the wind.

The hand trembled. It slid down first and then turned to the left and rose again. Their eyes all followed this pencil-point drawing an uneven line. This line crossed the first one he had drawn, rose a little, and then came down again. Then, as if wearied, the hand came to a standstill.

"*Je,*" said Clopineau. "Do you see? He's writing '*Je*', which means he wants something."

The *patron* seemed to be at the end of his strength. Large beads of sweat stood out on his forehead and ran down his cheeks, which were covered by several days' growth of stubble. He breathed deeply, compressed his lips, and his hand began to move again.

The others remained silent, and the only sound was that of the rain on the windows.

After another hesitation the hand started again, and suddenly it was Pablo who cried, "*Jeann!* Jeannette! He wants to see Jeannette. That's what it must be."

The *patron* released the pencil. His hand was trembling, and he began to shout again:

"Ay! ay! ay! ay!"

Pablo was already on the stairs.

"Jeannette, Jeannette! Come quickly!" he shouted.

He went back upstairs, followed immediately by the young

103

girl, who went and stood by the bed, her hands hanging and her mouth drooping open.

The *patron* was no longer trying to talk. His hand was stretched out on the counterpane and scarcely trembled. Large tears ran down his cheeks, mixing with his sweat.

"Kiss your father," said the *patronne*.

The little girl leaned forward and kissed his bristly cheeks. She stood upright again. He looked at her for another moment or two, and then he closed his eyes.

Pablo and Clopineau looked at each other, nodding their heads. Nobody spoke a word. Finally, since the *patron* seemed asleep, they left the bedroom without making a sound.

XIV

THAT night Pablo slept in the son's room, the door of which was opposite the room where the *patron* was sleeping.

"Since he's been ill," explained the *patronne*, "I sleep with the little one. It's easier to sleep and I rest better."

"And if he calls in the night you can hear him?"

"Yes, I leave the doors open; you must close yours. There's no reason why we should both be disturbed."

Once he was alone, Pablo sat on the bed and looked round him. It was more than two years since he had slept in a bed. The sheets were clean, but the bedding held the odour of another man. Pablo opened the window wide. Moths flew in. He put out the light and remained a long time leaning on the window-sill. He took deep breaths of the moist night air. Everything was dripping. He could see nothing in the darkness, but he knew that this window faced south. To the left was the slope of the hill which faded away far off on the plain stretching in front of him and away to the right.

Beneath the window there was the cemented pool where the ducks splashed about when they did not go as far as the stream. A little farther still were the vines which were not yet harvested.

Pablo thought of the harvest. The grapes there were left behind from earlier picking and were used for making spirit and mill-wine. All the best grapes, from the grafted plants, those which produced the good yellow wine, had now been brought in.

Pablo breathed deeply again and groped his way back to the bed. He undressed and lay down without putting on the light. He did not fall asleep immediately. He remained for some time with his eyes open, listening to the rain, which was the only living thing in the night since the wind had dropped.

He thought first of Mariana, and he realized that for some days he had devoted less time to her. The face she presented to him this evening was calm, as if in repose.

Pablo was lying straight on this very comfortable bed. He did not move, but felt the bed with every part of his body. For a long time he lay there like this, torn between the motionless image of Mariana and the sensation of wellbeing which the bed gave him. Finally, after a moment or two, he murmured, "The war is over."

But the word "war" immediately brought back into the room an image of Pierre. This bed in which Pablo felt so comfortable was the bed of a soldier who had left this evening with his water-bottle filled and bottles of wine in his two haversacks.

Pablo saw in his mind many soldiers. All had water-bottles in their haversacks or bottles in their hands. All waved to the women, even a long way off, who watched them going away.

Pablo had not seen this face of war for months. Usually it showed him the bloody face and the torn body of Mariana. There were always many ruins. Many smoking ruins, but never any soldiers.

Pablo had not noticed this until the present moment. In fact, he had never really evoked the war; it was of Mariana that he had always thought. Only of Mariana. But this evening, because he was feeling that he had really escaped from the war, he saw it again.

And that night he did not fall asleep until very late, after having passed in review the entire panorama of the war he had known. He had seen too many dead to be able to weep for them. All these dead were no longer men who had been crushed, burned, tortured, or shot. They were corpses piled in a huge common grave which was called war. The grave was closed, and all the wounds had ceased to bleed.

Isolated in one corner was Mariana. Mariana was now a face which had ceased to suffer. By dint of having sought in vain to imagine how she had died Pablo had ended by realizing that it

105

was not that which counted. He had the certainty that Mariana was dead, that was all.

Her face now seemed set for all time. Mariana now had a face. Pablo had been unable to save anything in his flight. Not even a photograph of Mariana. In the first days he would have given anything for just a picture of her. This evening, it was as if he had at last found again this photograph in the depths of his memory. A picture of Mariana who did not smile, but who did not suffer either. An image which would never change with the years.

Pablo looked at it for a long while. Then, voluntarily, he ceased to look at it. He realized that he could keep it in a corner of his heart and look on it whenever he wished.

Then, in the comfort of the bed, in the mist of drowsiness, lulled by the monotonous rhythm of the rain, Pablo felt that he was at home here, in this room where he could be alone with the image of Mariana. They were together. They could remain here, far from the war.

XV

THEY finished the harvesting in heavy rain, and the last two days were almost unbearable. The vines were on flat ground, on the far side of the stream. The earth was yellow—soggy clay which clung to the feet and to the buckets.

The highest trellises threw long shoots in every direction, all so thoroughly wet that even when the rain was not falling the pickers were soaked. Pablo himself was wet only to the waist, but sufficient for him to have to wring out his trousers.

He was considerably more tired than among vines on the slopes because of the soft earth and the level ground. He had got into the habit of long descents in a long stride with all the weight he carried pushing him along. Here he had to make a different effort, and weariness soon crept through his body, making other muscles painful.

Fortunately the grapes they were now picking would be used for red wine, and the *vendange* would not need pressing. When they got back to the farm they hurried to empty the *sapines* and then to go in and change their clothes. Afterwards they went down to the kitchen again, where the *patronne* was busy. Pablo sat down by the fire and stretched out his legs by the warm metal surface. Clopineau was already there. He did not need to change. He harvested in a hooded cape and managed to keep his clothes almost dry. He restricted himself to putting his feet against the open door of the oven to dry his socks, while his clogs steamed, standing on top of the hot-water bottle.

"You're brooding over my fire," said the *patronne*. "There's no chance of anyone stealing the stove, no matter what the weather's like this winter!"

Pablo had received his pay for the first week, and he had bought himself some tobacco and a pipe. He smoked one pipeful after lunch as he carried his first *bouille* of the afternoon. But the best one he had was in the evening, while he was waiting for his meal.

The *patronne* went out of the kitchen to milk the cows. Clopineau began to doze, and the only sound was the dragging of Jeannette's feet as she laid the table. When she had finished she went to stand by the sink and wait. Then all was silence. Pablo half closed his eyes and took little puffs at his pipe. The smoke rose slowly, mixed with the steam rising from the kettle. From time to time there was a loud thump; La Noire was stamping her hooves.

This was the one moment when Pablo managed not to think. Everything faded for him, becoming as grey and distant as the smoke from his pipe.

The *patronne* had decided to keep Clopineau working for her long enough at least to show Pablo the ropes so far as the main work was concerned.

"You'll be the teacher, in a way," she told him. "I'm not asking you to do the work, but only to show him what's to be done."

"That's all right, that's all right," replied the old man, winking. "I know what you're after."

"Well, Clopineau, you know very well I can't afford to pay two farmhands!"

"That's what I thought. But don't you worry, it suits me very well. You know I've got nothing to do for myself. While I'm here I'll be saving on wood for my fire, and I shall be fed. I ask nothing better."

The matter was settled, the old man asking for only ten francs a week for tobacco.

107

"You see," he explained to Pablo, "with the shortage of labour I could get something better-paid to do in the village, but that'd be odd days here and there, and I don't like that. I'm too old to like changing about here and there. And when I do work I like people to have value for their money. I haven't the strength of a younger man, so I'd crack up a bit and finish by only working one day in two. That's no life. Now, at least, I'm sure of eating every day."

"As far as the food's concerned," said Pablo, "there's nothing to grumble at here."

The old man nodded his head. "I can tell you," he said, "I've worked in practically every house around here. I didn't collapse from hunger anywhere, but I've never eaten as well as here. So far as that, you can count yourself lucky."

As he said this he began to laugh and rubbed his large hands together, making a sound like a rasp on wood. Then, leaning towards Pablo and lowering his voice, he said, "I can count myself lucky too. I'm only to be the teacher and do the talking, but I'm not the man to watch others work."

The old man did in fact continue to work as if he was being paid normally. As soon as the rain stopped, the beetroots and the maize had to be brought in. Pablo learned to handle La Noire and to plough. He was strong and put his heart into whatever he undertook. However, he did not always succeed at first try, and he became irritable. At times he was very upset. He swore away in Catalan, making both Clopineau and the *patronne* laugh.

"You'll manage it," said Clopineau. "You'll manage it. When you're working the soil you need strength and a good idea of what you're after. You've got both. All you lack is patience, but it'll come."

One day when he was working a nasty strip of ground where there were many roots of old apple-trees which had not been properly cleared, Pablo lost his temper more than ever before. He let go of the plough-handles and began to curse the ground, kicking at the stump the ploughshare had just turned up. The plough overturned, and the old man, who was leading La Noire by the bridle, halted. He waited for Pablo's rage to simmer down, and then, going over to him, he said, "You see, that sort of thing doesn't serve any purpose, and it's taking a great risk. If La Noire was a less even-tempered beast she might have taken fright and injured herself."

108

Pablo went over to the mare and caressed her neck and withers, which were moist with sweat.

"If she was hurt because of me," he said, "I'd never forgive myself in a hundred years."

"With animals, anger can be very dangerous," said the old man.

Pablo went back to take the handles of the plough. Clopineau followed him, and before returning to take the bridle he said, "You've got the right idea, you've got the strength, you're willing, but..."

He stopped and looked at Pablo with much goodwill and a little reproach in his eyes.

"Go on," said Pablo. "Tell me what you think. It will help me to know."

"I may be wrong, but I don't think you really love the soil."

Pablo did not reply. But the old man had not expected any reply; he had already returned to La Noire.

Motionless, his hands on the handles, Pablo stared at all the land around him. It was pale and bleak as if dozing below the grey sky. The sky was just an enormous grey cloud stretching between the two horizons. All was sad, even the smoke rising from the fields where the countryfolk were burning dead plants.

"O.K. now?" shouted Clopineau.

"Gee up! Gee up!"

La Noire stamped, twisting her chine and twitching her rump. The draw-hooks creaked, the coulter went deeply into the ground, and the plough started again to trace its furrows. A huge red wound opened along the side of another wound. The grass rose up, turned over, and plunged into the earth through which white roots twisted. At each stump encountered, Pablo gripped the handles more firmly, tightening his lips to hold back the oath which rose to his lips, despite his efforts to control himself. The shock travelled to his head, electrifying his arms and shoulders. Sometimes, by pressing so hard on the handles, he was no longer master of his body, and his feet were lifted off the ground. But despite all, by the end of the afternoon he had cleared this bad patch of earth without shouting or cursing once.

When they went back night was falling. They were sitting together on the back of the cart. Behind them the plough dangled against the rails. La Noire moved slowly in the narrow, deeply rutted lane. The old man led the way. With his elbows on his knees, Pablo looked at the sleeping land around him. The cart pitched heavily, and it seemed at times that the earth was beginning to dance like a huge, grey sea. Only heavy, chilled forms could be distinguished, hunched in folds in the ground or crouching at the foot of the slope. Everywhere the smoke from the fires of weeds mingled with the evening mist. Everything was coming to a standstill. The earth seemed weary of living under a sky which prevented it from breathing. For the earth this was not yet the long sleep of winter, it was the anguish before winter's sleep; it was like the regret for the harvests garnered and the dead leaves burning away. The mist smelled both of the brackish water and damp fires. Here and there a small red light winked in the centre of a field where huddled forms were sleeping.

"To love the land," Pablo said to himself. "To love the land..."
Was it possible really to love the land?

The word 'love' brought back to him the memory of Mariana. He knew that he would never love again. He had loved Mariana. He had loved the child she was carrying in her belly and who died at the same time as she did. Now there was no question of loving. Pablo was living. He had agreed to live, that was all. And he lived here because chance had brought him here. He was well off here. He suffered neither from cold nor from hunger, and weariness had become for him an ally. He knew it. He clung to it as a sick man clings to the medicine which eases his pain.

He did, of course, love everything around him. He loved it as he loved La Noire, for example, or old Clopineau. But that was not true love.

Little ever came back from his past except Mariana. Nothing else mattered. His work, his house, his food, all had been replaced. Without Mariana life here or back there would be the same. Here life in peace was possible; without the pestering of police, without the threat of prison and torture. Around Pablo now there were only silent people.

The *patronne* spoke little. She raised her voice only when Jeannette failed to do as she was asked. Pablo had also finally got used to the presence of this girl. She disgusted him less. She was there, like a dog staring always at humans, trying to comprehend what they are saying.

As for Clopineau, because he had been a farmhand all his life, he had got into the habit of never talking at table. He spoke only during work, and then only when it was essential. Otherwise it was only when they happened to smoke together while waiting

110

for the evening meal that Clopineau liked telling tales. But his weariness always betrayed him, and each time his eyes would close in the middle of a sentence, left suspended in mid-air.

If the *patronne* was there she said, invariably, "The old man's trying to do two things at once again."

Pablo would smile, but not answer, remaining isolated from the rest of the room behind the smoke from his pipe.

Sometimes, when they came back a little earlier from the fields, Clopineau and Pablo would go up to see the *patron*.

Since the weather had turned cooler the doctor had recommended that a fire be kept in the bedroom. They had found one morning an old iron stove which would burn huge logs. Jeannette had the job of keeping the fire going during the day, and she had never let it go out. The *patron* no longer shouted. When she had filled the stove, he would say gently:

"Ay ay ay ay."

The little girl would go over to him, and he would waggle his good hand until she took it in her own. They would remain like this for several minutes without moving, until the *patron* said:

"Ay ay ay ay."

Jeannette would then go back to her work.

If Pablo and Clopineau happened to be with him at the time, as soon as the girl had gone he would look at them, moving his good eyelid. The men would smile, and in the face of the *patron* they would see something indefinable which showed him to be happy.

One evening, because only one log remained in the wood basket, Pablo took it down to refill it. When he went up again the *patron* moved his body and made it clear that he wanted to say something. Pablo put down the basket and went downstairs to get the accounts book, some paper, and a pencil. Still with very great difficulty, the *patron* wrote: "wood".

Clopineau puckered his brow, and then exclaimed "That's it, I understand. He's worried about the wood."

He went over to the basket, picked up a log, went back to the *patron*, and, putting the log at the foot of the bed, held it with one hand while making with the other a chopping motion on the log.

The *patron* immediately moved his good hand and winked his eye.

"Soon," shouted the old man, "Pablo and me with La Noire.

111

The wood in the old mill combe. Don't you worry, we won't let you freeze."

Then, speaking to Pablo, he added, "I had a couple of words with the *patronne* the other day. Next week we'll find time for it. But you see how odd it is; he knows perfectly well that the wood we'll be cutting will be for the next winter, not this. He knows very well also that the woodshed is full. All the same, he is afraid of a shortage. He must feel that he's going to live a long time yet."

He stopped for a moment, appeared to think, and then, his eyes alight with joy, he went on: "That wood, young 'un, that's really something."

Pablo waited for a long time without saying any word, hoping for an explanation, but the old man said nothing more. He was looking neither at the *patron* nor at Pablo. He was looking into the distance, and the wrinkles of his face seemed to smile with just a trace of melancholy.

XVI

THE weather remained calm except for rare gusts of wind which changed the sky a little, tearing away a cloud or two without revealing any blue. The sun did appear, sometimes at dawn or in the evening, but before there was a chance to see it the clouds hid it again. Nevertheless the cold increased little by little, and one morning the *patronne*, as she was about to give water to the chickens she was fattening, found a thin layer of ice in the bowl.

"It's time for wood," said old Clopineau. "As soon as the sky smells of snow it's best to start cutting before too much falls."

As all the fields were in good order and there was nothing urgent to be done in the wine-cellar, where the fermentation was now slow and almost finished, they decided to tackle the job the next day. As he went off to bed that evening old Clopineau was rubbing his hands, and his eyes were bright.

"Be ready good and early," he said to Pablo.

Pablo woke very early, and when the old man arrived La Noire was already harnessed. They took only the time to swallow quickly a bowl of hot soup, and then they were off.

There was barely enough light to see by, but once they were

112

out of the village there was only one road. La Noire knew it well. She had only to be given her head.

The cold was biting. Sitting side by side on the seat of the cart, the two men had stretched over their legs the mare's blanket and the canvas cover. They remained silent for a long while, still heavy with sleep. Then, as daybreak began to light up the contours of the road, Pablo asked, "Where does this road lead?"

"It goes up towards Geruge."

As the road rose it became more winding. There was less land under cultivation, and soon there were only woods on either side. These were not tall woods, but plantations of young ash-trees and, more particularly, acacias. Beside the road, on a slightly lower level, the stream flowed along, sliding over stony patches from time to time and making a white sparkle of foam in the half-light of dawn.

Pablo looked at the old man a number of times. His eyes were going from one side of the road to the other, peering at the underwood, following for a moment the course of the stream, only to return quickly to the woods. He was drawing short breaths, like a dog trying to retrace a scent. Noticing that Pablo was watching him, he smiled.

"You'll see, my lad, what the wood really is: it hasn't anything in common with real forest, of course; it's what they call a vine-grower's wood. Acacia, you see, makes the best stakes. So they're the only trees we plant. When we're cutting we choose what we need for the vines, and the rest we saw up as logs for the fire."

As he was speaking his face became animated, and he began to wave his hands. Soon, in order to explain himself better, he took off his mufflers. His breath made a little swarm of tiny white clouds which floated one by one over his shoulder.

He talked about the great forests where he had worked in his youth as a cutter.

"One day," he said, "you must see them. They aren't so very far from here."

He remained silent for a moment, staring into space. Then, turning to Pablo again, he went on: "But even here it's good. You'll see. I guarantee we don't meet a living soul all day."

"Why did you leave the forest job?" asked Pablo.

The old man tapped on the place where his knees were under the blanket.

"My leg. In the forest, you know, you have to be absolutely fit

113

and strong to do a full day's work. You work in teams, and if there's one not up to it the others have to work harder to make up for him. It's not the same thing here at all."

"And you never go back to the forests where you used to work?"

The old man seemed surprised. "Go back?" he asked. "What for?"

Pablo dropped the subject. At the instant he asked his question he had realized that it did not make sense.

Now the day was fully come. It bathed the stripped woods with a mournful light. All was greyness. Nothing seemed alive except, rarely, a bird flying and disappearing among the trees. Very high in the sky, touching the clouds, there were flights of croaking ravens.

Soon the old man pulled the reins and turned La Noire down a lane on the left of the main road, between the woods. They went on a short distance before stopping on the level stretch, and then they climbed down. The old man turned the horse, so that the cart would be ready to leave, and began to unhitch La Noire. Pablo threw the blanket across the steaming back of the mare before giving her some hay.

"Now," said the old man, "the first thing is food."

"Already? But it's not yet midday," replied Pablo with a smile.

The old man laughed. He seemed truly happy, and his joy was like that of children playing at being workmen.

Taking his bill-hook, he began to trim the dead branches remaining from the previous cut, building a fire in the centre of the clearing. The flames rose quickly, consuming the handful of hay stolen from La Noire, attacking the brushwood and beginning to roar. In the stillness the smoke rose straight into the air, as high as the treetops, and then, cooling, it stretched into long banners which fluttered as if caught in the branches. The two men rubbed their hands beside the fire.

"Like this," explained the old man, putting a few big logs on the fire, "we'll have a fine pile of embers, and in an hour we'll be able to heat up the soup. The fire, when you're all day in the woods in winter, is the first thing to tackle. The rest comes afterwards."

Taking off their jackets, they put them on the cart, took their axes, and began the felling.

For Pablo it was an apprenticeship, and he soon learned that a felling axe was less easy to handle than a pickaxe. What was more, the plough had not hardened his hands as much as he

114

thought, and by midday his palms were covered with huge, burst blisters.

"I see you're looking at your hands," said Clopineau as they went back to the fire. "The axe is a real devil at the beginning; I don't want to force you to work, but I'll give you a bit of advice: persevere. If you stop for a day the trouble starts all over again. But if you avoid giving up you'll do fine. It's a question of one week, no more."

In fact, Pablo's hands changed quickly. The palms hardened and soon stopped being painful, though the backs were scratched and cracked. Pablo looked at them often in the evenings as he sat smoking his pipe by the fire. He felt the thickness of his callouses and rubbed them against each other. They did not yet make the same rasping sound as Clopineau's, but Pablo knew that the time would come.

He did not really think about it, but he was beginning to have no other preoccupation than the work they were doing during the day and that which they would be doing the morrow. Pablo now understood the old man's love for the woods. He even wondered at times if, without him, he would have come to appreciate fully all there was in the forest's silence.

The time he felt this most was during their meals.

They both sat by the fire, and the old man would take from the pan the bacon and sausage and place it on the upturned lid, which he set among the warm embers. Then he would take the loaf and cut the bread into the pot. They let it soak long enough for them to drink a glass of wine, and the old man would serve the meal. Then, eating slowly, Pablo would let his eyes wander over the greyness of the wood. The smoke of the fire left motionless blue traces everywhere. For long moments the silence was complete, and in this tiny valley, closed in by a low sky resting on the summits of the hills, the silence was different. It had a more delicate quality than that of the plain, for example, or the vine-planted slopes. The slightest sound took on a greater importance. A cracking of a twig, a spark exploding from the fire, the clinking of La Noire's bridle which she shook to beg a titbit, were all part of the silence. Everything seemed to be at the point where it could be most fully sensed.

Sometimes other woodmen worked above them or below. The blows of their axes and their shouts answered the sounds made by Pablo and Clopineau as they worked. The multiple echoes

115

made one, but the valley was never quite awakened. It had such a deep reserve of silence that noises never quite overcame it. They ran between the trees, but never leaped over their tops. One could sense that they remained there, as if held by the earth where they slept.

In the evening, to go down with the cart loaded with trunks cleaned of all branches, the old man took off La Noire's bridle and Pablo walked beside the cart, level with the brake-handle. He kept a solid branch in his hand ready to slip it between two spokes and block a wheel if the cart started to run away. From time to time he looked back. Behind them, with night rising from the smallest folds of the ground, the valley seemed to be closing itself, muffling itself in its heavy sleep.

This was winter. The land was bare and approachable. There was nothing to distract you.

Then, one day when they were in the woods, just as they were finishing a meal, snow began to fall. The old man had foretold it the previous evening, and in the morning, just before leaving, he had repeated again: "Tonight we'll come back with snow on us."

At first only a few flakes fell, each seeming to select a convenient spot on which to settle. Those which came near the fire melted before they touched ground.

"We'll finish stripping what's already cut," said the old man. "Then it'll be time to go."

"You must be joking; we can't leave at three in the afternoon."

"Let's get on. We'll talk about it again in a few minutes."

They set to work again with a good heart, striking hard to warm themselves and circulate blood which had become sluggish during the meal. After a moment or two Pablo, raising his eyes, saw that everything was already white.

"Well?" asked the old man with a laugh. "What did I tell you?"

"You were right. I think we'd better hurry."

They finished the stripping nevertheless, but they had difficulty in loading the cart. Their wet hands were stiff. The trunks slithered, and they were blinded by snow-flakes falling more and more thickly.

They returned to the farm slowly, and night was not far distant when they reached the house. As soon as she heard the cart, the *patronne* came out on to the doorstep.

116

"All well?" she shouted.

"Ah!" said the old man. "Were you worried about your mare? Anyone'd think you didn't know me."

Then he laughed, smothered as he was in snow, his head tucked in his shoulders, and the hood of his cape down over his eyes.

They rubbed down La Noire and gave her some hay before going in to sit by the fire.

"This time," said Clopineau, "it really is winter."

It was indeed winter, settling itself in all round the house. The fire continued to roar. The table was set. Nobody spoke. But it was warm within. This was not only the warmth of the fire. Life was there. All the life of the land had taken refuge in the house.

That winter was intensely cold. The snow remained, packed tight and hard as ice.

"There's more coming," said Clopineau.

More, indeed, came, and for a long time all outside work had to be abandoned.

But the men were not idle. There were the stakes to be sawn lengthwise, to be split, to be squared off, to be treated. There was wood for the fire waiting to be sawn up, in the woodshed. And then, when the tenacious wind chased them from the shed, they took refuge in the cellar, where there was always work to be done. Pablo was learning quite a number of jobs from Clopineau, who knew how to cope with everything.

"I think the *patronne* is satisfied," said the old man. "It may look as if all we've done is a lot of trivial odd jobs, just pottering about to pass the time, but it was all work that needed doing. Since his accident the *patron* hasn't taken much interest, and the boy had to be told how to do everything. It's a bad sign when a house starts to go downhill!"

The *patronne* was, in fact, a good manager. She always had some odd job or other to suggest.

"By the way," she would say, "while you're doing a bit of woodwork you might take a look in the stable and patch up the pen for the kids. I'm going to get some in the spring, and some of the planks are very shaky."

The men looked around, testing flooring, examining every part of the farmhouse and its outbuildings. Most of the time they finished by glancing at each other and winking.

"Come on," the old man would say, "no patching-up. While

we're at it, we might as well make it like new. There's no shortage of wood here."

In the end the house took on a brighter, cleaner, and more solid look.

"Bit by bit," said the old man to the *patronne*, "we'll be able to make you a proper little castle."

Everything was looked after. The stable, the barn, the tool-shed, the tools themselves which needed new handles, or sharpening, or cleaning. There was the plough, the harrow, and the reaper to be cleaned and oiled. But each time that everything seemed to have been done, something more was still found in need of attention.

"You'll never get to the end of it all," said the *patronne* with a smile.

"We will," declared Clopineau. "Only it isn't us who'll say when it's finished. The sun'll do that."

The sun shone quite often, but the sky stole all its warmth and the land remained icy. Over the whole Bressane plain there was no sign of life other than the smoke from chimneys and, marked in black on the snow, the road along which silent and tiny vehicles moved. Everything put out of doors froze immediately. Manure brought in warm from the stable steamed for a moment, and then, soon covered with frost, it became a solid block which the fork slipped across. The hens grouped themselves by the corner of the woodshed; motionless, ruffled, and huddled one against the other, they stayed there as long as the sun lasted. Then, as soon as it passed behind the corner of the house, they went in again to await their evening meal.

The *patronne* had knitted two mufflers and a balaclava helmet for her son, who had written from the front to say that cold was their worst enemy. Each time a letter arrived from him the *patronne* read it to herself in a low voice, and then, calling Clopineau and Pablo, she would say, "Come here, there's a letter from the boy."

They would leave their clogs behind the cooking-stove and follow the *patronne* to the room where the *patron* was lying. There, in a loud voice, she would re-read the letter. She stopped often to look at her husband. With just a movement of his eyes he was able to indicate whether he had understood or not.

Pablo listened sitting on a chair beside him. He listened watching the fire through the bars of the stove, or the wonderful frost

118

flowers made by the frost on the windows. What he heard seldom interested him. The boy wrote always about the same things. He spoke of shared parcels from home, snow-fights, and theatrical shows visiting the Army. He complained of the cold and the shortage of wine. He asked for more parcels, and ended his letters always with the same phrase: "A kiss for you, and I hope that Papa will be better in the spring."

As far as Pablo was concerned, the lad was on holiday. Many times he thought to himself that if the wine had been to his taste he would certainly not have found the holiday too long.

The *patron* remained in the same condition. He merely grew much thinner. His cheeks were sunken and he was paler. He now had the face of an old man. Since the weather had become very cold the *patronne* had insisted on his wearing a night-cap. Nothing was now to be seen of him except his face emerging from the sheets, and his seemingly shrunken head sunk in the pillows. He never asked for anything. Jeannette continued to look after his fire. With the north wind the logs burned more quickly, and she had to go up more often. As soon as she entered the room her father's eyes showed more life, and though he did not budge, his face lit up. Then, as soon as the little girl went away, his eyes became dull once more.

One day, seeing him thus, Pablo had the curious sensation that the *patron* was no longer part of the life of the house. He was a bit of winter which had entered the room and which the living tried to keep with them by feeding the fire.

This was stupid, and Pablo knew it. But from that moment on he often had the same idea. It was something like a wheel which had one spoke different from the others. When it was turning it was not noticeable, and one never thought of it. But when the wheel stops one thinks of it, and it is always that spoke which is in sight. Thus Pablo thought of the *patron*, winter, each time he happened to be in the bedroom, sitting in the same place where the thought had come to him for the first time. Otherwise he never thought of the *patron*. Indeed, no-one thought of him very much except at meal-times. It could not be said what Jeannette thought about. She had simply got into the way of going up to him each time that the fire needed fuel. There must have been something in her which told her the amount of time that a log took to burn away, varying with the way the wind was blowing.

Quite often Clopineau would say, for example, "We've put

119

this barrel on those two, but I wonder whether that's the way the *patron* would have wanted it."

But each time he made a gesture as if to say, "Well, there's not much chance of him saying anything, he won't even see it."

So, just as if there was no war on, just as if the *patron* really had been a bit of winter forgotten in the house, they continued to put in good order all that would be needed to welcome the spring which the earth was preparing during its icy sleep.

XVII

THE *patronne* and old Marguerite remained in the room while Pablo went down with the doctor.

The shutters were closed, and it was dark and cold in the kitchen. Standing in front of the sink, Jeannette was weeping.

"Poor child," murmured the doctor.

He crossed the room and went out into the courtyard. Pablo accompanied him as far as the gate.

"You came on foot?"

"How could I have managed to get here in a car? Haven't you seen the road?"

"No," said Pablo. "I haven't been out for two days. But last night, in my room, I could hear traffic all the time."

"It's even worse this morning," said the doctor. "You'd think everyone had gone mad."

Pablo did not reply. He stared down.

It was very warm. The midday sun whitened the dusty road. There was not a breath of wind.

"I looked after a lot of wounded last night," went on the doctor. "There was a chap who came from Dombasle with a bomb-splinter in his arm. I wanted him to stay for attention. Nothing doing. He was off straight away. They're the ones who're scaring people. Admittedly it's terrible the things they've seen, but I don't think the Boches will bombard us here. It wouldn't make sense. But everyone is trying to get away. When this wounded fellow had finished telling us all he'd seen my house-keeper, who's sixty-seven, wanted to take herself off."

The doctor remained silent for a moment. He turned his head

120

in the direction of the cemetery. On the other side, at the bottom of the slope, there was the highway. Pablo, following his example, looked as well. They could see nothing except the wall above which a few white crosses showed up against the blue, heavy sky. Beyond the cemetery the road should be visible. For a moment Pablo was tempted to go with the doctor as far as the bend, but already the doctor was saying, holding out his hand, "You'd better get busy with the burial immediately. With the heat the sooner the better, apart from the fact that people are so stupid that there's a chance they'll all be taking flight before nightfall."

The doctor went a little way, and then, turning round, he said, "During the funeral get the little one out of the way; that'll be the best thing to do."

Pablo remained for a moment at the edge of the road, his eyes fixed on the black silhouette of the doctor, who was walking along with his rather jerky step. After a moment the doctor began to gesticulate. He must have begun to talk to himself.

"Come on up and help us to dress him."

Pablo jumped. The *patronne* had just leaned out of the window to call to him. He turned round, finding it difficult to focus his eyes after staring so fixedly at the black figure which danced in the vapour rising from the overheated earth.

"I'm coming," he said.

He went to the kitchen and stood by the door to give his eyes a chance to become accustomed to the half-light. He then went across to Jeannette, who was still weeping.

"Don't cry," he whispered. "Don't cry."

But the child continued to sob. He stroked her hair several times, and then left her to go across to the stairs.

"I'll have to ask you to do something that's not very pleasant," said the *patronne* when he went into the bedroom.

"Don't worry about that."

He approached the bed where the *patron* was lying. The women had tied a large handkerchief round his head and under his chin to keep his mouth closed. His face was emaciated and almost as pale as the handkerchief.

"He'll have to be lifted while we dress him," said Marguerite.

Pablo went closer and leaned over the bed. It had been a long time since he had touched a dead man.

"The feet first," said the old woman.

Pablo's heart began to beat a little faster. Pearls of sweat

121

formed at his temples. He felt sweat running down his back and his chest. He took hold of the *patron*'s ankles. They were still warm. Pablo wanted to vomit, and he felt an urgent need to talk to give himself courage.

"Where I come from it's never the widow who does this," he said.

He had spoken without thinking.

"It's the same here," said the old woman. "But at this time of the year, with all that's going on, those who aren't among the vines have already fled."

They continued dressing the dead man, and then, when he was lying on his bed which had been covered with a fresh white sheet, Marguerite put a black rosary between his hands.

"Now you can close," she said.

The *patronne* closed the shutters.

"Give me a saucer," said Marguerite. "I've everything else I need, and you can light up."

While the *patronne* went down to fetch a saucer the old woman took from the larger pocket of her apron a twig of boxwood and a small phial of holy water. Once the candle had been lighted and the saucer placed on the bedside table, the two women made the sign of the cross over the body with the twig and then passed it to Pablo. Without a word he made the same gesture and put it down in the water. There was silence for several minutes. The women must have been praying, because their lips were moving.

"That's all right. Let's go now."

Since the shutters had been closed the old woman had been speaking in a whisper.

They went down, and the *patronne* said she was going off to make all the necessary arrangements.

"You'll eat with us?" she asked the old woman.

"If you'd like me to."

"Then I'll leave you to lay the table. I'm off."

As she went out she stopped by the sink and said to Jeannette, "You'll try to help Marguerite, eh?"

"Don't worry," said Pablo. "I'll give her a hand."

The *patronne* went out. The little girl did not move, but continued to sob. As they set the table Marguerite and Pablo looked at her from time to time. She had her eyes fixed on the end door and seemed lifeless except for the sobs which shook her rhythmically.

"She makes me feel ill," said the old woman.

"Me too. I feel sick to see her like that."

Marguerite came to a stop, putting down on the table the round loaf of bread she was holding, and went over to Pablo. Lowering her voice and looking towards the door, she whispered, "You'd think she understood."

"But of course," said Pablo. "I'm sure she understands."

"Oh, naturally, she's understood that her father is dead. But I think she understands what she's lost."

Pablo shrugged his shoulders.

"Didn't you see how, during the last few hours, he looked at her? He knew very well that no other person would be to her what he had been till then."

The old woman made a weary gesture and resumed her pacing up and down the room. After a moment or two, turning towards Pablo she said, "You must admit, a creature like her is no joke."

Pablo had also noticed the almost fearful look in the eye of the *patron* each time the little girl had entered his room during the time when he had been struggling against death.

This had lasted only a few hours, and the child had not appeared to notice anything wrong until the doctor came. It was only when she saw him that she began trembling and weeping.

Once more Pablo went across to Jeannette. "Haven't you a handkerchief?" he asked.

The child did not budge. Pablo went over to the cupboard, opened the door, and looked for a handkerchief. Then, returning to her, he wiped her eyes and her nose.

The old woman watched. "She's disgusting," she said. "You'd think she was only three years old. Three years!"

Pablo did not answer. He put the handkerchief in the pocket of the pinafore Jeannette was wearing.

"Come and sit down," he said. He took her hand. She followed him and sat on the chair he showed her.

"When she's like that she's no more life in her than a vegetable," Marguerite remarked. "As for me, the sight of that snot always hanging from her nose makes me feel sick."

Pablo turned round. He snapped rather sharply, "Then look elsewhere."

The old woman jumped, then, shrugging her shoulders, she went towards the door, the water-jug in her hand.

123

Pablo had sat on the edge of the table beside Jeannette. His hand caressed her hair slowly and gently.

Now she scarcely disgusted him any more. It was the first time he had made the gesture of wiping her nose. He had made it because he knew that she was crying too much to be able to obey. He had done it as one hides an object that one cannot bear to see. In that way one makes a gesture. One has courage for a few seconds, and afterwards one can look freely. That is all. Either the gesture must be made, or one must go away.

The *patronne* soon returned. She must have been running. Sweat was trickling down her face. She was red-faced and out of breath.

"Well?" asked Pablo.

She got her breath back, and then, in one burst, she explained, "I've seen the mayor. He telephoned for the hearse. Nothing doing. There's only the old man left. The two who act as undertakers left this morning."

"We'll easily find two men to lower the coffin."

"No, the old man doesn't want to come. He says that the road is too crowded. And the mayor said the same thing. It seems that even on foot you can't move against the heavy flow of traffic."

"Then the coffin will have to be carried."

"But there's no coffin either. The mayor went to see. There are none ready. I don't know what we're going to do . . . I really don't know."

As she said this she sank down on a chair and began to sob.

She had not wept before, but now all her tears seemed to come at once, and her entire body was shaken. Marguerite hurried to her side and tried to calm her, but to everything she said the *patronne* replied, "It isn't possible . . . I don't know what we're going to do . . . I don't know."

Her words were jerky and deformed by sobbing.

Pablo could not speak for a long time. Confusedly he tried to think. He walked mechanically as far as the door, pushed aside the sun-blind, looked across the sunlit courtyard, and then, returning to the *patronne*, he said, "You must eat something. That'll do you good. I'm going up to find Clopineau."

"Clopineau?"

"Yes. We two'll see what we can do."

The *patronne* stopped weeping for a few seconds and stared

at Pablo through her tears. Her eyes were wild, and she seemed to be seeing Pablo for the first time.

"Clopineau," she murmured again, and then began to sob anew.

"You're quite right," said Marguerite. "Go and look for him That's the best thing to do."

Pablo poured himself a glass of wine and cold water, which he drank before going out.

In the doorway he turned round. Jeannette was still sitting stiffly on her chair. She was looking at the end door and was still weeping. Behind her, an elbow on the table and her head in her hand, the *patronne* also continued sobbing.

Old Marguerite made a gesture to Pablo, as if to tell him to hurry, and then went towards the sideboard.

Pablo let the sun-blind fall behind him and found himself alone again in dazzling sunshine.

XVIII

PABLO walked for a long time without raising his head. He stared only at the white, cracked earth of the road. Now and then a lizard moved in the dry grass of the embankment, and Pablo jumped.

He went round the village, and soon reached the point where the pathway began to climb between the vines.

He went up like this as far as the third bend. There, stopping suddenly, he put one foot on the embankment and stared at the plain. The sun made it shimmer. The horizon remained empty, and the hills belonged neither to earth nor to heaven. They were a long, moving ribbon which rose from time to time like a great couched beast lifting its head for air.

At one moment Pablo thought of the last, raucous gasps of the *patron*. He saw again his hand twisting and gripping the sheet.

The sun overwhelmed everything. No sound came from the plain. But behind him a tongue of uncultivated land separating the path from the vines crackled under the sun like a fire smouldering. Crickets chirped to each other, cutting the heavy, almost unbreathable air.

Pablo had stopped there because he knew that by raising his

head he would see the distant end of the plain. He looked and saw no change. All he needed to do now was to go forward a few steps, to the end of the bend, or to climb on the embankment, and he would have a sight of the entire plain, from the foot of the hills to the horizon. He would see the village, still hidden by the vines. He would see the highway also. The highway first of all, because it was farther off than the village.

Pablo turned, facing the slope which rose in a straight line almost touching the centre of the sky shining like steel. Light was everywhere. It clung to the earth, enveloping each vine, each bush, each vine-stake. Pablo breathed deeply until he could feel the dry warmth moving inside his lungs. Beads of sweat rolled from his forehead and down his cheeks; he felt the saltiness of them on the edges of his lips. He remained like this for a long while. Then, resuming his walk, he went just far enough to sight the vines.

Now he could see everything, and at first view he had the impression that nothing had changed.

He stared at the highway more closely.

It was almost the same as on ordinary days. But under the double line of trees patches of shadow and light vibrated. They were shaken by a constant movement, by a long and single movement made up of a thousand vehicles.

That was all Pablo could see.

He then looked on the village side.

Nothing.

The clustered houses crouched beneath the sun and slept their midday slumber. Between the hot roofs the road showed white or dark purple.

Across the tops of the houses Pablo saw a black cat pass and then vanish behind a chimney, then, reappearing, jump across to another roof at an angle before slipping into a pool of shadow made by an attic window.

Around the farm a few chickens were moving. Others, in a motionless group, made a light patch in the shadow of the wood-shed.

He looked at the highway again; the long movement continued, trying to push to the end of the plain the patches of sunshine which stayed obstinately in place, between the plane-trees. By listening carefully he did finally hear a faint, vague sound which the hum of an insect was enough to drown.

126

Beside the road the sun continued to press down on the sleeping plain.

Pablo brushed his forearm across his sweaty brow and began to walk on.

When he reached the vines he climbed between two ranks and looked at the full extent of the vineyard. Since the morning the old man had worked well. More than half the vines had been tied. The new growth had been stretched along wires and attached to them by loops of withy. When Pablo came out from the vines and reached the level ground he saw Clopineau immediately in the shade of a group of hornbeams. The old man waved his hand.

"I heard you coming up," he said.

Pablo was out of breath. He let himself flop on the grass beside the old man, mopping his face.

"I don't need to ask why you've come at this time of day," said the old man.

Pablo nodded his head.

"Take this and drink up."

Clopineau offered him his flask, wrapped in a moist napkin. Pablo took a long swig. The wine was still cool.

"Last night," said Clopineau, "I didn't even think he'd last the night. Has he been dead long?"

"About two hours."

"And you want me to come down with you?"

Pablo explained about the departure of the carpenter and the others.

"If I understand you rightly, we'll have to make him a coffin?"

"Yes, we shall."

The old man sighed, lifted his cap, and scratched his white scalp before replying. "Poor old Lucien, to go like that!"

He remained silent for a minute, putting into his haversack the remains of his meal. Almost stupefied by the heat, Pablo watched without really seeing him.

"Won't make much difference," said the old man as he stood up. "I've already had all sorts of jobs, but a coffin, that's never happened to me before. Whereas wood, from planting to felling, shaping..."

He stopped suddenly, looked towards the highway, and, stretching out his hand, without shouting, his teeth clenched with anger, he added, "God above, what a rotten business! The war... The war... We can't even bury our dead!"

Still sitting at the feet of the old man, Pablo looked up. Those words had wakened him fully. He had fallen abruptly from a blue universe of mist where white shadows passed, from the dream of sunshine and warm earth in which he had begun to wander, half asleep.

The war. The dead. The millions of dead who could never be buried. The dead whom rain, wind, and sun would eat away little by little. The dead who would dig their own graves in the burning earth.

"Are you coming?" asked the old man.

Pablo shook himself. Clopineau was already going down between the two rows of vines, his basket in one hand and in the other his bundle of golden and shining withies. He was walking quickly, and his wicker-covered flask slapped against his buttocks like a soldier's water-bottle.

XIX

IT WAS seven in the evening when they finished the coffin for the *patron*. They had to abandon the idea of making a coffin in the traditional way, which was beyond their skill. Immediately he opened the workshop for them, the mayor said, "Use the tools, but not the machines."

"You needn't worry about that," said Clopineau. "So far as I'm concerned, anything mechanical...."

Once they were left alone, they made a tour of the workshop. There were masses of tools on shelves or hanging from lines of hooks.

"All that's too complicated," decided the old man. "I think we'd do better to take all the planks and nails we'll need and make it at the house."

Then all the afternoon they had worked at the rickety old bench installed in the shed. The ducks were sitting in a circle a few steps away and watching them from the corners of their eyes, without, however, ceasing to watch the circling bluebottles which they gobbled up when any strayed within a beak's reach. Several times the *patronne* had come with fresh wine. She no longer wept, but she had red eyes and her face looked tired.

128

"You think you can manage it?" she asked.

"We'll have to," said the old man.

And now it was finished. They had drilled holes so that the lid could be screwed on. They did not want to have to hammer the lid once the dead man was inside.

Pablo stood back a few paces. The sun, which was already low, appeared just at the end of the shed and tinged the white-wood coffin with yellow.

"To be honest," said Pablo, "it's only a box!"

The old man also stood back a step or two. He made a gesture of helplessness and sighed. "We've done our best. In any case, it's better than nothing. And then, you know, Lucien never was a man for luxury. I'm sure he'd have thought it very good."

Pablo looked at the old man, who had already begun unscrewing the lid. He was not joking. He was clearly convinced that the *patron* would have been pleased with his coffin.

"All the same," said Pablo, "it would be nice, wouldn't it, if we could put a cross on it?"

But the old man must have been thinking deeply about the *patron*.

"A cross! Not for him!"

"It's really the *patronne* I'm thinking about. In any case, it'll make it look more like a coffin."

They looked for two odd ends of wood. The old man planed them carefully, nailed the longer piece on the lid, and then, sawing the shorter piece across the middle, he nailed the two halves either side of it to make the arms of the cross.

"You're right," he said; "that looks better."

They put their tools away under the bench, and Pablo put the box on his shoulder, while the old man manœuvred the lid. As they reached the corner of the house Pablo placed the coffin against the wall.

"Wait a minute."

He went as far as the kitchen. "It's ready," he said, pushing aside the blind.

Old Marguerite blinked. She was alone with Jeannette, who had finally stopped weeping, but remained as if in a stupor.

"Come along, Jeannette! Get your basket; we're going to feed the rabbits."

The old lady took a bowl of mash. The girl took the basket of vegetable peelings, and they went out. Pablo made a sign for the

129

old lady to indicate which side of the house she intended to go round, and immediately they had gone he went over to Clopineau.

"All right now, we can go."

"Poor Jeannette!" sighed the old man before starting off.

Upstairs the *patronne* was waiting for them.

"The mayor must come when he's placed in the coffin."

"And the priest?" asked Pablo.

"He's been twice, and he'll be back about eight o'clock."

"Well, what are we to do? Wait?"

The *patronne* hesitated. She looked at Pablo and the old man and then at the coffin.

"It's not very handsome," Clopineau excused himself. "But what can you expect? We're not experts."

"It's wartime," she said.

She remained silent for a few seconds, and then, turning towards the body, she asked in a low voice, "D'you think it's beginning to smell?"

"Yes," said Pablo. "With the heat, it's natural."

"Then the best thing will be to get the lid on straight away, but don't screw it down."

The *patronne* opened the cupboard and took from a pile of sheets an extra-large one. She unfolded it.

"His mother embroidered it for us as a wedding gift," she said.

Pablo saw two complicated letters decorated with tiny flowers. The sheet smelled pleasantly of fresh lavendar.

While they wrapped the body several sobs escaped the *patronne*; these ceased as soon as they placed the lid on the coffin, which they then set on four chairs in the centre of the room.

Now that all was done they stayed there in the semi-darkness, looking at the coffin. After a moment Pablo turned to the old man. Clopineau lifted his head. His white pate made a patch of brightness. His eyes seemed to be asking Pablo what should be done. As Pablo gave no sign, the old man stared again at the coffin, then, in a very tremulous voice, he whispered, "Poor old Lucien, you won't get the funeral you deserve! We've done what we could, you know. We put our hearts in it. Our hearts were in it."

Pablo thought that the old man was going to burst into tears. He watched him. His chin was trembling. However, taking his eyes from the coffin, he turned towards the *patronne* and said, "Well, I think that's all we can do for the moment. Now that the

130

sun's gone, you'd better open the window a bit, and you'll also have to see about the vigil."

Two women from the village began the vigil with old Marguerite, while the *patronne*, Pablo, and Clopineau went to get some rest.

At two in the morning Marguerite awakened them. Punctual as ever, Clopineau had arrived. The three women again sprinkled the coffin with holy water, and then left in silence.

"I've made some fresh coffee," said Marguerite, the only one to speak before closing the door behind her.

The *patronne* took three glasses from the draining-board, and Pablo got the sugar from the cupboard. They drank their coffee in silence, all three seated and with their elbows on the table. The door was open and from time to time a breeze in the night lifted the blind and sent a breath of fresh air into the kitchen.

They had agreed not to watch close beside the coffin. Instead one of them went slowly upstairs every quarter of an hour or so. The *patronne* went first, then Clopineau. They stayed there for only a few minutes.

Soon it was Pablo's turn. He got to his feet and went up the stairs without any sound. As he reached the coffin, which was lit by a fluttering candle, he made the sign of the cross and remained absolutely still for a long while. The window was wide open, but the shutters were half closed. Many moths fluttered round the candle-flame.

Through the openings in the shutters a dull, rumbling sound came into the room. Pablo went over to the window and listened. The rumbling continued, always with the same regularity, the same dullness. Then he went downstairs and took his place again with the others. He remained for a moment looking at the others, and then said, "They're still travelling along the road."

"Yes," said the *patronne*. "Marguerite was telling me that a lot more people left the village today. It seems that the Boches have been in Paris since yesterday."

"Noémie says that a soldier told her they'd be at Besançon before tonight's over."

"Have many soldiers gone through?" asked the *patronne*.

"It seems that quite a few have," said the old man. "But I didn't go down to look."

"If only I could know where he is."

131

The *patronne* had said this very quickly, and her voice rose towards a strangled sob on the last two words.

"If only," she said again. "If only I could know."

Then, putting her head between her hands, she began to weep silently, with long sighs which shook her whole body and made two wisps of hair, which had escaped from her chignon, tremble against her temples.

PART TWO

PART TWO

XX

LITTLE by little the *patronne*'s grief abated. They had talked together for a while. Clopineau had tried to say that the vines were in fine shape, but each time one of them started a conversation it fell flat. All three of them felt a need to talk, but none of them could find words. Several times Clopineau's head dropped forward.

"You should go up and lie on my bed," Pablo had said.

But the old man would have none of it. Twice he went out to get a breath of the cool night air. On the third occasion Pablo went with him. They went as far as the road, leaned against the wall, and Pablo rolled a cigarette. The old man did the same, and they started to smoke in silence.

"The traffic's still passing," said the old man after a moment.

The hum on the highway continued. Pablo tried to drive from his mind the memories of flight which had been flooding back since they had begun this interminable vigil. He saw the frontier again, and the women and children. The dead wrapped in sacking who remained there, stretched out beside the road. Half-naked dead, their hands sunken in the mud of the ditches. Withered dead, swollen dead, and others who looked as if they might get up and move. Others, again, who continued their march, hanging on to the living. These truly had the faces of the dead. With only the light in their eyes still living intensely. But the moment this light died they had only to be laid out by the roadside for it to be realized that they had long been dead. They had not been killed by the blows of war; they had been fretted away, worn out, slowly drained of life.

In this disaster none knew clearly when life stopped and when death began. There were many still alive, sleeping among the abandoned dead; there were dead whom others tried to sustain, to drag along the road.

"It can't be long till daylight," said Clopineau.

"No, it must be three already."

135

Their cigarettes finished, they went back into the kitchen. The *patronne* came down from the bedroom.

"Would you like some more coffee?" she asked.

The two men nodded, and the *patronne* had scarcely served them before there were sounds on the stones of the courtyard. They looked at each other. Nobody moved. The *patronne* still held the coffee-pot, and her hand was trembling.

"It's the mayor," said Clopineau as the footsteps came nearer.

They sighed, and the *patronne* put the coffee-pot down on the table. The mayor came in. He was out of breath and red-faced. From the door he shouted: "The Boches are at Poligny! I've just had a phone call."

Since no-one spoke he repeated: "At Poligny! That means they'll be here in a few hours."

"Who phoned you?" asked Clopineau.

The mayor immediately flew into a temper and began to gesticulate, shouting, "How do I know? An officer. What does it matter? What we want is to save the village from being sacked."

"But what can anyone like us do?" asked Clopineau, keeping his voice steady.

The mayor looked at the *patronne*, and then at Pablo. "They mustn't find him here."

"What on earth does that matter?" asked Pablo.

The mayor began shouting again and waving his short, fat arms. "What does it matter? Good God alive, you sound as if you don't know that they're friends with Franco! If they find a Spanish Republican in this district they'll wreck every house and send the village up in flames!"

"But they don't know who I am," Pablo remarked.

The mayor seemed a little discountenanced. However, shouting louder still, he went on: "That's nothing to do with it; you must go. They might hear about it. I don't want to risk the life of every-one who lives here. You've only to join the refugees going through here on the road. You'll easily find a lorry to take you. Lots of them are only half full!"

They let him shout. When he stopped old Clopineau waited a second or two and then asked, "Have you got a lot of people for the funeral?"

"There's Junot, he got the grave dug yesterday evening. And I'll come, of course, to lend a hand."

"I think the priest'll be there too?"

136

"Of course, certainly."

The *patronne* seemed to be quite calm. She stood up and went across to the cupboard, took a cup, and placed it in front of the mayor.

"You'll have a little coffee, won't you?"

The mayor sat down, drew out his handkerchief, and mopped his face. When he had finished, turning towards Pablo, he said to him without shouting, "I honestly think it's best for you not to remain here. There are too many risks. There's no point in tempting providence; misfortune comes often enough as it is."

"I'll leave if you insist," said Pablo. "But not before the funeral."

The mayor raised his voice. "But didn't you hear me say that unless something stops them they'll be here in a couple of hours."

Clopineau said sarcastically, "Who do you think's going to stop them now?"

The *patronne* had poured out the coffee. "Drink up," she said. "It's not very hot."

"I'll leave after the funeral," Pablo repeated.

"Then he'd better be buried immediately," said the mayor. "There must be no delay, otherwise you'll never get away."

"You can't bury anyone at this time of night," said the old man. "Doesn't make sense."

The mayor banged his fist on the table. "What about the war?" he shouted. "Does that make sense? And to rush off along the roads, does that make sense? Of three hundred and forty-six local inhabitants, if fifty remain that's the absolute limit. Does that make sense?"

The others had not budged. Once again the old man let silence re-establish itself, and then, calm as ever, he explained: "First of all, what makes no sense is to shout in a house of death. Secondly, you're here shouting about those who've run away, yet you come here to make Pablo go. I just don't understand."

The mayor shook his head as if to say, "It's hopeless trying to make you understand. You'll never be able to." But Pablo was already saying, "All things considered, there's probably nothing against having the burial as soon as it's light. Then, if anything should happen afterwards, everything will be in order."

The mayor seemed reassured. "That's what we must do," he said. "I'll go and warn the priest."

He stood up, and then, before leaving, addressing Pablo, he went on: "You understand that what I'm asking is not that you

137

should go far away. The main thing is that you should leave the village. Once we see how things go, we'll see what can be done."

As soon as he had gone the old man growled. "That's it. You go somewhere else so that someone else can have the trouble, not him."

Pablo merely shrugged his shoulders. Until now he had felt no sense of fatigue, but suddenly his body was heavy with it. He was weary, very weary, with a host of memories of an exodus crowding in on each other.

"D'you think there's a serious risk in staying?" asked the *patronne*.

The old man looked at her for an instant before saying, "Do you want to leave too? The way the war's going it'll be all over in a week. And if that happens we may never see a Boche in the village. Off the road, like we are, what d'you think they'll want to come here for? They're only interested in the big cities."

"One never knows; people say so many things. A lot say they're a horde of savages."

"Listen, Germaine! The best way to get your house pillaged is to abandon it. I'm certain myself that, travelling the speed they are, they won't be fooling around looking in local cellars. You needn't worry about that."

The old man waited for a moment, then, walking towards the door, he went on: "If you want to go now I shan't try to stop you."

As he reached the doorway he lifted the curtain and turned back to Pablo.

"Coming?" he said. "If you don't want to lose time we'd better give La Noire a brush and get a cart ready."

They both went out. The dawn was already lightening the sky above the hill.

"You see," Clopineau explained, "it's bad enough already that we can't give him a funeral like others have, so we must give La Noire a bit of grooming and clean up the cart a bit."

"Which one shall we take?"

"The old break, I think. Once it's been given a rub-over it'll look better than one of the muddy old carts."

"You think it'll be all right?"

"Yes, if we take out the back seats it'll be long enough."

They had to move two other carts to pull out the break, which was at the far end of the barn. When it was out in the courtyard

138

Pablo took a broom to clean it out while old Clopineau brought the mare from the stable and began to brush her.

It was now daylight, but the sun was still hidden, yet it could be felt quite close, ready to show suddenly above the earth's rim. As soon as they had finished, the old man stood back a few paces. He looked at the mare's shining coat. He looked also at the old break which Pablo had freed from cobwebs.

"You know," he said, "as far as I'm concerned, to go like that, drawn by my own horse, at the hour that we leave for the vineyards, would be as good a way as any. A big fuss won't bring back the dead; it just costs the family a lot of money, and that's all."

The mayor arrived soon afterwards, accompanied by the *curé*, who had not been able to find a single choirboy and was carrying the cross himself. Two men followed, a few steps behind, one carrying the container of holy water and the sprinkler, the other the censer.

"I did think for a moment I'd call on old Marguerite," said one of them as they entered, "but as she came for the vigil, I thought that she must be asleep, so I didn't dare."

"You were quite right," said the *patronne*.

Everyone remained silent for a moment. They stared at each other, waiting for some lead. The *curé* was the first to make a move. Putting his cross in a corner of the room, he went to the door at the end. He was a man of about forty, small, but broadly built.

"Come," he said.

The men followed him.

"We mustn't make too much noise," said the *patronne*. "If the child woke up it would be dreadful."

They went up slowly. The window in the room had remained open, and the half-closed shutters let in only a sliver of early daylight. The candle was guttering.

"Better open the shutters; there'll be less risk of making a noise," said the *curé*.

He blessed the coffin and blew out the candle, while Pablo pushed the shutters open gently.

"Going down, there can be only two of us," said the mayor. "The stairway's too narrow."

"In that case," said the *curé*, "the big fellow must go first, with me behind."

139

As he said this he pointed to Pablo. Pablo took hold of the foot of the coffin and walked backwards to the door. On the stairs they had a lot of trouble. Pablo could feel the wood sliding through his fingers. There were neither handles nor any projecting moulding. He began to think they had made a mistake in planing the planks so smoothly.

Once they were downstairs, the others were able to lend a hand, and it was much easier to slide the coffin into the break.

On the doorstep the two women, with the sobbing *patronne* between, watched them.

The *patronne* had not changed her clothes. She had merely taken off her apron and put a black scarf on her head. The two other women were also wearing black head-scarves.

"Who is going to lead?" asked the *curé*.

"Me," said Clopineau.

"Would you like to carry the cross, Monsieur le Maire?" asked the *curé*.

The mayor went back into the kitchen and came out with the cross.

"You can take the censer," said the priest to Pablo. "We will put the holy water in the carriage."

He passed the container to Clopineau, who was already on the seat.

"Mind that none is spilled," he said.

"I will," said Clopineau. "I'm going to put it down in front of me, and I'll hold it between my feet."

The *curé* set out. Beside him walked Pablo and the mayor. The priest was reciting prayers. It had been decided to go directly to the cemetery to save time.

"I will ask you to celebrate a mass for him later," the *patronne* had said.

It took them less than five minutes to reach the cemetery. This was the older one, where the parents of the *patron* had also been buried. As they went through the gate Pablo thought of the evening of his arrival, and wondered where Enrique might be now. Then, looking straight ahead of him, beyond the tombstones, he found he could see the plain. From here he could see only two sloping meadows, the stream, two more meadows, and a field before the highway was reached. The sound of cars and lorries could be heard. Pablo looked between the crosses. The column of

140

refugees was advancing slowly. There were vehicles of every sort and many people on foot. Along the entire length of the road people were sleeping in ditches where they had almost certainly spent the night. Farther off, others were grouped round a fire. Then, once again, Pablo thought of the dead. Not so much because of the people lying in the grass, as because of those who were near the fire. Pablo thought of the coldness of death. Of the coldness which precedes it and warns those who have been marked down.

When they reached the edge of the newly dug grave they put the coffin on the ground, and Clopineau led La Noire forward a few paces.

"The grave-digger not here?" asked the *curé*.

"I don't know," replied the mayor. "He promised he'd come. But I see that the ropes are there, so he can't be far away."

The *curé* put the container of holy water and the sprinkler close to the grave. "We can't just wait about without knowing," he said.

"Do you really need him?" asked Clopineau.

"Of course not; we can manage it, the four of us."

They passed the ropes beneath the makeshift coffin and let it down into the grave. Once the ropes had been withdrawn, the *curé* blessed the coffin again, recited the prayers for the dead, and handed the sprinkler to the *patronne*. The procession was soon over. As everyone waited the mayor put his hat on again and asked, "Can you spare me now? I want to get back to my office. A little earlier the telephone was out of order; one never knows, I may be needed."

The grave-digger had left his spade and his pick close to the grave.

"If we could find two other spades, with three of us we'd soon be finished," said the *curé*.

"Come along," said the mayor. "There must be some in the toolshed."

The mayor took a couple of steps, and then, turning round, he stared at Pablo. "It's agreed, eh? I have your word. As soon as we're through, you leave?"

"Agreed," said Pablo.

The *curé* followed the mayor, and they were soon back with two spades.

"The women should go home," said the *curé*.

141

The *patronne* was sobbing. She went across to Pablo. "Well," she said, "what are you going to do? Are you leaving?"

"I promised him."

"What's all this about?" asked the *curé*.

Pablo explained what the mayor had feared.

"I think he's imagining things," said the *curé*. "I myself have done all I can to persuade people not to leave, and if everyone had behaved as I did, that would never have happened." He pointed towards the road.

"That's all very well," said one of the women, "but you've got to think of the youngsters. There are such stories going around."

"Exactly, there are too many stories going round. I think myself it is better to remain in your own home. In any case, even for the young it is too late now to leave. Where would they get? To Bourg, or to Lyons at best. Do you think that would put them out of danger?"

"Well then," asked the *patronne*, "what should we do?"

"I'm for home," said one woman. "My boy went off yesterday with his wife and the youngster. I'm going to take a bundle of clothing, and I'll go into the woods in the Geruge valley. They won't come looking for me down there."

She then went off, and the second woman followed her without a word. Pablo looked at the open grave, took a spade, and approached the heap of earth.

"Well," said the *patronne* again in a slightly trembling voice. "You're going, that's settled?"

Pablo made a gesture of helplessness.

"Listen," said the *curé*. "Since you promised, I realize that you feel you should leave. Well then, do as this woman is doing, go up into the woods, and then, as soon as it's possible, come back to the village. But don't fall into the stupid folly of going and joining the mob. That would be the surest means of helping to increase the general panic. What's more, it would lead nowhere. That those in the north rushed away can be understood, but now half of France is going to find itself crammed into the Midi. Either the war is going to end, or else there'll be a massive battle further south, and all these civilians are likely to hinder our troops. I think that the wisest thing is to avoid joining this crazy exodus."

"Very well," said the *patronne*. "I'll go home. I'm frightened the child may wake up."

142

"You'd better take La Noire. We've no further need of her," said the old man.

She took the mare by the bridle, and Pablo watched her for an instant as she walked away.

The sun had risen above the earth's rim and was throwing its light across the hillside, outlining with a glow of gold the break, drawn by La Noire, going towards it.

XXI

WHILE the men were filling in the grave three aeroplanes flew over.

At first this zooming sound, coming from the hill and seeming almost to touch them, made them duck their heads. Then, when it had passed, they looked towards the highway. The planes were flying off along the line of the road, as if they intended to brush the trees with the tips of their grey wings.

The three stared at each other for an instant, and then set to work again.

Like the others, Pablo worked silently. However, at the instant the roar of the planes had come over the hill he had felt a sudden cold sweat all over his body. He had thought of the grave, already quite deep. He had to make an immense effort to restrain himself from jumping into it. This terrible noise pierced him like a bullet, and once in his body it spread all through him. It filled him as it had filled the space between the sky and the plain.

This sound was poison to him. It had destroyed what calmness still remained within him just as it had shattered the silence of the morning.

Pablo was now gripping the handle of his spade. His clenched hands were trembling. He worked more vigorously. His sweat continued to run down.

A few moments passed, and the noise of the planes had ceased when they heard the sound of explosions across the plain. They looked, but they could see nothing unusual.

"You see," said the *curé*, "taking to the roads you run the greatest risk."

As soon as the grave had been filled in they left. When they

143

reached the house the *curé* took back his cross and censer, which Pablo and the old man had been carrying till then, and went on alone to the village.

Pablo and Clopineau entered the courtyard. La Noire was still harnessed to the break outside the kitchen door. As they approached they saw casseroles and linen in the back of the vehicle. While they were looking the *patronne* called to them from the first-floor window.

"Come up here, I need you."

As they went through the kitchen they saw Jeannette, who was eating a plate of soup. Places had been laid for them also. The *patronne* was in the bedroom. On the bedside table there still remained the candle and the saucer, with its twig of boxwood. The linen cupboard was open, and the *patronne* was pulling from it large piles of linen which she was placing in the centre of a blanket stretched out on the floor.

"What are you doing?" asked the old man.

"You can see, I'm getting ready what I want to take."

"You really mean to leave?" asked Pablo.

"Of course. Didn't you hear the bombs? If they're beginning that, d'you think we're going to wait here to be killed?"

"But where d'you think you're going?" asked the old man. "You know very well it's the roads and cities they're bombing. I'm sure what we heard was bombs falling on Bourg."

"And how d'you know they won't also destroy a village? A soldier who was going through told Mélanie Bouchot that, in the north, they burned everything. There's not a house left for miles and miles. Even isolated farms were hit."

"And d'you think you'll get far with all the crowds there are on the highway?"

"I've no intention of going on the highway. I want to go up into the woods. It's too late in any case to try to get away by the highway."

She hesitated for a second, and then, in a strangled voice, pointing to the bed on which could still be seen the hollow made by the *patron's* body, she snapped: "If it hadn't been for that we'd have been far from here a long time ago."

She pulled out another two piles of linen, which she put on the blanket, then, angrily, she ordered, "Come on, get hold of that and take it down to the break; afterwards come up for the mattresses."

144

Once downstairs, Pablo climbed on the break to get everything packed in.

"You stay where you are," said the old man. "We'll pass the mattresses through the window. What a shame, all the same, to see this! What a shame!"

The *patronne* had to be restrained. She was becoming frantic, wanting to take everything and turning the house upside down. The old man finally became annoyed.

"You're not making sense," he said. "You know perfectly well it's only a mare you've got, with a break behind her. That's not two pairs of bullocks harnessed to a cart. If you want to go a couple of hundred yards, and then have to throw off half you've loaded, that's up to you."

The *patronne* was in despair. Her face drawn, her hair in disorder, she rushed from one room to another, picking up objects here and there and putting them down again a yard or two away.

"Listen to me," said Clopineau finally. "If the Boches get as far as your house they'll need only to open the door. When they see the mess there is they'll hop off immediately, thinking that others have already pillaged the place."

Her nerves exhausted, she let herself slump down in a chair and began to cry. Pablo went across to her. "*Patronne*," he said gently, "if you want to go you mustn't wait any longer."

Old Clopineau sat down beside her and began to talk to her slowly, almost in a whisper. "This is what you should do," he said. "I've nothing to bother about in my old shack; leave me the keys, and I'll settle in here. If they come they mustn't find the house empty."

The *patronne* had ceased sobbing. With tears still running down her cheeks, she looked at the old man, nodding her head.

"Why should you take all the risk?" asked Pablo.

The old man smiled, saying, "Me? What do I risk? At my age they won't touch me, don't you worry. So you leave me, but you mustn't go into the Geruge woods. There's no point in making such a long journey, and, what's more, it's a road they may go along."

"Well, where d'you think we should go?"

"To Brûlis. The road is half overgrown with brambles, but with the break you should be able to get up there. La Noire's strong,

145

she's sure-footed, and I've never seen her jib at a hill. It'll be enough if Pablo takes a bill-hook in case there are any very large branches. That's all."

"And you think that's where we should go?"

"It's the best place. Once you're there on the level ground, you've the clumps of ash-trees and acacias, and, behind, the little combe with the Rougeins spring which is only five hundred yards down. And from above the old vines you can see the whole plain. From there you'll know what's going on."

The *patronne* stood up, went to the sideboard, opened the door, and came back quickly, carrying a leather case.

"These are the field-glasses which the *patron* used," she said. "We'll take them, and then we'll be able to watch better."

She had wiped her tears. Her face was still tense, but she no longer had a lost look.

"You haven't eaten," she said to Pablo.

"No, but that's all right. I'm not hungry."

"And the animals?" asked the old man. "You know I can't manage milking."

"We'll take them with us," said the *patronne*. "That's best."

"And what will you do with the milk up there?"

"We'll see."

Jeannette had not moved. Sitting on the other side of the table, her empty plate before her, her eyes never left them.

"Come along," said the *patronne*. "Come on!"

The child stood up and followed them. The animals were still in the stable. The *patronne* brought them out.

"Take La Noire and go ahead," she said to Pablo. "I'll follow with the animals."

"No," shouted the old man. "Just the opposite. Let the animals go first; the stuff they tread down will help La Noire to get along easier."

Driving in front of them the five goats and the cow, the *patronne* and Jeannette left the courtyard. Pablo let them get something of a start.

"Listen to me," said the old man. "I'm sure there's absolutely no risk. But one never knows, so in case I'm mistaken and I've anything to tell you, I'll ask Marguerite to come here and take my place long enough for me to come up to you."

He shook Pablo's hand and patted La Noire's neck, saying, "Hold her firmly during the climb, and if you feel she's slipping

146

don't hesitate to let the backside of the cart go into the hedge. That's always better than to harm your horse."

Pablo thanked the old man and shouted "Hup!" to La Noire. When he looked back, just before the crossroads, old Clopineau, standing in the doorway, waved his hand.

XXII

THE Brûlis land was truly wild. The vines had remained untouched for years, and the hedges had partly closed the road where no cart ever passed now. But despite everything they easily managed to reach the clumps of beeches and acacias marking the summit of the hill.

Once on the level ground Pablo pulled up La Noire and mopped his face. The sun was strong, and Pablo, on several occasions, had had to cut a way through with his bill-hook. There was also something else. First, throughout the climb, the nervous tension, the constant fear of a slip by the overloaded mare on the loose pebbles under her hooves. There was another fear also, which had not left him since the three planes had flown over.

He had tried to fight it, to avoid thinking of it, but, even when leading La Noire he was not able sufficiently to busy his mind.

Until this morning there had been the *patron*. There had been all the work connected with his burial. There had been this death to occupy them all. Until the *patron* was buried the war had remained in the background.

Then, in a flash, it was back. Since the three planes had flown over, since the distant sound of explosions, the war was close. Pablo felt it at his heels.

He felt it like he had felt weariness, for days and days. He felt it binding him. Pablo knew there was no question of fighting it. It was a tenacious malady, one of which doctors say, "It must take its course."

A little earlier he had really longed to take flight. He had felt the need of it. Now he was beginning to ask himself what had made them come here.

Leaving the horse to get her wind for a moment, he retraced his path as far as the line of beeches which bordered the upper limit of the old vines. Here one could really see the entire plain. The village was to the right, half hidden by a twist of the hill, but towards the south and west the plain stretched out in the sunlight.

The highway continued its interminable undulations.

Pablo stood still for a moment, looking over the motionless branches.

His anguish remained. He knew that in a few seconds all he saw there before him could be changed. The heavy silence of the sun could be shattered in an instant and the sky filled with dust and smoke. The terrible smell of gunpowder returned to the back of his throat, and suddenly he had the ridiculous sensation of having come here to have a better view of what would happen— to enjoy the war the more.

"Pablo!"

He jumped. His heart thumped stupidly in his chest. He turned round. The *patronne* was climbing up towards him. In the bottom of the little combe, filled with thickets, Jeannette was standing still, resting on her stick and watching the cow and the goats.

He returned to the break, where the *patronne* joined him.

"Well," she asked, "what d'you think of it?"

He looked around him. Apart from the little wood where they were standing and which bestrode the crest, separating the hill descending towards the plain and the slope going down to the combe, there was nothing but bushes, thin patches of grass, and heaps of stones.

"And the spring?" asked Pablo.

The *patronne* stretched out a hand and pointed to the spot where the animals were herded together.

"You see that strip greener than the rest," she said. "Well, that's where it runs. It's entirely hidden under the grass; but the water's clear and icy. Look, it comes out from under that rock a little above where the child is standing."

Pablo looked again for a moment, and then, thinking of what old Clopineau had told him, he said, "It looks as if we ought to be quiet enough here. I wonder if anyone is ever likely to come."

"Except for a few hunters, hardly anyone comes."

"The best thing, surely, would be to settle ourselves on the fringe of the wood. That way we'd have the shade and be less likely to be spotted from the plain."

148

He still had the same fear inside him, and, at the same time, he felt he was being ridiculous. Playing at hiding from something which did not exist.

Here all was silence. The heavy air carried no sounds. Only a few flies buzzed, attracted by La Noire, who shook herself in her harness occasionally. Taking her bridle, Pablo urged her forward slowly. There was no road here, and the break swayed on the uneven ground. Coming to a stop after a short while, Pablo asked, "Shall we settle here?"

The *patronne* looked round. "Here, or farther on, it's about the same thing."

Once the mare had been unhitched, Pablo removed her harness.

"I think we can set her free," he said. "I'd be very surprised if she wandered far."

They began to clear the ground, and, as if astonished to find herself free in this unknown meadow, La Noire stayed for some time close by, watching them.

"Off you go," said the *patronne*. "Go!"

The mare went off a few paces and began to browse on the edge of the wood.

When the ground had been cleared of brambles and the larger stones they made a large tent with the cart-cover they had brought. The trees served as pegs, and the cover was held by lengths of cord. Fixing this tent took them until midday. After that the *patronne* called Jeannette and got out the food. They ate in silence, too oppressed by the heat to speak.

Once the meal was over, time seemed to stand still.

At first Pablo tried to sleep, lying on the grass under the trees, but it was too hot and the flies, ever more numerous, did not give him a moment's respite. With eyes half closed, he looked at the *patronne*. Sitting at the foot of a tree, she had unfolded an old newspaper which had been among the packing material. She glanced through it and then put it down beside her. Afterwards she went back under the tent, where the heat must have been much greater. Coming out again soon after, she had walked between the trees and sat down farther off on a dead tree-trunk. She continued like that without stopping, so much so that Pablo ended by getting up also. He went first across to La Noire, who was no longer browsing but was standing motionless under the shade of the trees. He stroked her for a moment, gave her a crust

149

of bread, and then went over and joined the *patronne*. From habit, he asked, "What shall I do now?"

At the farm, as in the fields, it was the phrase he used each time he had finished a job.

The *patronne* looked at him. She gave a sad smile, lifted her arms, and let them fall back immediately on her apron, sighing. "What is there to do?"

"Of course," said Pablo. "Of course."

They remained still for a moment. Standing beside each other, their hands hanging, they looked about them, through the trees, at the combe where Jeannette, sitting in the shade of a bush, continued to keep watch over her little flock.

After several minutes the *patronne* sighed again and looked at Pablo, who sighed also. Then, without a word, they began to walk together towards the ridge. They went slowly, without deserting the shade of the trees, as if they were carrying a great load. When they reached the edge of the wood they slipped between two bushes and emerged above the old vines.

There all was like a furnace. The heat was coming as much from the ground as from the sky. The grass was brown between the old vine-plants, some of which still had their stakes. Farther off, below this place of brilliant light, the plain stretched away, looking almost grey. The highway was still alive with traffic.

"It looks as if there's less going along now," said Pablo.

"Yes, we should have brought the binoculars."

"Would you like me to go and fetch them?"

"No, that'll do later."

"I'm going now."

Pablo went off quickly, and soon reached the break. During the time he took to get to it, and while he was hunting in the jumble of things in the break, he had the feeling that he was breathing more easily. But as soon as he got back to the *patronne* his anguish returned.

One after the other they examined the highway for a long time. In the main pedestrians, cyclists, and horse-drawn carts predominated. There were a few cars and lorries, but hardly any soldiers. In the ditches objects and articles of every kind had been abandoned.

"If only I could know where he is," said the *patronne* again.

"You know very well, since he wasn't in the line itself he almost certainly left. He's possibly more comfortable than we are."

150

Silence returned—a silence which had been with them since they arrived. Its heaviness was added to that of the heat, and it was this which made the air so difficult to breathe. Even when they spoke the silence did not vanish. It retreated a few paces, but it could be felt all around, watching. It was beneath the hedges, in the wood, lying even on the hot earth, ready to return and weigh down everything. Their sighs told of the weight of this afternoon in which nothing seemed to be alive.

Even the highway seemed dead.

Pablo let his eyes wander over the plain, from village to village. He was not looking for anything, and yet something seemed to be missing from the land.

Looking again at the hill which sloped down before him, Pablo asked, "Why is this place called Brûlis?"

"I don't know, to tell the truth. My father said that in the old days every time that someone tried to cultivate this land the harvests were good because of the water under the hill; but at harvesting time everything caught fire. There are other old people who say that it was not burned by fire, but only by the sun. I think myself it was both: the hill faces south, it's the only one in these parts which does, and you can see how the sun strikes. So although the plants may well drink through their roots, they always end up by being grilled."

They returned slowly through the wood. For a moment the shade seemed quite cool.

"And the vines?" asked Pablo.

"Impossible now. It's too steep for a plough; a horse couldn't drag one. Everything would have to be done by hand. You can't manage that now, but it was possible in the old days. And also it's really much too far from the village. It's a pity because it used to produce the best wine in the district. But with the slope there's the problem of bringing up fresh earth on men's backs after any heavy rain. That's not a job you can get done nowadays."

Back at the tent, they stretched out on the warm grass. Pablo began to stare at the leaves above him and at the sky, and it seemed at moments that he might fall and go into it as if into a sea.

Soon he closed his eyes. Time had stopped. Everything had stopped. The war also would be stopped before it reached the plain.

151

XXIII

THIS was the first occasion since Pablo had arrived in this part of the world that time had stood still. He was like a blind man whose stick finds nothing to touch. He had never known this before. Even in the camp, in the lost days, there had always been Mariana. Of course, she still returned now. She always returned in a way, but she was elusive. She disappeared immediately he reached to hold her. Mariana remained the calm face of a portrait without a tear, but the portrait was transparent, impalpable, there was nothing to grasp. Two hours passed, but since the sky was empty, one did not see them pass. One did not hear them either because the wind had vanished. It had gone to the other side of the horizon with the last clouds, and since then it had not made itself felt. The trees waited, motionless. They were weary. They remained wilted, with all their birds held in their warm shade, and high above was the sun shining from all the sky and infiltrating everywhere.

Nothing was moving. No-one was speaking. There was only the buzzing of insects, but what they said unceasingly no longer made sense. It was a long cry more motionless than the silence. An interminable stroke of a saw through the heart of silence itself, and which would last as long as it did.

And, for hours and hours, this silence would weigh on his body.

Pablo would remain stretched out on the ground. He would remain there for a long time, and he would feel something forming inside himself. Something which grew little by little, making its way as his blood did through his veins, until it filled his entire body. Then he would no longer be able to rest. He had to get up. He would walk though the woods to the ridge. Sometimes the *patronne* followed him, but often she let him go alone.

He went with long strides, without hesitation, like someone who knows very well where he is going and has no time to lose. He would go like this through the row of bushes. And only there would he stop.

He would stare at the plain. The entire plain—in detail.

He would look at it for a long time. But above all else it was the road he stared at, and always towards its north end.

152

Twenty, or possibly thirty, times the first day. As often again the day after.

And always to see nothing but emptiness. Nothing but immobility. Because all this movement on the highway was a little like the buzz of insects; it was too regular, too monotonous to belong to life. It was something happening in the immobility of the plain like the continuous chirring of insects in the silence of the day and night.

For the night was as empty as the day. Pablo no longer had weariness to make him sleep. He was constantly between sleeping and waking, and never really slept.

Two days and two nights passed like this.

Three times a day they ate. In the evening they tied the animals in the wood and slept under the tilt. There was plenty of room. They did not see each other, or touch against each other, but Pablo, several times, went out silently, to stretch out in the open, on the earth itself. There he found emptiness once more. The sky into which he was going to fall. The sky where the stars were just a mist without life.

It was not possible to watch the coming of morning. Everything happened too slowly. There was no mystery to it any longer. In any event, to see morning arrive it must not be watched for steadily. The eyes must be taken from it. Something else must be done. To sleep again for a moment, or to begin some work. It is not by watching an empty sky that one can see the day advance. The day does not advance into an empty sky; it is the sky itself which becomes day. But everything is so slow that one has the impression that nothing is happening. The night draws back step by step, but there is nothing to hinder its retreat, or hold it back or go with it. And when the sun comes out from the earth one is waiting for it so much, the colour of the sky around is already so much sun, that there is nothing new. The earth scarcely appears surprised; so much still remains everywhere, on its tanned skin, of the burn of the day before.

Since he had been in the country Pablo had become too familiar with mornings. The morning had become for him like water and bread—a nourishment, a drink, of which one only thinks truly the day when one no longer has it. During many months he had formed the habit of discovering something new with each awakening, and now he no longer found anything.

153

The night no longer concealed anything; the dawn no longer brought anything new.

There was not even a moment when he could say to himself, "Ah! Here's the day. I'm going to have a look at the plain." He could go whenever he liked. Now, or in fifteen minutes' time, it was the same thing. There was only the awakening of the two women to mark truly the moment when the day had come.

So, on the third morning, when the *patronne* came from under the awning, Pablo got up.

"Well?" she said to him.

"I'm going up to take a look," said Pablo.

This was about all they said to each other throughout the day. Pablo knew that when he came back the *patronne* would say again, "Well?" and he would reply, "Nothing." Then he would return to sitting on the grass.

He began to untether La Noire, whom he caressed for a moment, and then, as she made off towards the spring, he went up through the length of the wood. It was already warm, and there was no trace of dew.

Once through the bushes, Pablo stopped. His eyes would run immediately along the length of the highway. Towards the right first, then opposite to the village, then farther on to the spot where everything became indistinct, where all detail was lost in a grey-green haze.

There was nothing. Nothing more was passing along. The highway was empty. There remained only, here and there, abandoned vehicles. Even on the small side-roads there was no sign of life.

Pablo hesitated, turned round towards the wood, looked again at the highway and the entire plain, listened with every nerve taut, holding his breath.

Nothing.

Then he went down again to the tent. He was walking quickly, and when the *patronne* saw him coming she asked, "Well?"

But she did not say the word as she did usually. Something had changed in the sound of her voice. Pablo took down the binoculars which were hanging on a tree.

"Come," he said. "Come."

Jeannette, who was standing in front of the tent, stared at them.

"We must untether the animals," said the *patronne*.

154

As soon as they were freed the little flock went down towards the bottom of the combe. Jeannette, picking up her stick, followed the animals.

"Let's go up quickly," said Pablo. "Let's go up."

"What is it?"

Pablo did not reply, and the *patronne* followed him without insisting. When they reached the ridge the highway was still empty. For a few moments they stared at it without speaking, and then the *patronne* asked, "What do you think that means?"

"I don't know."

"You think they are coming?"

"Most certainly."

"You think there's nothing to stop them?"

Pablo hesitated, listened for a moment, and then said, "I can hear nothing."

"I'd like to follow the ridge round the Jourdains wood. From there you overlook the village. Perhaps I'll see something."

Pablo looked at her. She seemed calm. He could not understand. His own legs and hands were trembling. Sweat was running down all over his body.

"No," he said. "If you like, I'll go. But I think it would be best to stay here. We mustn't show ourselves."

"But we can get along without anyone seeing us."

"One always thinks so. And that's how you can get yourself killed."

The *patronne* seemed genuinely astonished. She looked at him for a moment before asking, "Who by? There's no-one."

Pablo tried to recover himself. He wanted to stiffen up to stop his limbs from trembling. But something rose suddenly inside him. Something which had been building up for days and days like a fire of damp grass.

He caught hold of her arm and dragged her behind the bushes, shouting, "No, you mustn't. You don't know what it's like. It can come out of the blue. At any moment they can be everywhere and kill everything that moves in the fields without knowing what it is. They can kill all those who are in houses. All. All. They kill all. Because that is war. You have to kill. To kill everything living. That's the rule, you see.... You have to kill, you have to!"

He stopped, as if strangled. His anger was making his eyes moist and choking his throat. He stood there in front of the *patronne*, whom he was still holding and who was watching him

155

uncomprehendingly. He was there shouting, his voice raucous, his breathing heavy. And he could see himself. He saw himself as grotesque.

They were the only living things on all this immense earth, and he was afraid. He felt sick with fear. He was not ashamed of his fear, but he saw it as if it was in another man. He found it absurd, without foundation, but he could do nothing against it.

The *patronne* let him talk. Words came from him in bursts like boiling water which overflows. Then, suddenly, he stopped. His hands became limp, releasing the woman's arms where red marks showed, and fell to his sides. For a moment silence returned, heavier than before, and the *patronne* took Pablo by the arm to lead him back towards the encampment.

"Come along," she murmured. "Come along. We'll have something to eat. . . . That'll do you good."

Pablo was now drained. There was nothing left inside him, neither fear nor anger, nothing but a great humming deeper than that of insects, nothing but a white mist more blinding than the sun.

Like a child he allowed himself to be led back as far as the opening of the tent.

XXIV

THE bread was beginning to get dry despite the linen in which it was wrapped, but the *patronne* and Pablo ate small mouthfuls, slowly. They each held in their left hand a large slice of the round loaf, with its thick and very brown crust. With their thumbs they each held a piece of bacon on top. They cut off little pieces which they chewed in silence. From time to time they stopped eating to drink a glass of the cool wine which the *patronne* had gone to fetch from beneath the stone in the spring.

Pablo was not thinking. His head was completely empty, but his blood was cooling down little by little. He stared at the bread and bacon. He looked at the blade of his knife shining with grease. He looked at the wine with the sun glinting on it.

All this was peace. They were the things of peace. Things which war did not know, did not have the time to notice. And as

156

he ate, a little peace began to come back to him. It came slowly, also in little mouthfuls, and the cool wine began to warm up as it passed his lips. First it took away a little of the fever burning in him and left in exchange a freshness gained from the earth in the combe where the spring's flow was like a thin strip of sky. Then, as it went down into the belly, when it had become warmed itself, it gave back greater warmth. But it was a good warmth, which came from the earth and sky. From a more distant land, from an earlier summer lost in time when peace slept soundly on the burning slopes.

Pablo looked towards the end of the combe where Jeannette was standing by the bush. With her stick resting beside her, she was eating bread and bacon which her mother had taken to her as she went down to fetch the wine. Pablo could not distinguish her face, she was too far away, but he could imagine her features, the movements of her mouth. She must be staring at the corner of the meadow, always the same one, as she stared at a face or an object when they ate at home.

Jeannette, also, was peace.

Then Pablo looked at the *patronne*. She smiled at him, seeming to ask, "Is that better now?" He looked down and began to eat again.

He had almost finished his bread when he heard the goats bleating. He looked up. The animals had begun to run about. Two were coming towards the tent, the others going up the opposite slope.

"What's the matter?" asked the *patronne*.

They stood up. Jeannette was also running towards the other slope, but she was slower than the goats.

Pablo put down his bread and began to run towards the spring. As he went down the slope he met the two goats running wildly. When he reached the bottom Pablo jumped across the water at the place where Jeannette had dropped her stick. He was about to rush up the other slope to catch her when he saw a movement in the grass, a few paces from him. He hesitated for a moment, and then, snatching up Jeannette's stick, he advanced towards the snake, which was motionless. He could see only the body and the tail, the head being hidden behind a large stone.

Pablo came to a standstill, stood three seconds without breathing, and raised his arm slowly, very slowly. Then suddenly, whistling through the air, the stick slammed down on the ground.

There was an abrupt jerk of the stretched-out body which rolled up and twisted, showing its white belly. The stick struck twice more. Pablo then looked farther away: something was moving there also. Another snake was gliding between the tufts of grass. Pablo jumped forward, struck three times, adroitly, precisely, swiftly. But two other snakes were there, a few steps away, almost motionless, their shining eyes fixed on Pablo.

He stepped back a few paces, and then, looking towards the camp, he saw that the *patronne* had just finished tying up the goats.

"*Patronne! Patronne!*" he shouted. "Quickly, quickly, bring a stick!"

Almost immediately she was hurrying up the slope between the bushes. Pablo saw that she was carrying two sticks. Then, completely master of himself, he waited, watching the two reptiles. The *patronne* began to walk more slowly as she came near to him. He gave his hand to help her across the streamlet. She was red-faced and out of breath. Sweat was running all over her face.

"Are there many?" she asked.

"Two there, and there's some movement in the grass lower down."

The sticks which the *patronne* had brought were more flexible than Jeannette's stick. Pablo took one of them. Stretching out his hand, he pointed to a tuft of dandelions of which the stems were moving.

"See?" he asked.

"Yes."

"Then go over there. I'm going to try to get the two with one blow."

The *patronne* moved away to the left. Pablo walked softly towards the snakes. As he arrived within arm's length they began to crawl. Pablo wanted to strike before they could separate. He leaped forward, and the stick struck the ground. One snake twisted, but the other escaped between the grass. It covered barely a few yards, and already the stick was there. A sharp cracking sound and the reptile stopped, cut almost in two.

The *patronne* had struck from her side.

They finished killing the snakes which were still moving, and then inspected the ground all round. Nothing else moved. Then they looked at each other, and, after a moment's hesitation, they both began to laugh as they mopped their faces.

"How extraordinary!" said Pablo. "I've never seen anything like that before."

"It's the milk," panted the *patronne*. "The milk...I thought of it as I saw you hitting them."

"The milk?" asked Pablo.

"Yes, it's there that I do the milking. That's what's attracted them."

The first day the *patronne* had tried to make some cheese with the animals' milk, but up there it was not possible. So since then she had been milking without using a pail. She collected just the amount of milk she needed for the day and let the rest run into the ground.

"What's that one there?" asked Pablo.

The *patronne* looked again. "That's just a grass snake. The others are vipers. Don't you recognize them?"

"No," said Pablo. "Not very well."

They turned towards the slope. The goats had stopped on the edge of the wood, and Jeannette was close to them. Her mother made a sign for her to come across, but she did not budge. They looked at each other smiling, and the *patronne*, poking the snakes with the tip of her stick, explained how, at first glance, vipers could be recognized.

"D'you think others will come?"

"It's possible. We'll have to watch out."

"It's a good thing to kill them."

The *patronne* began to laugh. "You don't think that in normal times anyone amuses themselves by wasting milk on the ground just for the pleasure of killing vipers?"

They went up towards the wood.

"We'll go down and bury them," said the *patronne*. "Otherwise with the heat, some infection might start."

Arriving at the tent, Pablo picked up his bread and began to eat again. He was very hot, but he felt well. The weight which had been pressing on him for days had disappeared.

As the *patronne* rejoined him with Jeannette and the animals he said, "In a minute or two, I'll go out and have a look round. If there are any others about we'll take advantage of the occasion to get rid of them."

"I'll come with you. And tonight we'll keep the milk. Tomorrow we'll put it out on plates, so that the earth doesn't suck it up immediately."

159

"I'm sure we'll find others."

"But it's going to be very hot down below."

"We could make a shelter of branches, near the spring."

"That's an idea, yes. We'll have to see."

They talked for a long time. They started getting excited. Little by little they worked out a plan for a great campaign to eliminate all the vipers of the combe.

"I wouldn't have thought there could be so many," said the *patronne*, "but when you think about it, this is really snake ground about here. What's more, they're undisturbed."

They glanced all round the vale, staring at each pile of stones, scrutinizing the brambles in the hope of seeing other snakes show themselves.

"We've got to be careful because of the animals."

They looked for a spot where the little flock could be more secure, and the *patronne* called Jeannette over.

"You see," she explained, "on this side of the stream there's a place where there aren't any stones. Try to see the animals always stay there."

The little girl went off with her small flock, and they watched her as she went away.

"What we need," said Pablo, "is to get good sticks which can be held easily and are very supple."

He got the bill-hook and went to the other edge of the wood where the hazel-trees were growing. He chose the branches he needed and cut an ample supply which he stripped of their twigs. Each time that one had been prepared he made it whistle through the air and struck the ground with it several times. The grass fell flat, cut down as if with a scythe.

When he returned to the tent the *patronne* also tested some of the sticks.

"They are fine," she said. "Just what we need."

"Now I'm going to cut some branches to make a hurdle which'll give us some shade."

"I'll come with you. I'll put them together according to size."

They went into the wood, and Pablo began cutting branches.

The *patronne* had already assembled a considerable pile when, returning towards Pablo who was striking sharply with his bill-hook, she called out, "Stop! Come and look!"

Pablo stopped, his hand on the stick he was cutting. The sound of the last blow of his bill-hook rang down the combe before

160

dying away, as if absorbed by the heat from the sky and the earth. They listened for a moment, staring at each other.

A heavy rumbling sound was coming from the plain, just reaching the top of the hill.

Pablo planted his bill-hook in the branch he had not finished cutting and said, "Come along."

As they passed the tent the *patronne* snatched up the binoculars, and they went quickly to the top of the slope.

Once they were on the other side of the wood, they saw the highway immediately. Opposite to them it was empty. There were only the abandoned vehicles. Then they went forward a few steps to look more towards the north.

Over there, well before the road which linked the highway with the village, a column was advancing solwly.

The *patronne* stared for a moment through the binoculars, then she held them out to Pablo. She gave him time to adjust them to his own sight and asked, "Well, what is it?"

Pablo remained motionless for some seconds, and then, lowering the binoculars and turning to the *patronne*, he said simply, "I think there can be no doubt. This is it."

"What's out in front? Is it tanks?"

"Yes, there are four light tanks and lorries behind them."

"Look, look," whispered the *patronne*.

Pablo raised the binoculars again. Two motor-cyclists, grey-helmeted, had just stopped on the highway and were waiting for the column to come up.

"They must have come from the village, surely?" said the *patronne*.

Then both of them, without a word to each other, looked at the top of this twisted hillside which hid the village from them.

They remained thus for some seconds, holding their breath. Finally, the *patronne* asked, "D'you think they've done anything?"

"Well, there's no sign of smoke, and we didn't hear any explosions."

As the first tanks came close to the motor-cyclists they halted for a moment. The whole column slowed down, and then, as the motor-cyclists went off again, the whole column began to move once more. The motor-cyclists went ahead and passed opposite the Brûlis slope to disappear finally towards the south.

Taking up the binoculars again, Pablo, his eyes at the level of the brambles, watched the convoy pass. He could see clearly men whose chests emerged from the grey turrets. He saw also those driving the lorries. He passed the binoculars to the *patronne*, who watched the column pass and disappear from sight. After that Pablo and the *patronne* remained motionless for a long time. Two other lorries also passed, more quickly than the others. As they came level with abandoned vehicles they stopped, and men climbed down and pushed the derelict vehicles into the ditch. A few minutes later a motor-cycle squad went by, and that was all.

The sun beat down on the plain, which shimmered into the distance. The throb of engines had died away some time before, and only the buzzing of insects remained.

Pablo and the *patronne* stood for a moment face to face. Then, without a word, slowly, their eyes lowered, they went back to the camp.

XXV

THE remainder of the day was interminable. They began first by building a tunnel of branches near the spring. Then, before eating, they again went up to the crest to observe the highway. No convoys were passing along, but only an occasional lorry or an odd vehicle or two from time to time. Once their meal was over they went up again, then they returned to the shelter of their tunnel. They remained there for more than an hour without speaking, without making any gesture other than to brush away the gadflies which settled on them constantly. All the heat of the day accumulated in the bottom of this combe. It fell from the sky on to the stones and the stunted bushes, which threw it back to the centre. The spring also reflected the sun. All was light; everything prickled and burned the skin where sweat ran endlessly.

The *patronne* was first to be discouraged; kicking off her clogs suddenly, she walked down into the fresh water, saying, "It's not worth while stifling ourselves here. No more will be coming."

Scooping up the water with both hands, she splashed it over her face. Pablo did the same, and then they went up towards the wood.

162

There, at least, it was rather cooler, and the water which had run down their backs was still giving them a little freshness.

Nevertheless they were unable to remain still in one place. They went up at least twenty times to watch the highway. On almost every occasion the *patronne* would say, "All the same, I want to see what's going on round here."

But every time Pablo repeated that it was better not to take pointless risks. He no longer felt the unbearable fear, but he had a sort of fever. An irritation which sprang from everything, and which everything increased: more oppressive heat than on other days, the ever-present flies which never ceased to buzz around them, and time which failed to resume its normal course.

Time was no longer suspended, it was all to blazes. At certain moments it seemed to rush ahead, only to stop later and fall behind.

Finally, the sun began to descend towards the rim of the plain and set in a deeper purple haze than on other days. While the *patronne* busied herself with the animals and the meal Pablo went up again several times to the crest. When he told her that the horizon was very murky, the *patronne* said, "I'm not surprised. The weather has been absolutely unbearable. There'll certainly be a storm tonight."

They ate, then the *patronne* put Jeannette to bed and came out from the tent as soon as she knew that she was asleep.

"That's good," she said. "We can go now."

They passed along the side of the combe, rising steadily towards the summit. The *patronne* went ahead, stopping from time to time to listen. There was no moon, but the star-filled sky cast a shadowless light everywhere.

When they arrived at the back of the Jourdains woods they stayed for a long time listening. The village was quite close now. It was just on the other side of the wood and down the slope. But behind the trees, heavy with night, there was also the unknown: the mystery of the days during which so many things might have happened. They listened again, and then the *patronne* looked for the opening of the path which went through the wood.

Having found it, she paused again. Pablo moved up close to her and whispered, "It's the only path?"

"Yes."

"Then let me go first. I won't make a mistake."

"Why you?"

"Let me," he said.

He stepped past her gently and went under the vault of shadow. The night here was almost opaque, and he had to walk a little by guess. Each time he stopped he felt on his neck the rapid breathing of the *patronne* as she bumped into his back.

"I think it's to the right," she would whisper. "Or to the left. Perhaps straight on."

Pablo felt her speaking close to his ear, almost close enough for her lips to touch him.

Several times birds flew up. Pablo jumped each time. Then they suddenly saw ahead of them a light behind the trees and branches.

By instinct Pablo ducked, but the *patronne* said immediately, "It's summer lightning, but it's a long way off, over the Saône valley."

They emerged finally at the summit of the hillside planted with vines. The plain could scarcely be seen, drowned as it was in shadow.

"The storm's coming up," said the *patronne*.

Indeed, silent lightning was flashing along the horizon, and all the lower part of the sky was empty of stars. They listened for a moment, then the *patronne* advanced towards the right, hugging the edge of the wood.

"We'll go as far as the Briods' meadow; from there we'll really be able to see."

They walked on again for a few minutes as far as a piece of fallow land, which they crossed holding on to the brambles. On the other side was a quickset hedge taller than a man.

"There's a gap further along. We'll try and find it."

The *patronne* stopped a little later and, kneeling down, pushed a way between two hawthorns. Bending over in his turn, Pablo tried to get through, but the *patronne* had stopped moving forward. She was pressing herself to one side to make room for him, and, catching hold of his arm, she pulled him forward.

"Slide in beside me. We can't go down; the ground drops away."

He crawled in, his side pressing against the woman. Once he was in he saw that the meadow was very much lower down and that the hedge was planted on the summit of a piece of land rising almost vertically. Beyond the meadow there was a tumble

164

of vines and, immediately after, the trees on the road which led to the mill combe and the village.

The roofs were scarcely discernible, but Pablo felt them to be very near. It almost seemed to him that by hanging out a little from this leafy window, and stretching out his arm, he would be able to touch them with his hand.

Beside him the *patronne* wriggled. Pressing her mouth to his ear, she whispered, "You'd think we were very close, but at night it's misleading."

"There's not a single light showing."

"No, and yet, before, people didn't trouble very much."

Pablo thought for a moment, and then he said, "The Boches must have ordered all lights out."

"Then it means there are some of them here?"

"Probably."

They became silent. The lightning flashes were coming slowly nearer, and the night, rising from the plain, was moving little by little into the sky, hiding the stars.

"There must be a guard on duty," whispered Pablo.

The *patronne* moved again, and he turned on his side to allow her a little more room. Now, inside the hole in the hedge, they were almost face to face. Pablo felt the woman's breath on his cheeks and, against his body, the increasing warmth of her presence.

Below them there seemed to be nothing living.

The *patronne* had placed her hand on Pablo's arm. Suddenly she squeezed it very hard.

"Look down there," she whispered.

Pablo turned his head. Far, far off to the left, light was moving into the sky, a purple light with orange tints.

"What is over there?" he asked.

"That's the Lyons direction, but I don't know whether what is burning is this side of it or beyond."

They were silent for a moment, then she asked, "Can it be a town burning?"

"No," said Pablo. "To judge by the colour, it's no ordinary fire. It's probably a petrol-dump."

For more than half an hour they remained with their eyes fixed on the point of the horizon where the light of a great blaze flickered, sometimes lighting up the underside of clouds. It was the only living thing on the earth, and, in the sky, there were only the streaks of lightning which continued to flash as the dark shadow slid across the tissue of stars.

Finally, the fire began to die down. The sounds of rolling thunder became louder, and soon a breath of air began to move along the slope. All the hedge began to whisper, became quiet, then started again.

Pablo felt the woman shiver.

He sensed that she was pressing closer to him. Her bosom was warm and soft against his chest. Several times already their faces had brushed.

"We must get back," said Pablo. "The storm's coming."

"It's not here yet."

"Are you cold?" he asked.

"No."

Pablo climbed from the hedge first. Once he was standing, he bent down and took the hand of the *patronne* to help her up. Her hand was moist and trembling slightly.

"We'd better hurry," he said. "If the storm comes it may wake the little one, and if she finds herself alone she'll be frightened."

The *patronne* went ahead without a word.

Everything was now alive. Everything moved, everything made sounds. The wind was everywhere at once, and the wood was filled with the rustle of leaves.

They went through it very quickly. The nearest lightning flashes outlined tree-trunks which came out of the darkness for an instant and appeared to gallop in long lines.

Once they were in the combe the heat held in by the two slopes seemed to leap into their faces. They almost suffocated for an instant, but a moment later a lightning flash dazzled them. Almost immediately the air seemed to split, cracking like a giant tree falling on a pile of dry branches. They began to run, but the rain was already upon them. A few enormous drops first, which struck like hailstones, and then a flood of water.

By the time they reached the tent they were drenched.

Immediately he was inside the tent Pablo flicked on his lighter. The *patronne* had sunk down beside him. Half lying, resting on one elbow, she was trying to get her breath back. Water was running down her face, flattening streaks of hair over her forehead and cheeks. Her soaked dress clung closely to her heavy breasts, which rose jerkily as she gasped for breath. The flame of the lighter was reflected in her eyes.

166

"You see," said Pablo simply.

She smiled as she gasped for breath. "Yes, it came quicker than I expected."

Pablo turned towards the back of the tent. Rolled in her blanket, just as her mother had left her, Jeannette was sleeping open-mouthed.

A gust of wind lifted the canvas. The flame flickered and the lighter went out. Pablo tried vainly to get it to light again.

"No petrol," he said.

"That doesn't matter for what we have to do now."

Pablo heard her moving about. She must be undressing.

"Don't go to sleep in your wet clothes," she said. "You'll get your death of cold."

Pablo went towards the entrance of the tent.

"What are you doing?" asked the *patronne*.

"I'm just going to take a look at the animals."

He went out. The rain swallowed him, and the wind plastered his wet shirt against his chest. He took a few steps and then stood still. Little by little the freshness of the rain penetrated him. The blood beat less fiercely in his temples.

The worst of the storm had already passed, moving towards the mountain. Nevertheless the lightning was still playing among the clouds and flashing along the ground where the trees were swaying.

At each flash Pablo looked towards the animals. Tied up at the edge of the wood, the goats and the cow remained quite calm. But La Noire was restless, tugging at her tether.

Pablo went across to her and stroked her for a moment to calm her. Water was streaming down her neck and sides, and Pablo felt her shiver under his hand. He unhitched the mare and led her over to the tent. There he spoke to her again for a moment in a low voice. Then, as the storm moved farther and farther away, he waited for the rain to stop, went and fetched a large handful of hay, and spent a long time rubbing her down.

When she was almost dry he caressed her again, talking to her in a low voice. Finally, when he could feel that she was much calmer, he went back to the tent.

There he undressed silently and rolled himself up in his blanket.

XXVI

ONCE he was lying down Pablo began to shiver, but he soon felt perspiration enveloping him, although he had not moved about. He remained immobile for a long time listening to the wind, which was shaking the trees and the tent. It was no longer raining, but with each gust of wind drops of water spattered on the canvas.

Jeannette had not ceased snoring, but the *patronne* must have taken a long time to get to sleep. Pablo heard her turning over and sighing several times. He wanted to get up and go and sleep alone in the wood, on the damp grass.

Beneath this canvas he felt stifled. The storm had blown away all the sticky heat, all the weight of an interminable day tucked since nightfall at the bottom of the combe. Here also it was night, but a night different from that which dripped on the rocks and on the flattened grass. Between these two nights there was just a sheet of canvas soaked with rain, but sufficient to imprison air which it was difficult to breath and which hung heavily. Air which held the odour of bodies with sweat drying, the odour of open mouths.

There were above all these sweating bodies, which lived, which filled all the space.

And then, besides the bodies, there was also Mariana.

Mariana had come back this evening into this tent, more present than ever. Mariana no longer the serene visage of the portrait, but a sadder mask. Pablo had fought for a long time against this image, against a host of ideas which came to him, against the fever which took hold of his body at times in spells, like a burning wind which penetrates to the heart of a house.

Then, after a struggle, he ended by falling asleep, and he slept for a long time, an unbroken sleep.

When he awoke it was broad daylight and he was alone under the canvas. Outside all was silence.

He got up. His clothes were still damp. He looked for other things to wear in the pile of clothes at the end of the tent, then dressed in haste and hurried out.

The *patronne* was coming back from the combe, where Jeannette was already settled with her flock. When she saw Pablo she smiled.

"Good morning," said Pablo. "I overslept. You should have called me."

The *patronne* shrugged her shoulders and smiled. "For all there is to do!"

Her face was tense and her eyes had circles round them. Pablo looked at her for a moment while she was getting the bread out of the linen in which it was wrapped.

He wanted to speak to her, but could think of nothing to say. He turned towards the side of the combe where the sun was chasing small streamers of mist through the bushes.

"The storm didn't last long," he said finally.

"No."

The silence returned. The air hummed already with swarms of flies. The freshness of the earth crouched under the heat of the sky. The heavy heat was settling in again. Pablo felt it all around him. He felt it in himself with the weight which had oppressed him in the days past. There was, in addition, something else. Something difficult to define which came both from the silence of the *patronne* and from the return of Mariana. Above all from the return of Mariana.

For this morning again the sad face was there, immobile, but more intense. It no longer had the transparency which allowed light to fill it, which also allowed Pablo to go on living while looking at the world through it, breathing the air which came from beyond it.

"Come along," said the *patronne*. "Eat up."

He jumped. He went over to her, however, and took the bread and cheese she was holding out.

"Thank you," he said, and then went and sat on a tree-stump not far from the tent.

There he began to eat, staring at the bottom of the combe. After a few minutes he turned his head towards the *patronne*. She was looking at him, but she immediately turned her eyes away. He chewed slowly another two mouthfuls of bread and cheese. There was a sour taste in his throat, which increased as he ate. He soon stood up and went across to La Noire. As soon as he was close to her she pressed her muzzle against his chest. He looked towards the tent. The *patronne* had turned her back. Then, keeping her in sight, he cut his bread into small pieces and

169

fed them to La Noire. Afterwards, when she had eaten them all, he threw the rest of his cheese into some brambles. He caressed the mare again and went back towards the tent.

The *patronne* had not moved. Sitting at the tent-opening, her elbows on her knees, she was staring fixedly at a point on the hill on the other side of the valley. Her face was still tense and hard.

Pablo went and sat again on the tree-trunk he had left to go to La Noire, and fumbled in his pockets. When he had found three cigarette-ends he took a cigarette-paper from his pocket and rolled a cigarette. At the moment he flicked his lighter he remembered that it was empty. He thought of his matches, but they were inside the tent, where he could not go without disturbing the *patronne*. He took the cigarette from his lips, rolled the two ends between his fingers to close them, and slipped it into his pocket. Then he picked up a blade of grass which he began to chew.

They remained like this for almost an hour.

As time accumulated and grew larger, as the day enveloped the earth in heat and silence, the weight on Pablo's chest grew greater. It seemed to him also that something was happening between him and the *patronne*. Something which a slight thing could destroy; a little like one of those enormous ricks with over-dry grass which a tiny match can devour in a matter of seconds.

Pablo avoided moving, but every now and then he would look from under his eyelids at the *patronne*. Each time it seemed to him that she had shrunk farther into herself.

Indeed, everything seemed to be shrinking little by little. Each tree, each bush, each bramble, each clump of grass, seemed to be crouching towards the ground, bending its back under the weight of accumulating minutes piling up one by one in the hollows of the earth.

They remained there without thought, almost without life, waiting. At last, somewhere away on the left, right at the top of the ridge, there was a noise of tumbling stones. Nothing really, but enough to make them jump. Together they turned their heads.

Someone was walking in the bushes.

Pablo felt his heart beating. He held his breath. A shadow moved behind some branches, then nothing more. Again the shadow began to move and the branches were parted.

"Clopineau!" exclaimed the *patronne*.

They had both stood up at the same time, and they went to
170

meet the old man, who had seen them and was waving his hand as he came down through the wood.

"What news?" they asked.

The old man took off his cap and drew from his pocket a large checked handkerchief to mop his head where the sweat was plastering his few grey hairs.

"Let me get my breath..." he puffed. "Good Lord, but it's a climb. Long time since I've been up as far as this."

They went over to the encampment, and the old man sat on Pablo's tree-stump and swallowed in one gulp the glass of wine the *patronne* offered him.

"Well?" she asked again.

The old man wiped his moustache. His eyes were smiling. He took a deep breath and said, "Well, believe it or not, hardly a thing's changed."

"And the Boches?"

"First of all, it seems it's better to say the Germans, it's more prudent."

"But there are some?"

"There are quite a few. They're in the town hall."

"But what are they doing?"

The old man hesitated for a moment and looked at them each in turn before saying, "They're eating."

There was a moment's silence.

"They're eating?"

"Yes, that's what they do, mostly. But they pay. In French money what's more."

"But what do they eat?" asked the *patronne*.

"How should I know! What they can find, of course! Yesterday afternoon, apparently, there were four of them went to Juliette Rousset's place. She had a basket with three dozen eggs in it. They bought the lot. After that they went into the café, and they asked to have an omelette made. And, believe it or not, a thirty-six-egg omelette!"

Pablo and the *patronne* looked at each other.

"Three dozen?" she said.

"Juliette swore it, and Nanoux's wife at the café showed us the shells. I'm not joking—three dozen it was. And they ate them just like that, without any bread even."

The *patronne* appeared to be pondering for a moment, then she asked, "And at the house?"

171

"Your big black-and-white broody hen you thought was lost has come back. Fourteen chicks she brought with her. And yesterday evening I found out where she's been nesting; you'll never guess."

The *patronne* shook her head.

"Among the old iron piled up behind the woodshed."

"I certainly didn't think to look there. Still, what does it matter? Fourteen at this time's as good as none. It's too late. They'll never come to much."

"You wait and see. They're fully fledged. If you feed 'em a bit you could get 'em to a nice size before the cold weather starts."

They were silent for a moment, and Pablo asked, "Have the Germans been to the farm?"

"No, they passed by as they were going back to the main road. I was in the courtyard. They looked at me, but they didn't stop."

"And they weren't checking people's identity papers?"

The old man hesitated and then said, "What?"

"Did they ask people's names and ask to see their papers?"

Clopineau appeared surprised. He reflected for a few seconds and then explained: "But you don't understand. There were just twenty who came. If they'd tried to find out the name of everyone around they'd never have finished. And anyway, what good would it have done them?"

"Then we can come down again?"

"What do you mean, you can come down again? Why not? I don't think they're going to gobble us up. In any case, it's those who've left who'll be biting their nails, because nobody knows now what'll happen to them."

The *patronne* stood up, walked a few steps, and then, returning towards Clopineau, she asked, "Is there any news of the war?"

"Well, you know, there's plenty of rumours, but the truth, no-one knows."

There was a silence. Clopineau picked up his glass which he had put on the grass beside the tree-stump and held it out to the *patronne*, who poured some more wine for him, asking, "Who is at the house now?"

"No-one. I shut the doors, that's all."

"But..."

"What risk can there be? I've told you, everything's as if nothing had happened."

172

The *patronne* re-corked the wine-bottle and put it in the grass. "That's fine," she said. "There's no reason to hang about. Let's get everything together and go down again. I don't like to think of the house with no-one in it."

She began to busy herself, picking up a basket here and putting it down a little way off, walking between the tent and the break, then returning towards the men without doing anything.

"Good God," said the old man, "you're just as muddled as you were the other day. Listen to me, if you're so anxious to get down there again, you go ahead with the child and the animals. Me and Pablo will get everything else packed up and brought down."

She looked at Pablo.

"Clopineau's right," he said. "Of course you're anxious to get back to the house. You go on, we'll look after everything."

The *patronne* went down to the spring, and came back soon afterwards with Jeannette. They each had a stick to drive their flock towards the crest.

"And get us a good soup ready!" shouted the old man. "We'll need it when we get down."

She went off without a backward glance. The two men, standing in front of the tent, watched the little party moving away. As they arrived at the crest the *patronne*, who was hurrying the animals along, had already drawn away from Jeannette. She disappeared behind the line of bushes, and the two men could still see for a moment the little girl climbing through the wood with her jerky stride, swinging her shoulders and waving her stick from time to time as if to direct the animals.

For a moment she showed against the skyline, her stick struck the air once more, then nothing was left on the crest except the bushes glistening with light.

XXVII

IT TOOK two full days to get everything back in order. Two very busy days with scarcely time to glance through a window or to go as far as the courtyard when there was the sound of a car-engine.

"You see," said the old man, "they don't even look at us."

It was true. The few grey or green-uniformed soldiers in steel helmets or forage caps who went by on their motor-cycles or in small cars never stopped at the farm. Then after another week none were to be seen at all.

The war had passed by. It had followed the main road, lighting a fire far off on a stormy night to mark the end of another stage. That was all.

A few people had gone as far as Lons-le-Saunier, and they came back saying that down there also all had been uneventful. The Germans had had the holes dug by the French near the old Montmorot toll-gate filled in. They had also taken prisoner the few soldiers who had stayed behind, but apart from that nothing had been changed.

On the farm, as soon as the house was in order again, all work was concentrated in the vineyards to make up for time lost.

The armistice came while Pablo and Clopineau were busy with the second sulphate spraying of the vines. The armistice came with as little fuss as the war did, without delighting anyone and without causing any break in the work in the vineyards.

When Pablo and Clopineau returned home, blue from head to toe in their old, torn clothes, they began by changing and washing themselves under the tap in the courtyard. Then, while they waited for the evening meal, they went and sat on the kitchen doorstep.

They remained there without speaking, without seeing the night rising from the earth around them, making the air heavy just as fatigue made their legs heavy.

Behind them, in the kitchen, the two women were busying themselves preparing the meal and the mash for the animals. From time to time the *patronne* shouted an instruction to Jeannette. When the child failed to understand she began to shout for a few seconds, and then all became quiet again, and only the sound of clogs on concrete broke the silence.

When the *patronne* shouted very loudly the two men glanced at each other. They said nothing, but there was an understanding between them which they both sensed. Something like an agreement. Twice, when the shouts persisted and Jeannette began to cry, Pablo, without getting up, pulled aside the blind and glanced into the kitchen. On each occasion, as she saw him, the *patronne* stopped shouting. But once Jeannette began to cry it was sure to

174

last the whole evening. She wept right through the meal, sucking in her tears and mucus as she ate. Pablo avoided looking at her then, but just to hear her sobbing robbed him of appetite.

The *patronne* remained glowering and irritable, and she spoke only about work.

In the first days old Marguerite came every evening. As she came in she would ask from the doorstep, "Have you had any news?"

The *patronne* would shake her head and grunt, "No, nothing."

Then one day, when Pablo was in the courtyard about to leave, the old woman said, "It's not worth the bother of my coming back. It only turns the knife in the wound. When there's any news you let me know."

Many weeks passed like this. Then, one evening as they arrived, the two men realized that something had changed. As she heard the noise of the cart the *patronne* had come out on the doorstep. As soon as La Noire came to a stop she came out to meet them, saying, "At last! I've had a letter! He's a prisoner!"

The two men jumped down from the cart.

"There you are," said the old man. "You see! You see!"

And that was all. As on other evenings, the meal was silent. From time to time Pablo glanced at the *patronne*. Her face was less tense. Her brow less wrinkled.

When they had finished Pablo asked, "Does old Marguerite know?"

"Yes," said the *patronne*. "I went and told her."

She hesitated for a moment, looking at Pablo and the old man, then again at Pablo, and she added: "I went to tell her; she wept. She wept, and then, afterwards, we went to the cemetery together."

During their work the two men often talked about their dead *patron*. They did so without sadness. Most often it was the old man who would say, for instance, "If he was here he'd be very pleased to see that the planting is so thick and strong."

But talking never lasted long. The work was urgent, it governed every movement, the brain followed the hand. There was no time to spare for the dead. Now, however, it was different. They turned towards the end of the table, where the *patron's* empty chair stood, and the old man said, "We must find time to go there, one of these days."

"Yes," said Pablo, "we'll go."

That same evening, when old Clopineau had gone and Jeannette was in her room, and when Pablo himself was about to go upstairs also, the *patronne* kept him back.

"There's something I've got to ask you," she said.

"What?"

She seemed embarrassed. They were both standing between the end of the table and the kitchen stove.

"It's like this," she said, finally. "I know that you don't like talking about it, but I want to know what it's like in prisoners' camps."

Pablo breathed deeply. His face cleared a little. And then, after a few seconds his brow wrinkled again.

"You know," he said, "I can't really tell you. The French camps in Germany are probably not at all like those we were in."

"But do you think the French prisoners will be treated badly?"

Pablo hesitated. There was something in the *patronne's* eyes which suggested that it was this she feared. That she really wanted the truth from him.

"They'll be all right," he said. "There are the rules of war. Prisoners must be treated properly. And the camps are inspected by the Red Cross."

He reflected for a few seconds, and then added, "What's more, you'll have him back very soon after the war's over."

Pablo wished her "good night" and went to his room.

Once he had closed the door behind him he went and sat on the bed without lighting the lamp. In front of him the window was wide open. The summer night's air was almost still. He stood up and walked quietly across to rest his elbows on the window-ledge. From the side of the stream there came the sound of frogs croaking. In the garden, behind the gate, where the convolvulus climbed up, there were mole-crickets chirring, answering each other endlessly.

Pablo remained motionless for a long time. The moon had come up behind the hill and the plain was lighting up little by little. He could feel the day's weariness, but he had no wish to sleep. During the weeks he had been living like a machine, dizzy with work, he had almost ceased to think. But this evening his mind was full. With the remembrance of the prison camp, other images came to his mind, from farther off, but nevertheless more menacing.

One by one faces came into his mind, the faces of the dead.

176

There were hundreds of them, and he summoned them to his mind. There were so many that Pablo imagined his own homeland completely empty. A desert—with no trace of life. Here too the war had passed. It had done nothing. In his own land it had left nothing except the dead. For the living who remained it was death or the threat of death.

Suddenly Pablo started. The flooring had creaked behind him. He turned round and went back towards the bed. The *patronne* was coming up the stairs. He heard her close the door of her room, then all was silent again.

The dead, the thousands of dead, had gone. Here there were still living beings. There were even others elsewhere who might return from one day to the next.

A prisoner could be liberated. Or he could escape.

Pablo went to bed without putting on a light. He now knew this room very well indeed. Each piece of furniture, each object in it, was familiar to him. His body knew the bed which was shaped to him.

He turned on his side, facing the window. The night was still alive with sounds, but now on the large rectangle of clear sky shadows were passing, vague, without name or shape. One alone remained, fixed, motionless, like someone who waits; like someone who has made a rendezvous and knows for certain that the wait will not be in vain.

That night Mariana had once again all the serenity of a slightly faded portrait, piously treasured.

She had also regained her transparency, but the light within her was as pale and cold as a sun which abandons its attempt to pierce a December mist.

●　.

PART THREE

XXVIII

THERE was another hour of daylight left when they reached the top of the last row of vines. The sun was still full on the slope, and a spur of a small wood of alder-trees kept off the fresh wind blowing across the slopes.

"We're ahead of time," said old Clopineau, straightening himself up, his hand on his back.

"We've certainly done well," said the *patronne*.

The old man winked an eye in Pablo's direction and said, addressing the *patronne*, "Did you notice how the lad set about the pruning, though this is only his second spring."

The *patronne* smiled and nodded her head. Pablo slipped his secateurs in his pocket, saying, "It's you I've to thank, Clopineau. You've got the gift of teaching. You'd have made a wonderful teacher."

The old man began to chuckle. "Go on with you, and me only just able to read!"

They began to descend. Between the rows of vines the pruned shoots lay on the ground. Farther down, on the other side, Jeannette had begun to put them in little bundles which she tied together.

"Jeannette!" shouted the *patronne*. "Come down."

The girl stopped her work and rejoined them at the foot of the vine slope.

"She'll never get it finished on her own," said the *patronne*. "When we've finished the pruning we'll have to get on with bundling for a day or two, otherwise the vines will never be tidied."

She took a few steps towards the rows where Jeannette had already finished.

"You're leaving some behind," she said. "That's not the way to do a job. If someone's got to follow behind you all the time you might as well do nothing."

Pablo joined the *patronne*. A few vine-shoots remained on the

181

ground, but very few in fact. The *patronne* went over to the first bundle of shoots set down in the middle of the path between the vines. She picked it up by the withy and shook it. A few shoots dropped out. She put it down and, turning towards her daughter, shouted, "It's neither done nor not done, is it? Anyone would think it was the first time you'd ever seen vine-shoots!"

Jeannette stood still. Her arms hanging, her secateurs still open in her right hand, her bundle of yellow withies tucked in the belt of her apron, she stared at her mother without a word. Pablo saw that her chin was beginning to tremble and that her parted lips were wrinkling.

"What's left doesn't matter," he said. "They won't cause any trouble. It'd take a lot more than that to stop La Noire."

The old man had come across. "She should collect the cuttings without having to tie them," he said. "Since we'll have to lend a hand, she can make little piles, I'll do the tying, and we'll save time that way."

The *patronne* shrugged her shoulders and walked off grumbling. "When I think that her father wanted to teach her to prune! We'd have been bringing in the vine-harvest at the same time as the bundles of prunings."

Clopineau went across to Jeannette. Gently, in a soft voice, he explained to her how the tying should be done. When he had finished, to make it quite clear to her, he took her bundle of withies and tucked it under his own belt. Jeannette nodded her head and grunted. Going back to the *patronne*, the old man said with a laugh, "I'm wondering why you wanted her to learn to prune. Is it because you think I'm too old, and you want me to take her place tying up the cuttings?"

The face of the *patronne* remained stony. Looking at Clopineau and Pablo in turn, she rapped out, "With you two, she feels cushioned, just as she was by her father, and there's nothing can be done with her."

There was a moment of silence. Leaning back on a stake, Pablo rolled a cigarette. When he had finished he offered his pouch to the old man.

"Well," inquired the *patronne*, "are we going to start?"

Pablo looked at her, and then, turning his head towards the south, where the slope died away slowly into the plain, he said, "I think myself we should use the time we've gained to go and have a look at that land belonging to Mère Perrin."

182

"What good will that do?" asked the *patronne*.

"None, just satisfy my curiosity to see what it's like, that's all."

"It's been left for nearly five years," said the old man. "Can't be looking much."

"That's certainly true," added the *patronne*, "and if I'm not interested in buying it there's no point in going to look at it."

There was a short silence, then Pablo spoke again: "It would give us a chance to go home by the lower road and see how the corn is getting on as we go by. It's not that much farther round."

The *patronne* shrugged her shoulders, and then, picking up the basket which contained the remains of their midday meal and the empty wine-bottle, she set off, grumbling: "Since you're so anxious as all that . . ."

They walked quite a lot of the way without speaking. The path wound between two banks where the close-set grass was springing up through the layer of straw half rotted by the winter. The bushes were filled with squeaking and fluttering life. The day was beginning to fade, drawing across the plain a downy white mist.

They passed close to some vines where two women were pruning.

"Well," called out the *patronne*, "getting to the end of it?"

"We're doing what we can; the rest'll have to wait."

One of the women had stood up. The other woman, who was more elderly, continued with her work.

"Have you any news of your husband?" asked the *patronne*.

"Yes. He's still in East Prussia. And what about your lad?"

"Not too bad. With the parcels I'm able to send him, he's not suffering too much, he says. But they make them work hard in a factory."

"What are they making?"

"I don't really know. Something mechanical, I think, but he doesn't seem to find it too bad."

The *patronne* stopped. Then, as the other woman began pruning again, she added as she started to walk on: "Well, work hard! We're going round the lower way to have a look at our corn."

They walked on in Indian file. The *patronne* led the way, then came Pablo, looking at her broad back and the nape of her neck burned red by the sun. After him followed Clopineau, and, finally, Jeannette, who had caught up with them while they were speaking to the two women.

183

Once they were back on the road Pablo and the old man began to walk beside the *patronne*.

"There's some women who can never get to the end of their work on the land," said Clopineau.

"All the farms where one or two men are missing must be in the same state," said Pablo.

The *patronne* murmured, "Yes, we all have our share of misfortune."

"That's true," said the old man. "Of course it would be better if your man was still here and your son was back, but with us, you know, your land won't suffer too much."

"I know," she said. "I know."

Around them now there was on one side the rise of a hillside with lines of vines, for the most part in good condition, and on the other side the beginning of the flat land. Corn, oats, and barley were beginning to show. Between the large squares of different tints of green, long strips of freshly dug brown earth looked like islands of night in the evening light. Here and there a strip of land was still covered with dead weeds, maize-stalks, scattered and in heaps, with brambles straggling beside the furrows and climbing over mounds.

"You see," said the old man, "it's the beginning. If the war lasted another two years that land there would be ruined. It's certain that those who come back will have a hard job getting it back into condition."

The old man shook his head. His forehead crinkled into a myriad wrinkles, and the oblique light accentuated his features. The whole of his face seemed to reflect a deep sadness.

"And that's saying nothing of those who'll find everything gone."

"You think that the wives will sell the land?" asked Pablo.

"In 1914 there were many who hung on. But there were many who weren't able to do so. And you can take my word for it that at one time land wasn't worth much an acre. There were those who knew how to profit by it. Wars are like that: there's always some around to pick up what others lose."

They walked on silently. The road now skirted some three-year-old vines for which stakes had not yet been provided. The land was stony, but couch-grass was beginning to smother the side-rows, and shoots of brambles were showing tiny leaves between the clods. Twisted round the young vines was convolvulus

184

of the previous year, dry and shrivelled, trembling in the breeze. The old man stopped.

"That's the saddest of all," he said.

"Isn't that Léon Boisseau's last planting?" asked the *patronne*.

"Yes," said the old man, "the last."

"They still haven't heard anything?"

"No, but if he was a prisoner, or had got to England like some others, it'd be known. When the Germans came in his regiment was in the north, and apparently it was pretty well cut to pieces. With a wife like his, with her poor health, the land was done for."

The *patronne* began to walk on, saying, "She'd do better to sell while the vines can still be saved; afterwards it won't be worth much."

"What can you expect, she still hopes. And you make me laugh with your 'better to sell'. To sell, you've got to find a buyer."

They walked on. Pablo kept silent. He was looking at every piece of cultivated ground, at every vine, at every piece of fallow land. During the year and a half he had been here he had come to know most of the local land quite well. He had gone round quite a lot to work on various pieces of land for the *patronne*, all at different points of the compass. He knew all the strips of land well, but this evening he was seeing them as if for the first time. Until now he had learned to know the limits of each of the patches he had to work on, but the others had never interested him. Now he began to feel a desire to know them better. To know to whom they belonged.

He glanced at the old man several times. Finally, as they passed another vineyard which weeds had begun to invade, he said, "It's sad to see land going that way."

The old man nodded.

"That won't fetch much either," said the *patronne*. "It's too far out. Old Ravier and his wife can't get this far any longer."

After a lengthy silence Pablo asked, "You said, 'There were those who knew how to profit by it.' But do you think they should be criticized for buying land?"

"That depends on a whole lot of things," said Clopineau. "But it's always sad to see properties utterly neglected."

They arrived soon afterwards at a spot where the road was bordered by a hedge of hawthorn on the far side of the ditch. As the hedge opened on some fallow land, they left the road by scrambling across the ditch.

185

"Look," said the *patronne*, "that stretches as far as the two cherry-trees right up there."

They looked for a moment or two in silence. Half of the plot was planted with vines, and the stakes rose from undergrowth. The remainder of the plot had been neglected even longer.

"It used to be a fine patch of land," said the old man.

"Yes, and a wonderful situation. Makes you wonder why she was never able to sell, before the war."

"What can you expect? More and more the youngsters are leaving the land, and the old ones hesitate to take a chance. That's easy to understand."

"With a good horse that asks nothing better than to work," observed Pablo, "it'd not be difficult to get this far."

He hesitated, looking at Clopineau and the *patronne*, and concluded by adding, "Above all for someone like you who has already got fields in this part."

The *patronne* did not reply. The old man waited for a moment, and then, lifting his cap to scratch his head, he nibbled his moustache two or three times before saying, "Of course, there's something for and something against. Land is always land, but with this war no-one knows what the future may bring."

"The land, the land," said the *patronne*. "It's all very fine, but if you have to leave one day you can't take it with you. When the time comes to move you feel a lot happier if you've some cash put aside."

She paused for a moment, took two or three steps to avoid the dry weeds, and bent down to look at a vine.

"The vines are not all that old. I'm sure that by sacrificing one year, and by pruning them back hard, they would recover. But the job needs to be done soon."

"Exactly," said Pablo. "For heaven's sake don't delay."

He had spoken through clenched teeth. The *patronne* turned, looked at him for a moment, and then, her voice hard, she snapped, "I don't know why on earth you want me to sink money into this land. Anyone would think you didn't know what it was like to have to let everything go. If you had had land in your own country, what more would you have now?"

"Nothing more," snapped Pablo. "But nothing less either."

He checked himself. The old man looked surprised. The *patronne* took a step as if to go, but Pablo moved in front of her. His face flushed suddenly and he began to shout: "I can't see

186

what you're really afraid of! Whichever way the war ends, it will finish. And your land will still be yours. Whether you're French, German, or Chinese, what does it matter? But your hard cash tomorrow, or in a year from now, might quite easily be worthless. Your banknotes would be only worth making a bonfire of to keep yourself warm. You know that as well as I do."

He hesitated for a second. The *patronne* had not moved. She had become very red-faced, but she remained silent. Suddenly, turning round and walking back to the road, Pablo muttered, "Anyhow, it's pretty silly of me to try and explain anything to you. I'm wasting my time. I'm certainly wasting my time."

When he reached the road he slowed down to wait for the others. When they came up to him they began walking abreast, the three of them, not speaking a word.

Night was now coming out of the earth through every ditch, rut, and furrow. The sun had sunk into the haze on the horizon where a few russet clouds still lingered. The wind freshened, but it brought with it the smell of burning wood, of dung, and of freshly tilled earth. From certain fields a curious scent of grass and flowers rose.

As they passed along by the corn they halted for a moment and then went on again without a word. As Jeannette was already far behind them, the old man waited for her to catch up.

Pablo walked on, glancing from time to time at the *patronne* without turning his head. He gritted his teeth with suppressed rage. He had a seething feeling inside him, excited the more by the smell of newly turned earth around them. At each turn in the road, each tree, each hedge, there was a cry, a humming, a scent in the air, saying that all the land was beginning to live again.

Then, his fists clenched, Pablo needed all his strength to restrain his longing to shout aloud.

XXIX

DURING the evening meal they remained silent. Two or three times Pablo risked a quick glance towards the others, without even raising his head. Only Jeannette was looking at him as always with her empty, unmoving eyes. For her nothing had changed. The *patronne* and the old man sat staring at their plates.

As soon as he had lit a cigarette Clopineau stood up. "Well, it's understood," he said, "that tomorrow we deal with the vines at Rouleux wood."

"Agreed," said the *patronne*.

"Good night, all," said the old man. "I'll go straight up there in the morning."

He went out. The sound of his clogs died away in the courtyard, and silence returned. The *patronne* stood up and began to clear the table, while Pablo finished his cigarette. As soon as he had thrown the butt into the ash-tray of the stove he got up and went towards the end door.

"Good night," he said before going out.

"Good night," said the *patronne*.

Pablo went slowly up the wooden stairs of which every step creaked. As soon as he was in his bedroom he undressed and lay down. His window was open, and the breeze ran like a cool stream through the room. Pablo could feel it on his face like a cool hand. He tried to sleep, but he had too much simmering rage inside him. It was no longer the same rage as when he had shouted earlier in the day, near the fallow land. Now, above all, he was irritated with himself. He was annoyed that he had been unable to ignore matters which did not concern him. He was thinking of the early days of his life in the village. He remembered the fatigue which had absolutely numbed his mind, robbing it of thought. For a long time now his body had become accustomed to the work on the land. His hands had hardened; his back was strong. Some evenings he felt more weary than others, but he was never now an automaton which walked, which ate, which fell on the bed like a log, sinking into sleep the moment he lay down.

He turned about on his bed many times, seeking a cool place on the pillow to rest his head.

The *patronne* and Jeannette had come upstairs. He had heard the stairs and then the flooring of the landing creaking. Now there was nothing moving in the house except the breeze which came in waves over the window-sill, bringing into the bedroom the scents of the earth.

Pablo heard ten o'clock strike, then the half-hour, and then eleven o'clock. He still could not sleep. Not even that half-sleep which gives some rest. On the contrary, he thought more and more. Everything was upside down in his mind, and the sweat was running down his temples. Over himself he had only the sheet, cooled by the breeze, but even that was too much. Nevertheless he kept the sheet on to protect himself from the breeze which was heralding the spring.

He was unhappy to be no longer an automaton which does not think; he felt ill at ease also with all that the spring was bringing of life renewed. Weariness of the body is not only a cup which brings sleep, it is also an antidote. It is a remedy which prevents the sap of springtime entering the veins as the new air blowing across the body is breathed in.

For a moment Pablo thought of the stream. He had the idea of going down and bathing in it. The icy water coming down directly from the woods attracted him. But he thought of the walk, and of the staircase which would creak under his footsteps.

Many times also he saw the image of Mariana. But he thrust her away, trying to busy his thoughts with other matters.

In truth, he was no longer thinking. What was moving in his mind was something like the breeze turning about the bed. It was a mixture of everything in which nothing could be defined. For the wind was both a fragment of winter coming from the north with an after-taste of moist earth and a little of springtime, with all the scents, still indefinite, of the new life. And it was also the cold breeze of the night which gathered from here and there breaths of the warm air of the day which had remained in the slit of a ditch or behind an old wall.

There is air one breathes in, which is like the wine one drinks: mixtures make the brain muzzy.

Pablo felt all this in a confused way, without being able to do anything about it.

Outside the silence remained unchanged, but it was a silence which, however, said much. But what it said could not be heard; one could only sense it. And the silence of the house was equally heavy. It was not that of a house where fatigue had sent all to sleep.

Pablo turned over at least twenty times. He heard a half-hour striking, and then, before silence had re-established itself round the house, there was a series of loud thumpings. It was as if the house itself had begun to fight somewhere down in its foundations.

Pablo sat up on his bed. There were some other thumps, then the goats began to bleat.

"The animals."

Pablo thought immediately of fire. In one jump he was out of bed, and, slipping on only his trousers, he hurried out.

Without opening her door the *patronne* asked, "You're going to have a look?"

"Yes. What's going on?"

"I think one of the animals has got loose. I'm certain it's La Noire; she was fidgeting when I went to milk. It's the season that excites her. You need only close the main door and leave her in the courtyard. The night air will do her good."

The *patronne*'s voice was completely calm. Pablo went down. The floor was cold under his feet. At the bottom of the stairs he found his clogs and put them on. He had not put on a shirt, and once he was out-of-doors the wind made him shiver.

The mare had, in fact, managed to slip her chain. Once free, she had gone across to the goats, who had begun galloping round their small enclosure. Now La Noire was back in her box again, but with her rump to the rack. When Pablo went across she came out to meet him and nuzzled his chest with her muzzle.

"Gently, my darling, gently," said Pablo.

He caressed her for a moment, and she quickly calmed down. He took hold of the end of chain hanging from her snaffle, and, as he led her out from her box, he saw that she had lashed out at the feeding-trough of which the planking was either smashed or hanging loose. He led her out and, once in the courtyard, let her free. Surprised at first, she followed him across to the kitchen step. He stroked her again and went inside.

Upstairs, the window of the landing giving on to the courtyard was open. Pablo went over to it. The *patronne* was leaning on the window-sill. She turned round. "Weren't you cold?" she asked.

"No, it's a lovely night."

Outside there was a galloping sound.

"Come and look!"

Pablo went forward, and, leaning out of the window, he saw La Noire leaping about by the door, kicking up small bursts of sparks from the stones of the courtyard.

"Will she hurt herself?" asked Pablo.

"No, she'll just tire herself. In a moment or two she'll calm down."

190

The *patronne* moved a little. Pablo felt her against him, and his blood began to flow more quickly. The breeze had a hint of warmth in it, like a wind from the south. Like a wind from Catalonia.

"Couldn't you sleep?" she asked, turning towards him.

"No. What about you?"

"No."

They were silent for a moment. Down below, La Noire was still leaping about.

"Don't you really feel cold, like that?"

The *patronne* put a hand on Pablo's arm, near his shoulder. Pablo leaned forward slightly. His arms parted; the *patronne* pressed herself against him and their lips met.

They remained like this long enough almost to lose their breath, and then, turning round, Pablo took her by the shoulders and led her into his room.

They made love without a word, almost furiously, as if they really wanted to hurt each other. Afterwards they remained stretched out side by side, listening to the throbbing of their blood coursing more quickly under their moist skins. After a while the *patronne* shivered and sat up, leaning on one elbow.

"You're cold," said Pablo.

"A little, yes.... And I must go and shut the door of my room."

"Don't move."

He got up and hurried to close the door. When he returned he locked the door of his own room behind him.

The *patronne* had drawn the sheet and coverlet over herself. He slid towards her and pulled her to him.

"You don't find me too old?" she whispered.

"No," he said, "we're both young."

They remained for several minutes without speaking, then Pablo murmured, "La Noire is young too."

"Be quiet!" she said. "Don't make jokes about it."

"You haven't given me a chance to finish. I say La Noire is young. She is full of spirit. We are both full of spirit. We have so much spirit that it prevents us from sleeping."

"You're not going to complain about that, are you?"

They began to laugh and kissed again.

"You won't let me speak because you know what I want to say," Pablo went on. "But don't worry, I'll get round to it."

She sought his mouth to kiss him, but he struggled. Still

struggling, he went on, "And for all this spirit we have, there is land that needs it. Good soil that asks only to give. Just an effort is needed."

She gave up trying to silence him, and put her lips close to his.

"If you want land," she said, "buy it; you never spend anything, except for your tobacco. And if you haven't enough I'll advance you the balance."

"No," said Pablo.

"Why not?"

He hesitated. "For a lot of reasons. And the best one is that I haven't the right."

Taking him by surprise, she succeeded in kissing him. He let her continue, but as soon as she moved her mouth from his he said, "But if we did the opposite?"

"What d'you mean, the opposite?"

"I'll give you what money I have; you put the rest and you buy the land in your own name."

"They say that the Francs-Comtois are obstinate, but I can see that the Spanish are even more so."

"You're quite right. What's more, the Francs-Comtois have been obstinate since the time when they were Spanish."

There was a silence troubled only by the sound of the wind against the gable of the house.

"Listen," said Pablo. "I'm going to try to explain to you: you have money which is worth so much today. For example, with twenty francs you can buy..."

"Be quiet. You've already told me that. War always means devaluation. But supposing you had to leave, what would I do with all that land?"

Pablo sighed. "You think I'm going to go off."

She half-lay on him and, squeezing him very tightly, said, "No, no. I don't want you to leave. I just said that without meaning it. Even if the Germans started hunting Spanish refugees I would hide you."

"And then, you see, even if I went, even if you have to leave your land fallow, cultivate just enough for what you need to eat, but never sell your land. On the contrary, what you should do is buy as much as you can."

She did not reply. He waited for a few seconds, and then he kissed her. When their mouths parted she said slowly, as if speak-

192

ing to herself, "Tomorrow morning I will go and see Mère Perrin. I will go. I promise."

Then Pablo kissed her again, gripping her in his arms so fiercely that he almost hurt her, as if to show her the terrific strength he could feel in himself.

XXX

THE freshness of the dawn woke Pablo. He raised himself on one elbow, and immediately the *patronne* opened her eyes.

"We're crazy," she said. "It's day already."

With one bound she was out of bed and standing up in her long white nightgown which fell from her shoulders to her toes, showing only the curves of her large, strong buttocks. She went as far as the door, turned the key softly, and then, before opening, she said in a low voice, "It'll be best if no-one knows anything. We'll just go on as we were before."

"Of course," said Pablo.

She was about to leave when he made a sign to her to come back.

"Come back here."

He pulled her to him and kissed her.

"You know what you promised?"

"Yes."

She smiled again and went out. Pablo hastened to go down, and, once in the courtyard, he left his head for a long time beneath the tap running icy water. As he was wiping himself La Noire came round the corner of the house and trotted over to him.

"Well, have you calmed down?" he asked.

He laughed as he stroked her, and as he was doing so the *patronne* came out of the kitchen with her milking-pails. She went across to him and said softly, "Are you thanking her?"

They looked at each other and laughed.

"Yes. And I've been telling her she's gained something to use her strength on. A fine piece of land to get in good heart."

The *patronne* pouted her lips.

"And what about you?" she asked. "Have you still enough strength for the land? You didn't lose it all last night?"

Pablo puffed out his chest. Drops of water glistened on it, hanging on hairs.

"I'll show you," he said. "You'll soon see."

The *patronne* went into the stable. Pablo pulled on his shirt, picked up his soap and towel, and then went back to the kitchen. La Noire followed him as far as the step.

"Wait a minute," he said. "I'm going to fetch you a crust."

He went in. Jeannette was breaking vine-cuttings, which she was putting on the fire. Pablo usually said, "Hullo, Jeannette," and she grunted, with the tic moving at the corner of her mouth. But this time he said nothing immediately. He stopped and stared at the little girl. It seemed to him suddenly that he had not seen her for a long time. She also looked at him. They remained like this for a few seconds. Finally, hearing La Noire's hooves moving on the step, Pablo said, "Good morning, Jeannette."

The little girl grunted, and her tic started. Then Pablo cut a piece of bread and took it out to give to the mare.

Afterwards he prepared a snack of bread and bacon which he placed in a haversack with a litre of wine, and then he set out. In the courtyard, turning towards the stable, he shouted, "I'm going up. When you come back from seeing her come on straight up to us."

"Yes," shouted the *patronne*. "See you soon."

Pablo hastened towards the hillside, which was still in shadow and showed up darkly against the sun-filled sky. As he walked he breathed deeply. His legs felt a little heavy, but not what could be called weary. It was something indefinable which seemed to run right through his body, something which seemed a little like weariness, but taking away nothing of his strength. On the contrary, he felt very solid on his feet on the land, which was still half asleep all round him, and being awakened by the sound of his steps on the road. When he arrived at the main bend, where the road really began to dominate the plain, his eyes sought the reddish patch of the fallow land belonging to Mère Perrin. He found it immediately. It was between two well-kept vineyards and made a brighter rectangle against the shadow of the hill. Pablo smiled. He looked towards the farm where La Noire was browsing beside the wall of the barn, and then he walked on again.

194

The old man was already at work. He had pruned only a dozen vines, and Pablo thought that he could not have been there very long.

"Well, how goes it?" he shouted.

Clopineau turned round. "Well, well! No getting you out of bed, eh?"

Pablo began to laugh, got out his secateurs, and climbed up the slope. "But..." he asked.

The old man laughed. "Yes, I've worked the three rows at once; like that we'll all be near to each other."

They had the habit of beginning together and advancing at the same rate. This enabled them to talk to each other, and, when Pablo needed some advice, the old man and the *patronne* were near him. To have worked the three rows the old man must have been there quite a time.

"Nothing wrong, I hope?" asked Clopineau.

"No, nothing. But there's no need to continue a row for the *patronne*; she won't be along for quite a while. We'll certainly have time to complete at least one full row each before she gets here."

Pablo hesitated. He took hold of a vine-shoot and cut. Two, three, four snaps of the secateurs. Then, stopping suddenly, he put his hand on Clopineau's shoulder. The old man looked at him.

"What's the matter?"

Pablo stared into the distance. He lifted his hand and pointed with his secateurs towards the patch of fallow land. The old man stared.

"That's the matter," said Pablo. "She's gone off this morning to see Mère Perrin."

The old man nodded his head. "Well! well! You can reckon yourself pretty clever, you can. She's got a reputation for being very tough, that Germaine."

Pablo felt his face become hot. The old man looked away for a second, and then, staring down, he said, "I don't know how you managed it, but you're smart all right. That's all there is to be said. But smart you certainly are!"

They had begun to prune again, both of them, turning their backs on each other. After a few moments Pablo asked, "D'you think I was right?"

The old man did not reply immediately. He pruned two or three more small branches and then said, "Yes, you were right...

195

absolutely right. You are both young, the pair of you. And when you're young you can never have too much land."

Pablo tried to catch a glimpse of Clopineau's face, but the old man was bending over, only his back showing. They went on with their work without talking further until the *patronne* arrived.

They were almost at the summit of the slope when they heard her coming. They stood up straight. She must have run most of the way, and she was puffing. Pablo smiled at her and looked along the road. Jeannette was still a long way back, moving at her usual pace and carrying the basket of food.

At first the *patronne* said nothing. With one hand on a stake, she brushed the back of the other across her forehead. Pablo waited patiently. There was no need for her to say anything; her eyes had already told him all.

Clopineau was the first to speak. "I think you're getting a good bargain, Germaine. I can see by your face you're very pleased. And if you're pleased, that means you got a bargain."

Then, turning towards Pablo, he slapped him on the shoulder, nodding his head and giving a wink. "But this fellow," he said with a smile, "I've the feeling that once he gets an idea into his head he doesn't have it only where you'd think, eh?"

All three began to laugh, and then, still out of breath, the *patronne* said, nodding towards Pablo, "If I told you the life he's been leading me you wouldn't believe it. What's more, it was only to get a little peace that I agreed."

Pablo puckered his brows and pulled a face to make her understand that she shouldn't joke about the subject, then, without leaving her time to get a word in, he asked, "It's all right, is it?"

"Of course it's all right. We went to the post-office together to phone the lawyer. It's been arranged that we go to Lons tomorrow afternoon to sign the papers."

Pablo breathed deeply. He looked again at the *patronne* and turned to stare down the hill towards its meeting with the plain. When he had found again the reddish patch which was brilliant in the sunshine he half closed his eyes and murmured, "The day after tomorrow we'll be able to begin. The day after tomorrow."

Then, bending down to the next vine, he began to work again.

XXXI

THE next day the *patronne* left the vineyard immediately after the midday meal. Pablo climbed on to a mound to watch her going, and she turned several times to wave to him. The last time she stood still for a moment in the middle of the road, which, a little farther on, disappeared behind the hedge after a bend. When she was out of sight Pablo went back to sit beside old Clopineau and finish his cigarette. Jeannette was standing in front of them, her arms swinging, her secateurs open in her right hand. As soon as they stood up to go on with their work she followed them and continued to pick up the cuttings. Pablo glanced at her from time to time. She worked slowly, but seldom stopped. Sometimes she stood motionless, with a cutting in her hand at which she stared steadily. When she was there her mother would shout, "Well, Jeannette, going to sleep?"

The girl would jump, sometimes even dropping the piece of wood she was holding, and then begin working again. Pablo had never said anything, but he had noticed that Jeannette always examined the most twisted pieces of wood. As she stopped to look at another one he moved across two lines of vines and walked quietly towards her. When he was only a few steps away the little girl looked up. She had not quite the same look as usual in her eyes. There was in the depths of her pupils something like a faint gleam which might brighten. Pablo went over to her again and held out his hand towards the piece of wood she was holding. The tic moved at the side of her mouth; she grunted and gave him the piece of wood. He looked at it from all angles, holding it up to the light. Placed at one angle, the cutting looked like a sitting cat. Pablo showed it to Jeannette from that angle, saying, "Cat ... cat ... Minnie!"

As the child did not react, he repeated what he had said, and even tried to give a 'miaow'. Then, seeing that she did not appear to understand, he began to look at the piece of wood again. After a moment he showed it again to Jeannette and asked, "Rabbit? Bunnie?"

The little girl shook her head. Her mouth opened a little wider, and Pablo saw clearly the same small light he had seen before move again in the depth of her eyes. Then, bending down, he made the piece of wood move over the ground like a rabbit, jumping along. Jeannette soon crouched down with her eyes following Pablo's hand. Without stopping, he looked at her. Her eyes really were alive.

Pablo stood up and began to laugh. Jeannette grunted, and for the first time, he found that the tic by her mouth vaguely resembled a smile. He gave her back the piece of wood and returned to the vines.

While he had been close to the child he had forgotten the presence of the old man, who was waiting for him now and who watched him come back with a face all ready to smile.

"Well?"

"You saw?" asked Pablo.

"I saw. It looked as if she was pleased you went. I don't know, but she looked at you in a way I've never seen her look at anybody."

"Perhaps she's less stupid than we thought."

The old man lifted his hat to scratch his head, and then, after a long chew at his moustache, he went on: "What you're saying her father said to me quite often. But a father, well, he's a father. He never quite knows about his children; he always thinks them better than they are. However, he said to me many times, 'If I had the time to do it I could make her into a little girl who's just like the others.'"

"I know he loved her very much."

The old man looked at Jeannette and then at Pablo before he replied. "But Germaine never wanted to believe it, she didn't. And it seems to me that that's what counted."

Several times during the afternoon Pablo restarted the game with a piece of wood. He looked each time for a shape, and often he had to suggest two or three names before finding the one which made Jeannette's dark eyes light up and brought a smile to her drooping mouth. He tried people and objects in vain. Jeannette could see in the wood only familiar animals, those she looked after each day at the farm or saw in the village or in the fields.

When night approached they went down. They walked along without speaking. Pablo was thinking of Mère Perrin's land, but thinking much more about Jeannette. He was thinking of her rather like a man who has found a strange tool, certainly useful, but which he does not know how to use.

198

When they reached the farm the *patronne* had just finished un-harnessing La Noire. They pushed the break into the barn, and Pablo realized that it had not been used since they came back from Brûlis. The first time he had seen it in use was when it had taken the *patron* to the cemetery.

When everything had been put away they went into the kitchen.

"Well?" asked Pablo.

"Everything's signed," replied the *patronne*. "Everything's done. As I came back I went round to leave Mère Perrin at her house. She was very pleased. She hasn't much to live on, and now she's rather better off. In the square I met Marguerite. I hadn't the time to tell her about it, so I suggested she should come and take pot-luck with us."

She paused for a moment before adding, "As we're going to have more work, I thought I might ask her to come for a few days and help us to finish the pruning."

The old woman arrived soon afterwards, and, when the *patronne* had explained to her what she had been doing, she winked an eye towards Clopineau. "What do you think about it?"

"Me? I think they're right. It's a good thing for the young to have huge appetites."

The old woman stared at them intently, and once again Pablo felt himself reddening. He got out his pouch and rolled himself a cigarette, to keep in countenance. There was a heavy silence in the room, and all were standing still, waiting to hear what the old woman would have to say. Finally, pulling up a chair and sitting by the table, she said, "You can never have too much land, and while there are willing arms you mustn't hesitate. And now, Germaine, I hope you're going to open a bottle. I know your boy's not here, but as, after all, you're really working for him, the land you've bought had better be welcomed into the house. So, if there's to be nothing missing, you'd better open a bottle."

The *patronne* smiled and asked Pablo, "You know where the bottles of Brûlis are?"

"Yes."

"Then go and fetch one. And don't shake it too much as you bring it up."

Pablo went down. It was the first time he had touched this bin of bottles. In fact, no-one had touched it since the *patron* died, and the cobwebs tore like a grey veil when he pulled open the grille, which squeaked. The Brûlis was on the lower shelf. Pablo bent down, drew out a bottle, and raised it gently towards the light, keeping it horizontal. The wine looked clear, but there was so much dust on the bottle that little could be seen. He closed the grille of the bin and, holding the bottle horizontally, went up again slowly.

"Put it on the sideboard," said the *patronne*. "While we're eating the chill will be taken off."

They sat down at table. During the entire meal they talked a great deal. About the war. About the Germans, who were beginning to become less amiable than they were at first and were threatening to cross the demarcation line. Above all, they talked about work and the land. From time to time Pablo glanced at Jeannette. The tiny light no longer showed in the depths of her eyes, but she seemed less repulsive. Now, even when she was eating with her mouth open, he could continue to watch her. On her neck and cheeks there were traces left in the dust by sweat which had run down her forehead, but Pablo felt that this was not dirtiness, since it was only dust which the wind and sun had brought up from the earth. Clopineau had some on his face, the old woman too, and he himself had not washed when he came back, so he must also have a grubby face.

This evening only the *patronne* was different. She had slipped a blouse on above her grey Sunday skirt. Her embroidered collar showed the beginning of the separation of her breasts. She had no make-up on, her face was in repose, and her matt skin was clean. She had drawn her hair back in a bun, and not a wisp was showing on her neck. Several times their eyes met, and each time they were eloquent about many things the others could not guess. At one moment Pablo glanced at the clock, and then winked an eye in the direction of the old people. The *patronne* smiled and went out to fetch the cheese.

"I think the time has come to open the bottle," she said.

"This is indeed the moment," agreed Clopineau.

The *patronne* put the bottle and corkscrew in front of Pablo, who began to break the yellow wax seal with great care. When he had done that and was turning the corkscrew old Marguerite nodded her head, saying, "He knows how to do it."

Then, as he was filling each glass, she added, "Look, waiter, don't you know that's the boss's job?"

Pablo began to laugh. His face felt warm again. The *patronne* hastened to lift her glass and drink to the new land.

"And to the return of absent ones," said the old woman.

"And also to the end of the war," added Clopineau.

They talked about the wine. They talked also about the land. The *patronne* and Pablo continued to look at each other often, but they were less in a hurry now. The wine had to be finished, and they knew very well that a bottle of Brûlis is not drunk like a litre of rough, red wine.

At one moment, when the old man was speaking of the work wine demanded and of how things were affected with fewer and fewer men in the villages, Pablo stood up without a word and went to his room. The others looked at each other, and they were still looking surprised when he came back. He put on the table a thick catalogue which he began to open.

"Where did you find that?" asked the *patronne*.

"In the bedroom; it was on the chest of drawers; there's a stamp on it. Must come from the agricultural school where your son was taking a course."

"Surely."

They all looked at each other.

"And that's what we need," he said, pointing to one page.

"Whatever is it?" asked the old woman.

"Surely you can see, it's a wine-press."

"A press? Looks like nothing on earth."

Pablo began to laugh. "Everything's very clearly explained," he said. "You see this large, round wooden cage?"

"Yes, like a press lying down, but longer."

"That's just what it is. Only it turns on itself. Then as it turns the discs at each end move towards one another. That squeezes the grapes inside, and the juice runs into the big container below."

"And how d'you get it out of there?"

"You don't have to get it out," explained Pablo; "it comes out itself. Attached to the electric motor which turns it there's a pump, and, you see, you put this piping in the container and it's done."

They all looked at him for a moment or two without a word, and then the old man said, "Well, if I understand it properly, you only need a man to watch it."

"Not even that. When it finishes and there's no more juice the motor shuts itself off."

Marguerite began to chuckle. "That sort of gadget's all very fine on paper, but it costs a fortune, and once you've got it in your cellar you find it's useless."

"Surely not," said Pablo. "In the Bordeaux region apparently all the big cellars have them."

"Who told you that?"

"It's in another book in the bedroom."

"Did your boy talk about it?"

The *patronne* shook her head.

They went on arguing for a long time, but the two old people would not give way. For them a wine-press was a wine-press, like those there were in every cellar in the village.

"But don't you see," said Pablo. "You bring in the grapes, you press the lever, settle down to a quiet meal, and then go to bed. Then, while you sleep, all the work is done."

"That's all very well," said the old woman. "But I don't know how anyone could sleep with a machine like that going round and round in the cellar. Not me, anyway! I'd be too frightened that the thing would run wild and bring the house down."

The wine had made them gay, and all four of them burst out laughing. Then the two old people got to their feet.

"Don't forget," said Clopineau, "if you want us really to get down to it on your new land tomorrow morning, this is no time to spend the whole night at table."

The old people went out, and as soon as Jeannette had gone up Pablo and the *patronne* kissed each other.

Tomorrow there would be land to clear, but they felt that they could not wait till daybreak to use the energy given to them by the wine so warm inside their bodies.

XXXII

They had agreed that all five of them would work, and the following day the dawn had scarcely shown in the sky before Clopineau was there. Pablo had just finished washing under the tap in the courtyard.

"We're going to have the weather we need," said the old man.

"Some bright sunshine and a bit of a breeze to keep it from getting too hot."

"You think so?" asked Pablo.

"I'm certain. You'll see; the breeze'll come up with the sun."

The old woman arrived soon afterwards, and Clopineau asked her, "What sort of weather are we going to have, Marguerite?"

She did not even bother to glance at the sky. "Good weather for working," she replied.

"You see, Marguerite thinks so too."

Pablo turned towards the woman. "What d'you mean exactly?"

"Well, a fine day with enough wind to freshen you up and blow away the dust."

"You'll have to teach me how to know the weather."

"It's easy," said the old man.

"Tell me what makes you say the breeze'll come up with the sun."

The two old people looked at each other, and it was Marguerite who replied, "My word, a whole lot of things, and nothing. You see, you feel it. The light dew, the colour of the sky, the air, I don't know, things like that can't be explained."

The old man nodded in agreement.

As he dressed Pablo stared at the hill, the sky, and the plain. He took little sniffs of the air, like a dog on a trail, but nothing told him that a breeze would come up with the sun. Then he looked at the two old people with a touch of envy in his eyes.

Immediately after breakfast they harnessed La Noire to the open cart. They loaded the plough, picks, forks, secateurs, saws, and the basket containing lunch. Once all had been loaded the *patronne* shut the farmhouse doors, and they all got on the cart. They sat on the tail-board, legs dangling, and the old man took the reins.

The sun was not yet up, and the sky was just beginning to turn yellow along the irregular line of the hill. The last traces of night still lingered, and there was no-one in any of the fields. From every house-top a thin line of white smoke was rising, and these clear threads seemed to be the only life on earth.

La Noire went at her regular pace, pulling along the cart which lurched like a boat. Nobody spoke. Marguerite seemed to be dozing, Clopineau and Jeannette did not take their eyes from the shining rump of the mare, whose nostrils were steaming. Side by side, the *patronne* and Pablo glanced at each other from time to time. At one moment she leaned towards him to whisper in his ear, "I'm absolutely all in, dead-beat."

He smiled. He too could feel in his limbs the strain of the night, but he could also feel a deep strength dormant in him, ready for anything. He opened his hands, looked at them, and felt his corny palms. Then he turned round and looked at the plough, the chains of which were clanking. The ploughshare gleamed like a little bit of sky set down on the cart.

They went as far as the fallow land without a word. When they reached it the sun was not yet in the sky. It could be felt, quite close, but Pablo thought he would have time to take La Noire from the cart and harness her to the plough before it showed. He had suddenly thought of this, and it seemed to him to be very important. He would force the coulter of the plough into the soil at the very moment the sun showed itself. The sun would be the signal. He would watch, and when he saw it appear he would shout "Hup!" and he would press on the handles with all his strength.

Pablo pushed the plough forward, and the *patronne* held it so that it could be let down.

"Wait," shouted the old man. "I'm coming."

"Unhitch the mare," shouted Pablo. "Unhitch her."

The old man began to loosen the straps of the belly-band. "Anyone'd think you'd got a fire in your pants," he said, with a laugh.

Pablo had already pushed the plough to the beginning of the first row. The *patronne* watched him with a smile.

Now La Noire was in place. They hooked up the traces, and Pablo, passing the reins behind the nape of his neck, stayed there without moving. On his neck he could feel the cold of the leather which would be burning him later. The old man remained a few seconds without saying anything. La Noire, at first still, was tugging now, stretching her neck to reach a tuft of wild oats of which the green tips were showing through dry brambles.

"Well," said the old man, "what are you going to do?"

"It won't be for a few moments yet," said Pablo.

He continued to stare at the summit of the hill. He had located exactly the point where the sun would show. This was just between two clumps of acacias which seemed to be running along the crest and letting the yellow light be seen between their slender trunks. The others did not understand. The *patronne* and

204

the old woman also came over. Sensing that he would have to give some explanation, Pablo, without taking his eyes from the two clumps of acacias, asked, "So, it's understood, eh? You'll do just as I said. I'll go up once, to make a start, and you'll do the rest with the picks and then give a final raking to clear the rubbish."

The crest was lighting up. Pablo became silent. Still time to count four. The yellow was turning to white. Pablo's heart was thumping. The others had not yet understood exactly, but they must have felt that this was a very important moment. A serious action. They did not know, but they kept quiet, a little as if they were in a church at the moment when they should bow their heads.

"Hup! Hup! La Noire!"

It was done: the fire began to show between the legs of the animals poised on the crest, the sun appeared, showing the very tip of its polished top like a shell. The mare stretched her neck and tensed her haunches. Her hindquarters swelled, moving under her skin which glistened with golden glints. There was a crackling sound, as if a fire had been lit.

Everything was in this crackling. The scrub crushed by La Noire's hooves crackled like brushwood; the wood of the plough groaned like a log in a fire.

Pablo had raised himself on his toes, all his weight on the plough. His strength welled up from his loins. He felt it rising through his body, moving into his shoulders like a stream disturbed by an eddy and going down through the veins of his arms into his hands. From them it passed into the wood of the handles which were vibrating. The whole plough quivered with his strength; it was his strength, there before him, in this shining steel which would open a long wound in the earth. The plough was alive with Pablo's blood and the blood of La Noire. These three were a single force biting into the soil.

The earth was hard and firm, and the weeds spread traps over every foot of the ground. The mare moved slowly, but she never stopped. The brambles wound round the coulter, tangling up the plough, but La Noire tensed her shining hindquarters and broke them off. All the old vines shook, and it was as if a signal had flashed ahead along the wire, to tell the brambles: "Look out! Hang on! Here comes someone who doesn't spare his elbow!" But the warning was wasted. La Noire went forward, weeds up to mid-leg, like a ship moving through smooth water.

205

She continued like this, in one long pull, to the top of the slope.

There, only there, Pablo looked up.

The sun was shining on the hill. It had half swallowed the acacias, which now looked afire. Large patches of gold glittered all down the slope to float round Pablo among the vines where everything was moving. The breeze had risen. Pablo had not noticed it; he felt it only now as he turned sideways to get a breath of air.

As he turned he saw a shape out of the corner of his eye. He turned a little farther. The *patronne* was standing behind him, watching him.

They remained silent for a moment. The two old people and Jeannette were still at the bottom of the slope.

"Have you been following me?" asked Pablo.

"Yes."

He could not think what to say, and it was she who spoke.

"Turn La Noire. I want to do the return trip."

"You?"

"Yes."

"No."

"Yes, I want to."

"It's not a job for a woman."

"Just one row. If I don't go deep enough you can stop me."

Pablo smiled. He felt like grabbing her in his arms, but from down below the old people were staring up at them. He turned La Noire round and got the plough in line. Then, pulling off the reins, he passed them round the neck of the *patronne*, at the back. He saw her shoulders rise. She must be filling her lungs to give herself strength.

"Hup! La Noire!" she shouted.

Her head sank into her shoulders; for a moment her whole body floated from left to right, as if she was going down on one side. Then, as if the whole plough had dug itself into the earth, she bent forward, straining, filling her chest, and rounding her back.

Pablo followed a few steps behind her, his eyes on the nape of her neck where the black strap was leaving red marks.

She had a lot of jolts, but not a single halt.

When she came to a standstill at the end of the row her face was running with sweat. She was laughing. So were the old woman and Clopineau, who came across saying, "You just had to

206

plough your own row! When I saw you going off behind him I thought that was probably your idea. And you're quite right. It's a good thing to get to know with your own land."

"Yes, she's right," said the old woman. "To trace your own furrow on the first day across the new land is like having ha'pennies in your pocket the first time you hear the cuckoo."

They all laughed, but Pablo had already turned the plough and was off again towards the slope where the woods had taken their proper shape again after the sunrise.

There was light everywhere, and all over the land there was the laughter of the breeze blowing through the wild grass. Here, in the fallow land, because there were a lot of obstacles the breeze was delayed. It jumped each line of vines, falling afterwards between them, disturbing the brambles, and swirling a little way after the plough before escaping across the plain.

XXXIII

FOR five days they worked on the new land. Sometimes the *patronne* would say, "We must be mad; we're getting near the end of pruning-time and there are still four rows to be done. We'd have done better to have finished off there."

But Pablo insisted on continuing. He joked, saying that with youngsters like Marguerite and Clopineau a couple of acres became no more than a pocket handkerchief. Everyone laughed and set to work even harder.

Five days from dawn to sunset. Five days battling against the weeds clinging to the earth and the vines, replacing broken or frail stakes. Finally, at the end of the fifth day when they were going back, before crossing the ditch separating the vines from the road, they remained still, without speaking for a moment. The sun had disappeared, but there was still light enough to see the rows as far as the cherry-trees. They remained silent. The old man spoke, finally: "It's fine," he said. "It's much better than I'd expected. He'd have to be a very clever fellow who could say to me now, after looking at those vines, 'They remained untouched for more than five years.'"

It was true. The land was clean. Even the shaky stakes had

been replaced. The light wood of the new ones made bright marks which could be seen going farther and farther, like buoys marking a complicated route on a calm sea.

Of all the weeds and rubbish there remained only a huge heap of ash, still warm, in the centre of the field adjoining the vines. Pablo had even ploughed the level land that was not planted with vines.

"That's a good thing too," said the old man, pointing to that part of the land. "You've turned it all over; you won't sow anything till a year's passed, but you'll turn it over again and all the weeds will be well and truly dead. It'll be a good, clean piece of land, rich and well rested when you sow it. Myself, I'd put clover down. I'd leave it two years, and then I'd plough it in, green. They can say what they like, but it's the best way of manuring."

They took the road towards the house. On the cart they had the old stakes which would still make good firewood. During the last part of the journey, each time they passed a strip of land belonging to the farm the old man would say, "Your wheat's looking fine, but next year I'd plant potatoes here."

They would go on a short distance, and he would speak again: "Look at those vines; they're making too much growth. Better have a look at them in daylight."

Pablo laughed. "You're quite right, but I wonder how you manage to see it as late as this."

For night had fallen. They were keeping on the road because La Noire could find her own way, but all round them there was nothing but a vast plain of shadows, stretching as far as the edge of the sky, where there was still a tiny hint of day. On their right the hill looked like a hunched-up, formless mass. Ahead, as they approached slowly, the village could be distinguished by a strip of light from a poorly blacked-out window. From time to time a door opened, suddenly throwing a large rectangle of golden light which had quickly vanished. They all pulled the leg of the old man, who continued to comment on the fields and vines beside the road.

"You can laugh," he said. "But if I talk about land it's because I know it like the back of my hand. When I go past a piece of land I always ask it if there's any news, and since I came along this way this morning I can tell you how it is, whichever piece you like to name."

He pretended to be annoyed, but he was happy. Pablo could

208

feel it, and encouraged him to talk. He loved to hear him talking of the land. First, because what he had to say was useful, and there was also the pleasure of listening. The old man could talk of nothing except the land, but at least he spoke well. Words came to him like a clear spring leaping from the rock. Sometimes Pablo found himself listening without paying any attention to what was said. It was like music, between day and night, between wind and sky. Pablo let himself dream, feeling to himself that it was the dying day which was accompanying him and telling him stories. The others were also listening, and it was not till they came to the first house that the spell was broken. At that time many had finished milking and were moving churns into store. When the cart passed them they would call out, "Well, well! Look at the night birds! Like us to lend you a lantern? Just look, they work blind now!"

They laughed. They all laughed, on both sides, but sometimes Pablo sensed a little jealousy among those who had men away at the war.

He thought of this sometimes, but never for long. Work held him, hardly allowing him time to breathe. Also he had his eyes on other land. He now knew all the land in the district, and he knew those who risked having to sell one day. He never spoke of it. He was like a cat which waits because it is its nature to wait rather than to chase.

Here the earth had to be given the labour it demanded—the utmost arms could give. After that there was the wait for harvest-time, and nothing could change the time for preparing the *sapines*. All that could be done was to hope that they would be well filled and that, from year to year, more and more would be needed.

But no-one thought of this. It was there in the evening and the wind; in all that happened on the land in the twilight hour. It was written or whispered somewhere, but in the secret language of the vines and of the furrows, where the wind rests a second before leaping in one long flight to where the sky rests on the earth.

Pablo had, in addition to his work on the land, another task almost every day: the *patronne*, like all who lived here, wanted "to put something by". Each time that a barrel of wine, a calf, or some goats were sold she looked at the banknotes, counted them many times over, and went up to her bedroom. For her no

209

investment was sure; she preferred her wardrobe. Then there was an argument, a wrangle, a dispute, or a harping on the subject. Each time Pablo struggled anew, and each time some part of the notes became a plough, a strip of land, or a new machine.

The *patronne* always finished by giving way. There was something young and lively in her, something which helped her to understand. But as a counter-balance, she had an eye which wandered always towards the wardrobe, where a pile of sheets hid a pile of notes. The difficulty was to get her to admit that a note might lose all its value in a few hours. Even when she admitted Pablo's argument she did not seem entirely convinced.

The old man also did not always understand. Each time that he saw fresh equipment arrive, or a new strip of land added to the others, he would say, "The money! It's good. It's very good. I'm all for buying land. But you should always put something by for a rainy day."

Pablo smiled. What the old man thought was of no importance.

Time slid by smoothly, one season pushing another along, one piece of work begetting others.

All round were other men who were also working hard, but farther off there was the war. The papers were full of it, people talked of it, letters spoke of it, but it was far off. The war had left them aside, and the sun rose behind the hill and sank beyond the plain without seeing it. The war was beyond the horizon, and the breeze blowing between the rows of vines smelled only of the warm odour of stables and the friendly smoke of wood-fires cooking an evening meal.

All the evenings were one long evening, and the days one long, single labour. Even when the weather was bad the days were filled with jobs needing to be done inside the house which had accumulated during the weeks of sunshine.

Sometimes, on wet evenings, when Pablo came earlier to sit in the kitchen, he would keep the fire going so that the mash for the animals kept boiling. When he took a log from the basket he liked to look at it. He questioned it, and before giving it to the big kitchen stove to devour he made it tell him its story. Some logs knew the smallest secrets of the woods. The life of creatures whose passage was marked on the bark. Here it was teeth-marks, there peck-marks, elsewhere it might be the silvered trail of a snail. On other logs there was only the living pattern which could be a world in itself, a pattern which seemed to be everything and

210

nothing. Pablo lingered over the logs because they were something which told him everything they wanted to tell him.

Then there were the logs which had had two lives. The first, their lives as trees, were too remote to be spoken of, but it was their second lives as logs which told a story and warmed Pablo's heart, because these second lives were the simple existence of a vine-stake, but often it held a secret. A secret between Pablo and the old worn wood, split, eaten away by rain, with metal staples and the rusty traces of old wire marking it. All this showed that the wood probably came from a vineyard recently bought, where the stakes had been replaced, the trellising renewed, and the vines given a new life.

It was of no importance, but it was enough to make the song of the fire consuming that wood take on a different note.

Pablo remained for long spells listening, eyes half closed, while around him Germaine and Jeannette continued their comings and goings in the large kitchen.

PART FOUR

PART FOUR

XXXIV

THE snow began to fall at about four in the afternoon. It had been threatening in the sky for a week, but there had been too much wind.

At first they paid little attention to it, but as the flakes began to sting their necks and ears they looked to the north.

"I think we're in for it," said the *patronne*.

"Yes," agreed Clopineau. "And you know what they say, 'When there's wind with snow, you never know.'"

"I thought it meant that there might be a lot of snow or very little?"

The old man hesitated and looked at the *patronne* before replying. "You're joking. Of course, it can mean almost anything, but I think it means 'No-one can tell how long it'll last.' And that's true. When it comes like this, fine and thick, without stopping the north wind, you never can tell what will happen. Everything becomes confused, and it takes a clever one to foresee what'll come."

Pablo looked round him. The snow was flying between earth and sky without settling, and yet the ground was already white. The horizon had been blotted out and the plain had disappeared. It was difficult to see as far as the end of a row of vines before everything dissolved, becoming white and grey, earth and sky confounded.

They picked up the roll of wire, the hammer, and the staples, and then took the road to the village. They walked along without talking, heads tucked into their shoulders and leaning a little to the right, the side from which the wind was coming.

As they arrived in sight of the house the old man said, "I don't think it matters now; the worst of the job's done. And now you've got some vines you'll be making wine when I'm pushing up the daisies."

"You're probably right," said the *patronne*, "but in any event you'll certainly drink some of the wine. With the plants we've put in, and with land like that and all the work we've done, I'd be very surprised if we don't get good wine."

In the courtyard the snow was swirling round and piling up against the house. At the angle, where the wind was diverted by the stonework, the ground was free of snow.

They kicked their boots against the doorstep and, as the *patronne* opened the door a gust of warmth, smelling of woodsmoke, swept into their faces. During the very cold days, when the three of them wanted to go out together, old Marguerite would spend the afternoon with Jeannette. She would bring her knitting and settle down beside the fire. It was very pleasant for them to find the soup warm and the table laid when coming back to the house.

But this day they were too early: the old lady had not begun to get anything ready for the meal. When they came in she looked at them without getting up from her chair. Her dry old hands were resting on her knees, and her knitting was lying in her lap. She was not as alert as in other days, and her eyes were vague as she looked between her half-closed eyelids. This evening she was staring at them as if they had returned from a long journey.

They shook their clothing and went towards the fire, hands held out. Then, without standing up, the old woman asked, "Did you see him?"

They looked at each other. She went on: "Henri. Did you see him?"

"Henri?"

"Yes. Pablo's friend. Haven't you seen him?"

There was a lengthy silence. Pablo looked round the room. It was already dark, and the stove threw a large rectangle of light on the floor. One leg of the table was in the light from the grate. The top of the table was brightened by the last of the daylight coming through the window. It was a cold light which seemed to slide over the polished oak without bringing it alive. At the far end of the room Jeannette was seated. In front of her she had a pile of shelled haricot beans which made a bright patch on the wood. The little girl did not move, and Pablo could not see her face. He realized what must have happened. She must have smiled when he came in. Pablo looked again at the ceiling, where small circles of light were dancing. He needed nothing more. After a few seconds the *patronne* asked, "Is it true he came?"

216

"Yes. He was looking for Pablo. I wanted him to wait here, but he wouldn't have it. I think he went to the café."

"What exactly did he want?" asked the *patronne*.

"I don't know. I think he'd had a drink or two."

The old woman waited for a moment, sighed, and then went on: "Anyhow, he now speaks French quite well. You can understand him. But he didn't make a good impression on me. He told me how the Germans made him work for them, but he managed to escape. If I understand him rightly, he's in hiding. Didn't sound very good to me. Not good at all."

"And he told you he'd come back here?" asked Pablo.

"At nightfall, he said. I told him you wouldn't be back before. I didn't think the snow would come so soon."

"It's the wind," said Clopineau. "You know how . . ."

"Yes, I know, but all the same."

The *patronne* turned towards Pablo. "Well," she asked, "what are we going to do?"

Turning to the old woman, Pablo asked, "Which café did he go to? The one in the village, or the one just outside?"

"I don't know. I didn't ask him."

"In that case," said Pablo, "the best thing is to wait for him. I don't want to go rushing round in this sort of weather."

"And if it's true the Germans are after him? What's going to happen?"

"In any case, they won't find him this evening," said Pablo. "We'll have to wait and see."

It was as if there was something like an embarrassing presence in the room. Something which had slept long and was now re-awakening. Despite everything, Pablo felt calm. He had a curious sensation: the feeling of being both present and elsewhere, of being at the same time Pablo and someone else.

The *patronne* went across to the door and pressed the light-switch. They all blinked for a moment in the light, and then they looked at each other. Pablo tried to recall the presence he had felt, but the light had chased everything away. Nothing remained. It had passed like one of those spring-time winds which are full of life but too feeble to do good or harm. So long as they are there they sow life everywhere; once they are over the enclosing hedge their passing cannot be remembered.

Pablo went and sat opposite Jeannette. He watched her for a moment, smiling. The little girl grunted and then smiled back.

217

"Have you done all those?" asked Pablo.

She nodded her head and grunted again. Pablo put his hand on the pile of white beans which he began to spread over the table. He made a big oval of them, and then made two little holes and another larger one in it.

"The eyes . . . ," he said, "the mouth."

Putting some haricots on each side of the oval, he went on: "The ears."

Jeannette watched each of his actions, and as the pile of haricots changed form her eyes became more alive. When he had finished Pablo asked, "Little man?"

Jeannette nodded her head and grunted. For a long time now Pablo had known how to read her face. When she smiled he knew that she had understood what he had said to her. Pablo could not have said whether Jeannette's manner of grimacing had changed a little or whether she had learned to understand, but for him each movement of the tic by her mouth now had a special meaning.

He piled up the haricot beans again, and then, taking Jeannette's hands, he put them on top of the pile.

"Go on," he said. "You make the funny man. You."

She began to spread out the beans. Now it was Pablo following every movement of Jeannette's hands.

The *patronne* had begun to prepare the meal. The old woman picked up her knitting again.

"What do you think about it, Germaine?" she asked, after a long silence.

"What do you expect me to think? We'll just have to wait."

"For my part I think that fellow's got trouble written all over his face. First of all, he's unhealthy, you can see that. I said the very first day: he's a man it's better not to have in your home. That sort always get out of everything. Misfortune never gets a hold on them. But as it is always with them, it falls on others."

"You can't turn people away just because they aren't big, strapping fellows," commented old Clopineau. "After all, perhaps he just wants a bit of money. You never know. Afterwards he'll be off."

"He'll be off telling everyone there's a Spaniard here," snapped the old woman. "And before a week's up Pablo will be arrested."

Pablo turned round. "D'you think nobody knows I'm here? D'you think that for more than a year, while the Germans have been in the 'free' zone, there wasn't anybody in the village to tell them? If no-one's been to arrest me it's because no-one wanted to do so. The Germans have other fish to fry at present. They've got the Americans on their back in North Africa, and here all the men in the Maquis."

"Exactly," said the old woman. "They're worse off every day. But you never talk to anyone. You're here working, without taking any notice of what's going on round you, so, obviously, you don't see anything."

Pablo remained silent. Yes, he knew that the pattern of the war had changed. He knew also that it had spread almost everywhere, but he had always tried to ignore it. From the *patronne* he knew what her son said in his letters, but apart from that, practically nothing.

"There are times," added the old woman, "when we wonder if you just pretend to know nothing about it."

Pablo looked at her, looked at the *patronne*, and then stared down. He remained like that for some time. No-one spoke. The wind shook the shutters and the door. The fire roared, devouring the logs which had nothing more to say. This evening the logs burned without telling the story of the forest or of the vines on the slope, all golden in the sunshine.

The war was here. Until now Pablo had tried to ignore it, but it had come into the room. Now he could no longer act as if he did not recognize it. He knew it, and it was this thought that occupied his whole mind, which prevented him from listening to the song of winter and the fire.

He remained like this without moving until the moment a hand tugged at his sleeve. He started and lifted his head. Jeannette was looking at him, her lower lip drooping. On the table she had made again in beans the large, white, laughing head.

XXXV

THEY had almost finished their meal when the sound of footsteps outside the door halted them. Pablo felt the blood running faster in his veins. The *patronne* turned pale. Her hands were trembling.

"There are several of them," she whispered.

There were three knocks on the door. Then a silence. Pablo stood up, looked at the entrance door, then at the stairway to his room. In the space of a second a whole film flashed through his head: he was going up, going into Jeannette's room, opening the window and dropping on to the roof of the woodshed. From there he was going through the meadow as far as the hill. The snowstorm was all round him. No-one could possibly follow him.

This happened very quickly, very clearly, but he made no move.

Someone knocked again, and the door opened. Immediately the *patronne* shouted, "Come in, and close the door quickly, it's such a cold, filthy night!"

Two men entered at the same time as a great gust of wind shining with snowflakes.

Pablo felt all his blood rushing to his face.

Enrique and the mayor turned down their collars, shaking their snow-covered coats.

"Come and warm yourselves," said the *patronne*, standing up.

They saluted her. For a moment or two everybody was speaking at once, then silence returned, broken only by the sounds of the wind and the fire. When the warmth had taken the numbness out of their hands the two men sat at the table.

"Have you eaten?" asked the *patronne*.

"No," said the mayor, "but my wife is waiting. I shan't stay. I just came with him."

"Me, I'll gladly eat, if I may," said Enrique, laughing.

It was true that he spoke French with a very strong accent, but it was easy to understand what he said. The *patronne* put a plate in front of him. She brought also two glasses, and Pablo filled them with wine.

"Thank you," said the mayor. "Your very good health."

They emptied their glasses, and then, as the *patronne* brought in the rest of the meal, the mayor spoke slowly, seeking his words.

"As I can't stay ... I should be obliged if we could talk a little now ... if you don't mind."

He looked at Clopineau and old Marguerite, hesitated, then looked at them before saying, indicating Enrique and Pablo, "I would prefer it if we three could talk together."

Clopineau wiped the blade of his knife between his thumb and forefinger and put it in his pocket. He held out his glass to Pablo, saying, "That's fine. I was just going back, anyway."

Pablo poured him a half-glass of wine, which he drank in one gulp.

"You understand," mumbled the mayor, "it's not that I want... I don't mean...."

Old Marguerite interrupted him. Standing up, she snapped sarcastically, "Anyone would think we were spies."

She went towards the door, threw her shawl over her head, and pulled on her clogs. Clopineau wrapped himself in his hooded cape and went out behind her.

"That's unfortunate," said the mayor. "Old people get upset over a trifle; there's no knowing which way to take them."

"Do you also want me to go?" asked the *patronne*.

The mayor shrugged his shoulders. "Of course not," he said. "I know you're not one to rush off gossiping to everybody. Only old people, without meaning any harm, often say more than they intend to."

"You might have put it to them differently."

The fat man sighed. "If you think it's easy for me!"

The *patronne* had filled Enrique's plate with soup, and he was eating very calmly, as if all that was being said had nothing to do with his presence there. The mayor looked at the three of them, coughed twice, and then said, "I haven't the time to explain everything to you. He will tell you what happened. What interests me is that he mustn't stay here. Too many people know about him already. He should never have gone to the café in the first place and talked to people he didn't know. Especially the café on the main road. In the big room, when I arrived, there were a lot of fellows from Lons I didn't know. Hadn't any idea who they were. No, that was something he shouldn't have done."

As he was speaking his voice rose, his face reddened, and he began to wave his plump hands.

Enrique stopped eating for a moment, looked him straight in the eyes, and almost shouted, "Are you going to shut up? I've already told you that your speeches turn my stomach."

Then, quite calmly, he began to eat again. The mayor had become silent. Pablo looked at him for an instant and said, "Monsieur le Maire, I think you should explain to us what you want. What's done is done; there's no point in going back over it."

"No, but if tomorrow the Gestapo comes looking for him and it's known that I was in contact with him, it's me who'd be in the cart."

Enrique began to laugh. "You need only do the same as me," he said. "Join the Maquis. That'd make one more."

The mayor clenched his fists. The muscles of his jaw swelled beneath the skin. "I don't need any advice from you. I know where my duty lies. I have the responsibility for the district, and ...and..."

He stopped, stared at them one after the other, and then added: "And the Maquis have no complaints about me. If it was otherwise I wouldn't be here, nor you either."

Enrique turned to Pablo and said in Catalan, "This big blockhead expects a medal for bringing me here from the café! What a clown!"

Enrique laughed. He had obviously had a lot to drink.

"What's he saying now?" shouted the mayor.

"Nothing," said Pablo. "He's had a few drinks, that's all."

Enrique frowned and clenched his fists, turning towards Pablo. But Pablo remained calm, looking at him with a smile.

"Eat up," he said. "It'll do you good."

Enrique cut himself a slice of bread and began to eat his potatoes.

"Well," asked Pablo, "what exactly is he to do?"

The mayor coughed again. "Well, it's like this. He wants to join the Resistance. I'm all in favour, but it's something you have to show a bit of discretion about. But as for me, as I said, I'm all in favour. I can tell him where to go, but with him not knowing the countryside, in the middle of the night with the weather what it is, he's certain to get lost."

"But he doesn't need to go right now," said the *patronne*. "They aren't going to come looking for him tonight, are they?"

The mayor started to shout again: "Ah! No, no! No more talk. I don't want him around any longer. He might keep quiet, that's to be seen, but talkative as he is, it's hardly likely!"

Enrique went on eating, sneering from time to time and muttering insults in Catalan.

"And where are you thinking of sending him?" asked Pablo.

"Up near the Epaisses Wood, on the plateau."

The *patronne* began to laugh. "And you expect him to go up there tonight? You can't be serious. It's a good ten miles, even taking the short cuts, and what's more, you need to know them well!"

"There's no question of that; he need only go up to the place where wood is being cut at Vaux. There are empty huts there where he could spend the night. Tomorrow he'd have plenty of time for the rest of the journey. Don't you see, once he's up there he won't be taking any risks. Particularly if he goes while it's still snowing. His tracks will be covered immediately. Afterwards it'll be another matter."

"D'you hear him?" sneered Enrique. "He thinks of everything. Got a brain, that chap has!"

Once again he had spoken in Catalan, and the mayor stared at him, choking back his anger. "I risk getting slung in jail for him, but despite that, he doesn't give a damn for what I say."

"It's not that," said Pablo. "He's just joking, so don't pay any attention to him; he's always like that."

"Listen," said the mayor. "I've no time to waste. If the Germans start looking for him they'll come here. As far as I'm concerned, I shall know nothing. I brought him to you because this is where he used to work, and that's all. For the rest, you'll have to manage the best you can. But it's certain they won't be satisfied with a glance at your false identity card. They'll set about finding out who you are, and when they know you're Spanish also you'll be in a pretty hole. So the best thing, I think, would be for you to go with him."

Pablo stepped back a pace. He was about to speak, but the *patronne* snapped, "He should go to the Maquis with Enrique? Are you in your right mind?"

The mayor looked at her, smiling and nodding his head.

"It won't suit you at all; I know that."

The *patronne* was worried; very quickly she recovered herself and shouted, "I don't give a damn for what you think. What happens in my house is no concern of yours. I need my foreman because my husband is dead and my son's a prisoner. And that's that!"

This time the mayor exploded. Standing up suddenly, he slapped the table with the flat of his hand, shouting, "And I don't give a tinker's cuss for what goes on here, but I'm not going to tolerate any longer having a man in the village who's no right to be here. I've been too weak. If there's trouble for all of us because of him I'm the one who'll get the blame."

When the mayor struck the table Jeannette had begun to sob. Pablo stood up, went across to her, and, taking her by the hand, led her to the door to the stairs.

"Go up to bed," he said to her gently. "Go up quickly, and don't cry. It's nothing. Don't cry."

Jeannette went up sobbing, and Pablo walked back to the middle of the room.

The *patronne* and the mayor, standing on either side of the table, were staring at each other. Enrique was eating steadily, looking at them from time to time without interrupting his chewing.

"I don't think you'll get anywhere," said Pablo. "We've got to give some thought to this."

"There's nothing to think about," retorted the mayor.

Enrique interrupted: "He's right. You've got to come with me; that's the only possible way."

Pablo stared at Enrique, but it was the *patronne* who spoke. "Why are *you* interfering? If you'd never come we wouldn't be in this difficulty."

Enrique turned to her and laughed. Then he shouted in Catalan, "If we hadn't come, some four years ago, you wouldn't have a Spaniard in your bed every night."

"Enrique!" shouted Pablo.

"What did he say?" she asked.

"There's no need to make a drawing," went on Enrique, still in his native language, but turning towards Pablo. "But what does it matter? What we've got to do is to get rid of that idiot. After that, we'll see. So tell him you're coming with me. Ask him to explain where we're to go and tell him to hop off. Afterwards, I'll be able to look after myself."

"What's he talking about?" asked the mayor.

Pablo did not reply. He reflected for a moment, and then, turning to the mayor, he said simply, "My friend's right. I'm going to leave with him."

"No!" shouted the *patronne*. "You've no right to leave me. I won't be able to find anyone for the work . . . my son is a prisoner."

Then she stopped suddenly. Her face became contorted. Her chin trembled, her harsh stare passed from Enrique to Pablo, and then to the mayor, before returning to Pablo. There was a long silence. Pablo put his head down and said in a very low voice, "I must go. . . . That'll be best. I must go."

The *patronne* was on the verge of tears. Anger made her face hard. Her thin lips moved all the time. Almost without parting her teeth, she snapped, "You're a lot of cowards. Women who're left alone can only starve to death ... can only sell their land."

"We will help you..." stammered the mayor. "I'll see if I can find someone."

The *patronne* stared at him. Her moist eyes shone with hatred. The mayor looked down. Pablo had continued to look at her. As soon as she turned towards him he winked one eye twice, saying, "You must try and understand, *patronne*. We don't realize it ourselves, but it could be dangerous for the village if I'm here."

She did not reply immediately. Her face changed slowly. Pablo winked again, and he nodded towards the mayor. The *patronne* sighed and sat down. The mayor lifted his head and looked at them in turn. Now it was she who was staring at the table.

"I know it's hard," said the fat man, "but things can't go on as they are. All the village knows. Even the gendarmes know he is a Spaniard and that I gave him a false identity card. They'll keep quiet, of course, but it only needs some idiot to let out one word and everything will be in a mess. You must understand, Germaine, the way things are the war can't last much longer, so it's better to try to avoid complications."

The *patronne* said nothing. Her forehead had become flushed. As soon as the mayor grew silent she stood up and went to the door at the end of the room.

"If he's got to go I'd better put some things together for him."

She went out. The wooden stairs creaked and then became silent. The fire, on which no fresh logs had been placed for some time, was no longer singing. The three men were silent. After a few seconds Pablo decided: "I must go up too to get my pack ready. I'll get you to tell me about the road to take and who to contact, then you can get off home."

The big man leaned on the table and put a finger on the polished top. "You know the road to the Moulin wood?"

"Very well."

"You take it right to the top."

He stopped suddenly, took his watch from the pocket of his velvet waistcoat, and then, shrugging his shoulders, he went on: "Lord! Here it is, almost eight. My wife'll eat without waiting for me. If you want to get your things together I'll explain afterwards. Give me a piece of paper, and I'll get it all written down. Then we can go out together, and I'll walk a little way with you."

Pablo turned to Enrique, who burst out laughing and shouted

225

in Catalan, "If I understand rightly, you've won the confidence of everybody in this delightful little village."

While he laughed loudly the mayor asked Pablo, "What is he saying now?"

But it was Enrique who replied. "I was saying that back home we'd call that slinging people out to be sure that they'll go!"

Then once again he began to laugh, while the mayor muttered some words of excuse.

Pablo did not listen. He was already going out through the small low door when Enrique stopped laughing to shout to him in Catalan, "Take your time. But after the third tumble have a thought for us."

The door clicked behind Pablo, but the sound of Enrique's laughter followed him to the top of the stairway.

XXXVI

THE *patronne* was sitting on the bed. When Pablo entered she stood up, remaining silent. Her eyes alone asked: "What are you going to do?"

He went forward and put his hand on the old chest of drawers on which were piled books and catalogues of agricultural machinery. He did not speak.

Here, the sound of the wind was muted, but wild scurries of snow could be seen flying against the windows like thousands of insects surging out of the night.

"You've put the lights on and not even closed the shutters," said Pablo.

She turned her head towards the windows. "In weather like this there's no-one about, least of all on the side where the fields lie."

Pablo opened a window. The snowflakes burst in immediately with a blast of cold air. He leaned out to close the shutters. He could see nothing except the rectangle of light shining down from the window. His shadow, with arms outstretched, spread across the snow like a great crucifix. Farther away was the night, the emptiness where nothing was alive except the interminable howling of the wind.

226

Closing the window, he turned round.

"Has he gone?" asked the *patronne*.

"Who, the mayor?"

"Yes."

Pablo began to laugh. "Do you think him as stupid as that? He'll leave at the same time as we do."

She stepped forward and stood against him. "You're not going!"

Pablo did not reply. Then, taking him by the shoulders, she looked at him, saying very quickly, "A little while ago you gave me a wink. You made out you were trying to make them believe you were leaving."

Pablo sighed. "Of course. I thought I could do it. But if I come back it'll begin again. He seems determined about it this time. And after all, it would perhaps be more sensible."

"Then you're going away? You're going to fight? You'll leave me alone with all this land! With all this land you've made me buy! And I haven't even enough to pay a man till next harvest."

He had known what she would say. It was exactly what he had thought himself each time he had realized that he might be forced some time to go into hiding. A few minutes ago, at the moment he was walking up the stairs, the words and laughter of Enrique had put another thought in his mind. There was that also, of course. They slept together. It had been like that for eighteen months. And they still often made love, particularly when there was not too much work, when the land did not drain all their energy. But Pablo knew that this was not what mattered most.

"We must find a way," he said. "I must try to live somewhere not too far away. Like that, in the daytime I can work on the land, especially the plots which are well away from the village."

"Listen, you must stay. You go with them as far as the plateau, and then afterwards come back. You mustn't go off without thinking seriously about it. We'll find something."

She was speaking quickly. Pablo could sense that she was very attracted by this idea.

"We should have thought about it earlier," he said. "Then we could have arranged something."

She kissed him and said, "You mustn't go."

Pablo shook his head as he murmured, "We never have time to think about anything."

227

She stepped back a pace to be able to see him better, and then she said, "It was you who wanted all this work."

He smiled.

"What's more," she went on, "there's something else."

"What?"

"One day you told me that you never wanted to fight again."

"It isn't fighting again if you're just hiding to avoid being captured by the Boches."

"But there are those who are fighting. There were some killed near Doucier the other day."

"That was on the road."

Pablo reflected for a moment, then he added, "What's more, I'm a Spaniard. The French can't force me to fight."

"That's true, but it makes no difference. I think the risk will be less if you stay in this part of the country. On your own you'll be able to hide more easily than if you're with others. And also, if you refuse to fight, they won't want to keep you."

He began suddenly to laugh. "I wonder why we're arguing, because I don't want to go anyway."

The *patronne* laughed also, and then asked, "And your pack? I'd better get one ready, because of the mayor. You can leave it somewhere as you go along and pick it up on your way back."

"You need only take a very old bag and put in things for Enrique. He doesn't look as if he's much in the way of clothes."

"I'll put in some of my husband's old things. And then, if that doesn't fill it enough, I'll put in some old newspapers. You'll only have to throw them out somewhere on the way."

"That's fine, and I must take some food. And as we'll probably sleep in the huts, you'd better put in a blanket for me."

He moved away.

"You'll have to bring the blanket back."

"I'm going down," said Pablo. "If I stay here they're going to think..."

As he opened the door the *patronne* asked, "If you were really going, would you have gone down to them again so soon?"

Pablo grinned. "No," he said, "certainly not."

"Well!"

"Does it matter what they think?"

"D'you think the mayor hasn't any idea? I know very well what they say round here. But if only they knew how little I care what they say."

Pablo went out on the landing. Once again she said to him, "Listen."

He went back in and closed the door.

"I'm worried about how to behave in front of them. It'll be better if I don't come down. Tell them that I'm annoyed. I'll get your things ready; you come up for them in a minute or two."

"Right you are," said Pablo.

"Wait, wait...When you're coming back don't come through the Moulin valley. From the log cabin go through the woods and remain under cover as much as you can. It'll take a long time, but you'll have the whole day ahead of you. When you get up on to the crest go just above the vines and find a spot from which you can see the house. If there is any danger I'll close the shutters of this window."

"You think of everything."

"It's better to be careful. I don't think there's anything else to worry about, but all the same, there's no point in taking risks which can be avoided."

"It would probably be better for me to wait for nightfall before coming back."

"Yes, that's true. If only because of the mayor."

Pablo thought a little more. As they kept talking, something seemed to be coming back to him from a long time ago. The *patronne* came across.

"What's the matter?"

"It's not going to be much of a life, lying hidden like that," he sighed.

"We'll find some solution. You'll see. I'm certain."

Her voice had trembled a little. They looked at each other in silence for a moment, then she said, "You promised."

He nodded agreement, turned towards the door, went forward a few steps, and then asked, "And if the shutters are closed?"

"It's more as a precaution I suggested that. I'm certain there'll be nothing."

Pablo did not move. With his hand on the knob of the door, he was looking at the *patronne* with a sad smile.

"If the shutters are closed," she added, "go up to Brûlis. I'll find a way to send up someone to tell you where you should hide."

He opened the door slowly, went out on the landing, and turned and smiled before closing the door behind him. Once he was alone in the darkness he remained still for a few seconds.

Inside the bedroom the floorboards creaked as the *patronne* walked about getting his pack ready. In the well of the stairs he could hear, coming from the kitchen, the voice of the mayor and Enrique's laugh.

XXXVII

On a page from an exercise-book the mayor had made a sketch-map of the plateau, showing the position of the two valleys, the villages, and each farm. He had marked the road to be taken, showing many landmarks on the path from the hut at Vaux to the Epaisses wood. He had given them also, but not written on the paper, the name of the man they should ask for when they arrived and the password they were to give.

They had pulled on their bags. The one Enrique had was more a bundle, none too well tied, which he was able to sling across his back, and it was held by an old belt. Pablo recognized the material rolled round it; it was one of the jackets they had been given four years earlier when they left the camp. He had worn his own out long ago. All patched and darned, it was useful now when treating the vines with sulphate. His own bag was both larger and heavier, and the *patronne* had attached two very thick cords to it as shoulder-straps.

Enrique had put on a jacket which had belonged to the dead *patron* and, over that, an old, shabby pelisse with the leather still serviceable. He had wrapped his head in a large muffler. Pablo was dressed as he usually was when going to the woods on the coldest days. He knew that like this he would be comfortable.

Before opening the door Pablo turned back and looked round the kitchen. Everything was in order, and the fire was almost out.

"Ready?" asked the mayor.

"Ready it is."

"Then it's clearly understood: you'll ask for Fox on behalf of Uncle Clement."

"That's all right; we remember," said Pablo. "You're sure that the hut is in the woods immediately after ours?"

"Absolutely sure. I came through there a week ago coming back from Bornay."

230

"And you're sure also that the hut isn't occupied?"

"Quite sure. No-one has had any work up there this year."

Pablo took a step towards the door, turned about, and asked again, "The hut hasn't fallen down, I hope?"

"I've already told you it hasn't."

Pablo was about to open the door when Enrique went across to the mayor, took him by the collar of his lumber jacket, and shouted, "If you've played a trick on us and we have to sleep in the open I warn you that we'll be meeting again."

The mayor had stepped back a pace. "I give you my word," he said.

"Fine," said Enrique. "We'd like to believe you."

They were now close to the door. Enrique began to laugh unpleasantly, and then, looking at the mayor again, he said to him, "Your word! That's easily given, but if you could give me some tobacco that'd be better."

"I've two packets," said Pablo.

The mayor pulled out a packet of cigarettes and opened it. They each took one which they lit, then the fat man offered the packet to Enrique, who slipped it in his pocket, thanking him.

"I don't think you'll be short of anything up there," said the mayor.

Pablo opened the door, and they let themselves out. The wind swept in with a minor snowstorm. He switched off the light and closed the door behind them. Once they were in the courtyard they stood still for a moment, their heads tucked into their shoulders, trying to get their breath.

"Good God!" said Enrique. "You can't see a thing."

"You'll soon get used to it," said the mayor. "Come along."

They set off.

The snow was already deep. In some places, against walls at the corners of houses, the wind had formed drifts which came up to their knees. In other places the road was swept almost clear and was very slippery.

Pablo walked behind the mayor, stepping in his footprints. Enrique tried to keep up beside him.

"Walk behind," said Pablo. "You'll find it's easier."

"We'll never do the journey in weather like this."

He grumbled on again for a minute in Catalan, but as nobody answered he became silent.

In the village the wind was gusty. It moaned through the

telephone-wires, shook the shutters, launched icy clouds which seemed to be swept from the roofs. In certain places it could not be felt at all, and they then breathed more deeply, like men about to dive. Then, as soon as it whistled again, they tucked their heads in and walked, noses in their upturned collars, without breathing, almost until they were breathless.

"I'm going to leave you to go on," said the mayor.

They stopped by a wall. They could scarcely see each other. Only the mayor still had his cigarette, of which the red tip whitened with each squall. He held out his hand.

"Good luck. I think we'll be seeing each other again soon."

"I hope so," said Pablo.

"And remember," growled Enrique, without bringing his mouth outside his collar, "if you've been having us on, it won't be very funny for you."

"I'm easy in my mind," said the mayor.

They shook hands.

"How far is it from where I was working with Clopineau to the woods of Vaux?"

The mayor hesitated. "Two or three kilometres," he said, "not more."

"That's already something. That makes about seven kilometres from here."

"Once you are in the valley you'll be sheltered most of the way."

"How lucky we are!" jeered Enrique. "Doesn't it make you want to come with us, instead of staying here where the wind is blowing?"

"Let's go," snapped Pablo. "I hope we'll be able to see well enough to find the hut."

"Certainly you will," said the mayor. "It's immediately at the beginning of the cleared space in the wood."

They began to walk on. This time Pablo was leading. The snow was still very fine and dry. It opened easily beneath their boots. But for the moment the road led north, and there was nothing to break the wind which was following the hillside, whistling like a huge blade on a whetstone.

Despite his balaclava helmet, Pablo felt the cold numbing his ears. He tugged at his fur collar, but the cords of his pack stopped him from getting it as high as usual. In the pack almost half the weight must have been old newspapers. Pablo thought for a

232

moment of stopping to dump them, but the village was still quite near, and the wind here was blowing too hard.

"This is what he calls sheltered, that pal of yours!" snapped Enrique after a moment.

"Wait a bit. We'll be in the valley just after the next bend."

They walked on for a few minutes, and then, when the noise was almost enough to make them giddy, it changed. To the shrill whistling there was added a rumbling sound, far off, coming from somewhere ahead. Finally the whistling of the wind lessened and the rumbling sound came nearer. They had the feeling that the sky rolling above them was hurling a load of enormous logs about.

"Now we're in the valley," said Pablo.

There were still great gusts of wind heavy with snow battering them on one side and bursting through the trees, but they could hear them coming. It was a little as if a log had fallen from a load in the sky and had rolled down the slope and up the other side of the valley to join the clouds again the other side. When they sensed it coming over they doubled up with their heads tucked well in. The trees cracked, weeping snow and threshing all their branches, leaving on the ground in one moment all the snow accumulated since the previous gust. This fell in powder like fine salt being emptied from a tin.

"Rotten muck!" shouted Enrique. "We're going to look a regular couple of scarecrows by the time we arrive."

Pablo did not say a word. Even when his companion asked him to slow down he went on at the same pace. He knew that this was the only way to avoid fatigue.

When they reached the point where the road passed under the sheer rock-face the wind could no longer be felt.

"Wait a minute," said Enrique. "My pack's cutting through my shoulder. I want to put it the other side."

"Change it over as you go along. Mustn't stop."

"Yes, stop, just for a minute."

Pablo stopped. Enrique panted. "I don't know how you do it," he said. "I'm all in."

Pablo had started to free his pack, to get rid of the newspapers, when Enrique asked, "So it's agreed, eh, you stay with me?"

They could not see each other so well in the shadow of the rock.

"And is it true," Enrique went on, "that woman of yours was angry?"

Pablo still did not reply. He tightened the cord he had begun to untie.

"Come on," he said. "We mustn't stop; we'll get numb."

Enrique grumbled, but as Pablo made off he hastened to catch up with him.

The snow seemed to be falling less thickly, but the wind kept swinging from one side of the valley to the other, shaking the loftiest trees. At moments there were long ripping sounds as if cloth was being torn, then a time with only the scuffle of twigs being shaken. The wind must be lying quietly on the snow to rest for a moment, and then, gathering itself in the depth of a combe, it leaped out again and stung the invisible sky which wailed. Afterwards it could be heard on the other side, very far off, in the direction of the plain, pursued by sounds like a whiplash.

Beyond the places where he had worked with Clopineau, Pablo did not know the road, but he had only to go on between the woods. It was impossible to make a mistake. All that was needed was to see the open space on his right, and then he would find the hut.

The cords of the pack were making his shoulders sore, and several times he thought of the newspapers. Each time, however, he tried to keep his attention on the road. He did not want to think of anything else. There was the road going forward from bend to bend, and behind there was Enrique following, swearing from time to time and shouting, "Not so fast, for Pete's sake! I'm all in."

Pablo pushed on obstinately, without slowing down at all. However, they came to a spot well sheltered by the high slope, and Enrique stopped again and shouted, "Stop! I can't go on!"

Pablo turned back. Enrique was leaning against the earth wall and had allowed himself to sink down until he was squatting on his heels.

"You'll lose the use of your legs," shouted Pablo as he drew near.

But Enrique did not budge.

"Come on, get up! We're almost there."

"I've heard that tale before."

Enrique could scarcely speak. Pablo thought again of the newspapers. He could throw them away and carry Enrique's bag. He hesitated, his hand on the knot in the cord. Then, leaning towards Enrique, he said, "Come on, give me your bag and get up."

234

He took the bag and grabbed his comrade's arm to help him to his feet.

"I can't carry you, you know."

Enrique breathed deeply. "You're a good bloke," he whispered. "It's you who's going on, and what's more, carrying my bag."

"Come on, don't worry. I'm used to walking. Come on."

They started off again. Pablo went a little less quickly. From time to time he turned to ask, "How's it going? All right?"

"O.K.," puffed Enrique.

Pablo felt his right shoulder becoming paralysed under the double weight of the two bags. He thought of the newspapers and then of Enrique. Then, each time, he finished by thinking of the road. When his shoulders became too painful he thought of the sulphate bottle or the grape-picking. He repeated to himself twenty times, thirty times, the same phrase, to the rhythm of his steps.

"Weather like this ... in any case ... could do nothing ... weather like this ... in any case ..."

It finished by having no sense at all, but nevertheless it was a string of words which occupied his head as the road occupied his feet. After the turning there was another, and after the other yet another.

"Is it still ... far?" gasped Enrique.

"I don't think so."

"This cold ... Can't get my breath ... and at the same time I'm soaking ... with sweat."

"That's why you mustn't stop."

They marched on again for a long while before reaching the cuttings. Finally, by the sound, Pablo realized that the trees were less numerous. He pushed on farther. On his right the snow rose up from the road to be lost in the night, with only here and there the thin, supple line of a sapling swaying. The rumbling was still there, but it contained more distinct crackings; the nearer sounds had diminished.

Pablo left the road some twenty yards from the last trees and began to climb the side of the hill. He went forward slowly, his hands groping, searching with his feet for a good foothold among the old stumps which were hidden by the snow. Behind him Enrique was groaning more and more.

Suddenly Pablo stopped.

"This it?" asked Enrique.

"Shut up!"

They listened. The wind up there was regaining its vigour. Another twelve yards of climbing, and it would be coming straight at them.

"Well, can you see anything?"

"No," said Pablo, "but I can hear something."

Enrique became silent again, then he began to laugh derisively.

"What's got into you?" asked Pablo.

"The cemetery business ... You're going to play the cemetery lark again. ..."

"Shut up! There's no cemetery here. That noise of corrugated iron could only be coming from the hut."

Enrique sneered again. "We're going to land on a dump for night-soil or something like that."

"Will you shut up?"

Enrique became silent. Pablo held his breath. He searched the night with eyes which had tears in them from the cold. All was white, then grey, then black. And even the white was that of the night. However, each time the wind dropped a sound of moving corrugated iron mixed with the sound from the valley. They needed to know exactly where it was coming from.

Three times Pablo listened to it again.

"I'm going to sleep here," said Enrique.

"Come on. It's down there."

Pablo walked again, going obliquely to the right, towards the wood. He took a few steps and stopped. The sound was closer. Ten paces. There it was. Below them.

They went down a little way and found themselves suddenly in front of a plank door. They had not seen anything because they had climbed a little too far and because the roof of the hut was against the bank of the stream.

"We could easily have missed it."

Pablo felt for the handle. His hand first met the corrugated iron which the wind was shaking, then the catch. He lifted it and pushed the door open.

"It'd be funny if there was someone in there," jeered Enrique.

"Come on. Let's go inside."

Pablo closed the door behind them and felt for his lighter.

236

XXXVIII

First there were two sparks, then the wick caught light. They looked round immediately. The hut was almost square. The walls were of planks, and the roof of corrugated iron sloped towards the back, where there was a swinging bail covered with dried ferns. Pablo went forward. In a corner there was a small, square iron stove. He touched the rusted pipes and tapped them. A little soot fell.

"That ought to work," he said.

Enrique had gone across to a table, close to the wall. He bent down.

"There's even some wood," he said.

"What we forgot was a candle. My lighter won't last long."

"That's just it. If we have a fire it'll give us some light."

Pablo extinguished his lighter. "Let me do it," he said.

He untied his bag, put it on the ground, and began to feel for the cord which closed it. The snow had stiffened everything, and his fingers were numb. Enrique had now brought out his own lighter. He flicked it on.

"Don't bother," said Pablo. "I can manage without a light. We'd better economize on the lighters, we'll need them."

Enrique flicked off his lighter, saying, "It's damn silly that no-one thought of a candle."

Pablo fumbled in his bag. The newspapers were at the bottom. He pulled out a big handful, all pressed closely together. Perhaps the *patronne* had thought that the mayor would carry the bag part of the way. Pablo took one paper, which he unfolded, tore into pieces, and stuffed in the stove. Afterwards he put in the ferns and bark. Enrique did not budge. Pablo felt him crouching beside him. His breathing was still jerky and rather harsh.

From the hut the storm was no more than the deep growling of a torrent racing through a gorge. The sounds of the corrugated-iron door rattling and the sharp whistling of the wind driving over the snow were dominant.

"That's it. Now you can light up."

Enrique flicked his lighter, the flame jumped up, trembled, and then approached the paper sticking out from the stove. The

237

paper curled up, a more yellow flame licked the iron, hesitated, curved several times towards the interior, and, folding over suddenly, began to zigzag like a lizard between the ferns.

"Talk about drawing!" said Enrique.

"With a wind like this and a chimney which goes straight up, it's bound to."

There were, however, several blowbacks; two large clouds of smoke billowed into their faces, and then the fire really began to crackle. The pieces of bark writhed, the ferns danced before falling apart, and sparks exploded to die out on the dry earth floor. Pablo put in another handful of dried ferns, then two large logs, which soon began to dribble sap as they whistled gently.

"This wood hasn't been here very long," said Pablo.

"Who cares, so long as it's warming?"

They were sitting on the floor itself, extending their legs towards the blaze. The opened front lit all the lower half of the hut. They remained for a moment or two without speaking, then Enrique asked, "What about some grub?"

Pablo stood up and got from his pack the cloth in which the bread and meat had been wrapped. He also got out the bottle of wine, holding it out to Enrique, who uncorked it and drank a mouthful.

"God almighty!" he said. "It's stone cold!"

He stood up and, taking a long strip of bark, lit it and began to poke around the part of the cabin still in shadow.

"What are you looking for?"

"If we could find a saucepan we could have hot wine."

He moved several empty boxes, opened an old meat-safe which was full of spider-webs, looked under another upturned case, and finished by finding a frying-pan and two saucepans. He took the smaller of these and went near the fire to make sure that there was no hole in it.

"It must be dirty," said Pablo.

Enrique rubbed his hand round the inside. The saucepan was dusty. He had to get some snow and melt it in the pan to clean it; once the dirty water had been thrown away, he began to warm half the bottle of wine.

"You see," said Enrique, "I did right to tell you to bring some sugar."

Pablo began to laugh. "You're always the same," he said. "When it's a question of your belly, you can be relied on."

238

Enrique opened his bag and brought out a metal mug. "Aha!" he said. "That's something else you forgot to bring."

Pablo did not reply. Since the fire had begun to crackle he had felt a deep warmth starting to seep into him as the air warmed in this hut where huge shadows danced against the walls. It seemed to him that he already knew this hut. He had felt an impression almost of wellbeing, with Enrique warming wine for the two of them. Then Enrique had spoken of the forgotten mug, and the feeling had vanished like a dream. There was still the flame, with its song, the planks with shadows dancing on them—the planks which held the wind and snow at bay—but Pablo felt a new coldness in the depths of his being.

He looked at Enrique, who began to laugh, saying, "Good Lord, Pablo, a little while ago, when the mayor was around, I was a bit drunk. Now I feel better. You're a nice bloke. I'm glad to have caught up with you, you know, really glad."

Pablo stared at the fire. It was above all the fire which could be heard now, the fire and the saucepan, which had begun to jiggle about. Enrique remained silent for a moment, and then said, "I can understand you feeling a bit sick at leaving your woman. I can understand. It's natural."

He stopped again. Pablo was not looking at him. He could no longer take his eyes from the half-burned log lying on the cinders with lively flames leaping towards the opening of the pipe above. Enrique coughed violently several times, and began suddenly to talk more quickly and loudly.

"You know, I've had a rough time. Those sods gave me real hell. They're the same sort as Franco's lot. It'd give me real pleasure to clobber a few. They've now got all the world against them. It's no longer just a matter of time; we've got to set to seriously. In a show like this, guerrilla warfare, you can cause as much trouble as bombardments and all the rest. And it's guerrilla for us. Then, one day, when the time comes, it seems that all the civilians are going to be armed. There'll be a special signal, and in all the occupied countries, at the same hour and the same minute, everyone will get his man. In the street, at the cinema, in the cafés, everywhere: a knife between the shoulder-blades and it's finished."

He rubbed his hands, and his eyes gleamed.

He got up on his knees to reach the saucepan. "It's hot," he said.

239

He filled the mug and handed it to Pablo.

"No," said Pablo, "you drink first."

"No, no, you first."

Pablo took hold of the hot metal mug, took a small sip, and handed it back to Enrique.

Enrique also took a mouthful. "That certainly warms you!"

He put the mug on the floor between them and went on: "You'll see, as soon as the Boches are beaten everyone's going to turn on Franco. We'll be able to go back home again. And it's there that they're going to be made to understand a thing or two, those who're having a good time now. It may even happen in Spain at the same time as here. Those of us who can get there will also have their own man to kill when the signal's given."

He appeared to reflect, his hand, held towards the fire, fell back on his thin thigh, and he said, nodding his head, "If only one could choose one's own man... If only..."

He drank another mouthful of wine and passed the mug again to Pablo. "Go ahead, it's just right now."

The wine was still very warm, but it was drinkable, and Pablo felt the welcome warmth going down with a slight burning sensation.

"Don't you think that's how it'll happen?" asked Enrique.

"Certainly, certainly."

Pablo looked at the flames again, and then, handing the bread to Enrique, he said, "Take this if you're going to eat."

"Aren't you eating?"

"No, I'd rather lie down straightaway."

He stood up, unfolded the blanket, and went over to the hanging-bail. He stirred up the bracken, from which a little sweet-smelling dust rose. In a corner were two goatskins which he rolled up to make a bolster. Then, kicking off his boots, he put them near the stove, beside their bags, which were steaming, and went back to lie down. Lying on his side, he looked at Enrique, whose silhouette was outlined against the firelight. He looked even thinner than in the past. His neck was thin, and his over-large ears seemed to be parting from the sides of his head. Still eating, he was continuing to tell the story of all he had done during their separation. His volunteering for the Foreign Legion, all the trouble he had before getting in, and his flight to the south.

"You see," he explained, "I said to myself, down round Col-

240

lioure, they all speak Catalan, and I'll be able to look after myself all right. But then when the Boches came into the free zone, that's where they started. So I had to get away. I'd been told about chaps who were resisting near the Massif Central. I wanted to go there, but I got pinched at Castelnaudary, a town near the forest, when I was almost there."

"The Germans got you?"

"No, French gendarmes. But those bastards sent me to Montpellier, and I was forced to work for the Germans."

He stopped long enough to refill the mug and take a drink. "Want some?" he asked.

"No, thanks."

"Well, then I worked for them. But it was hard. They wanted to fortify the coast; they were frightened of a landing. And then one day the news got round that they were going to send us all to Germany, into factories. Then I chanced everything to get away, and I managed it."

He became silent. He had finished eating, and Pablo watched him removing his boots and making up the fire.

"Close the front," he said. "It'll burn more slowly."

Once the front was closed there were only two small squares of light on the floor, halfway between the stove and the hanging-bail. Enrique went forward, and Pablo moved aside to give him more room. They lay down side by side and pulled the blanket and their coats over themselves.

"Comfortable?" asked Pablo.

"Not too bad. We may be pretty high up here, but we can't grumble."

Pablo closed his eyes. Enrique remained silent for a moment, and then began to talk again of what he had done. Afterwards for a long time he talked about the war. Pablo did not listen to him; he could hear only the sound of the words. Words in a language he had not heard for a very long time.

He was not thinking. He did not want to think. Little by little Enrique's voice became softer, more distant, but it remained noticeable enough to prevent him from thinking.

XXXIX

W<small>HEN</small> they got up, the wind was no longer blowing, but it was cold in the hut.

"The fire's out," said Enrique.

He lit his lighter, took a piece of wood, and poked the ashes. A few red embers showed and flickered for an instant.

"What shall we do? Light it again?"

"No point in it. We've got to leave."

Pablo opened the door. The overcast sky made the snow look grubby.

"It didn't keep on all night; if you look closer you'll see there's still some trace of our footprints."

Pablo turned towards Enrique. "Do you really think they would have followed you and searched for you in the village?"

Enrique began to laugh. "A lot of cock! I just talk like that because I can see our footprints, and I think about that filthy storm which lasted just long enough to freeze us to the bone. I don't think at all about the Germans. They decided to forget about me long ago. They don't worry much about one bloke when they can easily pick up thousands of others."

While listening to him Pablo had rolled up the blanket. He went over to his bag. The moment had come to pull out the newspapers, to give the rest of the underwear to Enrique, and to say to him, "I'm going to show you the road to take," or, rather, give him the mayor's sketch plan, since they each knew equally little about the road to be taken.

Enrique sat on a box to pull his boots on.

"They're almost dry, but damned stiff," he said. "The snow doesn't do leather any good. We ought to have stuffed 'em with paper."

There was a moment of silence. Pablo did not move. His back turned, crouching down in front of his open bag, he was trying to think.

"We didn't think of it," Enrique went on. "We should have stuffed 'em with bracken."

He stood up, stamped his feet several times, and asked, "What are you doing? Need a hand?"

Pablo pushed the rolled blanket into the pack. "That's it," he said.

"Don't stick the bread in; we'll want a bite of something before we set out."

They ate, standing on the doorstep. Slowly the snow began to look whiter, but the sky remained grey. The light seemed to cling to the ground and crawl along as if unable to rise any higher than the tops of the trees.

Everywhere was silent. Down below, on the other side of the road, the forest was spellbound. For long minutes nothing moved, then there was a slither, a cloud of whiteness floated towards the ground, a branch flicked upwards. From time to time one branch would hit another, and then there would be another slither of snow, another white cloud. The branch would tremble for an instant, and then all became motionless again.

As soon as they had drunk their last mouthfuls they set out. Despite the frost the snow remained powdery, and their boots sank into it. Enrique walked for a moment beside Pablo, and then dropped back to follow in his footsteps.

From time to time there was a great loud cracking sound which echoed and echoed in the forest. Birds were rare, and since they flew low the first tree-trunks hid them immediately.

They walked for fifteen minutes before reaching the outskirts of the wood. When they came out on the plateau Pablo stopped. He had the mayor's map quite clear in his mind. It was there, opposite, they must go. To cut between the houses away on the left and the huge, isolated farm where a plume of white smoke rose directly heavenwards.

"I'd like to go over there," said Enrique, indicating the houses. "There's sure to be a café. We'd be able to have a drink of something hot."

"No, it'll be better to avoid houses. One never knows."

"Surely you don't think there are any Germans in a little backwater like this?"

"There could be some gendarmes about. And not all countrymen are especially friendly to the Maquis."

"To hell with the countryfolk! It isn't written all over our faces that we're trying to join up with the Maquis."

"Obviously not, but two men with packs, two men who don't belong locally, are bound to be suspect. People are very wary these days."

"Is that how it is in your backwater?"

Enrique finished speaking with a sneer. Pablo wanted to shout to him, "Go on alone and fend for yourself." He contented himself with shrugging his shoulders.

"Upon my word," said Enrique, "you've become a proper country bumpkin."

Pablo had begun to walk on. He could not return to the farm before nightfall; he knew that once he was on his own he would walk much more quickly. What was more, he could cut through woods, straight towards Brûlis. He had never been that way before, but it must be woods and fallow land all the way.

So he could go on with Enrique till midday. That was it. Till midday. Afterwards Enrique would not have a long way to travel alone.

Now it was enough to walk along counting one's steps. Trying to keep the same rhythm. Trying not to think of this monotonous march across this white plain.

The sky was still grey, but there were occasionally sudden changes. In some places it became duller, with almost black shadows. Pablo tried to guess at the time, but the light gave him no help. From time to time he looked back without stopping. For a long while the black line of the Vaux woods marked the horizon, thinning in places, and then, when the land incurved, the black line disappeared. The sky was now like a great dirty wall set down on the snow. Ahead of them the ground rose towards an enclosure. The mayor had indicated it on his map; they had to bear to the right. After the crest there should be the deep combe, with three farms and their pastures and drystone dividing walls.

Pablo felt that midday could not be far off. He sought a landmark. Something on this blank, white expanse. Something like an island for a stopping-place. Soon a clump of birches showed up. "There," thought Pablo. "That's where I'll stop."

When they neared the clump of trees he slowed down. The crest was now only a few yards ahead, and the small wood must straddle it.

"Shall we stop?" asked Enrique.

"At the top," said Pablo, without turning.

A few yards below the summit they entered the wood. Little by little the combe came into sight. This was certainly the place. The dark stone walls . . . the stream . . . a farm. A second. A third.

244

Each had a smoking chimney. Their courtyards were clean and tidy, and on the roads the mark of wheels could be distinguished.

Pablo stopped.

"Are we going to have a bite?" asked Enrique.

Pablo sighed. He had not thought of that. "If you like," he said.

"We'd better find a trunk to sit on."

"No, it'd be better to eat as we walk up and down. Cold can be treacherous if you don't keep moving."

They put down their bags and cut some bread and cheese. It was icily cold, and they ate very little. Pablo felt his stomach contract. Now it was over. He must not go a step further with Enrique. During all the time they remained there Pablo thought of the land, the farm, La Noire, Germaine, Jeannette, and Clopineau.

They passed through his mind, not as if in a film, but like a series of photographs. Silent photographs which seemed as frozen as was everything around him on this plateau, in this combe where there was nothing living except the thin thread of smoke which writhed upwards above each of the three roofs.

"Look," said Enrique.

Pablo had seen. A door had been opened. A man came out pushing a broom and sending up a white cloud of snow.

"He's sweeping out the stable-litter," murmured Pablo.

The man went in again and came out as before four times. Now there was a brown patch on the snow with a little steam rising gently from it.

"We'd better finish the bottle," said Pablo.

They both took a drink, and Pablo tossed the empty bottle on the snow. Afterwards he breathed deeply, hesitated as if before plunging into icy water, and then, bending down, pulled the blanket out of his pack. He also pulled out various items of clothing and put everything on the snow.

"What are you doing?" asked Enrique.

Pablo pulled out the packet of newspapers and flung it down by the empty bottle.

"What are you doing?" asked Enrique again.

Pablo stood up, looked straight at him, and then said in a voice which trembled slightly, "It was because of the mayor."

"Because of the mayor?"

245

"Yes, to make him think I was also leaving for a long while. If my pack hadn't been well filled he'd have been suspicious."

Enrique's face changed suddenly. His forehead wrinkled and his eyes half closed. He clenched his fists. He opened his mouth as if to speak, and then, after a few seconds, he burst out laughing.

"Sweet bloody hell!" he shouted. "God almighty! I'm a bigger bloody fool than you are!"

"Enrique," Pablo began, "you must understand...there's..."

"Don't bother. I understand all right. When a bloke's gripped by the short hairs he knows he can't do anything about it. I might have known it just from seeing your old girl."

Pablo also raised his voice. "Enrique, it's not that."

He stopped suddenly. There was a brief instant when the whole plateau seemed to echo these words spoken too loudly. Then the silence surrounded them again, coming from the depths of the land and running through this little valley.

Enrique nodded. His face relaxed. He pointed to Pablo's pack. "So you lugged all that stuff this far for nothing."

He began to laugh. Pablo thought that the *patronne* had told him to bring back the blanket. He looked again at Enrique. Enrique with his hollow chest, his skinny body, his shortness of breath.

"No," he said. "This is for you. You can put your bag inside mine. Now there aren't any newspapers, there's room."

They looked at each other for a moment without a word. Pablo felt for an instant that he wanted to embrace Enrique. He also had the certainty that Enrique was thinking the same as he was. Yet they finished by both looking down towards the bag.

"I'd have liked to have gone farther with you," said Pablo, "but I have to get back before nightfall."

Once the bag had been closed, he opened the map, explained again to Enrique what the mayor had said, and then helped him to tie the cords round his shoulders.

"That all right?"

"It'll do," said Enrique, smiling.

Pablo held out his hand.

"Au revoir," said Enrique. "And thanks. You're really a good sort."

Pablo lowered his head. He felt his face redden. Enrique shook his hand and moved away.

246

"If you need anything!" shouted Pablo.

"Okay!"

Enrique went through the small wood, and then began to skirt the crest to get round the combe with its three farms. Pablo watched him for a long while as he moved between the trees. It seemed to him that he was staggering a little under the weight of the pack, which gave him the gait of a strange animal, with a thin body and thin legs supporting an enormous head.

XL

WHEN Enrique had passed out of sight Pablo remained motionless for a moment. He was looking at a distant point on the horizon where everything became blurred, where the dark sky and the white land made a grey haze which moved a little like a heavy sea. Then Pablo shivered. Automatically he put his hand to his back to push up his bag, but he had nothing to carry now. His back was wet with sweat. He jerked his shoulders, turned about, and went off in the tracks they had made and which were, on all the space he could see, the only sign of life.

As soon as he saw the Vaux woods he left the track to strike off to the left. Seen from here, the forest was one single dark line, like a thick line drawn by a grey crayon, with another lighter one above it. Pablo did not know this stretch of country. There were no landmarks he recognized to give him a bearing. He walked by instinct, certain that he was going straight towards the slopes near Brûlis.

He walked with a long, supple stride, his body scarcely leaning forward. He applied himself to breathing all the time in the same rhythm. His mind was occupied only with the smooth working of his body.

In order to avoid any detour he had to climb over four barbedwire fences. Each time he took the opportunity of looking behind him. The double track of his passage stretched away straight as a bow-string. Before reaching the woods he saw on his right the houses he had already seen that morning. He calculated that the distance was about right, and he went through the clump of acacias without turning from his path. The ground was now uneven, and the descent was broken by bushes, ditches, and old cross-paths. He had to make many detours, but he was confident that he was still moving in the right direction.

Here a few birds gave a semblance of life to the woods. Flights of crows winged overhead. Soon the sky seemed to clear between the trees ahead of Pablo. It was as if a river had been disturbed and the grey had turned to yellow.

Pablo marched on. He crossed a long strip of fallow land where the weeds crackled as he trod them down. At times he was up to the waist in weeds, with brambles catching his feet. After that came another group of acacias, a slope, a hedge, and another slope with overgrown bushes, their twigs like a thousand pencil-marks against a sky in which the light was increasing. Pablo could feel its approach. He almost ran to get up the slope, went between two clumps of bushes, and emerged at the top of the combe at Brûlis, at the exact spot where Jeannette had come to hide, the day when they killed the adders. At the bottom of the combe the spring leaping from the rock was etching a black and sinuous line in the snow. Pablo went down, slipped and fell, and then went off again up the other slope after having jumped the stream. When he reached the clump of trees where they had camped he stopped for a few seconds. He was breathing hard and he was very hot. Above him, behind the line of bushes from which they had often looked at the road, the clouds had parted, showing a patch of bright sky.

Pablo walked on, and when he reached the top he stood still. At the foot of the hill the whole plain was shining: he stared at the road. He paused for a moment to look at the huge white expanse which the black roads crossed, and which the villages punctuated with purple-coloured patches from which white or black smoke was rising.

Nobody had come, so he could go back; the shutters would certainly be open. He began to follow the line of the crests, remaining constantly in the shelter of thickets or hedges.

Finally, from above a great vineyard at the point where the hill curved a little to the east, the village appeared.

The sky had clouded again, but a last ray of sun lit up the houses. Pablo did not have to look for the farm. In the blue-grey haze rising from the snow there was something like a small, still flame.

Nothing moved outside the house. The sun was causing the

248

golden sparkle on the window with open shutters. Smoke was rising from the chimney, and for a moment it seemed to Pablo that the odour of warm soup and the smell of a wood fire was rising to the summit of the hill.

He breathed deeply and remained leaning against a vine-stake, his eyes fixed on the tiny, distant light. Suddenly the light vanished. The sun had disappeared. Down below him, far away, the earth and the sky seemed almost one again.

Then, without haste, Pablo went down through the rows of vines.

He had done nothing to quieten his blood. He had not tried to get his mind clear, and yet he felt calm; scarcely tired at all. He was going back to the house at the end of the day, and tomorrow there would be more work to be done.

XLI

DURING the following days there was a lot of wind from the south and great masses of clouds which brought rain at nightfall. The downpour lasted just long enough to wash away the snow.

"The weather's with us," said Clopineau, rubbing his hands together. "It's going to be a bit of a splash, but if the wind holds the ground will soon be dry enough for us to get on."

The wind wavered, swung to the south-west, and then began to blow directly from the east. The old man continued to rub his hands.

"We couldn't have hoped for anything better," he said. "This is just what we need, and I'm sure it's going to last."

He was right. The sky became free of grey clouds, and, in one night, the wind made it bright and clear.

Pablo had to stay shut up indoors for only four days.

Four days of stamping round the kitchen like a lion in a cage, without daring to approach the window. Four days of climbing up the stairs every time there was the sound of clogs in the court-yard.

"You'd do better to stay lying down," said the *patronne*. "You make me feel giddy clumping round the fire."

She said that, but she said it with a smile. It had been her idea, and she had arranged everything, had arranged it in her mind during Pablo's absence and explained her plan to him and Clopineau the evening he returned. At first Pablo had said nothing, but the old man had immediately approved the idea.

"Brûlis, it's just right! We've got everything that's needed to build a hut for you up there where you'll be as quiet as a mouse. It's the most forsaken corner in this part of the world. I've always said so."

The *patronne* added, "And I'm sure it'll be only for a short while. As soon as the mayor has calmed down a bit you'll be able to come down again."

"Then it's not worth bothering to build a hut," Pablo said. "I'll be able to manage with the tarpaulin."

But the *patronne* and the old man insisted.

"At this time of the year we always have a cold spell and snow. That's no joke. In any case we've plenty of time to spare now."

Then, on the morning of the fifth day, Pablo left for Brûlis well before dawn. He cut across the fields, and, as soon as it was daylight, the old man and the *patronne* arrived by road with La Noire and a load of building materials.

"You didn't see anyone?" asked Pablo.

"No. After all, we've certainly the right to bring up stakes for the vines."

They had hidden the tarpaulin and tools under the stakes which would be needed for the construction. As for the rest of the wood, they had only to cut it. They could chop down trees and saw them up when they were there.

They began in fact by cutting down trees, because they had decided that the hut should be in the centre of the little wood.

"That way anyone would have to be on the top of it to see it."

They took five days to build the hut, but it was well built and solid, with two thicknesses of logs for the walls and one for the roof, which was covered with galvanized iron. They had put in a small stove for a wood fire, but, of course, Pablo would be able to have a fire only at night or, at a pinch, when the wind was in the west, because of the smoke.

Pablo sensed that the *patronne* was happy to be able to keep him with her. He knew very well that she thought more of her land than of the two of them, but he thought particularly of the vines which would really need him.

As for Clopineau, to see him taking so much trouble over this hut, and to hear him laugh and joke, made Pablo think of him as a child. He was playing at building a hut. In fact, when the building was finished, and when Pablo's mattress had been placed on the hurdle, the old man went and sat on it, saying, "You watch out. The day you come down I'm going to come up here and settle in. At least I should be sure of being able to die in peace."

So long as the bad weather persisted no-one noticed that Pablo had returned, but when work became possible again, all the village soon knew that he was passing his time among the vines. The *patronne* did not wait for the mayor to call; she went to find him. She even went several times. Then, one day, she waited an hour at the municipal offices. That same evening she went to Brûlis to tell Pablo, who was waiting for her, sitting right at the top of the road.

As soon as he saw her coming he realized that she had good news.

"Well?" he asked.

"Let me get my breath back!"

She was flushed, and her whole face was shiny with sweat.

"You came up too quickly," said Pablo. "Come and have a glass of wine, that'll do you good."

They went as far as the hut, and the *patronne* drank a half-glass of wine. Then she explained with a smile: "It wasn't easy, but this time you can come back, and no-one will say anything."

"Why's that?"

"Everything's O.K."

"I don't understand."

She hesitated a moment, looked at him, and, standing up, walked over to him. As there was only one stool, he was sitting on the edge of his bed. She sat down beside him.

"Now explain."

"There was only one way to manage. The mayor told me about it the second time I went to see him, but I didn't want to talk to you about it until I knew it would work."

"And what is it?"

"The Spanish consul is a friend of the Prefect. He'll sign your papers."

"The Spanish consul?"

"Yes, he's at Lyons, but he comes often to the Prefecture at Lons."

Pablo knitted his brows. He looked at Germaine for a second, and then said, "But he's the Franco Government consul."

She pulled a face to show that she did not understand much about all that. Pablo spoke more loudly. "You know very well who I am! And I know those people will never agree to give me a permit."

"But that's just what they're going to do."

Pablo stood up and began to walk about the hut. "But I don't want it! I didn't fight against them and I didn't get away to give in now. Perhaps they're reduced to that now to try to get men back into Spain. But I'm not having any!"

As he continued to speak his voice rose. Germaine watched him march up and down the tiny cabin, where he could not take more than four steps without turning round. She had never seen him like this before.

Since they had lived together, Pablo had never really been angry. But sometimes there was something which seemed to be disturbing him. Something which he scarcely recognized, but which he had difficulty in putting away from him.

When he became silent his face was pale and his hands were trembling. There was a long silence, and then Germaine said, "You haven't understood. You get carried away without reason."

"What haven't I understood?"

Pablo had shouted, but he broke off sharply. Sitting on the stool, his back against the log wall, he asked in an almost normal voice, "What is it I haven't understood?"

"Why the consul is doing it."

Pablo said nothing. She waited a moment, and then went on: "The mayor himself saw him at the Prefecture, and he told me exactly what was said. The mayor explained that all you wanted was to work. He swore that he knew you well and that he had never believed that you had fought."

"And he believed him?"

"He said, 'There were plenty like that who were led away, and went off in the same way because they were frightened.' He also said, 'I know perfectly well that all those who are really dangerous have joined the Maquis.'"

This time Pablo did not shout. He looked down, remained quite still for a moment, and then went towards the door. A torrent of memories rushed through his mind. The death races against the armoured cars of the Franco troops; the shattered houses; the

252

dead bodies of children; the face of Mariana, of thousands of beautiful and innocent Marianas; the camp; the rats; hunger; and then, clearer and nearer, the grotesque silhouette of Enrique going off in the snow. Skinny, stunted Enrique; Enrique the death-dodger, who went out to fight, his big bag on his back and his knife in his pocket. His knife with one blade and a cork-screw.

Dangerous Enrique!

Outside, night was rising slowly from the bottom of the combe where all the bushes were of the same shape and colour. In front of these bushes the images passed, confused, slow or quick, almost as vague as the bottom of this little valley, the colour of moist earth and twilight.

Pablo remained like this for a long time. Then, when the night had fully invaded the valley, he heard Germaine get up and walk quietly round behind him. She put a hand on his shoulder. "Come along" she said. "You can come down this evening; now it's only a question of days before you get your papers."

She closed the door of the hut. Pablo followed her like a docile animal. He did not speak; his hands were scarcely trembling. He no longer felt any anger, but only an impression of an enormous emptiness.

Around them was the land sleepy with evening, wrapped in shadow and seeming scarcely to breathe.

They walked like this to the village without speaking. For Pablo there was no more scent, no more wind, nothing living on this hillside where the winter seemed to have returned with the ending of the day.

As he reached the courtyard he stopped. The door of the stable was ajar. He went across to it. As he moved a warm odour came to meet him.

When he reached the barn he moved the door silently. La Noire began immediately to shake her chain and stamp her hooves. Clopineau, who was giving her some hay, shouted, "Whoa, there! What's got into you?"

The mare lifted her head and tried to turn in her box. Then Clopineau looked towards the door. Pablo went forward. They looked at each other without a word, and Pablo slipped between the swinging-bail and the mare. He remained there for a little while caressing and talking to her.

Clopineau had filled the racks, and now La Noire had begun

feeding. The two men left the stable, and when Pablo crossed the courtyard it seemed to him that something had awakened in the night. Something impalpable which rose from the earth.

They went into the kitchen. The *patronne* had begun to serve the meal. "Come along," she called out. "That's the third time I've told you to add an extra plate."

Jeannette went to the cupboard, took out a plate, and came back. The two men had stopped by the door, and she looked towards them. When she saw Pablo she stood motionless with the plate in her hand and grunted several times.

"Well," said the *patronne*, "have you made up your mind?"

She went towards the table. Pablo went forward also.

"Good evening, Jeannette," he said.

She grunted again, and her face lit up. She was smiling. She was really smiling.

Then Pablo went and sat down. He put his elbows on the table and looked at the steaming soup.

Opposite him, though busy eating, the old man talked to him about the land and all there was to do.

Pablo did not listen to him, but the sound of his voice was like an echo of the song of fire in the stove and the murmur of the night closing round the house, of which every part creaked.

PART FIVE

PART FIVE

XLII

THE lorry turned off the highway into a straight, bumpy earthen road, going dead slow. At the moment the road entered the wood the driver put on his brakes. A man holding a tommy-gun came across and waved a hand, saying, "O.K. On you go."

The driver changed gear.

"Well, well," said the man with the tommy-gun, "you're bringing a new 'un? With all those coming in now it's obvious that the end's in sight! There's no chance of the wind turning, they all know that."

"He's a pal of the Spanish chap who used to be with us," said the driver.

Pablo had not spoken. The lorry began to move along quickly despite the potholes and the ruts. The earth was dry and the bumping made the lorry clatter loudly. Above his head Pablo could hear, knocking against the side, the Lewis gun manned by two men standing behind the driver's cab. He looked round. A piece of vest was still fluttering against the little window, and beyond was a white cloud which hid the trees. Even the casks and the sacks stacked in the lorry were already the colour of the road.

"Soon be there," shouted the driver.

There were three more turns, and then a crossroads guarded by four sentries. The lorry slowed down, took the road to the left, and stopped in front of a house built in a clearing. Behind the house two tractors and three lorries were parked under the trees. The driver turned and backed in beside them.

"Always have to park like that," he explained, "ready to drive off. You never know when there might be an alert."

The lorry stopped. Pablo and the driver climbed down. The man with the tommy-gun had already jumped down, as had his companion, who went straight into the house.

"We unload this lot?"

257

The driver jeered. "You're cuckoo! That's not our job. They'll send a fatigue party to shift that lot."

Three men had come out of the house. The driver went towards them, and then, turning round, he asked, "Are you going up to the camp?"

"Yes," said the man holding the tommy-gun.

"Then take this new chap with you."

Pablo picked up his pack, hitched it over his shoulder, and followed the man. They took a path which went up through the woods. Soon they could hear many voices and noises of cans and saucepans. The ground levelled off, and Pablo saw the first tents between the trunks of oak-trees. In front of each tent there were men sitting on the ground, eating from mess-tins.

They stopped soon afterwards at a group of three tents.

"This is it," said the man.

"What d'you want?" asked a lad of about fifteen.

"I want Enrique."

"Enrique!" shouted the lad.

The flap of one tent was lifted. Enrique came out smiling.

"It's you. I knew you'd come up. How's everything?"

"Fine!" said Pablo. "And you?"

"I'm O.K."

They had spoken in French. Pablo noticed it.

"Come in," said Enrique.

They went in. Inside there was a plank set on two casks, which served as a table, and other casks were being used as seats. A man was sitting on a camp-bed, eating.

"Here's my pal Pablo," said Enrique.

The man put his bread down on the bed and held out his hand to Pablo. In his other hand he was holding a tin of food. "Have you had anything to eat?" he asked.

"Yes, thanks very much," replied Pablo.

"That doesn't matter. Open a tin for him, Enrique. He's going to keep us company."

"No, I assure you..." said Pablo.

"Don't worry," Enrique interrupted.

Pablo did not insist. He took the bread and the tin of meat he was offered.

"It's American tinned stuff," said Enrique. "When we first had it we found it very good, then we got fed up with it, and finally we got used to it."

258

"It's worse for tobacco," said the other. "You don't eat tinned meat very often, but tobacco's different, and we've only got theirs."

They ate for a moment without speaking, then Enrique said, "I haven't explained things to you yet. That chap there's Lieutenant Dubois. He's the chief of our group."

Pablo looked at the man. He was small and thin, a little like Enrique, but he had a paler face and his hair was cut very short. His appearance was hard and firm.

"Yes," he said. "Your comrade's often spoken to me of you, and I've been wanting to meet you."

"'Till now," said Enrique, "that hasn't mattered much..."

"I didn't mean to suggest he should have come up earlier," said the lieutenant, raising his voice. "I said it only because it's true—he's talked a lot about you to me. On the other hand, I've always agreed that we should have only the number of men we need. Even now, if we had only half the number that'd be best."

He broke off to drink. Pablo turned towards Enrique. Enrique looked at him for a moment and then burst out laughing.

"What's the matter with you?" asked the lieutenant. "Off your head?"

"No," said Enrique, "but I am looking at his face and then thinking of my message."

"What did you say exactly?"

Enrique turned towards Pablo. "Have you got the piece of paper?"

Pablo felt in his pocket and brought out a piece of crumpled paper. The message was written in Catalan. Enrique read it in translation in a loud voice: "I want you to come up straightaway. We need you. It'll be for some days."

The lieutenant began to laugh in turn. "Of course," he said. "It may seem funny, but we do need him."

He stopped, took a can, and filled the mugs on the table with wine. Then, turning towards Pablo, he explained: "You see, we haven't got enough weapons for all the men who've come to us lately, but that's not very important because if we did have them we couldn't hand them out. Most of those who've come are mere kids, and we've got something better to do than to give lessons. The main thing is that we've got a good free group. So if I could change the youngsters I've got for fellows like you I'd give ten of them for one like you."

He began to laugh. Enrique laughed also. Pablo looked at them for a moment, and then he mumbled, "You're exaggerating. There's not much I know how to do."

"Don't be modest," said the lieutenant. "Your friend told me what you did in Spain. We know what chaps like you can be worth here."

Pablo had stopped eating. He drank a few sips of wine, and it tasted sharp.

"You're a good type," said the lieutenant. "Every time we've sent someone to you you've looked after them. Actually, of course, it was more useful to us that you should stay in your own place. But now the big effort's pretty near. The Americans are coming up the Rhone valley, and we don't want them to liberate Lons and the countryside around. That's our job. It's for us to do."

"You want to attack the town?" asked Pablo.

"We certainly intend to do so."

"But you know there are still a lot of Germans there, according to rumours."

They began to laugh as they looked at Pablo.

"Don't you worry," said Enrique. "We've got more information than you have, and the day we attack, all the different groups will be in it together."

Pablo remained silent. He would have liked to go out and get a breath of air. The others started to eat again. They had put a slice of cheese and some apples on the table.

"Eat up," said Enrique.

"No, I'm all right, thanks."

"Apparently you know the F.M. and grenades?" said the lieutenant.

"A bit," said Pablo quietly.

The man appeared to reflect, then, speaking to Enrique, he explained: "Tomorrow you'll show him all the various weapons we have here. I'm going to post him to section three. Bertrand and Godard are the only two old hands. We've never seen the others in action; it'll be useful for them to have a chap like him with them.

As soon as they had finished eating, the lieutenant gave Enrique some instructions about the night guards, and added, indicating Pablo, "No guard duty for him till tomorrow, and the same treatment as the long-service chaps. Explain the regulations to him and take him to number three."

260

They stood up. The lieutenant shook hands with them, and they went out. Once they were outside, Enrique made for a tent a little way off, between the birches.

"You can start off by getting rid of your pack, then we'll do a tour of the camp."

The tent was a large lorry-tarpaulin which hung right down to the ground only on one side. In front, and at each end, planks held upright by small stakes made a surround some eight inches high. Inside there was straw, empty sacks, blankets, and a pile of mess-tins, mugs, and clothes. Four rifles and three tommy-guns were lying at the back of the tent. Only one man was there, sitting under a tree and reading a scrap of newspaper.

"Where are the others?" asked Enrique.

The man stood up. "I don't know, chief. They went down towards the post."

"What's your name?" asked Enrique.

"Marcel Buatois."

"This chap's Pablo. We were together in Spain. He'll teach you how to blow up a tank."

"I know. Godard told us he'd be coming, but we hardly hoped he'd be posted to us."

The youngster seemed very young. He was tall and thin, fairhaired with smiling eyes. Pablo noticed that his handshake was firm.

Enrique had picked up a branch. Without bending over, he moved some of the clothes with it, pushed a mess-tin aside, and poked the straw over.

"Have to make a place for him," he said. "And then you'll fish around to get him some fresh straw. It's disgusting here! I'd better have a word with Godard."

He spoke loudly in a dry, peremptory tone. Buatois did not reply.

"Come on," said Enrique, "we'll go on a tour."

When they had walked a few paces Pablo asked, "What exactly are you, here?"

"Sergeant-major," said Enrique. "That's to say, I stand in for the lieutenant when he's absent. I also lead all the difficult patrols with the shock groups."

They walked a little way without speaking. Pablo looked at the forest where shadows seemed to come out of every trunk. There were no coppices here, but huge trees of which the

261

branches formed a thick vault speckled with tiny spots of clear sky.

Enrique went on: "You know, the war in Spain thrills them. If you'd come at the same time as me you'd probably be a lieutenant now with a group under your own command. What put me back a bit at first was my accent. Not so much because they couldn't understand me, but they didn't much like to be ordered around by a foreigner."

They walked on. Pablo did not speak. He was looking at the trees. Soon afterwards they found two men crouching behind a fallen tree-trunk.

"O.K.?" asked Enrique.

The men stood up. One was holding a carbine, the other a tommy-gun. There was a haversack between them. Pablo thought that it probably contained hand-grenades.

"Here's my pal Pablo," said Enrique.

"You've talked about him often enough," said the man who was holding the tommy-gun.

"I always told you he'd be with us for the big day."

They went on, leaving the sentries to continue their watch.

"That," explained Enrique, "is Post Two; farther on, to the right, is Post One. These are the two most dangerous because of the thickness of the woods. We put only our best men up here. The one who spoke to me is one of our old-timers; the other is a youngster, but he's also very good. The other posts are in the skirts of the forest; that's not so tricky. We used to have only one man on guard, but now there are enough of us to post them in twos. That's good for the youngsters. And anyway, we've got to find something for them to do, but if you put them on their own they get scared a bit and are always firing. When we tried to post 'em singly we often had four or five alerts in a night. There are also advanced posts round the forest, but that's too far to go now; you'll see them some other time."

"You've never been attacked?"

"Not here. It's too far from the road. They don't like getting into the forests. But where we were earlier they encircled us almost completely. Someone had informed on us. Fourteen chaps were lost, all youngsters who didn't know that part very well and weren't able to get away in time."

They walked on for a moment without speaking, and then Pablo asked, "In fact, you've only been in a battle once?"

262

Enrique stopped, looked at him, and shook his head before saying, "Honestly, you don't seem to know much. Haven't you ever heard of the attacks on German convoys?"

"Yes."

"Well, that was some of our work. And it wasn't a picnic, I can tell you. We often had quite a few wounded, and even some killed."

Ahead of them the wood was brightening. They soon reached a large clearing where all the trees had been felled. There was still wood lying about, the remains of that which had been used to make small huts for the sentries. Enrique introduced Pablo to many of the men. Each time he spoke of the war in Spain and how Pablo had been, on the Madrid front, a specialist in attacking tanks. Pablo stared at the ground each time. They continued their tour as far as the house where lorries were parked.

"Here's the guard-house," said Enrique. "You'll sleep here tomorrow if you're on guard duty. The drivers also sleep here, and the gunsmiths have a workshop here. It's here also that we keep the prisoners shut up."

"You've got prisoners?"

"Not at the moment. We never keep 'em for long."

Enrique made a gesture of lifting a rifle to his shoulder. Pablo said nothing. They went on a little farther, and then returned to the camp. Night had fallen almost completely, and many electric lights were shining inside the tents. Enrique stopped, shouted, and the lights were switched off.

In the tent where Pablo was to sleep the others had already settled down.

"You there, Godard?" asked Enrique.

A voice came out of the darkness. "Yes, we've left a place for your pal. Right at the end, on the left."

Enrique led Pablo to the far end of the tent. "Well, here you are; try to get yourself settled. Good night."

Pablo sat down on the straw, which crackled.

"Got enough room?" asked the man beside him.

Pablo recognized Buatois' voice. "Yes," he said. "I'm okay."

"Your pack's just over there."

Pablo felt around and found his pack at the end of the tent. He also noticed that the straw was not packed down.

"Thanks for the straw," he said.

"That's okay; if there's anything you want just ask."

"No, I'm all right. Good night."

"Good night. One thing, if you get up to go out and pee don't go too far because of the sentries."

"I know; Enrique told me."

XLIII

THERE was still some movement around the camp. Shouts, sounds of weapons, and washing-up. Under the next tent men were talking in hushed voices. Little by little all became silent. Then there were several minutes of almost complete silence.

Lying on his back, motionless, Pablo listened. There was nothing to be heard except a little crackling of twigs, a faint almost imperceptible sound of branches rubbing together.

Then, slowly, the forest started to come to life. The hooting of owls and the cries of birds unknown to Pablo came through the night. There was not a breath of wind, and yet all the forest was in movement. It was like a multiple, regular breathing, and in addition, there was a soft chorus of nibblings, beating wings, and whisperings.

Never had Pablo spent a night in such a forest as this. He thought for a moment of nights at Brûlis. Of silence. The great silence of the plain. Here there could never be silence. The forest was alive with the life of every animal, of every plant; it was even alive with the sleep of all these men lying inside makeshift tents.

Several times Pablo had the feeling of a presence near to him. It seemed to him that an animal must be there, a few inches from his face on the other side of the planks. He raised himself on his elbow and looked. There was no moon, but a milky light filtered between the boles and floated under the branches. Pablo raised himself farther. On the ground something was shining. Something like a glow-worm, but thick and long. Pablo stared at this light for some minutes. The glow seemed to move. A little farther off there was another light. Pablo sat up still more. He was about to get up when Buatois asked him quietly, "What's the matter? D'you need something?"

"No," said Pablo. "No, thank you."

"The first few nights no-one sleeps well, but you soon get used to it. So long as it doesn't rain we aren't too badly off."

While he was speaking Pablo was still watching the light. It had now stopped moving. He hesitated for a moment, and then, lowering his voice still further, he said, "I don't know what it is, but there's something shining in a very queer fashion over there, on the ground."

Buatois did not bother to raise himself. "That's phosphorescent wood," he said. "I've never seen so much before. The whole place is full of it round here. Haven't you ever seen it before?"

"No."

"It's half-rotten wood all eaten into by worms."

Pablo lay down again.

For a long time he tried to put some order in his thoughts, to make up his mind what he should do. What he should say to Enrique in the morning. Until now people had arranged things for him. The men had come, as they had before many times, but this time, in addition to barrels of wine and sacks of potatoes, they had also taken Pablo. They did not even need to say anything. They had handed him the note from Enrique as they handed their usual requisition order. Pablo had prepared his pack, said *au revoir*, and climbed into the driver's cabin, next to the driver. He had done all this naturally, without hesitation, without reflection.

Since it had been known that the Americans were very near, everyone was living in a mood of deep excitement which had reached the most isolated farms. Work continued, but at the same time there was a mood of waiting for something. Nobody knew just what, because no-one knew exactly what was going to happen, but they knew they were near to being liberated. They spoke of it only a little, but the waiting was there, present everywhere, almost palpable. Also, without noticing it, the men themselves were not quite the same.

Pablo thought of the other calls of the men of the Maquis coming for food. Many times they had spoken of Enrique. Many times they had said, "You'll have to come one of these days." But each time Pablo had merely smiled. He winked his eye like someone who had foreseen everything, was fully prepared, who knew what was going on and awaited only the hour for action.

Once also the Germans had come. They had searched the entire village, house by house. When Pablo had shown his

Spanish identity card, a loyal subject of Franco, the officer had patted him on the shoulder, saying, "Maquis, terrorists, all communists."

Then again Pablo had smiled and winked.

That was all. All that Pablo had seen of the war was the air squadrons on their way to bombard towns of which he did not even know the names; with the passage quite near to them, on the main road, of reprisal units going up to pillage and burn the villages of the Haut-Jura where resisters abounded.

But for themselves, too near to the plain, too far from the towns, they had always had their work, a work of both sorrows and joys, almost as in peacetime.

Nevertheless tonight Pablo was there, lying under a tent where soldiers were sleeping. By stretching his arm a little he could feel the cold steel of a rifle-barrel. A short way off, in a haversack, there were hand-grenades.

For a long time he tried to fix his thoughts on the house. Everyone must be asleep. Tomorrow morning Germaine would almost certainly go with Clopineau to finish the sulphating; that certainly could not wait. Pablo thought again of Jeannette. Of the kitchen with its big, shining table. Of the cellar with its lines of casks and the wine-press. The beautiful new mechanical wine-press. The press which had cost three-quarters of one year's harvest and had been used for only one year. He thought also of La Noire and her foal they had sold.

For Pablo that was everything: the house, the furniture, the people, the land also. Everything was there, a little in disorder, a little like things stuffed hastily in a sack at the time of a hurried departure. But everything was as present as this forest with its myriad sounds, as these men sleeping, as these weapons sleeping also.

Several times more Pablo turned about. He did it slowly to avoid disturbing the big chap sleeping next to him.

Far off the engine of a car protested on a winding road. The birds continued to answer each other. A nightingale sang interminably a song which flowed through the night like a cool stream through black rocks.

Each of these sounds brought its own image. They entered into Pablo, took shape, lit up, added themselves to all the sounds he had brought with him from the village. Now there were so many that they ran together, forming a world of life and of sleep, of sunshine and of night, which kept him from thinking.

A little while later steps approached the tent. An electric torch sent its beam over the faces of the sleepers. Pablo closed his eyes and saw the light pass over his closed eyes. The torch went out, and the steps died away into the thousand sounds of the night.

XLIV

In the morning, thanks to the clearing towards the east, the camp was full of sunshine. The light flowed down the leaves and spread large bright patches on the grass. Men moved round incessantly, washing was hanging on lines strung between trees, and everyone was gossiping or whistling, just as if it was a fairground with only the music missing.

Pablo strolled around for a minute or two looking for Enrique, but the youngster he had met the previous evening near the lieutenant's tent told him that Enrique was out on patrol. Pablo went back to the tent. Buatois was there.

"Godard's looking for you," he said.

"What should I do?"

"Wait here, he wants to show you the weapons."

Pablo sat down on the straw beside Buatois. They remained a moment without speaking, and then Buatois asked, "Did you sleep well?"

"Yes."

He looked at Pablo for a few seconds before saying, "I hear that you saw some dreadful things during the war in Spain."

Pablo did not reply. He shrugged his shoulders. The other went on: "I've the impression that Godard's very proud that you've been put in our group."

Pablo sighed. For a few moments there was just the murmur of the camp and the rustling of leaves through which the morning breeze was playing with a thousand flutterings of sunlight. Then, as Pablo still failed to speak, Buatois asked, "Is it true that there were as many Germans and Italians against you in Madrid as there were Franco troops?"

Pablo turned towards the youth, who was looking straight at

him, with something in his eyes which suggested a child saying, "Tell me a story."

"Listen," said Pablo, "I don't like to talk about it. I'd like to please you, but, you see..."

Pablo tried to find words to continue, to explain something he had never explained to anyone else. When he found no words Buatois began to laugh. "You know," he said, "I haven't been here very long, but the old-stagers have told me that your friend Enrique can talk for hours on end on the subject. You're certainly not like him."

"You mustn't get annoyed with me," said Pablo. "It isn't the same thing for me."

The other had stopped laughing. He looked at Pablo's face for a moment, and then said, "I understand. I understand."

Pablo wanted to speak, to get the conversation round to another subject. "What's your job in ordinary life?"

"I'm a student."

"Of what?"

"I'm doing my second *bac*. After, I don't know, I may study medicine."

He became silent for a moment, and then, returning to his thoughts of the war, he said again, "That doesn't matter, but it seems odd for an old soldier not to want to talk about what he did. My father was in the '14 war, and I've heard him talk about the war a hundred times. I know it all by heart, yet I went on listening all the same. And when he was retelling anything he never varied what he said by a single word. In the end I was convinced that it was the worst things that had happened which he remembered best. I don't know exactly what you did, but I'd be surprised if you had a worse time than him. That's why I can't understand why you won't talk about it."

The lad stopped. Pablo sincerely regretted that he could not tell him of the things he had done. He hesitated a long time, and then said, "I didn't suffer as much as all that. Only, you see, I lost everything back there... even my wife."

He had spoken these last three words in a very low voice. Yet Buatois had understood. His face flushed. He made an awkward, unfinished gesture with one hand.

"I'm sorry," he said. "Do forgive me."

"There's no harm done," said Pablo. "You couldn't possibly have guessed."

They remained for some seconds staring at each other. Around them the camp and the forest bustled with life. Below was the life of men, above was the life of the trees and the wind. And everywhere, on the land and on the men, the sun moved in tiny patches of light as numerous as the gaps in the leaves which gave a sight of the sky.

"In fact," said Buatois without raising his eyes, "for us to be here is normal, but for you it's very different."

Pablo stood up and walked a few paces in front of the tent. A little earlier he had spoken almost against his will of the death of Mariana. He had done so to free himself; because he had been able to think of nothing else he had thrown out words as one throws anything that comes to hand between the legs of a pursuer. Now it was something different. It was yesterday's refrain beginning anew, and it was going to continue with the others. Pablo thought for a moment. What he must do was leave. He must explain to Enrique that he could not do what was wanted of him, that he did not want to be the Pablo he had been made out to be to everyone in the camp.

Pablo felt his anger rising, filling him with the words he would say. They came easily these words. They would come again when Enrique was there.

Pablo went across to Buatois again. "When the patrols return," he asked, "where do they go?"

"Down below, to the guard post."

"I'm going there."

"And if Godard comes here?"

Pablo hesitated, longing to say that he didn't give a damn, but he went off without a word and without looking back.

The patrol returned to the post a few minutes after he had reached it. He went across to Enrique immediately. The words were there on his lips, ready to come out.

"So you're here," exclaimed Enrique. "That's perfect."

"I want to tell you ..."

Enrique turned to his men. "You, Ravier," he shouted, "nip up quickly and get the old hands of the third and fourth groups together, with ten of the least stupid of the new recruits, and send 'em down here."

The man put down his rifle and started running towards the camp. He had barely taken ten strides before Enrique shouted again: "Hey! Ravier!"

269

The other stopped. "What?"

"Nine men only, there's one here!"

He turned back towards Pablo.

"Listen..." began Pablo. "There's something I've got to..."

Enrique interrupted him. "This isn't the moment, old man. Troubles always come when the lieutenant's absent. We've had a message that German motor-cyclists are on the Champagnole road, and there seems to be some movement also on the other side. I'm going off with my lads, and you're going to have your first outing."

Then he gave a hearty laugh.

"But I..." said Pablo.

Still smiling, Enrique replied, "I'm sorry, I'd hoped to leave you in peace for your first day, but the lieutenant's gone off with a party of twelve, and I'm short of experienced chaps. I need you."

Pablo stared at the ground. The equipped men began to come down the path. They formed a circle round Enrique and Pablo, and when they were all present Enrique explained what they had to do. He put Godard in charge of the second patrol. When he had finished speaking the two groups separated. Buatois walked across to Pablo. "I'm glad we're both in the same patrol," he said.

His eyes were shining. They seemed to be the same blue as the sky, with sunshine in them.

"I don't know," said Pablo.

"Hey! Godard! Is he on the F.M. with me?"

Godard came across. He was a tall, thickly built man of about thirty. His big, hairy hands were grasping a sub-machine gun.

"Yes," he said. "You know the 29 because you had them in Spain."

"Yes," said Pablo. "I know it."

"Buatois knows how to load it," said Godard, "but he's never fired one."

Buatois held out the sub-machine gun to Pablo. A loading-clip was fitted to the gun. Buatois was wearing a haversack slung across his back.

"It's not loaded," he said.

"I can see that," said Pablo.

Godard gave the order to march, and he went to the head of the file, which started to march slowly inside the edge of the wood.

270

As the sun rose higher the wind began to drop. At times it stopped at a cluster of fir-trees on the edge of the forest. It could be sensed because of the constant fluttering of the leaves. It was still breathing deeply, like someone who has run too quickly. Then, suddenly, it started again. It moved through the spoiled hay from which tiny clouds of pollen rose, shining in the sunlight. It moved scarcely at all into the interior of the woods. Occasionally it stirred a few branches on the skirts of the wood, just taking a glance at the blue shade. Then, as if frightened by so much mystery, because it was now a day wind, a wind meant to move beneath the sun, it veered away. The branches became still, drooping towards the grass before slumbering again. There was little dew left, and it was better marching in the shade than in the sun.

When they were crossing a small strip of grassland, to cut off a corner of the wood, the men began to feel sweat running down their faces. No-one spoke. They remained in Indian file, wavering sometimes, stopping sometimes, going on without a sound.

Pablo was sixth in the line. Buatois was behind him. All the men ahead were armed with tommy-guns and grenades. Those at the end of the file each had a rifle and also carried F.M. chargers.

When they arrived at the point where the forest met the road they found a look-out man. Pablo recognized the spot where the lorry had stopped when he had first arrived.

"Well, what's this about motor-cyclists?" asked Godard.

"I heard them."

"You heard motor-cycles, eh? There's nothing to indicate they were German."

"From here I can't see the road. My job is to guard the path. I did hear them, I tell you; anything else ..."

The man shrugged his shoulders. Godard hesitated. "But anyway it was you who gave the warning?"

"Yes, it was some chaps from a farm who came and told me."

"From which farm?"

"I can't tell you; I didn't know them."

"And they did really tell you the Boches had come from Lons?"

"Definitely. Coming this way, there's nowhere else they could have come from."

Godard gave a shrug of irritation. "Come on," he said, "step it out."

271

They stretched out in skirmishing order to cross the large meadow which separated the wood they had just left from another less thickly wooded. The grass came up to their waists. Every now and then, at a signal from Godard, they stopped and crouched motionless for a few seconds. They stared across the meadow. The grass was almost completely still. The wind was dying away, stirring from time to time the ears of wild oats.

When they were again under trees Pablo asked in a low voice, "Where are we going now?"

"Down the road, I guess," said Buatois. "We're now in a wood where we haven't any sentries."

They were moving more slowly and stopping more often. The silence of the wood was troubled only by bird-song or the rustle of their brief flights between two branches. Pablo could feel the silence sinking into him in long, slow waves in rhythm with the flow of his blood.

The ground became hummocky. Each time they reached a rise in the ground they stopped behind it and waited before going on. Then they could hear the heart of the forest beating, as though the earth was breathing.

As they went forward the air was a little cooler. Despite this, however, Pablo could feel sweat running down his spine. The wood and steel of the gun in his hands had become so damp as to be slippery. But he could not do anything about it. His hands had put themselves on the gun when it had been handed to him, simply because it was a gesture which they knew so well. But that was all. The rest did not follow. Pablo could feel it. He felt it in the trembling of his limbs when he had to stand up to set off again; he felt it in his throat where the bitterness of gall remained for a long time.

The ground soon became level again, with fewer hummocks of grass.

"Not far now," murmured Buatois.

When they were some twenty-five yards from the edge of the forest, which showed framed in sunshine between the violet trunks, they stopped again. Godard went on accompanied by one man.

Kneeling behind his weapon, Pablo watched their progress. He rubbed his hands on his shirt several times to free them from sweat. Taking out a handkerchief, he also mopped his forehead. He glanced quickly at Buatois. The youngster looked quite calm.

272

He was watching the two shapes moving farther and farther away, almost at a snail's pace, stopping at the foot of each tree.

Pablo's eyes also followed them. Then, in proportion as these two shadows grew smaller, and as they approached the lacy patch of light, Pablo's heart beat faster. He was waiting. But he was not waiting for the gesture which Godard should make to call them forward. He was waiting for something else. Something he had felt inside him for some seconds and which was now very clear indeed. More than twenty times already the film had unfolded in his mind. Godard and his companion reaching the edge of the wood. They straighten up slowly to get a longer view. And then, as they are upright, a burst of fire flings them both to the ground. And the explosions give the signal for butchery. All the Germans encircling the wood begin to move forward. The circle closes little by little, and no-one, absolutely no-one, can come out alive. Pablo turned his head several times, staring at the undergrowth. Nothing really moved, yet everything was alive. Everything seemed to be living in the presence of the death which was hidden there, which was around them, which was behind each of the pillars supporting the vault which gave the wood the cool freshness of the tomb. Crouched as he was, Pablo could smell the earth itself. His hands were touching the cold, damp earth, mossy in places, sleek as the surface of the road a little farther on.

Perhaps they would be left to rot, without even earth to cover them. Pablo had seen so many of these corpses which slowly collapsed into the earth which sucks them away little by little. In a few minutes, possibly, he would also be a corpse.

In a few moments he would feel his life going from him. He would possibly feel it exactly as Mariana had felt it.

Mariana!

It had taken the presence of death to bring back before him the face of Mariana.

Now she was there. Transparent, but present. There was the form of her face without any of its colouring. The colouring remained that of the undergrowth. In this face, from beyond this face, two bluish forms moved.

Soon they became still. Pablo held his breath. His hands moved again to his weapon.

He would have to kill and to be killed.

An interval.

273

Even the birds had ceased to sing. Even the smell of the earth was no longer rising.

All was silence. It would suddenly vanish in a flash. A steady volley. A volley, and everything would suddenly become alive. To live vividly, for a few seconds only.

"Quick...quick...!"

Pablo's lips had scarcely moved.

Even the face of Mariana was absolutely still.

Suddenly the two shadows moved. They became gilded, luminous. Godard's arm rose and fell twice.

Every man began to march again. Pablo felt the air coming into his lungs again. His back was icy cold, his shirt sticking to his skin.

His hands, still moist, tightened on his gun; they gripped it very tightly, so tightly that they almost trembled.

XLV

PABLO knew now that fear had penetrated him. He could feel it. Throughout his body he felt it like a many-clawed animal. It pressed on his lungs, tightened his stomach, and twisted his guts like a bad wine which refuses to go down. Pablo was sick with fear. He had been like this throughout the whole time ever since he joined the patrol, and he had been the same since they returned. He was unable to eat. Fresh water alone seemed good to him.

"Don't drink so much water," Buatois had said to him. "It's not good to drink it on its own: it comes from a tainted source."

Pablo had tried to smile. Then, to avoid questions, he had gone off to sleep in the tent. Lying with his eyes closed for two hours, he had listened to the sounds of the camp. The camp had a warlike voice. With the return of the patrols, there was a constant sound of weapons, of orders, of shouts, of voices talking. No-one had seen anything suspicious, but the menace remained.

From time to time Pablo opened his eyes and stared at the forest. With so much noise in the camp, there was nothing to be heard of the woods, but it was enough to see them to realize all the dangers they could hold. Beyond them was almost the un-

274

known. Beyond the line of guard-posts death could be hiding behind each tree-stump.

There were, certainly, advanced posts on the skirts of the entire wood, but Pablo had seen when he was patrolling that they were so widely spaced that in the middle of the night a battalion of well-trained soldiers could get into the wood.

The night was closing in. It had begun by filling the ditches. Slowly, without a sound and with a thousand tricks, it was encircling the camp, creeping up to each tent. It could not be seen moving, but it was enough to close one's eyes for five minutes; when you reopened them it was possible to see just how much more territory the night had won.

That sapling, a little way down, which a moment ago was a long thread of light hanging from above, had disappeared. It was now nothing more than a steely-blue line in the shadow of the great lichen-covered beech.

Pablo closed his eyes again and waited, forcing himself to keep them closed for two, three, four minutes, and then looked again. The shadows had deepened. There were now only a few spots of light among the highest branches. The rest was a light which belonged as much to the night as to the day.

Many times he thought of the hayloft in the barn where a man had hanged himself. He saw again the hook covered with spiders' webs which caught the light of his lantern every night. He saw again the *patron* stretched out in the middle of his bedroom. The plank coffin nailed roughly together. He saw again, above all, Mariana.

For him that was the sign that death was walking near. Pablo thought again of Jeannette. Of the old doctor at Saint-Agnes: "This child senses death like a dog does." Was Jeannette weeping this evening? Did she sense that Pablo was about to die? Poor, poor Jeannette!

Two or three times already Pablo had felt the urge to go away. To leave everything, his pack and his blanket, to go off from the camp as if for a stroll and then make his way through the woods. He knew he could find his way by instinct, and not rejoin the road until he was close to the village.

He knew the direction. He would make no mistake, he was certain. He would have to walk for a very long time, but for that his legs would find fresh energy. But there were the sentries, and the advanced posts. They were probably too sparse to protect the camp fully, but close enough to each other to prevent Pablo from getting away.

Germans or resistance fighters, these men had guns. They held death between their hands, and it was death Pablo feared. A death which might loom up at any moment. A death which had entered him already and made him ill. He had already got up several times and gone away from the tent, but it was not to run away. It was because fear was turning his stomach.

The night continued its advance. Each minute there was one of the more distant trees which faded into the mass already swallowed by the darkness.

Despite this, the sounds of the camp continued almost at their usual rhythm. Sometimes there was the sound of a particularly loud shout, or else a burst of laughter spreading from group to group of the men. Several vehicles arrived. A lorry came and manœuvred into a parking space, and then a few moments later there was a short silence followed by much noisy talk. Dominating the hubbub, Pablo recognized the lieutenant's voice, shouting orders. He sat up, leaning on one elbow, and looked towards the centre of the camp. He saw the light in the lieutenant's tent, and the men there seemed to be dispersing slowly.

Soon some of the group came over, talking together. Pablo felt Buatois settling down beside him.

"What's been going on?" he asked.

"A lorry-load of supplies had just come up. The chaps on it brought a prisoner with them," Buatois told him.

"A German?"

"No, a Frenchman. He's a chap from Champagnole. There are quite a few who know him."

"What's he done?"

"They don't know. They're going to question him."

"D'you mean they arrested him without any reason?"

Buatois hesitated. The sounds of the camp were more muted now; the men were talking inside their tents.

"There's no need to worry about that," said Buatois. "He's certainly got something on his conscience, because he did a bunk when he saw the lorry."

Pablo said nothing. He looked towards the spot in the wood where the last ray of sunlight had shown; now all was finished. The day was dead. Pablo stretched himself out once more.

"Going to sleep again?" asked Buatois.

276

"Yes, why do you ask?"

"You know very well we're on guard-duty."

Pablo sighed.

"We'll be on together," said Buatois. "I'm very glad about that."

"At what time?"

"It'll be our turn in half an hour, but we must go to the post now."

They put on their equipment and went down towards the house. No-one was sleeping there. The drivers, the gunsmith, and the man on guard-duty were chatting outside the door. When Pablo and Buatois arrived Godard, who was in command of the guard, gave them their orders. Afterwards they went into the old stables to spread their blankets.

"It's best to have nine to eleven," explained Buatois. "Afterwards you have the whole night to sleep, since we don't go on again until 5 A.M."

Pablo thought of the day. At five o'clock it would be daylight. But till then there were eight hours during which death might come soundlessly to them.

He sat down on the straw.

"Feeling queer?" asked Buatois.

"Yes, I'm a bit tired, that's all."

Pablo stood up and looked at the stable. The swinging bails had been removed, and there remained only the manger and the rack. They had placed their blankets at the far end to avoid being disturbed.

"Like this," said Buatois, "we've our heads towards the manger, and I've found that very satisfactory. Above there are the drivers, who also sleep on straw, and, since the flooring is pretty poor, every time they move you get a shower of dust on your head."

Buatois put out the light and then went into the courtyard. Pablo left the group and went and sat at the foot of the wall. Through his shirt he could feel the warmth of the stones. He thought of the sun down below, the one which would ripen the grapes all along the slopes. He thought of Germaine also, and of Clopineau and Jeannette. Today they had probably finished the plantation near the Trois Haies road. A splendid, vigorous plantation. But in a few days, if there was any rain, the grass would be up again. The whole job would need to be done anew.

Pablo remained for a long time with his eyes fixed on a vague

277

point in the dark wood. Then, suddenly, a bitter laugh rose in his throat. A laugh which remained in his throat, held by the bile which had been there for two days. A laugh which meant: "You may die from one minute to another. What the hell can it matter to you whether the weeds are growing up among the vines?"

Pablo stood up and walked away to be sick, but all he could do was spit. His belly was empty.

As he came back to the house he saw men going into the stable. A voice shouted: "Shut the door so that we can have a bit of light!"

Other men stayed in the courtyard.

"Ah! There you are," said Buatois. "I've been looking for you." He held out a carbine to Pablo.

"Is that what I have to take?"

"Yes, for guard-duty one takes a tommy-gun and hand-grenades, the other a carbine."

They began to march towards the wood.

"We take the first watch Post Four," explained Buatois. "You'll see, it's cushy."

They went past the first three posts, numbers one and two in the obscurity of the woods where the men could be scarcely seen, where the only light was from scraps of phosphorescent wood which they scattered by kicking them. Post Three was near the clearing, but quite a long way from the camp. Post Four was also on the edge of the woods, but only some twenty-five yards from the first tents.

As soon as Godard and the reliefs had gone Pablo looked towards the wood. Someone was talking loudly in one of the tents, and he recognized the voices of the lieutenant and Enrique.

"They must be questioning that bloke," whispered Buatois.

They became silent. The voices were now quieter. Pablo went forward a few steps. From his new position he could see the light. He could also hear better.

"You can see," the lieutenant was saying, "that we can come to an understanding. We all know what it is to be in urgent need of money. Between ourselves, it's not much, is it, a thousand francs for a camp where there are, after all, a hundred and fifty men? That doesn't make 'em worth much by the pound."

There was some laughter. Someone spoke, but Pablo could not understand what he was saying. Afterwards, still laughing, the

278

lieutenant went on: "Come on, tell me, how much did they offer you for me?"

A silence.

"Come on, tell me; let's have a laugh. It's always funny to know how much someone thinks you're worth."

There was another silence, and then there was the sound of Enrique's voice.

"Talk, come on, you bastard!"

"Shut up," shouted the lieutenant. "I forbid you to touch him. He's told us all he knows, and that's the end of it. He's behaved like a skunk, agreed, but it's not for us to judge him. There are courts for that. Anyhow, he's not the only one to have made a mistake. This is war, you know. In any case, I've nothing against him personally. On the contrary, I'm sorry I had to hit him pretty hard a little while ago. But now we're friends. . . . That's right, isn't it, we're friends?"

The man must have spoken in a low voice; Pablo could hear nothing.

"Come on," said the lieutenant, "untie his hands and give him a glass of wine, that'll buck him up."

"Instead of a glass of wine I'd give him a couple of bullets through his head right now," shouted Enrique.

"Indeed. Well don't let anybody try it, or there'll be the devil to pay!"

There was again a long silence. No doubt they were all drinking.

"Well," said the lieutenant, "how much did they promise you for my scalp?"

A loud burst of laughter followed the man's reply.

"I thought you were worth more than that," said Enrique.

"That'd burn me up, lieutenant," said another. "A thousand francs for the head of a group is a bloody insult to the whole lot of us."

"Now, wait, there's no need to get worked up," said the lieutenant. "A thousand francs for him, together with what his pals pick up, begins to count."

For a moment they were all talking at once, then the lieutenant's voice rose, harsh, angry, spitting out his words.

"So you admit there are many of you. You were trying to make a monkey out of me earlier. Come on, give us all the names, and be quick about it."

279

Again Enrique shouted, "Talk, you bastard, talk!"

The man moaned several times and then shrieked. There was a brief silence, and then a man's voice said, "I think you hit him a bit too hard, lieutenant. He's out cold."

"Go and get a handful of straw and take off his boots. We'll soon bring him round."

Pablo took a step towards the tent.

"Stay here," whispered Buatois, taking hold of his arm.

Pablo stood still.

"Come on, we're not at our post, and we could be in trouble," Buatois went on, pulling him back.

They returned to the clearing.

"It's disgusting," said Pablo. "I'll have to see Enrique."

"Be quiet. Perhaps it is disgusting. It sickens me too. It's a filthy job I wouldn't like to have to do, but that fellow there must have accomplices. He must know who they are. If I've been told aright it was he who betrayed the camp we were at before. That's to say he's responsible for fourteen of our chaps being killed. That's also disgusting."

Pablo said nothing. Behind them the sound of voices continued. Soon afterwards the man gave a loud scream which stopped suddenly. Pablo listened again. No voices could be heard.

"D'you think they've killed him?" he asked.

"No, surely not. There's still a lot more he can tell them."

Men were now coming out of the lieutenant's tent. Pablo heard them walking away, talking together, and then there was silence. A heavy silence, but only for a few seconds, as if all the forest had stopped breathing to listen with Pablo to hear whether the man was still groaning.

Then, quickly, everything became alive again. Pablo and Buatois sat side by side on a huge tree-stump. They listened. They looked.

Nothing moved, yet everything was moving. Under the clear light of the stars which fell in soft waves like threads of mist, every bush, every silhouetted tree, was alive.

Every screech of an owl woke an echo and brought a reply, and the reply also had an echo. It was an endless dialogue from tree to tree, from branch to branch. All was alive, all was so clear, so evident, that it was not possible to feel fear.

But it was what could not be seen, could not be heard, that

was to be feared. It was what might surge out silently from the trees from one moment to another.

So long as the prisoner was being interrogated Pablo thought only of him. Now his fear was again upon himself. A fear against which nothing could prevail. Pablo was lucid, most lucid. He could feel it. He told himself that he was the same man who had fought in Spain. The man whose record as a *dinamitero* had been told and retold by Enrique before he came. He repeated this to himself. But each time the face of death came before his eyes again. The face of death with the features of Mariana.

All the clearing, all the woods, were peopled with thousands of Marianas bleeding and in pain. All of them were at the same time dead and dying, all were struggling against a death which had already lived long in them.

Now and then Pablo looked at Buatois. Buatois was calm. With his tommy-gun across his knees, his chin in one hand, he seemed to be studying the night. A score of times Pablo felt the urge to say, "You see, down there, a helmet. . . . There's a rifle being raised." Twenty times he refrained.

Buatois was still a lad. He was the latest to join the group before Pablo. But Pablo was there as an old soldier. "You put a youngster with an old hand," Enrique had explained. "If you put youngsters together they get scared, they're shooting off every five minutes."

Fear. The fear which gets inside a man and never comes out again. Which can come out only through the wound out of which his life will ebb away.

"Is one frightened of death to the very last second?"

"What's that you're saying?" asked Buatois.

Pablo jumped. He had spoken aloud without realizing it.

"Nothing. I was thinking about something."

Buatois began to laugh. "So you think in Spanish, do you?"

"What d'you mean?"

"You spoke in Spanish."

Pablo must have spoken in Catalan. He said nothing. There was a long silence, then Buatois moved. "Still another hour," he said.

Pablo did not reply. He was motionless, paralysed by all the coldness of this night penetrating him, freezing the sweat still running down his body. For another hour he remained like this, clenching his teeth to keep them from chattering, and sweating out his fear in great drops.

281

XLVI

WHEN they reached the house Godard switched on his torch to help them to find a place. At the moment when Pablo and Buatois bent over to spread their blankets he laughed.

"You'd do better to pull out a bit nearer the centre; sometimes the chap up above feels like a pee."

Pablo looked upwards towards the ceiling.

"No," said the other. "Not as high as that, in the manger, like a little Jesus."

Godard's lamp lit up the manger. Pablo stood up. The prisoner was lying there on his back. The lamp did not light up his face, but only his blood-spattered shirt. His feet were outside the manger; they were tied together with wire and attached to a bar of the forage-rack.

"Well, get to bed," said Godard.

Pablo stretched out his blanket and rolled in it. Godard went out.

The darkness was complete. There was the sound of men snoring. Others were breathing heavily. The prisoner moaned. He tried to move three times. Each time his head hit the side of the manger, and he groaned more heavily.

Pablo was trembling. He could feel himself becoming feverish. Sweat was still running down his body, but between sudden bursts of feeling very hot he shivered.

The prisoner was still trying to move. The wire round his ankles grated on the iron bar of the rack. Despite himself, Pablo found himself thinking of the barbed wire in the cemetery, the night he arrived at the village.

The man began to moan more loudly, and Pablo realized that he was gagged.

"Shut that bloody row!" shouted one voice.

"Belt up!" cried another voice.

The man became silent. Pablo now thought of the forest. He thought of the clearing where death moved, silent and invisible, between the trees. Death with the colour of night; the same which had that afternoon the colour of burned undergrowth or of meadows bright with sunshine. Here in the stable it was less present. It was only in the manger to which the prisoner was tied.

Pablo raised himself gently.

"What are you doing?" asked Buatois.

"Nothing."

Pablo remained motionless for a few seconds, staring into the night in the direction from which the moaning was coming. Then, taking his blanket and stepping over the recumbent bodies, he went towards the door.

"Where are you going?" asked the sentry as he walked out.

"I feel sick. I'd have to keep on going out, and that'd wake the others every time. I'd rather sleep outside."

He settled himself in a thicket for a moment, and then, rolling himself in his blanket, he stretched out by the wall, a few paces from the sentry, who asked, "What time are you on?"

"Five o'clock."

Pablo was silent. All round him the night was breathing, talking, trembling. Shadows everywhere moved between the branches, between the trees, between the piles of firewood to take this little, miserable remainder of life which trembled inside him.

Occasionally the sentry marched from side to side of the courtyard. Pablo saw his boots pass near to his face. Beneath his cheek he felt the ground tremble.

Everything was trembling in the night. Everything had the same fever as he had. Fear had penetrated the earth and the trees; it had even entered the heart of stones; warm in the sunshine a little while ago and now frozen. Fear sweated out of the walls. It ran on the ground like a storm of rain and rose to the branches like a mist.

All the night throbbed with fear. All sniffed, all scented death. Soon, when the moon rose above the earth, men, trees, and stones would start to howl at death like dogs. And death would have only to strike at random to silence those who shrieked.

There would be more dead, many more dead, hundreds, thousands of dead. Dead who would have the dolorous face of Mariana.

"What?"

"Not feeling too good?" asked the man, leaning over Pablo.

"What's the matter?"

"I don't know, but you were yammering in Spanish; I couldn't understand what you were saying."

"It's nothing," said Pablo. "I must have been dreaming."

The man marched off. Pablo snuggled nearer to the wall and pulled his blanket over his face so that he should not see this night where death and fear were making their round of the forest.

XLVII

THE day rose on the circle of trees. In the clearing every bush and twig sparkled. The oaks, the elms, the white-trunked birches and the hornbeams, their branches more twisted than ever, had beneath them a few strips of night still clinging to the brambles which struggled between the tree-stumps. Pablo kept shutting his eyes, but the dance continued inside his head. And in this strange dance dozens and dozens of Marianas were involved, each one more beautiful, more dead, than the one before.

"Better see the medico," said Buatois. "You're trembling like a leaf."

Pablo shook his head, gritting his teeth, clenching his hands on the barrel of his rifle, the butt between his feet.

"Have you ever had malaria?" asked Buatois.

"No."

"That's funny, you've got exactly the same symptoms as my father, and he suffers from malaria."

Pablo was no longer looking at the end of the clearing. He was not looking at anything. He could see only this dance, this whirl of trees, of earth, of faces coming back to him unendingly.

Yet he could still think. His mind was more orderly than it had been in the night. Beside him was Buatois, who was on watch. And now the night was ended and the Germans would not come. His fear was still with him, but it was no longer a death a few steps away from him which he feared. It was something far greater. It was something impossible to define but which was more inside him than around him.

It was almost an hour since they had come on guard again when Enrique came out of the wood and walked towards them. Pablo saw him mixed with everything which was already turning over in his head.

"You managed to get yourselves the best post," said Enrique, sitting down beside them.

"Yes," said Buatois, "here there's an open view—no risk of a surprise."

There was a silence. Inside Pablo's head every word reverberated. For a moment he thought he was at the farm, in the cellar,

284

and that he had just climbed into one of the big barrels to clean it. Now, in this clearing where the shining morning echoed with the songs of birds, Pablo heard words sounding as if he was deep in a huge barrel.

"Well," said Enrique, "we did a good job. If we keep this militia chap talking we'll soon know the names of all the gang which denounced pretty well all our comrades who have been arrested in the last two years."

No-one spoke. The birds continued to call from the trees. Inside Pablo's head the echo rolled, the sounds ran together.

"It's a pity we didn't nab him sooner," said Enrique; "it's a bit late now."

"You've had some news?"

"Nothing definite, but I think the Americans will be here in a week."

"Then we'll get on the move?"

"Yes, for sure."

Enrique remained silent for a moment, and then, nudging Pablo with his elbow, he shouted, "D'you realize, a month from now the war may well be over. After that it'll be our turn."

He remained silent for a moment, and then, speaking in Catalan this time, he added, "Just think of it, Pablo, going back to Spain and finding those bastards who did for us. Finding the sods who burnt my place down. Can't you see yourself looking at the rats who slaughtered your wife?"

Pablo wriggled his head. A head in which meaningless words were echoing. In French or in Catalan, it was all the same thing. The words were like so many notes of music struck at random and thrown on the wind to be carried from one side of the clearing to the other.

Mariana! Enrique had never known Mariana. No-one in France had ever known Mariana.

Mariana was a Christian name which said death. Since then there had been other things. There had been the hillsides with their vines, a black mare, a child with a drooping lip and dead eyes, a woman as strong as a man. All that was something like an island of peace in a world of war and of death. It was down there, in the sunshine, on the other side of the wood.

He had only to stand up and to walk in a straight line.

Mariana would never live again ever!

In Pablo's head words rang. Words which escaped from

phrases spoken by Enrique: "War...killing...liberty...liberation."

Others rang in his head also, leaping from phrases spoken by Buatois: "Peace...the need to fight for peace..."

There was also a long dialogue of mixed-up words, broken by those which the echo sent back:

"War..."

"Peace..."

"Spain..."

"Vengeance..."

"Liberation..."

And inside Pablo's head these words became mixed with others which rose out of his fever: "La Noire...La Vigne...*Patronne* ...Jeannette...Clopineau...Fear...Fear of the war...Fear of death."

The sun was now above the woods and shining straight down on the clearing. He was going to walk south. It would be enough to walk with the sun. In a way, it would be enough to follow the sun.

Enrique and Buatois were still talking. Pablo could sense them near him. He stood up. The trees and the sky turned more and more quickly. Pablo leaned his rifle against the tree-stump, between the two men. He took one step...a second step...a third step.

The trees, the earth, and the sky rotated more and more swiftly.

"What's the matter with him? Is he drunk?"

Enrique's voice filled the whole clearing. Pablo hesitated, took another step.

"No, he hasn't drunk anything. I think he's ill."

Another three, four, five paces.

"Where are you going?"

Pablo stood still. This time the earth and sky were turning round him. He was going to plunge into the sky above the trees.

"Oh!"

That was the last thing he heard, together with the almost imperceptible sound of hurrying feet.

At one stroke the night had returned, in the wonderful clarity of a clear morning.

PART SIX

PART SIX

XLVIII

DISCHARGED as "physically unfit", Pablo was free. The certificate signed by the doctor, countersigned by the lieutenant, and carrying the stamp of the Free French Forces was in his pocket. The Free French Forces were the Army, and in the Army, when it was a question of issuing documents, nothing ever moved very quickly. He had had to wait for a week. A whole week after the liberation of the district. A week in this forest where a part of the group still remained.

In the very first days Enrique and the Maquis band had packed up immediately to follow the army of liberation. There remained now only youngsters newly arrived or reserve officers who had hurried to put on their uniforms as soon as the last trailing German was out of sight.

These fellows, when it came to the question of documents, were experts, and during the past fortnight Pablo had remained lying in his tent. Life had come back to him, and the forest no longer held any fears, it simply oppressed him. He looked often towards the south-west. Down there, beyond the trees, there were the hills sloping down to the plain. And on those hillsides the sun was filling out with sugar the already swollen grapes.

Pablo had waited for an entire week, but the certificate was now in his pocket, his pack was on his back, and he was walking through the woods.

When he reached the point where the wood joined the road Pablo jumped the ditch. A sentry was standing there. He was a young fellow Pablo did not know.

"Where are you going?"

"I'm off home."

"Where's your permit?"

Pablo pulled out the document. The man looked at it, and then, looking up, he asked, "Were you wounded?"

"No," said Pablo. "I'm ill."

"Oh!"

There was a silence. Pablo folded the paper and put it back in his pocket.

"And they let you go off on foot? They wouldn't even take you as far as Lons in a car?"

"No, there won't be a lorry for two days, so I preferred to get back home walking.

"Cheerio," said the man.

"Goodbye," said Pablo.

He began to walk on again. Around him was a group of meadows separated by jutting spurs of the forest which came often to the verge of the road.

No, Pablo had not been wounded. Others had been wounded, others had been killed in the attack on the town. But at that time Pablo was lying in bed. Sick and fevered. From inside his tent he heard the bark of bazookas and the yapping of hand-grenades. When Buatois came back he told him about the attack. It had lasted only a few hours. "Pity," Buatois had said, "that you couldn't be there."

Yes, a pity, but a man cannot fight when he is ill. A man cannot fight when his legs refuse to bear him.

Pablo thought suddenly of the forest. The forest so much like the one close to him now. He stepped off the road and went towards the nearest trees. The shade was cool. The meadow had just been mown, and the wind was full of the smell of hay. They had stopped here the day they went on patrol. They had watched the border of the other wood for a long time before crossing the open space.

Pablo breathed deeply. He had walked quickly, and sweat was running down his face. He put down his pack, got out his knife, and cut from a hazel-tree a branch which he then stripped of its twigs.

Around him everything seemed to be breathing smoothly. All was calm, and the trees swayed gently in the breeze. He remained for some moments standing still in the sunshine. He was alone. Absolutely alone. Nothing could come out of the shadows of the wood. No gun could be aimed at him. His blood ran calmly in his veins; he no longer felt in the depths of his throat that bitterness which had prevented him from smelling and enjoying the scents carried by the wind.

He picked up his pack and made his way back to the road.

At the moment when the sun was immediately above his head

Pablo was already beyond the Révigny valley. He had preferred not to follow the road, and it was in the heart of the forest that he stopped to eat the bread and the bar of chocolate he had brought with him. Around him all was still. The wind was moving only in the depths of the valley, between the trees bordering La Vallière. Pablo sensed this from time to time by the movement of a tree-top, the fluttering of leaves. But here there was only the huge sun shining down on the wilting grass, gliding between the hornbeams to spread patches of light on the dust of the pathway.

Because he had not walked for several days Pablo could already feel weariness moving up his legs and reaching his back. But this weariness was a friend. It moved in his muscles without ever making him really uneasy. It did not oppress his chest or touch the beat of his heart.

Since the morning he had been walking through meadows and woods, always breathing easily. Not for a moment had he had the feeling that death was riding round the bend of a path. Each time he had seen a man in a field he had waved an arm, shouting, "How's it going?"

Every time each man shouted back, "Could go quicker."

Or else: "Bit dry, but nothing to grumble about."

Now he set off again, still following the course of the sun, which had already begun to go down. Once past the village of Moiron he would make his way to Vaux, and then, after Geruge, he would find the first acacias. This time he wouldn't have to hide as on the day when he had come back after taking Enrique up. He would take the road. He would pass along by the cuttings. The saplings must be splendid. Once he was out of the woods the village would lie in front of him, on his left, the range of hillsides all lined with vines.

Once there, he would have only a few minutes to walk before reaching the farm. Night would be very near. Germaine would be back at the house, and Jeannette would be setting the table. Clopineau might still be with the cattle.

Pablo stood up. His legs were numb, and his pack seemed heavier. He walked on, nevertheless, and soon got into his swing again.

No, he had not been wounded. He was walking now as he had done in the past, and his illness had left him only a little fatigue which some work would soon shift.

291

He thought many times that Enrique, Buatois, and the others must be marching also, somewhere, in the direction of Germany.

Had they had to fight? Had they had men killed, wounded? At Lons, before retreating, the Germans had set fire to part of the town. They had shot many people. For an instant the face of Mariana came before Pablo's eyes. There must be somewhere other Marianas breathing for the last time.

Far from here, to the north and the east, under the same sun in woods like these, there were certainly, at this very minute, men and women dying.

Here the war had passed. It had followed its path from which Pablo had stood aside. It had left behind debris, dead bodies, empty places, but it had gone.

Pablo walked on. The sun was going down. In an hour he would be marching on facing the sun. He would truly be walking towards the sun. He was tempted, for a moment, to go off to the left and straight through to Brûlis. He thought how, if he did so, the plain and the village would appear before him suddenly. Immediately he would be able to see all the farm's land. He hesitated. No. It would take too long. Once he was at Brûlis he would have to go back along the hillside road as far as the farm. He had found his marching rhythm again, but his weariness was still with him, despite all, demanding that he take the shortest route.

He started to walk again.

No, he had not been wounded. He had not fought.

As he went through Geruge, Pablo saw that garlands had been strung from house to house, flags were at the windows, and, on the square, there was a flower-decorated platform for musicians. He went across to a young lad.

"Is there a fair on?"

The boy stopped chewing. "No, but since the liberation people dance nearly every evening. There are soldiers who come. Americans and French. And the chewing-gum they give us!"

Pablo thanked him and resumed his march. When he left the village the sun was almost at the level of the tops of the first firs. On the plain all must be copper-coloured.

Pablo bent his head forward because of the sun.

No, he had not fought. He had not been wounded; at this moment he was walking. He was returning to the lands which awaited him.

292

XLIX

W HEN he reached the courtyard of the farm Pablo stood still. It was almost night. In the kitchen the lamp was lit and the shutters were still open.

He had taken the footpath to go round the village, and he had walked quickly, more and more quickly as he neared the farm. He had almost run, thrust along by a great happiness which was welling up in him and began almost to burst out as he caught a breath of the house.

Then suddenly, at the moment he was about to enter the door, his joy froze. He did not dare to go on. He looked towards the window, but from where he was he could see only a corner of the table. His heart began to beat heavily. He took a deep breath and looked towards the stable. There was light down there also. Germaine must be milking. Clopineau was probably feeding the animals. Pablo thought of La Noire. He hesitated for a moment, then he began to walk to the kitchen.

As he came level with the window he stopped. Jeannette was alone, standing motionless by the stove. The table was not yet laid. He went on to the door, which he opened gently.

As soon as he walked in, Jeannette turned. Pablo smiled. Jeannette's hands began to tremble. Her entire face came alive, and she opened her mouth to grunt.

Pablo walked towards her. "Good evening, Jeannette!"

She did not move, but grunted several times. She lifted her hands towards Pablo. They were dirty. Pablo took hold of them, however, and, pulling the little girl towards him, he kissed her twice on each cheek. She grunted again, and when he went to step back she caught hold of his sleeve to keep him near.

"Poor little Jeannette," he said. "My poor little Jeannette."

Pablo waited for a few seconds, and then, when she was a little calmer, he said to her gently, "You've stopped washing yourself, have you?"

Jeannette twitched her mouth, and, swinging her shoulders, moving at her usual pace, she went towards the sink.

She washed slowly, turning her head from time to time towards Pablo, who smiled at her. He went across to her.

"That's good," he told her. "Very good. Had you already forgotten that you should wash?"

As Pablo went back towards the table, clogs sounded on the doorstep. The *patronne* came in, with Clopineau following.

They stood still for a moment, and then the *patronne* moved forward.

"Good evening, Pablo."

"Good evening, *patronne*.... Good evening, Clopineau."

"So here you are," said the old man. "We were wondering if you'd gone off with the Americans."

"No. I came back as soon as I possibly could."

The *patronne* had put down her pail of milk. "Come along, Jeannette, lay the table," she said. "Pablo must be hungry."

"How did you come?" she asked.

"On foot."

"On foot from right up there?"

Pablo laughed. "Yes. Otherwise I would have had to wait two days longer, and I thought there was probably a lot of work to be done here. How are things at the moment?"

The *patronne* and the old man hesitated. Then the old man said, "Very good. The vintage will be good, I think."

Pablo emptied his glass. He looked at the *patronne*, but each time their eyes met she looked away or lowered her eyelids. She had her hair up. A stray wisp was fluttering against the white nape of her neck. Pablo suddenly felt a longing to be alone with her.

"I'd very much like to have a look at the animals," he said. "Will you come with me, *patronne*?"

"No, no. You go. I've got to get the food ready."

Her voice had a curious note. Pablo stood up and went out.

At the stable all was clean and in good order. La Noire had begun to whinny immediately he opened the door. He stayed close by her for a little while, then went back to the kitchen.

By now night had fallen. The evening coolness was coming down. Pablo felt the chill of his damp shirt sticking to his back.

"I must go up and change my clothes before we sit at table," he said.

He had almost reached the far door when the *patronne* brought him to a stop:

"Wait!"

Pablo turned round. She took a few steps towards him. He

294

smiled. "Are you frightened I won't be able to find my own way?"

He stood aside to let her pass. She lowered her eyes.

"No, there's something I must explain. All your things are in there."

She had not gone as far as the door to the stairs. Turning to the left, she went round Pablo and opened the cupboard. As she stood with her back turned Pablo stared at Clopineau. The old man shrugged his shoulders almost imperceptibly and also looked down.

Finally, after an interminable minute, the *patronne* moved away from the cupboard. Her eyes were glistening. She returned to the table, and then, beginning to cut bread to go in the soup, with her head still down, she explained: "My Pierre has come back. He wanted his room. So, till you came back, I put everything there, in the cupboard."

Pablo shut his eyes for a second. He had just the same feeling he had had in the clearing. It seemed to him suddenly that everything in the kitchen had begun to turn. But no, he opened his eyes and, leaning towards the shelf of piled linen, took out a shirt and changed. Then, returning to the table, he took his usual place opposite Jeannette.

The table was now laid. At the end of the table, in the place of the *patron*, which had remained so long unused, there was a white plate. Against the fumed oak of the table it made a bright splash from which Pablo could not take his eyes.

Suddenly the old man asked, "It wasn't too tough? Seems you were in a battle."

Pablo could not think; at first he was surprised and felt empty, with Clopineau's words echoing curiously in his head. Then, immediately afterwards, someone he had long forgotten forced himself into his mind, almost tangibly. One of the men who had been killed near Madrid, at the time when many had fully realized what was happening. He was a man about fifty years old who kept repeating, "There is only one reason to fight, one only —the hope that the war being fought will be the last. It's only when one knows there will never be a last one, that one war always begets another, well, then . . ."

Pablo did not even look up towards Clopineau. He remained silent and motionless. The old man did not insist.

The soup was ready. Steam rose from the soup-tureen towards

295

the lamp and sent a faint shadow over the table. The white plate seemed like a smooth pond with a patch of light mist pierced by the sun above it. The mist assumed a thousand shapes, had a thousand faces flowing into one another. Some came from near-by places, others from afar and days gone by. They passed constantly from one side to the other of this circle of light, seeming to disappear but always coming back. When Jeannette or the *patronne* walked by the table the mist moved and the swirls gave the shadows a different life. The forms moved more quickly, or hesitated for a second; the faces grimaced, smiled, seeming to mock.

Pablo was not thinking. He was waiting. His clothes were on a shelf in the cuboard—well pressed and ironed. He had only to put them in his pack, put his pack on his back, and go.

He would have to stand up and take ten steps to stop in front of the cupboard, put the linen in his pack, take his hazel stick, and go. He would have to do that all in one movement, without stopping, without looking at anyone.

"I don't think he'll be very late, but if you are hungry we can begin without waiting for him."

Pablo jumped. He turned to the *patronne* and said, "I'm in no hurry."

"Well, for my part," said the old man, "since it's ready, I'll have my soup. I don't like being late getting to bed."

The patronne served Clopineau. "Are you sure you don't want to eat immediately?" she asked Pablo.

He held out his plate. The mist was now rising towards him. On its way it brushed against his face. It smelled deliciously of smoked bacon and cabbage. At the camp he had often thought of this smell mixed with that of the wood-fire. He looked towards the kitchen stove. In the hearth two logs were blazing. To one side there was a large basket full of logs he had cut the previous winter. Some were grey, with no bark on them, fretted, and with many marks of staples and rusty wounds. These had come from the old posts dragged out of land they had bought to bring back into cultivation again. Pablo could see these patches of land, one after the other. All well placed, all cleaned up, replanted, manured, and clean as a whistle.

Several times he looked at Clopineau. The old man, however, was eating without lifting his head, without saying a word, sucking his moustache between each spoonful of soup.

"Aren't you eating?" the *patronne* asked.

296

Pablo picked up his spoon. "Yes, I'm just going to start."

He stirred his soup for a moment, and then, before putting the spoon to his lips, he asked, "So the prisoners have returned?"

"No," said the woman, "but Pierre escaped more than a month ago. He was in Switzerland, so he was able to come back as soon as the Boches had gone."

Pablo began to eat. It now seemed to him that he had been afraid without any reason. The son had returned; he had taken his own bedroom again. That was all. Pablo looked towards the *patronne* again, and this time it was a moment or two before she lowered her eyes. Pablo tried to guess what she was thinking, but he could only see that she was sad.

"Everything went well for him?" he asked.

"Yes."

"He didn't have too much to grumble about?"

"No, towards the end he was on a farm, where he ate fairly well and there was no fear of shelling."

They became silent for a moment. Pablo ate another few spoonfuls. He now felt almost happy. Almost relaxed.

"And the plots of land," he asked, "has he seen them?"

She nodded her head and looked down.

"What does he think of them?" asked Pablo.

She did not reply. Clopineau had finished his soup. "Pour me half a glass of wine, and then I'll be off," he said.

Pablo poured the wine.

"Don't you want anything else?" asked the *patronne*.

"No, that'll do me. It's later than usual, so I don't want too much in my stomach, or I shan't sleep."

Once again Pablo felt a twinge of distress. The old man swallowed his wine and stood up.

"Well, good night, everybody," he said.

He went out, and Pablo listened to the sounds of his footsteps fading into the night. When there was no longer any sound other than the purring of the fire Pablo looked at Jeannette, then at Germaine, and then at Jeannette again.

The little girl's eyes had not left him since he arrived. Each time he turned towards her he saw her mouth part and her eyes widen. Jeannette's whole face smiled. Germaine remained melancholy. Pablo waited a little longer before asking, "What's the matter? Anyone would think that something was wrong."

Germaine stood up, went as far as the stove, and stirred the

297

potatoes, which were cooking in the cast-iron saucepan. Then, returning to her chair, she sat down heavily and put her elbows on the table. Pablo waited. The silence hung over them like a frosty night. Germaine moved her lips twice almost imperceptibly.

"Come on," said Pablo finally. "If there's something to be said you must say it."

She lifted her head, heaving a sigh. "He's going to get married."

She stopped again.

"Well, that's quite normal. He was engaged before he left."

"Yes, yes, yes, it's normal," she said, very quickly. "It's normal to get married, but it's not normal to ... to ..."

She stopped. Her chin was puckered, and her lips were trembling.

"Well, tell me ... what is it?"

Suddenly, with every word sounding strangled, she cried, "They don't want to stay on the land. He's found a business he wants to buy in Lyons. It's her who's put the idea into his head. They want to go to the town. And they're going to sell everything to buy this business. Everything ... everything ..."

She was not weeping, but the words were strangled in her throat. They stopped there to turn into sobs which she held back by an effort of will. Her whole face was contorted.

For what seemed a long time they stared at each other. Pablo had put down his spoon. His fists were clenched. A grimace passed over Germaine's face.

"He's at her place.... They had to see the business broker again. Tomorrow they're all going to come.... With her parents too. And those who are going to buy the.... And the broker!"

She had almost shouted the last phrase. However, her eyes remained dry. Pablo waited for a few seconds before asking, "And you? What about you if they sell everything? What are you going to do?"

At that she hung her head.

"What are you going to do?" Pablo repeated.

"They're taking me with them."

She had said this in a voice Pablo did not know. A voice without anger, without sadness, without hate. A voice which pronounced empty words.

They were motionless for a long time, then, when she lifted
298

her head, Pablo saw two large tears run down her bronzed cheeks. He looked at her for a long time without speaking.

In a few days she had become an old woman.

Pablo waited a little longer, and then, standing up, he walked as far as the cupboard and looked back.

"May I sleep over the way, just tonight?"

Germaine nodded agreement without looking at him. Then, without haste, he looked for the lantern, lit it, put his clothes in his pack, and went out.

L

THERE was no moon. The night was dark. All the light of the stars remained in the sky where it flickered like a springtime mist. The wind coming from the hill was still warm with the heat of the day still lying on the ground. It smelled of the forest, it smelt of the sunburnt stones of the hillside. It smelled also of the village with fires lighted for the evening meal; the village where the open stables puffed into the night the odours of sweating animals and fresh manure.

The village was alive—the life of the wind mixed with the life of man as it passed through.

Pablo stood still. He pressed the glass of the lantern against his thigh, the better to see the night.

Now he could breathe. Just to have found again the night wind made him feel less weighed down. He crossed the road. The wind was everywhere about him. It was one of those weak but steady, even-tempered winds. A wind like marathon runners who move always with the same long, supple stride, following the rhythm of their well-regulated breathing. For a moment Pablo thought the wind was like those dogs which are always under your feet; sometimes they irritate you, but when they are not there you hasten to call them. You can do anything with the wind about you. You can spend days working, nights on guard, or asleep, or making love.

Pablo turned round and looked at the house. He thought of the spring wind he had felt on his bare chest, the night he had got up to go and see La Noire. He thought of Germaine, and of the first purchase of their first piece of land.

A little while ago, when he was going across to the cupboard to collect his things, he had felt a great emptiness inside him. Now he was almost calm, almost unconcerned. The house was to be sold, together with all the land, perhaps in several lots, perhaps to someone who would tear out the vines; Germaine was going away. Everyone would go.

Pablo turned about suddenly. A light was coming along the road. He remained still, the glass of the lantern firmly against his thigh.

The son was coming back. He put his bike under the window and went in. For a second his silhouette was framed in the rectangle of light, and then the door was shut.

Now, once more, there was nothing round Pablo but the night. A night which held its poor, flickering light very high, a night which did not light up the earth. The light which fell from the window on to the ground was dirty. Only the wind continued to live. Nevertheless, in the wind something had changed. The scents it was bringing were less warm, less distinct. They were blending together to become only the smell of a forest far away, more mysterious, rather wild.

Pablo breathed again for a long time this breath of the earth before taking the few paces which separated him from the old barn.

When he reached it he put down his lantern, lifted the latch, then set his back against the door. When it opened, a little dust fell from the ceiling. Picking up his lantern, he went in and pushed the door to without closing it entirely.

Nothing had changed here. Pablo shone the beam of the lamp everywhere, bringing it to rest on the hook smothered in cobwebs. The hook of the hanged man. The lantern trembled slightly. Pablo looked at the stairway, returned once again to the hook, then went up slowly. The steps still creaked. Above there was a little more straw than when he had come with Enrique. The musty smell in the lower room rose as far as this. He opened the shutter, put down the lantern, and then, getting out his blanket, he spread it on the straw. Taking off only his boots, he lay down.

The night scarcely touched the tiles. It was there, however, all round the barn, living and almost warm. Pablo could feel it.

Little by little it became more heavy. It was round Pablo too, it was even below him. Different, less mobile, and more humid. The smell of it came up between the floorboards and up the stairway. It battled with that from outside which came in through the opening and flowed under the roof.

As he had gone into the barn Pablo had awakened the night.

This night which was rising had brushed against the cold walls, the iron hook, the black beams. That which came from outside had run across the warm earth, between the grasses, between the lines of vines, between the firs on the hill. From everywhere it had pilfered a little of life.

In the room below the night was imprisoned. It was a night which remained unchanged even during broad daylight. It was not like the other which encircles the earth every day before returning. It remained there, squatting between four walls to keep its smell of death.

Still motionless, Pablo listened to their struggle. They fought with subtlety and dexterity and almost without a sound. Faintly, from time to time, there was a rustling, a sigh, a stifled moan. Sometimes a slight, a very slight creak. Nevertheless they were fighting. Pablo could feel it, and as the struggle continued a vague fear grew in him, pressing little by little on his chest.

The two nights were fighting, but it was a whole world against another world.

It seemed to him even, at moments, that he was dreaming wide awake, and that his dream was grotesque. Yet the fear was always there, pressing on him.

As he lay down he had rather hoped that weariness after his day of marching would help him to sleep; he now knew that here also there was a battle. His fatigue was still there, but so was fear, and for the moment fear was the stronger. It was keeping him awake, his eyes open, attentive, watching the slightest move of the two nights.

But the nights had already been fighting for a long while, and neither one nor the other showed the smallest sign of weariness. Pablo passed a hand across his forehead. He knew that his fever was coming back.

He sat on the straw, felt for his boots, and pulled them on. Then, without taking the lantern, he groped his way down.

Once he was outside he began to walk in the direction of the hill. Thus he had the wind directly against his face and chest. He

301

could feel it enveloping him, singing in his ears before running off across the invisible plain.

Here there was no longer any battle of the night. There was only a night where the trees, the vines, the houses, could barely be seen, a night where life flowed like a fresh spring from the summit of the hills where the trees sang.

Pablo walked like this for a long time.

Then, when he felt the air freshening, when his fatigue seemed to him to be spread through his entire body, he returned in the direction of the barn.

He had walked without thinking, not seeking to get some order in his mind, but the walk and the freshness of the wind had done the work.

As time passed the heat mist dispersed and the brightness of the stars grew greater. The houses stood out more whitely against the background of the plain; the roads ran between the vines like large, pale ribbons. There was no longer any light in the village.

Pablo had almost reached the barn when he saw a shadow move against the wall, at the side of the barn door. He stopped, waited a moment, and in a whisper he asked, "Who is it?"

The shadow moved again. "It's me.... I was looking for you."

Germaine came over to him. "Where were you?" she asked.

"I needed a breath of air. I went for a walk."

They walked a few paces along the path. As they got near to the door of the barn Pablo asked, "What do you want?"

"Come along, I must talk to you."

She entered the barn and went up first. Once there, she settled down on the straw. "Sit down," she said.

Pablo sat down beside her. There was a short silence, and then he asked, "Well, what is it you want to say to me?"

She hesitated for a few seconds and then whispered, "It's terrible. It's terrible, you know."

In the darkness her hand pressed down on Pablo's hand. By the sound of her voice and the way she was clutching his hand he knew that she was going to cry again. He tried to think of something to say, but his head was empty. Or, rather, in his head there was nothing other than the song of the night wind, the song of the hill.

"If you had been there, perhaps I wouldn't have given in," she said. "But all alone.... And he had been away for such a long time."

302

Pablo could think of nothing to say. He was thinking of Germaine. Solely of her. A little earlier, in the kitchen, he had seen her aged, wrinkled, fatter, and stooping.

"Do you think there is anything I can still do for you?" he asked.

Germaine had let go of his hand. There was a silence.

"What are you going to do?" she asked.

He gave a derisive laugh. "Me? What d'you think I *can* do now? Tomorrow I'll go away."

"You can't go like that."

"What d'you mean, like that?"

"For months and months you were never paid."

"Did I ask for anything?"

"No, but what's due's due."

Pablo thought for a moment before saying, "If I didn't ask for any money it was because I wanted you to go on buying land. Let's say it's rather as if I'd made a bad investment."

"Why d'you say that?"

"Because it's true. I have always worked with you as if I was working for myself."

"But why d'you talk of the land? You think what's happened to me is not bad enough?"

The last words almost stuck in her throat.

They were distorted sounds like half-formed words and cries. She was going to weep. Pablo knew it. He had known it even before she came here. He knew also why she would cry. He knew everything at this moment. He imagined what must be passing inside her mind, and he tried to find something to say.

He searched his mind for words to comfort Germaine, and at the same time he thought of his own distress. He reviewed all that he had done with her. He thought of all the land bought piece by piece, all the projects he had still in mind, and yet within himself he could not find any trace of bitterness.

Beside him Germaine wept softly. He could not see her: he scarcely heard her, but he could imagine her face, that of an almost old woman down which tears must be running. He imagined her heavy bosom, sagging, her thick, rounded shoulders shaken by sobs.

All that was outside him. Tonight he felt as hard as the stones of the old wall.

"Since the matter is settled," he said, "there's no reason for

303

tears. The moment you agreed you had only yourself to blame. But what I cannot understand is why you are selling everything. You could have sold just enough for what they needed, and you at least could have stayed."

Germaine sniffed and coughed several times. "That wouldn't have been enough," she said. "It had to be the house and the land. The business agent said so: one without the other and the whole value is lost."

"Of course, it's not a farm and a few fields you're selling, it's a domain. A great domain. It is an industry in perfect working order, with tools and machinery in excellent condition, with . . ."

As he continued to talk his voice had hardened. He stopped suddenly, waited a moment, and then, spacing his words, he asked, "But perhaps that's what you've come to ask? For me to remain, to be handed over with the machinery? It is done, I believe, to include the farm-workers in the sale."

Germaine had ceased sobbing. She waited for some seconds before replying. The light coming in through the opening was more milky than it had been earlier. A trace of pale light was mixed with the night wind, and now they began to see each other. Pablo was lolling on his side. His moist eyes shone. Since she could not bring herself to reply he snapped, "You didn't explain to your son what a domain like that represents? You didn't try to make him see reason? And what's more, is there any law that can force you to sell your lands because he demands it? I don't know French law, but it seems to me that you must have a right to a say in all this."

Pablo was now angry. There was no sadness in him, but a sour bile rose in his throat. Now he almost shouted, "When I think that I thought you strong, and you let yourself be manœuvred like that!"

He stopped suddenly. Germaine had begun to weep again. To see her like that, and to hear her, made Pablo think of Jeannette.

"And Jeannette?" he asked.

"Jeannette?"

"Heavens! Hasn't she any rights also? And what's more, what are you going to do with her? Surely you aren't going to take her to the town with you?"

There was a long silence. Germaine lowered her eyes. Pablo waited, his eyes fixed on her hair where a large hairpin shone. Finally, without moving at all, Germaine murmured, "Pierre

304

wanted her to be treated. He said that if she was sent to some nursing home..."

"You're going to lock her up, eh?"

"No, she would...I mean, it's a hospital."

Pablo caught hold of Germaine's arm. For a moment he squeezed it in his hand, without saying anything. Then, without anger, but in words that hissed, he exclaimed, "You don't give a damn for the child! None of you give a damn! You just want to get rid of her."

He had wanted to shout. To threaten. He was on the point of saying, "There'll be none of that!" but he restrained himself.

He himself was no-one. Nothing more than a Spanish refugee, in a more or less regular situation. He was a man who could be sent out of France without any reason being given. They would not have to throw him out, since he had left work voluntarily.

Had left to fight the Germans!

Suddenly Pablo thought of the woods. Of the clearing. The pain of his fear gripped his stomach just for an instant. Everything passed before his eyes. The liberation. The dances in the villages. The celebrations. The battles. The departure of Enrique and the others. He saw again the grotesque silhouette of Enrique carrying his enormous pack and disappearing across the snow. Enrique, the fighter.

Mariana!

Mariana and millions of other dead.

No, Pablo had not fought! Not this time. He had not been able to do so.

Germaine was no longer weeping. The minutes slipped by. On the tiles the night was passing, rumpling a mourning band with a scarcely visible sheen. It moved away slowly, coming from behind the hill to travel to the far side of the plain.

Far off, on the Moulin wood side, the night birds were crying to each other. Behind the barn there was a cat fight which lasted a long time, with screechings like those of a new-born babe being strangled.

Everything passed through Pablo's head without order, but not pell-mell. After the burst of anger which had escaped him earlier he felt weak. A shiver ran down his spine. Germaine, still not moving, sighed several times.

"Well," he said finally, almost in a whisper, "what is it you came to ask?"

305

She too spoke in a low voice, trying to find her words. "We can't sell before the harvest . . . November, certainly . . . so if you could . . . that is, if it's possible . . . I wanted to ask you . . ."

Pablo interrupted her. "I'll do it. I'll stay as long as necessary."

Germaine stood up. She went as far as the stairway. Her foot scuffled on the floor, seeking the first step. There she stopped and spoke again. "I would rather you didn't talk about it to Pierre."

Pablo laughed mockingly. "I know how to behave with a boss!"

"No," she mumbled, "it's not that. But you must understand, he's my baby."

Pablo had barely heard the last word she had murmured almost without moving her lips, and yet just this word . . .

Pablo shook himself abruptly, like a dog coming out of water. Down below the door was just being shut. Germaine had come in slippers. He did not hear her walking away. He rolled himself in his blanket and stretched out, his head on his pack.

There was no longer any conflict between the night in the barn and the night outside. There was only a night weighing silently on Pablo. It was not really cold, nor did it smell truly of the hill. It was a flavourless night, almost entirely dark, in which only a few faces made patches of light.

Among these faces there were above all the faces of the dead. More immediate than the others, there was the face of Jeannette, a dirty face, scarcely more alive than the others.

LI

THE sun was not yet in the sky when Clopineau and Pablo reached the vines. La Noire, after several days in the stable, had pulled well, trotting across each piece of level road, lengthening her stride on the rises.

As soon as they reached the vines the old man began to lift up loose shoots and attach them to the trellises. Pablo unhitched La Noire from the cart to harness her to the plough.

"It's a good job you're back," shouted the old man. "The weeds are beginning to get the upper hand."

306

All along the road they had scarcely spoken, except for remarks about fields they passed.

Pablo took hold of the handles. "Off you go, my beauty," he shouted. "Up like lightning!"

The horse started off, willing and powerful as ever.

When they reached the summit of the vineyard Pablo turned round. The breeze was carrying between the vines a long cloud of dust raised by the plough. The sky shone, very clear, right across to the horizon. The plain stretched away, still in shadow. The smoke rising from the village chimneys joined up and settled as shadows unravelling at roof-level.

Since he had got up Pablo had not yet really thought. He had reviewed his night. The face of Germaine, her strangled voice. But he had not thought. He had managed to occupy his mind otherwise.

But now that he had at his feet all this land which stretched out of sight, a deep sense of melancholy filled him. A melancholy which had come on him suddenly, without warning, simply at the sight of this awakening plain.

He looked at the village, the farm, the barn of the hanged farmhand where he had slept. Then for a long time he stared at the highway. The black highway bordered with trees, their trunks marked with white at the bends of the road. The highway along which he had seen the war pass. It came from the end of the plain. It stretched along at the bottom of the hills and disappeared before reaching the town. There it divided. One branch went up to the mountains and the other towards the north. It was from there that the war had come. It was towards there that the war had gone. One day, also, Enrique and the others would return along it. Along there would come those still alive. They would return marked by the war to parade in the beflagged streets and to dance in the squares with living girls.

For an instant there passed over the plain images of death and ruin. Stones tumbled down and streets spattered with blood. Banal images like those in popular weeklies. Images which had become banal because of repeated wars. Despite himself, Pablo rubbed his hands on his trousers as if to wipe them. Then he looked at them for a moment without seeing them. Then suddenly, shrugging his shoulders, he took hold of the stilt of the plough and made La Noire turn.

From that moment on he tried to avoid stopping. The work

307

was not heavy for the horse, and the descent gave him a chance to get his breath back.

Finally, on the stroke of ten, it was the old man who came out from the vines, shouting, "Isn't it time to stop for a bit of food?"

Pablo finished his descent and joined Clopineau, who was sitting on the side of the cart, facing the plain. For some hours the sun had been strong, and they could feel on their shoulders its good, frank warmth.

"Aren't you hungry then?" asked the old man.

"Yes, a little."

Pablo opened the basket. Germaine had prepared everything for the day. They began to eat in silence. The old man stared at a point on the horizon. Pablo looked at the village. The old man turned towards him to pour himself a drink or to cut himself a slice of bread. Pablo took no notice of him. He knew that the old man would start talking. He waited, and the old man did in the end ask, "Well, what are you going to do?"

Pablo finished munching his mouthful of bread and said simply, "Carry on."

Clopineau pursed his brow. His wrinkled forehead showed that he had not understood. After a moment he asked, "Carry on what?"

As if to himself, Pablo whispered, "Carry on living."

The old man smiled. "Come on. Don't be funny. I think we know each other well enough for you to be able to speak frankly. First of all, has she told you all that has happened?"

"Yes."

"Well, then, where do you come into all this?"

Pablo waved a hand towards the plain. The old man looked for an instant, and then, a little annoyed, he began to talk.

"But heavens above, it doesn't make sense, all that! You know perfectly well I'm not blind. I've known for a long time that you weren't just a farmhand, in the house. I'm not an innocent little choir-boy, you know."

Pablo laughed derisively. "So what? I'm not going to say to the son, 'You haven't the right to sell this farm because I've slept with your mother'! Can't you see what a farce that'd be?"

"I thought you were more intelligent. So you don't realize that this scamp has led his mother by the nose! That she allowed herself to be cheated like an idiot! But it would be all right if you gave her a straight talking-to for once. If you explained what a farm like hers really is, with all the land you've added to that which her father left."

"But he doesn't give a damn for all that!"

"Of course he doesn't give a damn for all that. But if you explained to him that if he let you and Germaine go on working he could live on velvet, perhaps he'd change his mind. I know that lad very well, I do. He's not bad at bottom, but they spoiled him. He's lazy and a trifler. And his future wife will probably be the same. They want to go to the town because they think that there all the good things of life will just fall into their laps. That's all. Nothing more!"

Pablo was still staring towards the limits of the plain. The blue line of hills became sharper as the sun moved higher. Where there was water it shone, the houses speckling the greenness with splashes of red and white. When Pablo blinked his eyes the plain looked like a vast, flowering meadow.

Searching now among the surroundings of the village, Pablo counted the pieces of land belonging to the farm. The original lands and the new ones; he looked also at the pieces of land which separated them; all those which he had hoped to buy or exchange to unify the domain. For some moments he remained thus, reflecting. The old man had stopped eating, but he did not speak. A few paces from the cart La Noire was grazing on the grass of the slope.

Since Pablo still did not speak, the old man ended by jumping down from the cart.

"Anyhow," he said, "do something. There's still time for the moment. But later, when the agreement's made, that'll be another kettle of fish."

He was standing in front of Pablo, who was still bent forward over the side of the cart. Pablo looked down.

"All right," he said. "I'm going down."

He jumped from the cart, tied La Noire to a fence-stake, and, turning to the old man, shouted, "I'll take the short cut. An hour from now I'll be there."

He plunged into the vines which went down the other side of the hill and began to descend with long steps between two lines of vine-plants.

He had not, as in the days of dressing the vines with copper sulphate or vintaging, a full *bouille* on his back to push him along from behind. But he felt a greater strength than ever. A strength he had not known for years and years.

When he had had to labour to bring the land into good heart, to clear it and to plant it, he had found great reserves of strength in himself. But that which had suddenly come to him was different. He did not know when, or how long ago, he had used it, but it was long, long ago.

Nevertheless he found it young and new, ready to serve again.

Throughout his journey he cut straight across meadows and vineyards. As he approached the house he clenched his fists, as if to assure himself of this strength he had found he still had in him.

The farther he descended, the smaller the plain seemed, the more vast the sunlit sky seemed to grow. Everywhere there was a warm light, and the wind which was blowing snatched a bird's song from every hedge.

LII

BREATHING rapidly, dripping with sweat, Pablo stopped in the courtyard. His strength was still there, very alive and warm like an animal ready to pounce.

He took time to breathe two or three times, and, already, it seemed less alert. Then, without further delay, he walked towards the kitchen door. He went in.

Empty!

The cast-iron pan was on the stove where a log blazed.

Pablo felt his impatient strength quiver. He went as far as the end door, opened it, and shouted up the stairs:

"Pierre! Pierre!"

Above there was a sound of footsteps, the noise of a door.

Not for an instant did Pablo think of Germaine or Jeannette. He waited with his hand on the door. His heart was still beating very quickly, but his breathing was already much more steady.

Steps crossed the landing, and Pierre appeared. He stopped at the edge of the first step and leaned forward to ask, "What is it? I thought you were up at the vines!"

Pablo swallowed his spittle. "No, I've come down. I must talk to you."

310

"Not now, I haven't the time. I'm just finishing dressing, and then I've got to go off."

Pierre turned away and disappeared.

Pablo remained a few seconds without moving, then he went up the stairs. The door of Pierre's room was open; Pablo went in.

"I apologize," he said, "but I must speak to you before you go out."

Standing in front of the mirror, Pierre was tying his tie. He turned round, his hand stretched out, smiling.

"How are you? How did things go with you?"

Pablo shook his hand. "Not too badly. And you? Did you have a difficult time?"

Pierre turned back to the mirror and straightened his tie. "No," he said. "It wasn't much fun a lot of the time, but I got away in one piece, that's the main thing."

The young man had changed. He was larger, thicker too. He had the red face of his father, with, however, in his face, and particularly his eyes, something rather harder which made him also look somewhat like his mother.

"But," he said, sitting on the edge of the bed, "I really must thank you. You helped my mother a great deal while I was in Germany."

"Exactly," said Pablo. "That's more or less the subject I want to talk to you about."

Pierre was now occupied in pulling on his shoes. He smiled, saying, "Yes, I know, my mother told me she owes you a lot of back pay. Don't you worry, it'll all be paid."

Pablo's strength moved in him. The animal arched its back, its muscles tautened.

"Listen, it's not that I've come about. It's something more serious."

Pierre stood up, saying, "Well, we'll see about it later. For the moment I've other fish to fry."

Pablo stepped back, shut the door, and put his back against it.

"If you will let me speak it'll take a couple of minutes, that's all."

The other had screwed up his eyes and clenched his fists. He was smaller than Pablo. For a moment he seemed to be weighing him up, then he said, "Very well, but make it snappy."

"It seems that you intend to sell . . ."

"It's more or less done."

"That's impossible. Nobody would sell a domain like this. Do you realize what it represents?"

"Yes, several million francs."

At this point Pablo began to shout. "I'm not talking about cash. I'm talking about work, all that had to be endured to do it."

Pierre interrupted him. This time it was he who shouted. "You don't say so! Have you come to read me a lesson? Do you think I've any lessons to take from a fellow who lived in clover while I was so stupid as to fight and to become a Boche prisoner? What did you do all that time? Sold wine and everything else on the black market to buy more land."

"But..."

Pablo could not go on. Pierre shouted too loudly, and he could feel his strength going.

"You did work, and it's just as well. You didn't think you were going to be looked after for doing nothing."

He stopped to take breath, and then, in a lower voice, he added, "And when I say looked after, I know what I mean."

Pablo sighed. Pierre was no longer shouting. He had even stopped speaking. But Pablo found nothing to say. With a few words the youngster had killed all the strength he had thought so firm.

"What did you fiddle, eh?" went on Pierre. "Make no mistake about it, I know just what went on. While others risked their skins you built yourself a little kingdom. If I'd been knocked off during a bombardment, that would have fixed things very nicely for you, wouldn't it?"

Pablo did not reply. There was silence for a few seconds. They remained staring at each other. Pablo's hands trembled. Suddenly, at a wild speed, a film ran through his head, in which he made a jump forward, catching Pierre by the throat, forcing him to the ground, and shouting, "Don't sell or I'll kill you! Swear to me that you'll never sell this land!" The other jeered at him. Then, holding him with one hand, Pablo hit him in the face. The other no longer shouted, and Pablo struck again, again, and again! Blood ran on the floor; Pablo's fist was all bloody. And when he let go of Pierre's dead body, the gendarmes were already there. Everybody began to insult and curse the Spanish refugee who had just killed an ex-prisoner. Then, while they took Pablo away, Pierre's body was laid on the bed in which his father had died. Once dead, he truly looked like his father.

312

Pablo passed a hand across his forehead. In front of him Pierre was still standing alert, his fists on his hips, his eyes hard. Pablo dropped his head. There were a few more moments of silence. Pablo looked at nothing, but his eyes took in the whole room. Behind Pierre there was the window wide open on the vista of vineyards and fields. In the rectangle of sky a lark rose, swooped three times, and disappeared.

"Well," said Pierre, "I think we have nothing else to say to each other."

Pablo shook his head, but did not move. Pierre went back to his bed, picked up his jacket, and put it on. Then, returning to the door, he said, "Very well, let me pass. I'm going to be late."

Pablo stood aside and opened the door. The young man went out and down the stairs first. Pablo followed, but when he reached the kitchen Pierre was already going through the door to the courtyard.

The *patronne* was standing by the table, busy with moulding cheeses. When she saw Pablo crossing the kitchen she stopped, made a movement of her chin as if she intended to speak, but Pablo looked away from her, and she remained silent.

As he reached the threshold he saw Pierre near the door, bending down and pumping up his bicycle-tyres. He went forward. Jeannette came out of the woodshed with a basket of vine-shoots. She looked at him and smiled. Pablo smiled back and took the road to the vineyards.

He walked without looking back, without raising his head towards the hill.

The sun's heat was now intense, but Pablo did not feel it. On his shoulders there was something else, weighing them down.

Several times he raised his open hands and stared at them.

Between his eyes and his hands, between his eyes and the blinding bright dust of the road, between his eyes and everything he tried to look at, there was a mist in which images of life and death were mixed together.

The face of the *patron* lying in his makeshift coffin, that of Pierre, obstinate and mocking, that of the *patronne* which had no precise expression, that of Mariana also, who tried at times to find a place in the front rank. And also another, unmoving, frozen in her dirt and her smile, frozen in her tears. A poor face from which Pablo had so often looked away when the sun shone on the drippings of her nose towards her partly opened mouth.

313

That face did not thrust forward. It remained at the back, letting the others jostle for a share of hatred or regret.

LIII

WHEN he reached the vines Pablo started work again without saying a word. The old man did not question him. At midday they ate in silence, sitting side by side in the shade of alder-trees. Then, until evening, they continued their task, regular and tireless, like good machines.

Pablo, on three or four occasions when he reached the end of a row, stopped long enough to follow with his eyes the tortuous twisting of the highway. He had no thought, nor had he said, "One day I'll take my pack and I will go in such a direction with the idea of doing this or that." No, he had decided nothing. However, he had looked at the highway several times; this highway which he had never followed very far except with his eyes. This highway he had seen the war pass along.

Then, at the distant end of the plain, the evening mist rose where the sun was now sinking before disappearing.

When they reached the farm it was not quite night, but the day was already half-way across the world.

They were sitting side by side, their legs hanging down, in the front of the cart which La Noire was pulling with her slightly heavy tread.

Today nothing had happened except a day of work beneath the sun.

At one moment, towards the middle of the afternoon, Pablo had clearly seen a black car pull up outside the house. Some people got out. Then the car had been driven along the best of the roads, slowing down at certain places. Clopineau had probably noticed it also, but he said nothing.

Now they were going back, and they knew they would find the table laid for the evening meal.

When they reached the courtyard they unhitched the mare. The old man led La Noire away while Pablo filled the racks with hay. Afterwards they went in to sit at table.

314

The *patronne* was stirring the soup. Jeannette was just sitting down in her place.

"Well?" said the *patronne* after a moment.

"It's finished," said Pablo. "All is clean and bright. Tomorrow we'll do those on the Berchut slope."

His voice was soft, absolutely calm.

The *patronne* served the soup and sat down. She coughed two or three times. She stirred her soup, cutting the bread and vegetables with her spoon. Her forehead was wrinkled, her eyebrows knitted.

Pablo sensed that she wished to talk, and he had a longing to say, "Come on, what are you waiting for, the way we're placed?" But no, he said nothing. He was calm. He felt well; a little dull like the plain beneath the evening mist. He had time, all the time in the world ahead of him.

She ate a spoonful, and then, coughing again, she said, "They came ... this afternoon."

Pablo looked at the end of the table. No place had been laid for Pierre. He had not noticed this before. The *patronne* made it clear. "He will not eat here this evening. He is dining with his future parents-in-law."

Clopineau continued to eat. Pablo ate also. From time to time he glanced at the *patronne*. Her eyes never left him, and her look seemed to say, "Help me. I must speak." But Pablo made no move.

Finally, after a few minutes, she made up her mind. "It's settled ... everything is settled. They will come in on November the 1st."

Pablo nodded his head to show that he had understood. The *patronne* went on, still with a break between each phrase: "There are five of them. They have two sons and a daughter.... So, of course, they won't need anyone."

Again he gave a sign that he had understood. The old man stopped eating. "That doesn't matter much to me. I'm refusing a day's work from people all over the place most of the time. At my age I don't need to do much to be sure of my food and tobacco."

Pablo had turned towards him. The old man became silent for a moment, and then, without looking at the *patronne*, he said: "But for Pablo, it's much more difficult."

He chewed his moustache. Pablo shrugged his shoulders. The *patronne* coughed again. They turned towards her.

315

"I think that can be arranged," she said. "I thought . . ."

Pablo interrupted her. Still calm, but in a rather hard voice, he said, "There's nothing to be arranged. I know what I have to do. On the 1st of November I shall be gone."

"Why?" she asked. "If we can arrange something else."

He kept silent. The old man had put his elbows on the table; he was waiting, his eyes half closed.

"You heard very well what Clopineau said: around here a man who wants to work need never worry about anything."

"That's true," said Clopineau, "but daily work, for an old chap like me, is all very well, but for someone with more needs . . ."

The *patronne* did not let him continue. In a more assured voice she went on: "A man with plenty of strength, with a fine horse and willing to do jobbing work in a district like this where there's a shortage of labour and tractors are useless, he's in a better position than a day-labourer."

For a moment Pablo closed his eyes to listen. This was not so much to pay attention to what she was saying, but to listen to her voice. She was talking as in the days when it was a question of buying extra land. He opened his eyes. She had sat up. He noticed that she had put on a fine dress, no doubt to receive her visitors and the broker.

"What's that you're saying about a horse?" said the old man.

She sat up further and, staring at Pablo, said, "There are two things agreed. The people who are buying will not take the Brûlis land and hut. They will not take La Noire either."

La Noire. Pablo had not thought much about La Noire in all that was going on.

"Why not?" he asked.

The *patronne* seemed to hesitate, then she said, "The money owing to you will be paid. That's understood, there's no more to be said. But in addition we are to give you the Brûlis land and La Noire."

She waited for a moment before saying in a slightly lower voice, "I know very well that La Noire is no longer young, but still . . . she can still make the journey again. And Brûlis, with the hut done up, and with another at the side for the mare . . ."

Pablo began to laugh. The others looked at him.

"Why d'you laugh like that?" asked the old man.

He did not reply, and, turning to the *patronne*, he asked, "Can we have the next course? I want to get to bed."

316

She stood up, served the haricot beans and bacon, and they began to eat again. After a moment the old man asked, "Well, what d'you want to do then?"

Pablo shrugged his shoulders without speaking.

"There's nothing else to be done," said the *patronne*. "It's surely a better solution than to go off without anything in prospect."

Pushing his chair back suddenly, Pablo stood up abruptly and shouted, "I didn't ask you to bother yourself about me, did I? I'm not asking for charity! I may be pretty low, but not that low."

His chair had fallen over. Jeannette began to cry. He looked at her, his hands clenched. Her eyes had never left him. She was weeping as always, her mouth open, her face almost unmoved, her shoulders scarcely disturbed by her sobs.

"Be quiet," said her mother. "Be quiet."

Pablo bent down and picked up the chair. He stood for a few seconds, his hands on the chair-back, his eyes fixed on Jeannette, and then he sat down.

"Don't cry, Jeannette," he said. "Don't cry, my little one."

But Jeannette continued weeping.

"Come along," said her mother. "Up to bed, that'll calm you down."

The little girl stood up.

"Go up," said Pablo. "There's nothing to worry about, go along. It's nothing."

When she had gone Pablo, turning to the *patronne*, asked, "Well, what have you decided to do with the little one, finally?"

Germaine sighed. "That's also been arranged," she said. "She will not go to the asylum at Bourg. She will go to the nuns at Lons. She'll be better looked after. That'll make it further for us to come to see her, but at least, when the fair's being held, she'll have people from round here to call and see her."

Pablo lifted his head. Germaine looked at him. Her eyes were more shiny and her voice less assured. They ate the cheese in silence; the two men each rolled a cigarette, and then, as they both stood up, the *patronne* asked, "Well, what have you decided?"

Pablo blew out a puff of smoke, looked in turn at the old man, Germaine, Jeannette's empty place, and then again at Germaine, saying, "We'll see. I need to think about it. We'll see."

Then he followed Clopineau, who was walking towards the door.

317

LIV

Work continued. Each passing day made the grapes a little heavier with sunshine. Soon the time of the wine-harvest would come, and the cellar had to be prepared and the vines to be kept in good order.

The season moved along, pushing forward the lives of men as it pushed forward the life of the vines.

Clopineau, Pablo, La Noire, and, sometimes, Jeannette continued the work, always at the same speed, always treating the land in the same manner. The *patronne* seldom accompanied them. When she did go with them there was embarrassment for them and for her.

With the days drawing in and the nights which had become cooler there came again time to sit down in the kitchen, once the animals had been cared for, to smoke a pipe while waiting for the meal. It was always the old man who gave the signal. Pablo followed his example, filled his pipe, and lit up.

Her milking done, the *patronne* came in and began to do the cooking. The old man would already be dozing. Pablo would look at him, look at Jeannette, and then at the *patronne*. There was always the steam rising from the saucepan, always also pipe-smoke, but the steam remained steam and the pipe-smoke remained pipe-smoke. Neither one nor the other ventured far from its source; everything in this kitchen was the same at the same time of day. It was the evening, it was the time for a pipe and for sleep, but there was something missing in this room. Something had gone, something Pablo had never noticed *before*, but the absence of which upset everything.

The first evening he remained in his chair until time for dinner. The following day, as soon as he had finished his first pipe, he went out in the courtyard. The third evening, after food had been given to the animals, he said to the *patronne*, "Please call me when the meal's ready."

She nodded, and Pablo walked off. He went round the house. On the other side, against the outhouse with a work-bench, there was a stump used when stakes or posts had to be given a pointed end. Repeated axe-strokes had hollowed it slightly. Pablo sat on it, with his back against the wooden wall. It was almost like an armchair. The warmth of an afternoon's sunshine was still in the wood, and Pablo felt it penetrating him. He filled his pipe and lit up.

Before him was the whole length of the plain and a sight of the hillside where night was wrestling for a last scrap of the day's warmth. Silence had come also. The silence composed of the thousand sounds of the evening. Above, here and there, stars were showing in the sky. Others shone above the plain, singly or in groups. More still twinkled.

So it was on many an evening, between the end of work and the time when the *patronne*, coming out on the doorstep, shouted, "Food's ready."

Pablo had said nothing on the subject of Brûlis, and no-one had mentioned it to him again. In fact, he did not think of it himself. He was living in waiting for the last day. He waited without impatience, almost without apprehension.

However, when he was alone in the evening, he often looked towards one point in the night. There was nothing over there except the mass of a hill, a little darker than the sky. Nevertheless by dint of staring at the same point he finished by seeing something like a vent in a triangular form appear. Sometimes he thought of a corner of the sky someone had tried to force into the hillside to split it like a thick log. Other evenings he thought of an arrowhead driven into the ground. This arrowhead seemed to say, "Up here, you see, it's here, the land they call Brûlis. A piece of land nobody wants because it doesn't fit in with the present age. It is too far off. At the moment no man can be found to cultivate it. Yet there is good land here."

Each evening there was a moment when Pablo kept silent with all his strength to listen to this triangle of sky which pointed out to him one spot of the earth. And every evening the triangle of sky found something new to say.

Yet it never invented anything. Most of the time it confined itself to talk of things Pablo had long known, but which he had forgotten. It spoke of the land, it spoke of La Noire, it spoke about men also. Men whom one could see from far off as Pablo had seen them when they were on the highway of the plain, with all their equipment for war and for death.

When Pablo's thoughts turned to the highway, when they

began to seek to rejoin those who had gone, there was always a moment when the darkness became deeper, where the highway itself joined the night. Then Pablo would turn his head, and immediately his eyes returned to the little triangle of sky wedged in the hill.

Pablo saw Spain again only two or three times. But each time he found again war and death. Then he pushed away the thought. He did so without any sense of shame. He had brought nothing with him except the image of Mariana.

Other memories also came back; those of the forest where death hid behind every tree. Then Pablo would feel the blood rising to his face. Sometimes he even hung his head or stared questioningly at the night around him. Sometimes he looked about him, to the left, where he could see Pierre's window. But Pierre was not there. Pierre was hardly ever there. Yet from the window a few words came, words hard as flint: "While others risked their skins."

Then Pablo would sigh. He would shake himself like a dog trying to shake off dried mud from its coat. Then there was always a host of images which returned, a swarm of words which murmured—Mariana. The man lying in the manger his feet tied, his face bloody. Spain again, here once more there was fighting. The highway which led to the north, towards men who were either dying or killing.

There was all that, and even, in Pablo's hands, the feel of a rifle moistened with sweat. Other words also came, brought by the fresh, night-coloured wind. These words had strange tonalities. They were sometimes like a spoken choir, a choir made of voices from far and near. But always they had a tone of reproach, evoking battle, liberty, duty, courage.

Pablo shook his head. He looked at the plain and the hillsides veiled in shadow. Sometimes also another picture came into his mind, the hook in the ceiling, the hook of the farmhand who had hanged himself.

Then he would stand up. He would walk quickly through the meadow, as far as the hedge. Then he would come back, only to go again. He would go on like that for a long time, his teeth clenched on the stem of his pipe, his hands clenched so tightly that his nails dug into his horny palms.

However, he ended each time by coming to a halt, his eyes fixed on the triangle of sky.

Then he would sit down once again on the stump and close his eyes.

His pulse slowed little by little. Around him the land was now asleep. Far, far off to the north, farther away even than the other side of the earth, men were continuing the war.

But here it was a peaceful night which enfolded the hills and the plains where the next wine-harvest was ripening.

EPILOGUE

On the last Sunday of November Pablo rose just before dawn. He groomed his mare, took from the table the haversack he had prepared the previous evening, and went off along the crest path. This was the first time in a month that he had left Brûlis.

When he reached the point where the hillside incurved a little the sky was already clearing. The grey mist weighed down in the distance, but a bright winter light flowed between the clouds and the hill. Pablo slowed his pace. With a touch of his hand he pushed round to his back the haversack which was slapping his side.

Twenty yards away to the left was the hedge from which they had watched the village, the *patronne* and he, one night when a great light lit up all the far end of the plain and a thunderstorm had risen, blotting out the stars.

Pablo halted; he shrugged his shoulders twice. Then, going along the border of the little wood, he walked on quickly.

The sky cleared for a moment, showing a less grey light which seemed to be draped on the vines and the waste land of the hill. On the left, in the hollow, the village still scarcely free of night was beginning to show smoking chimneys. Without stopping Pablo looked at it several times. He felt a little fear; no, not that, just a little twinge in his chest.

He began to walk again, still following the crests, and the village was soon behind him. On the road the wind, jumping the hedges, pursued rust-covered leaves.

Pablo continued walking for two good hours before reaching the town. As he reached the first houses he asked to be directed. It was simple—a wall, a second wall, and then the first street on the left.

Before the façade of closed windows behind bars he remained still for a while before deciding to ring the bell. Finally he pulled the well-polished handle. There was a wait. The door opened, and he went in. The door closed immediately behind him, and he

323

found himself in a tiny room with a very high ceiling and badly lit by a small light-bulb nearly at the level of the almost black ceiling.

Pablo felt his heart contract.

A step came nearer, deadened by a partition. A wooden grille opened, and Pablo sensed the shadow of a face behind the wooden bars. A part of the grille pivoted, and an opening appeared in front of him. He took a step forward.

"Write on the slate the name of the person you wish to see and also your own name."

Already the shadow was moving away from the grille and the opening closed. Pablo looked at the recess. There was a slate placed on the ledge and a piece of chalk hanging from a string. He went across, wrote two names, and stepped back. The ledge disappeared.

Several minutes passed in a heavy silence which came from the grey walls, a silence which had not really been broken, but which had been here for ever and ever.

Finally, on the right, another door opened, and Pablo went into a room slightly larger. Here, too, it was gloomy and cold, but there was a table, a bench, and some chairs, and the old, polished wood gave it at least a little life. Pablo sat down, his haversack on his knees, and began waiting again, with this silence still around him like a fog.

Then, after quite a wait, there was a fresh sound of footsteps approaching, and a key was turned in the lock of a low door. Pablo stood up. The door opened, and Jeannette came in.

As soon as the door was closed behind her she took one step, then another, and stood still. One more step, and she hesitated again. Her face showed misgiving. Her eyelids fluttered; her mouth puckered; she took a step forward, then lifted her hands and smiled.

Then Pablo walked towards her. He took her in his arms, hugged her to him, and kissed her twice on both cheeks.

After that he stepped back a pace and turned his face away long enough to wipe away two tears on the cuff of his sleeve. Then, taking Jeannette by the hand, he led her across to the table.

"Come and sit down," he said. "Come and sit down."

Jeannette sat down facing him. She grunted again two or three times, and all her face was one continuing smile. Pablo had just

324

put his haversack on the table, and, while he opened it, the little girl watched every movement of his hands closely. He brought out apples, some nuts, two packets of sweets, and a box of biscuits.

"Those," he said, pointing to the biscuits and the sweets, "were brought up to me by Clopineau, from the village shop. You know Clopineau? You remember him?"

She grunted, nodding her head. Pablo began to laugh.

"And, you know, he sends you his good wishes, Clopineau. He would come to see you, but he is very old. This is a long way. Some of the others promised to come, but visits aren't allowed on market-days, so they would have to come specially on a Sunday. They haven't really the time. You know how it is, with the land and the animals and everything."

Jeannette was still smiling. Pablo got out from his haversack another little paper packet. He opened it and drew out a partly dried bunch of grapes.

"You see," he said, "I have gleaned these. These are grapes from Brûlis. It's full of weeds, but a few still ripen all the same. You'll see, they're so sweet you'd think they were made of sugar."

Pablo became silent for a moment. He had not spoken so much for days and days. He unwrapped a sweet which he held out to Jeannette. She began to suck it, and it seemed to Pablo that she was truly happy. He hesitated for a moment, then as the silence closed in, chilling the room, he went on: "The new people have been there a month, you know. Immediately after you left they arrived."

He puckered his eyebrows, watching Jeannette eating her sweet, and went on more quietly, as if speaking to himself: "We left the day before, La Noire and me. I had taken the cart with an old trolley and a good plough. Before that I had already made one journey with hay and my own odds and ends."

Jeannette put out a hand towards the bag of grapes. Pablo gave her one, which she began to eat. She chewed always in the same way, opening her mouth very wide; nevertheless Pablo's eyes did not leave her.

"You know," he said, "so far I've had a lot to do to build a stable for La Noire and get myself more or less settled. But next year I think I will, after all, get the old vines back into good shape."

He began to laugh and added: "I will bring you some grapes,

325

and perhaps it will be possible for you to come out for the vintaging."

He fell silent for a moment. He could see his hut. He thought of the wood stacked up for the fire, the hay for La Noire. Soon December would come to whistle across the plain, dragging winter behind: up there everything had been prepared.

"What's more," he went on, "La Noire and I have a lot of work in the cuttings in the woods, three times more than we could ever manage between now and the spring. Everyone wants us. I haven't put my nose inside the village since I went to Brûlis. But every time Clopineau comes up to give me a hand he tells me of this person or that who needs a man with a good horse for a day's work."

Jeannette had finished her grapes. Pablo watched her all the time, and he was happy to have found her well and clean. He watched her still for a moment or two without saying anything, and then, putting his hand in his haversack, he drew out a distorted piece of vine-wood which he placed on the table. Jeannette leaned forward a little. Her face had suddenly become serious. She stared at the little piece of wood. Her hand moved forward slowly at table-level, like an animal.

She first touched the wood with the tips of her fingers. Then, taking hold of it, she picked it up and examined it, turning it from side to side and back again. Finally, after a minute or two, she put it down on the table. There was a smile on her face again. She lifted her face to Pablo. Pablo seemed to be thinking for a moment. His lips moved several times, then he said, almost in a whisper:

"La Noire ... La Noire. ..."

Jeannette grunted. Her hand trembled a little, and her face relaxed. She then took the piece of wood again and made it move along the table.

"La Noire," repeated Pablo. "You see, it's La Noire. It really is La Noire."

Then, as the little girl moved the piece of wood round the table, Pablo began to speak more loudly. He made it sound as if he was really talking to La Noire, and each time that he cried "Hup!" the piece of wood moved more quickly. Each time that he said "Whoa!" the piece of wood became still.

They continued the game for a while. Afterwards Pablo drew out other pieces of vine-wood.

There were some which Jeannette pushed away after she had examined them closely. But there were others which she lined up beside La Noire. There were cows, chickens, ducks, and even a cockerel.

"I'll find you others," said Pablo. "There are two old vine-gardens I've been asked to grub up. That's going to make a big pile of wood. I'll certainly find you some others."

But Jeannette seemed tired. She had her expressionless face once more. For a long time Pablo looked at her, motionless and silent.

Finally, putting back in his haversack the pieces she had not wanted, he stood up. The little girl stood up also. Over her grey frock she was wearing a large blue pinafore. Pablo said, "We're going to put all this in your pinafore pocket."

Jeannette lifted the two bottom corners of her pinafore, just as she did in the fields when collecting wild salads. Pablo put in the linen pocket the fruits, the sweets, the biscuits, and the pieces of wood.

"Bye, bye," he said.

Jeannette's face puckered a little. Pablo stepped forward, bent over to avoid the lump made in her pinafore, drew Jeannette to him, and kissed her.

"Run along now," he said. "Run along. I will come every Sunday, I promise. I promise you I will come every Sunday."

The little girl did not move. She stood with one hand holding her pinafore up and the other hanging limply by her side. She looked again like the little girl Pablo had seen the night of his arrival in the village. The difference was that she was clean. But she had scarcely grown at all, her chest was still completely flat, and her face that of a child of twelve.

Pablo raised one hand and made a slow gesture, repeating in a low voice:

"Run along. I'll come back."

Jeannette turned on her heel and went off, still at her usual pace, her feet slightly apart, her shoulders moving from right to left.

Behind her the door clicked. Pablo looked round him. He was alone. However, the door by which he had entered began to open. He went into the other room, walking carefully because of the silence which was closing in again and which he found even heavier.

He waited for a moment in front of the other door, which opened on to the wind of the grey street.

The clouds were now scudding along at roof-height. The wind which was raking the street carried with it a few spots of rain.

Pablo looked once again at the grim front of the building and murmured:

"Every Sunday."

Then, hugging the walls, he went off with his rather heavy stride.

Once he was outside the town boundary he stopped at the first bush, drew out his pocket-knife, and, looking for as straight a branch as possible, cut himself a stick.

The wind had dropped. The rain was falling more heavily, plastering the dead leaves to the road.

With his head down, a little hunched, a little bent, Pablo began to walk on.